QUANTUM MAYHEM

Also by Lesley L. Smith

Temporal Dreams
Neutrino Warning
Kat Cubed
Reality Alternatives
Conservation of Luck

The Quantum Cop Series:
Book 1: *The Quantum Cop*
Book 2: *Quantum Murder*
Book 3: *Quantum Mayhem*

The Space Operetta Series:
Book 1: *A Jack By Any Other Name*
Book 2: *A Jack In The Dark*
Book 3: *A Jack For All Seasons*

Quantum Mayhem

By Lesley L. Smith

Quarky Media

Boulder Colorado

Quantum Mayhem

Published by Quarky Media, PO Box 3332, Boulder, CO 80307

ISBN: 978-0-9973131-8-5 (ebook)
ISBN: 978-0-9973131-9-2 (print)

QUANTUM MAYHEM

For awesome female scientists everywhere…

Chapter One

I was working in my office in the Gamow physics tower when I was interrupted by a call on my cell phone.

The caller was my roommate, Ben Willis, aka hot cop (I really needed to quit thinking of him like that since I had a boyfriend). "Hey, Ben. What's up?"

"Hey, Madison," he said. "Are you busy?"

I looked at the stack of papers to grade on my desk and my giant to-do list on the pad of paper next to it. But Ben was a pretty awesome roommate; I owed him a lot. "Depends. . . I might not be busy if you need help with something."

"The police chief up in Nederland called," Ben said. "He said he has a situation that might call for the quantum cop." Ben was developing a reputation as the first line of defense when it came to quantum crimes. I'd discovered how to affect reality using quantum physics; unfortunately, others had deciphered how to commit crimes using this knowledge.

Damn. Since I was the quantum cop, I definitely needed to help him. "When can you pick me up?"

"I'm next to the south door with my bike." We'd ridden his awesome motorcycle to crime scenes before.

"Sweet! I'll be right down." I almost--but not quite--ran down the many stairs. I was excited about solving a quantum crime and serving justice and not at all about hugging Ben as we zoomed up mountain roads on a beautiful fall day.

Outside, the weather was unseasonably warm and pleasant for the beginning of November. The sun shone brightly, and a light breeze blew colorful fallen leaves across the sidewalk.

Ben stood right outside the exit on his bike, on the sidewalk.

Around thirty, he did that sexy, shaved-head thing that some guys did. He looked as hot as ever in his sexy leather jacket, all muscles, not an ounce of fat on him. Darn it.

He smiled under his mirrored shades and saluted as he saw me.

"Where are we going?" I asked.

"Caribou, Colorado," he said. "A former silver-mining town, a ghost town. It's up in the mountains, near Nederland. Should be a fun ride today." He handed me a helmet.

The drive up to Caribou was fun. Correction: it was wonderful. We motored up the highway like NASCAR racers-- at least it felt like it. A few Aspen trees still clutched their sunny yellow leaves, and the various pines stood majestically as we zoomed by.

I had my arms wrapped snugly around Ben, and I leaned into his back. The roaring wind was a powerful presence hammering at us. But in the bright sunshine, it just felt exciting as we drove up and up the mountain.

Eventually, we drove up a dirt road, seemingly in the middle of nowhere, and Ben turned off the bike. We were in a vast empty meadow filled with brown grass and the skeletons of last summer's flowers, surrounded by snow-sprinkled mountains. Pretty.

A man standing next to a battered pickup truck waved to us. He wore a warm-looking jacket with a shearling collar. If I had to guess, based on his sparse white hair, craggy face, and worn hands and neck, I'd say he was pretty old.

"Ben," he called out. "Thanks for coming. Is this the physics lady?" He pointed at me.

I nodded as I got off the bike. Standing there next to the bike, my body still vibrated from the ride.

The temperature was a little cooler than down the hill in town, so the warm sun on my skin felt good.

"Yep," Ben said. "This is Professor Madison Martin, the quantum cop. Madison, this is Chief Goodwin of Nederland." He stowed the two helmets.

"Nice to meet you, sir," I said, holding out my hand.

We shook, and he frankly looked me up and down. I couldn't tell what his conclusion was. At least he didn't say I didn't look like a physicist, or I did look like a soccer mom, which was what people usually said.

"Ben, here, told me you were the quantum cop," the Chief said. "But not how it all works. Can you help me out?"

"Sure." I nodded. "Quantum physics is the physics of very tiny things."

Ben joined us. "The short version, Madison." He said that like I was going to get carried away talking about physics. He knew me pretty well.

"Suffice it to say, the universe follows the rules of quantum physics," I said. "Basically, everything can be described as a probability, and it takes a human mind to collapse the probability wavefunction and instantiate a reality."

"What?" the Chief said.

Ben interrupted. "The bottom line is if you really understand this, you can control reality. It's like a superpower. Or magic." I didn't like the words 'superpower' or 'magic,' but Ben and I had had this conversation before.

"Can you do the physics magic, Ben?" the Chief asked him.

"I'm trying to learn," Ben said. "It's a little tricky, but hopefully, I'll get it soon." He glanced around. "Anyway, What's the trouble here?"

Chief Goodwin waved his hand around. "You're looking at it."

I examined the beautiful mountain meadow with a narrow dirt road and lots of dried grasses and wildflowers. Some kind of bird of prey glided over us under the enormous indigo sky. "I don't see anything," I said. "I mean, it's pretty and all, but. . ."

"Exactly," the chief said. "The town is gone. There were a bunch of old wooden structures and some stone buildings and foundations."

I started getting a bad feeling. Stuff disappearing did sound like quantum shenanigans. But I shouldn't jump to conclusions, right?

Ben shook his head and scowled as he unzipped his leather jacket and shrugged it off. He placed it on the bike's seat. Underneath, he had on a form-fitting black t-shirt. Good thing I'd stopped thinking of him as the hot cop because I might have been distracted.

"Granted, they were old and rundown and all, but still," Goodwin said. "This is a historic site. It's not right." He paused. "Did you know a prospector named Conger discovered gold downstream in 1861 and followed the gold right up Coon Trail Creek to here?"

He knew a lot of history for a chief of police; I was impressed. "I did not know that. Neat," I said. "Is there still gold around here?" I looked around; I wouldn't mind seeing some gold in its native habitat. Or silver, for that matter.

The two men glanced at me with downturned lips and then continued their conversation.

"Who reported it?" Ben asked.

"Some scientist types," Chief Goodwin said. "I think they said they were archeologists. From the university." He looked to me. "Do you know them?"

Archeologists? Why would I know them? It wasn't like every one of the thousands of university employees knew everyone else. "Gosh, no. I can't say that I've had the pleasure."

"Anyway," Ben said. "Did they give you any other info?"

"Yeah," Goodwin said. "They sent me some pictures." He swiped his phone and held it out in front of him. "This is what the place looked like just a few days ago. They were studying it."

Ben and I stepped to his phone and squinted, trying to see the image.

Goodwin swiped.

I could barely make anything out in the bright sunshine. "Can you email us those pix?"

He nodded and started typing. "Crap. Not enough signal. Usually, it's decent around here. Can I send them later?"

"Sure," Ben said.

"So why do you think it was quantum stuff?" I asked.

"Come on." The chief turned and started walking away. We followed him.

Our shoes crunched on the stones and gravel in the dirt road. We left the road and walked up what seemed to be a dirt walkway. But it ended abruptly at nothing.

Goodwin pointed. "The biggest stone building was here."

There was no building now. I crouched down on the walkway. It ended suddenly in a packed dirt rectangle covered with piles of sand. I carefully poked one of the piles of sand. "It feels like sand." I turned around to face the two men who stood behind me. "Are you sure there was a building here recently?"

"Yes." Goodwin held out his phone.

I stood and squinted into the screen. An old stone building was centered in the picture, and the tree in the picture looked exactly like the physical tree about ten feet from the foundation. Tree, check. Building, not so much. "Huh."

Ben leaned over and checked out the picture and then the tree.

"Okay," I said. "So that is weird. But it's not necessarily quantum mayhem." It was very probably, but not totally necessarily, quantum mayhem.

"There's more." Goodwin pointed at another space in the clearing. We followed him over there. A dirt walkway led to a pile of sawdust. Goodwin swiped and held out his phone.

Sure enough, the picture showed a rickety wooden structure with a familiar background. Again, there was no sign of the building presently--with the exception of the sawdust.

I got a chill, and I didn't think it was from the wind that had sprung up.

"There's a whole bunch of these piles of sawdust," Chief Goodwin said.

"Is it quantum stuff, Madison?" Ben asked.

"Can't be sure." I was pretty sure. I shrugged. "Anything else?"

"Oh, yeah." Goodwin led us over to another open space.

As we approached, this time, the ground seemed to be covered in something shiny. We walked right up to it and stared at mounds of shiny goo. "What was this?"

"A bunch of trees and plants and stuff," Goodwin held out his phone again and showed us a picture of a bunch of trees and plants and stuff.

I crouched down next to the goo. I didn't want to touch it. It looked slimy, glistening in the sun.

I stood. "Okay, you're convincing me." Darn it.

"We should take a sample," Ben said.

I took a step back. "Knock yourself out. I don't do goo."

Ben took a small plastic evidence bag and latex gloves out

of his jeans pocket and scraped some goo into the bag.

"Anything else?" I asked Goodwin.

"Yeah. It's a little further away." He pointed at a path through the grass.

The three of us tramped along, not saying anything.

I didn't know why they were quiet. I was quiet because I was mystified. Why come out in the middle of nowhere and wreck everything? Why destroy a whole town? What was the point?

After several minutes, Chief Goodwin stopped abruptly. I almost plowed into the back of him. He pointed down. "Look."

"Look at what?" There was nothing there. Literally. It was a giant hole in the ground.

"This is where the mine was," he said. "It used to be a relatively small opening, with a wooden structure and a warning sign blocking it." That was not what it looked like now.

Now, it almost looked like a modern-day strip mining operation had taken place here. Or maybe a huge sinkhole. Or a quarry. The point was there was an extremely big hole in front of us.

"I'm guessing it wasn't like this before?" Ben asked.

Goodwin held out his phone. I could just make out a small, rickety-looking wooden structure about the size of an outhouse with a big sign, 'Danger. Do not enter.' There were no holes in the ground visible in the picture.

I crouched down next to the gaping chasm.

"Be careful!" both men said.

I jerked at the loud voices.

Ben added, "Don't fall in."

"I won't," I said. "Unless you guys startle me again." I leaned over the edge, and the edge of the hole looked weird, kind of spongy. "Gloves?"

Ben handed me some latex gloves.

I put them on and carefully touched the edge of the hole. The earth felt spongy.

It felt familiar. Crap. It felt like holes that had been made in the past, using quantum mechanics to collapse the probability wavefunction. That was a mouthful, so I called it q-lapsing.

In the past, similar holes in things like bank vaults had been made by criminals, technically my criminal former students. I frowned. Would this never end?

I stood and pulled off the gloves. "Okay, you totally convinced me. Something quantum happened here."

"So, can you catch them?" Chief Goodwin asked.

Ben and I glanced at each other. It was unlikely with so little info. "Uh, we'll try," I finally said.

Ben said, "Maybe I should take more samples."

Chief Goodwin departed with instructions to call him as soon as we identified the bad guys.

I resisted the urge to tell him not to hold his breath.

Ben scurried around, taking samples of spongy earth, sawdust, and sand.

As the sun started to go down, I sat on a big rock and thought. Who knew how to q-lapse? Me, my boyfriend Andro Rivas, my grad student Alyssa Long, FBI agent Lisa Baker, the physics department secretary Nancy Hernandez, and my former students Griffin Yin and Arjun Chatterjee.

Everyone else was dead. Sigh. Knowing how to q-lapse was not good for your health--even disregarding the possibility of an aneurysm if you did it too much.

About a year ago, I had been trying to teach other FBI agents how to q-lapse until one of them turned evil. Could yet another agent have figured it out?

There was also a minor chance my current quantum mechanics students had figured it out even though I'd been extra careful this year.

And then there was the pesky issue of the webpage controlreality.org that basically explained how to control reality using quantum mechanics. So, technically, there were potentially thousands, if not millions, of people who knew about q-lapsing. I needed to get rid of the webpage if it was back. I took out my phone but, like Chief Goodwin, couldn't access the web.

Ben stomped up. "Gee, thanks for helping."

I tapped my forehead with my finger. "I am helping. I'm trying to figure out who could have done this."

"I guess that makes sense." He placed a bunch of evidence bags into the inside pocket of his leather jacket and started putting it on.

The sun was slipping behind the higher peaks. The temperature was dropping quickly as the sun set.

"So, what'd you figure out?" he asked.

"I'm still working on it," I said.

"What do you think happened here?" he asked. "What was the point of all this? Of destroying a ghost town?"

"I wish I knew." All I knew was it wasn't good. I shivered.

Chapter Two

The next morning, Wednesday, I handed back the papers to my quantum mechanics students that I'd stayed up late grading (after pondering the disappeared ghost town for far too long). I still had the toothpaste-green basement classroom that made everyone look a little like the Incredible Hulk.

As usual, the nerds slouched at their desks, showing off a variety of t-shirts, jeans, sweatpants, and the like. They were all around twenty years old, juniors or seniors, mostly physics majors.

Zhang Wei groaned when I gave him his paper. "B! How could you give me a B?" Zhang was my overachieving trouble-maker this semester. He thought he was brilliant. In his defense, he did seem pretty smart.

I smiled. "I gave everyone the grade they earned."

Even Grace Harris, my first female undergraduate quantum mechanics student (yay!), groaned and said, "A-minus?" She was usually much more polite. She also seemed pretty smart.

I returned to the front of the classroom.

I faced them and smiled some more. "Well, that's why we have so many homework assignments, so you can drop the lowest ones."

Grumble, grumble.

"Anyway, let's get back to work." I turned to face the board. "Last time we talked about wavefunctions."

This year I was being super-duper careful not to teach them how to use quantum mechanics to control reality.

I glanced back at them. They still didn't look happy.

"Maybe we should do a quick review. We can describe particles or systems of particles with something called a wavefunction. Think of the wavefunction as a mathematical representation of the particle. Wavefunctions are continuous and normalizable. Recall, continuous basically means the same thing as a continuum, like space." I took a small step away from the board. "I can move in space a little or a lot." I took a big step. "It's all a big continuum."

"Like the spacetime continuum?" Grace asked.

Most of them snickered. One guy started humming the Star Trek theme.

"Yes!" I said. "Exactly like the spacetime continuum. And normalizable means the total probability of finding the particle somewhere is one hundred percent."

And we were off.

After class, I went back to my office in Gamow Tower. I set all my stuff down, including new homework to grade, and woke up my computer to check my email. Thus, I was working when I was rudely interrupted by what appeared to be a ghost. It resembled a person-shaped patch of fog.

"Mwahh," the shadowy figure said. *"Mwooh."* It seemed to be made of mist or whatever else ghostly ectoplasm might be made of.

I jerked back in my chair.

Then I heard something else. "Madison," Andro said in my office doorway. Andro was the handsome physicist from the office next door, aka my boyfriend. He was tall, but not too tall, and very fit. He had shiny, floppy, dark brown hair and the most gorgeous blue eyes in the universe. He was staring down at a sheaf of papers in his hand. "I can't believe you got this accepted for publication. The first scientific article about q-lapsing. Good for you. But aren't you worried about it leading to more crimes?"

"No," I said. "Criminals don't read physics journals. But, ah. . ." I pointed at the ghost.

Andro's attention was firmly fixed on the papers.

"Moooh," the ghost said in a spooky way.

"Look out, Andro!" I yelled. He was walking right towards the spectral figure, still staring at the papers.

He finally looked up with his beautiful baby blues. "Ack!" He backed into the doorframe. "Is that a ghost?"

I stood up. "No. There's no such thing as ghosts. Right?"

"No," he said.

"No," I said. "No ghosts. Definitely not."

"Ellp mmmm," the definitely-not-a-ghost said.

And then it disappeared.

Andro and I remained staring at the spot for some moments. Finally, I sat back down and said, "So, that happened."

"Yes, it did." He walked towards me, carefully bypassing the spot where the apparition had so recently been. He sat down heavily in one of the rickety guest chairs in front of my desk.

He sighed. "What do you think it was?"

Good question, very good question. I raised my eyebrows. "With our luck, it had to be some kind of quantum thing, right?"

"Yeah." He nodded.

"Because there's no such thing as ghosts."

"Right. No ghosts."

Something about this whole incident was troubling. Okay, more than one thing was troubling. "Did it sound like it might have said, 'Help me'?"

Andro rubbed his strong chin. "Hmm. Yes, maybe so. What are you thinking?"

"What if someone's in trouble and needs help?" I asked.

"Knowing you, you'd try to help them," he said.

"How?" I asked, holding up my hands.

"Good question," he said. "It'd have to be someone who can q-lapse, or can mostly q-lapse."

"I agree," I said. Something was nagging me, something I hadn't considered yesterday up in Caribou. . . "Did I mention there might have been an instance of quantum mayhem up in Caribou, Colorado?"

He stared at me. "No. What's quantum mayhem?"

"Basically, a whole town was destroyed." He looked alarmed, so I added, "It wasn't a regular town though; it was deserted." I glanced at the area where the ghost had been. "The whole ghost town was destroyed." Were the ghost and the ghost town related?

"Is that where you were yesterday afternoon? Caribou?" he asked.

"Yeah." I nodded energetically. "Ben and I caught a case, a

quantum case."

"I hope no one was hurt," he said.

I shook my head. At least, as far as we knew, no one was hurt.

"Tell me about it," he said.

"That's basically all we know right now. The town was destroyed, probably by q-lapsing."

"Not much to go on."

"Nope." Darn it. It was very little to go on.

"What about the not-a-ghost then?" he asked. "How do we help?"

"If it was a q-lapser, we need to call all the q-lapsers and see if they're in trouble!" I grabbed my phone. "Will you call Alyssa?" Alyssa was my favorite grad student, quite motivated. Okay, she was my only grad student.

He took out his phone. "Can't you call her? I think she has a crush on me."

In truth, she did have a crush on him. If she had one failing, it might have been that she was a little boy crazy. "Okay," I said. "You call Agent Baker, then." Agent Lisa Baker was one of the FBI agents who knew about the quantum menace (crimes committed using quantum physics).

"All right." He dialed.

I dialed. Alyssa's phone went straight to voicemail. Oh no.

Andro was talking. "Agent Baker? Yes, this is Professor Rivas. I'm just checking in. Is everything okay?" He paused. "No, it's not suspicious that we're checking in with you. No, nothing's going on."

He paused again. "We as in me and Madison, er, the quantum cop, er, Professor Martin." He held out his phone. "She wants to talk to you."

I took his phone.

Agent Lisa Baker immediately said, "What's wrong?"

"Nothing's wrong," I said. "Why would anything be wrong? Nothing's wrong."

"I don't believe you," she said.

I pictured her typical no-nonsense, graying blonde ponytail and nondescript dark pantsuit. It was difficult to pull one over on her. "We may have seen someone q-lapsing, but the person seemed to be in trouble. We're checking that it's not you."

"I didn't q-lapse recently," she said. "Who else could it be?"

"Good question," I said. "Can anyone else at the FBI do it?" I'd tried teaching the agents in the Denver field office how to q-lapse, but only one besides Lisa really took to it, and he'd turned to a life of crime.

"Not that I know of," she said slowly. I knew she was thinking about her former partner Nate, too. Poor Nate had died in a hail of bullets last year because of said quantum crime spree. "I'll double-check and get back to you." She hung up.

I handed Andro his phone back. I still felt bad about Nate. If I hadn't taught him to q-lapse, he'd still be alive.

"Why didn't you call Alyssa?" he asked.

"I tried. She didn't pick up."

"Uh oh," he said.

Uh oh, indeed.

He stared at the time on his phone. "I have to go. I have class in a little while, and I have to do a little more prep." He stood.

I stood. "I hope you're not planning on leaving without a kiss."

He grinned, leaned over the desk, and planted a delicious kiss right on my lips.

"Mmmm," I said.

He leaned away. "That's your cinnamon roll sound."

"What can I say? You're my cinnamon roll."

He frowned a little. "Nope. Try again."

We'd been trying out pet names for each other--at least I'd been trying out nicknames for him. "My jelly doughnut?"

He shook his head.

"My bear claw?"

He hesitated for a second but then shook his head again. "Let's stay away from the whole baked goods arena."

"Aw. Snickerdoodle?"

"No, *mi amor*." He already had a great pet name for me. He started walking away, smiling.

"Twinkie. No wait, Ding Dong!"

He walked out the door, but I heard him laugh in the hall.

I snickered for a moment. We were in a good place, dating,

and had exchanged the l-word, but didn't feel the need to get engaged or anything like that.

He was focusing on his new-to-him daughter, three-year-old Sophia. She was adorable.

And I was focusing on my career; I'd only been an assistant physics professor for about fifteen months, and I'd had some rocky bits. I needed to impress my boss, Professor Chen, the department chair.

Anyway, I needed to find Alyssa and make sure she was okay. I'd taught her to q-lapse, and I felt like she was my responsibility.

If I was Alyssa, where would I be? Hhmm. . .

She might be here talking to me, her graduate advisor, but obviously, that wasn't the case now. Unless she had been the ghost. Ugh. She might be teaching her class (she was a teaching assistant), but it wasn't time for it.

I could go down to the physics office and ask the secretary, er, administrative assistant, if she knew where Alyssa was. She knew everything. She was the real power behind the ergonomic chair of the department chair.

I started to walk down the many, many stairs; I needed to get some coffee anyway. As I walked and thought of coffee, I realized the q-lapser might be administrative assistant Nancy Hernandez. She might be in danger. There was no time to waste.

I stopped and gathered my wits, concentrating. I thought about all the quantum mechanical possibilities. I focused on the possibility where I was already in the physics office. I concentrated and collapsed the quantum wavefunction to instantiate the reality in which I was where I wanted to be.

"Dammit!" Nancy said, jumping in her chair. "Don't do that!" She was a beauty pageant-worthy, twenty-something Chicana that all the physicists were intimidated by.

My head hurt a smidgen from q-lapsing. "Are you okay?" I asked her.

"I would be if you didn't q-lapse in here and scare the crap out of me," she said.

Jeez. I was just trying to help. I turned to the coffee machine, grabbed one of the mugs, and poured myself a big serving. I took a sip and felt myself relax some. My head hurt slightly less. I smiled at her. "So, you're fine?" In hindsight, I should have just run down the stairs instead of q-lapsing down here. Or called. I did have her cell phone number. Well, hindsight's twenty-twenty.

"Yes," she said slowly. "Why do you ask?" Nancy had turned to the dark side a little. She'd fallen under the spell of Nate-the-evil-FBI-agent and done some questionable things. I don't know all the legal details, but she only got a slap on the wrist. She was on probation, and one of the terms of her probation was she wasn't supposed to q-lapse. At all. Ever. Never ever, with extreme prejudice.

If I accused her of q-lapsing, she might take offense. She might get worried her probation would be revoked. Probably with good reason.

I had thought we might be friends, but after everything that'd happened, it didn't look like it would happen.

"Madison," she said.

"What?"

"Am I in danger or not?"

"I'm not sure what's going on," I admitted.

"Well, what do you think is going on?"

"I may have just seen a ghost upstairs."

She stared at me. For a while. You could have heard a pin drop--if anyone still used pins anymore.

"What?" she finally said.

"Never mind," I said. "I'm looking for Alyssa Long. Do you know where she is?"

She glanced at the large old clock on the wall. "Did you try her office?"

"She has an office?" Why hadn't I known that?

"Obviously," Nancy said. "She's a grad student, employed here at the university; of course, she has an office. You're acting like you didn't know that."

"Of course, I knew that." I didn't know that. "Uh, remind me, what's the room number?"

She passed along the number, and I hustled down to the basement to Alyssa's work space. Unfortunately, no one was there, either. Damn. Considering the small room had five cluttered desks in it, it was a little surprising. How could none of her officemates be around?

I tried her cell again.

Voice mail. Damn.

I stood in the hall, not sure what to do next.

I thought I heard, *"Mmmm."*

I twirled all around, but I didn't see any homo sapiens or any ghosts either. I didn't see anything but boring hallway.

"Hello? Is anyone there?"

No one answered me.

I stood there outside Alyssa's space for a few more minutes.

What would a real cop, a non-quantum cop, do?

I wasn't sure, but my roommate was a real cop. And he knew a lot about q-lapsing. I called him. "Ben?"

"Madison?" I heard a lot of yelling in the background.

Oh no!

Was he under attack?

Chapter Three

I immediately q-lapsed and landed in the middle of my apartment, surrounded by yelling, cheering men with flushed faces, and holding beer cans. Judging by the hotness of all of them, these were Ben's cop friends. They all faced me.

They did not look like they were in trouble.

They did look very surprised. Possibly, they weren't used to women popping into their midst out of thin air.

I searched the crowd for Ben and found him, not in trouble, after all, staring from the phone in his hand to me. He seemed startled.

Our crowded apartment was a pretty generic two-bedroom for a university town, with beige carpeting, off-white walls, and a large combination family room kitchen.

As usual, when I q-lapsed, I had developed a headache. Q-lapsing used some special quality of the human consciousness to instantiate reality, and it taxed the q-lapser's brain. The weirder or more improbable the reality, the more it hurt the brain.

When my arrival registered, the commotion stopped momentarily as everyone stared at me. Within moments, however, the cheering and yelling erupted again. Apparently, they all knew about q-lapsing and weren't scared. I guessed that made sense since they were buddies with Ben. He started walking towards me.

"Woo hoo!" Everyone was animated and smiling. Clearly, no one was in distress.

In the background, some cheesy music with an insistent bass beat played. *Boom. Boom. Boom.*

"Take it off, babe!"

"Seriously?" I asked. "That's kind of disrespectful, isn't it? I mean, I'm flattered, but--"

Ben grabbed me by the arm and started dragging me towards my bedroom. "What are you doing here?" he asked in the doorway.

"What am I doing here? I live here," I said as the two of us stepped into my room. "What are you doing here? I heard yelling. What are all these people doing here in the middle of the day?"

Through the doorway, I finally saw the woman in the center of the crowd, a buxom blonde who'd been behind me. Wearing only a sequin-encrusted bikini, she reached behind her neck and started untying her top. "Ohh. . . This is a bachelor party?"

"Yeah," Ben said. "Evan's getting married this weekend. And you're kind of throwing a damper on things."

Taking in the rowdy crowd of twenty-something men, as far as I could tell, nothing was damped--unless it was Ben. He did seem a little annoyed as he stared at me.

"Sorry." I held up my hands. "When I heard yelling, I thought you were in distress. Excuse me for coming to help my friend." I paused. "Why didn't you tell me you were having a party here today?"

"I didn't think you'd approve," he said, looking down, and scuffing his shoe on the carpet.

"Why wouldn't I approve of you having a party in your own apartment?" Ben had been a real stand-up guy and let me move in without first and last month's rent and without a security deposit last year.

He shrugged. He was clearly embarrassed.

"I'm a little surprised to see such a rowdy party in the middle of the day, but I don't disapprove," I said.

"The guys are all on the job, and some of them are working the night shift," he said. "That's why we're having it in the middle of the day."

"It's your apartment. Do what you want."

"Thanks." He smiled. "Yeah, I guess I'm being a little stupid. Do you want a drink?"

My head hurt a little. I did need a drink, but not liquor, something with caffeine. "No, thanks," I said. "I should get back to work. Sorry for bothering you."

"Wait. Why would I be in distress?" he asked. His brain was not firing on all cylinders; possibly, he'd been enjoying some adult beverages before I arrived. "Is it something related to that town being destroyed?"

I had no idea if the non-ghost was related to the destroyed town. "It'll keep. I'll tell you later." I grabbed some cash from my dresser top and a sweatshirt from a drawer. "Get back to your party, Ben." I shooed him back to his friends.

He seemed all too eager to go back.

I put on my sweatshirt, snuck through the family room, and out the door. I stopped at Boulder Brews across the street and got a triple shot mocha. Taking a sip, I sighed. Now that hit the spot. I walked over to the bus stop on the corner and sat down on the bench to wait.

I sipped and watched the traffic go by. The last few stained-glass leaves rustled on the fall breeze. I tried to relax my brain. I took a deep breath. Sip. Breathe. My headache faded away.

I really needed to quit q-lapsing when it wasn't an emergency. The problem was it wasn't always apparent what was an emergency and what wasn't.

A ghostly figure asking for help did seem pretty serious, however. Who could it be?

Another q-lapser I hadn't contacted was Griffin Jin. That kid better not be q-lapsing. That kid better not be in trouble. We'd come to an agreement: I wouldn't turn him in to the FBI as long as he didn't q-lapse.

He'd committed some crimes with the original quantum criminal, his best-friend Luke Bacalli, about two years ago. And then last year, he'd gotten dragooned into helping the evil FBI agent, Nate Sawyer. In between there, he'd been incarcerated without a lawyer, charges, a trial, or anything else official and kept under sedation.

He had started out as my student. I felt a smidgen responsible for all his troubles. If I hadn't (inadvertently) taught him how to q-lapse, he'd probably be graduated from college and starting some glamorous, high-paying new career in the tech industry by now.

I pulled out my phone and dialed Griffin.

He answered immediately. "Oh, thank God, Madison!"

"What's wrong?" I started preparing to q-lapse.

"I'm being haunted!" he wailed. "A ghost won't leave me alone!"

I didn't think he was being haunted for a minute. I did think something quantum was going awry. "Calm down. There's no such thing as ghosts, Griffin."

He shrieked. "I think I see it right now! It's coming for me!" He shrieked again, and I heard a loud thump.

"Calm down, Griffin," I said.

He didn't answer me.

"Griffin?"

No answer.

"Crap. Griffin! If you can hear me, answer me!" I put my coffee down on the bench beside me. Did he need saving? Did I need to q-lapse to California? I took a deep breath.

If I'd learned anything today, it was not to q-lapse without thinking. Think, Madison.

Think.

I had a brainstorm: I could call Griffin's girlfriend, Sadie. I did.

She answered right away. "Professor Martin? We didn't do anything wrong."

Well, that was suspicious. Clearly, they'd done something wrong. But, one thing at a time. "Uh, I'm calling about Griffin."

"Oh, right," she said.

"Is he all right?" I asked.

"Yeah," she said. "I'm looking at him. He's sort of cowering on the floor."

"On the floor?" I said. "That doesn't sound good. Are you sure he's okay?"

"Yeah," she said. "He claims he's being haunted, but I haven't seen anything. Hey--" She paused for a moment. "Does q-lapsing wreck your brain? Did all the quantum stuff do this to him?"

Yikes. I didn't think so. On the other hand, I did also see a ghost today. And so did Andro. And we both knew how to q-lapse. "I don't thi-i-ink so."

Think, Madison. I picked my coffee up off the bench and took a sip.

"So, what did you guys do that you weren't supposed to do?" I asked.

"Nothing," she said very quickly. Too quickly. I didn't believe her for a minute.

"Oka-a-ay," I said. "I guess, take care of Griffin. I'll be in touch. If you do see the ghost, try to record it with your phone." Darn. I should have recorded the ghost I saw.

"Yeah, right," she said. I could tell she didn't believe Griffin had seen a ghost. "Bye." We hung up.

I sat on the bench.

I sipped my coffee. Look at me, all thoughtful. Yay, me.

Something funny was going on, though.

Sip.

Look at the leaves fluttering in the wind.

The bus arrived. Boulder had an awesome public transportation system. Buses ran, like, every fifteen minutes.

I got on, swiping my Eco-pass. (I got it free as a university employee.) "Hey," I said to the driver.

"Hey," he said back.

I sat down near the front. In the middle of the day, the bus was mostly empty. Two possibly-homeless guys sat in the middle of the bus with possibly all their belongings in satchels at their feet.

Sip.

In the back, three teenaged boys tossed a football back and forth, laughing. Why weren't they in school? I shrugged. I wasn't the school police.

Sip.

I checked my phone and saw those pictures had come in from Chief Goodwin. Could what happened in the town be related to the ghost? Sadly, I had no idea. I scrolled through them but didn't gain any insights.

Sip.

What did Andro and Griffin, and I all have in common? Besides q-lapsing?

Sip.

Uh oh. I knew what we had in common.

Besides physics, we had Luke Bacalli in common. Luke had been my best quantum mechanics student and became a very talented q-lapser. Unfortunately, Luke had turned to a life of crime.

I thought I'd killed Luke in a big quantum battle about two years ago. I still felt guilty about that. Did heroes feel conflicted about meting out justice? I'd be fine with putting people in jail, but death seemed extreme--especially without any kind of trial.

On the other hand, I also thought I'd caught a glimpse of Luke about a year ago when Nate was busy being a criminal. We'd thought Nate had been impersonating Luke. But now I wasn't so sure. What if he wasn't totally dead?

Uh oh.

"Miss?" the bus driver, a heavy-set guy, asked me. "Are you all right? You don't look so good."

I didn't feel so good.

Chapter Four

When I got back to my office, my grad student Alyssa Long was waiting for me--and not happily. The corners of her lips dragged down dramatically. "You called?" she asked. Her t-shirt read, 'Bitches Love Science.'

"Alyssa!" I said. "Are you all right?" I waved her inside, leaving the door open.

"Yeah." She frowned. "Why wouldn't I be all right?" So, not in danger. Yay.

I decided not to get into the whole debacle of quantum crimes starting up again. "I was just checking in."

She looked suspicious. Or, maybe my perceptions were colored by my guilty conscience. If not for me, no one would have discovered q-lapsing. No one would have been hurt by q-lapsing.

I smiled. "So, what can I do for you?"

"Did you forget our research meeting?"

Yes. "Of course not." My mind raced. What had we been discussing last time? She was supposed to be writing up her results section. "Results. Show me what you've got." I pointed at a chair, and we both sat down.

She got out her computer and scrolled to the appropriate place.

About an hour later, Andro started to walk into my office but backed off when he saw Alyssa.

I nodded at him to indicate I'd talk to him when Alyssa and I were done.

"And that's about it," Alyssa said a little later.

"It looks great," I said. "As we discussed before, your method is totally solid. Your model simulates the detection of the new neutrino particles. But." I resisted the urge to smile at her. I was doing entirely too much smiling lately to cover stress. "You don't have enough data yet. You need to run your model at least a thousand more times so you can get some good statistics."

She exhaled loudly. I carefully ignored her grumpiness. I knew better than to get sucked into her moodiness.

"And, hey," I said. "The physics department seminar today is on neutrinos. I expect to see you there."

She nodded. "Yeah. You told me before." She started gathering her stuff together. "I better go try to start some runs before it begins."

"Excellent idea," I said. "Overall, you're doing really well, Alyssa. Keep it up."

As soon as she departed, Andro poked his head back into my office. "Where'd you go this time?"

Ah. I hadn't told Andro I'd disappeared because I'd thought Ben might be in trouble. "A bachelor party."

He sort of laughed and choked at the same time. "What?"

"Ben was hosting a bachelor party."

"What!" he said. Now he sounded a little mad. "Why would Ben invite you to a bachelor party?"

"He didn't invite me. I called him, and there was a lot of yelling at the apartment. I thought something was wrong, so I q-lapsed over there."

"You really shouldn't q-lapse so much," he said. "It's dangerous."

We'd had this discussion many times. Andro thought q-lapsing was an interesting phenomenon but that it should be kept on a theoretical basis. "You're not wrong," I said. "But I thought people were being hurt."

Seemingly mollified, he grinned a little. "So, how'd a bunch of cops take a woman appearing out of mid-air in the middle of their party?"

"I'd have to say pretty well. They asked me to take off my shirt, of course," I said. "To shake my money-maker."

He raised his eyebrows as if asking, 'Did you take it off?'

I snickered.

He joined in.

"You know I wouldn't strip in front of a bunch of cops," I said.

"It's not dignified enough for the quantum cop. I might have to work with these guys in the future."

"Hhm. Stripping. What an interesting idea." Now his grin looked a little evil. "Do you know how to strip? I'd like to see that. I'd really like to see that."

I couldn't help grinning a little evilly back at him. "I think that could be arranged. If you reciprocate, of course. When?" I could not keep track of his schedule with his daughter Sophia.

"I was supposed to have Sophia tonight."

Bummer.

"But her mom asked me to switch."

Now, a huge, happy grin spread across my face. "Excellent! Your place?"

His grin matched mine. "Yes. I'll make dinner."

"Excellent. I'll bring beer." What a perfect division of labor. Wow. My mood was improving at an exponential rate.

"In fact, do you want to go home early?" he asked.

Was he implying a little afternoon delight? Wow. "It sounds fun, but I have to go to the seminar today," I said. "It's on neutrinos. Aren't you going?"

"I was planning on going, but I could be convinced otherwise," he said.

"I have to go. I made Alyssa promise to go."

"Aw," he said, eyes twinkling.

I resisted his charms.

At the appointed time, Andro and I walked down to the seminar vicinity together. Outside the auditorium, refreshments had been laid out on a table. We got there early enough that there were still some cookies. I snagged one and shoved it in my mouth.

I was debating eating another one when someone said, "Madison? Madison Martin?"

I turned around to spy a vaguely familiar-looking white guy about ten years older than me. "It's Peter, Peter Cox." I must have looked blank because he continued. "We met at the APS conference a couple of years ago. You gave that excellent talk--"

"Oh, Peter!" I didn't recall him, but I liked anyone that called me excellent. "Sure. How have you been?"

Andro waved to me and went off to talk to some other colleagues.

Peter nodded. "Good. Say, I wanted to say I was happy to see your paper finally got accepted." He took a step closer. "I'm a reviewer, and one of the other reviewers was really nasty. It was totally unprofessional."

The sugar rush must have been making my brain slow. "What now? You were a referee for one of my papers?"

He nodded. "Yeah. And this other reviewer was just vicious."

Vicious didn't sound good. "About my paper?"

"Yeah," he said. "I complained to the editor about it."

"Do you know who the other ref was?" I asked.

"No. Sorry, no idea," he said.

Finally, I knew at least part of the reason I'd been having such a problem getting papers published lately.

Someone near the door to the seminar room said, "Let's get started, folks."

I grabbed another cookie and entered.

Alyssa waved at me; she'd saved me a seat. I went and sat next to her. (Andro had to fend for himself.) "Thanks," I said. It was easy to differentiate the students from professors in the crowded room via wardrobe: students tended to wear t-shirts, and faculty tended to wear button-downs.

Professor Chen introduced the speaker, a scientist from the IceCube Neutrino Observatory, the particle detector at the South Pole. He dimmed the room lights.

The speaker clicked past his intro slide and said, "A neutrino is a very small electrically-neutral elementary particle, sort of like a tiny neutron."

Alyssa whispered, "Could he be any more basic?"

"It's good to start at the beginning, so we're all on the same page," I whispered back.

The people around us said, "Shhh!"

Sometime later, Alyssa poked me. "Are you asleep?" she whispered.

Yikes. I'd fallen asleep. Well, I had been extra busy the last couple of days. "Of course not," I whispered. "I'm concentrating, thinking deep, important, neutrino-y thoughts."

"Shhh!" folks around us said.

"So, in conclusion," the speaker said, "we have discovered a diffuse all-flavor flux of high-energy astrophysical neutrinos."

They had? It sounded interesting. Diffuse meant they couldn't tell where it came from. All-flavor meant they detected all the currently-known types of neutrinos. High-energy astrophysical neutrinos meant they came from outer space.

The speaker said, "Any questions?"

Everyone started clapping.

Alyssa's hand shot up.

The speaker nodded and pointed at her.

She lowered her hand and said, "When you say all-flavor is that Standard Model flavors?"

He nodded.

"How do you know there's not something more exotic in there?" she asked. For her Ph.D., she was studying the possibility of neutrinos beyond the Standard Model.

The speaker smiled. "Great question." He turned back to his computer. "I brought some extra slides." He started clicking through extra slides at the end of his presentation.

Then he grimaced and stepped backward. He seemed to be taken aback by something next to him. "Ugh. . ." Somehow he tripped over his feet or something and fell on the floor.

You didn't see that every day, a seminar speaker falling on the floor.

The front of the auditorium erupted into gasps, 'Is that smoke?' 'What's that?' and 'Oh, my God.' People stood up from their seats. Some leaned towards the mystery, trying to get a better view. Some started leaving the theater, while others actually jogged towards the disturbance in the front. Everyone under thirty had their phones out, recording everything.

"What is it?" Alyssa asked, holding her phone up. "Smoke? Is there a fire?"

We were standing to get a better view. "I don't think so," I said. "I don't smell anything. Do you? And the fire alarms and sprinklers would go off."

It was hard to see in the seminar room, what with the crowd and the dimmed lights, but it looked like a ghost stood in the front of the room.

Oh, no. Not again.

"Is that a ghost?" Alyssa asked.

"No," I said. "There's no such thing as ghosts."

Someone turned on the room lights. The thing looked like a person made of mist; it was the same shape and size as a man. It looked exactly the way I would imagine a ghost would look--if there was such a thing.

Could it be smoke?

Someone had helped the speaker up off the floor, and they had backed up against the wall in the front of the room, joining about a dozen people staring intently and/or recording as the case may be.

Then the not-a-ghost said something that sounded like, *"Boo."*

The crowd jerked back.

Seriously?

As Alyssa and I cautiously approached the front of the room, Professor Chen peeked in through one of the doorways near the front. He looked like his paradigm was exploding.

And then, just as Alyssa and I joined Andro where he'd been seated near the speaker, the not-a-ghost said, "Madison." That clinched it; it definitely wasn't smoke. Smoke didn't talk.

Alyssa's head whipped around to face me. "Did that thing just say Madison?"

"No," I said. "You should probably go, though, Alyssa." I pointed at the back exit behind us.

"No," she said. "I want to see what happens next. This is exciting."

I exhaled. Having a grad student was surprisingly like having a kid. "Well, step away a little, at least."

She reluctantly moved back a little.

"What do you want to do?" Andro asked.

"I guess I have to go talk to it," I said.

It still floated in the front of the room, sort of bobbing up and down.

The others in the room were talking softly amongst themselves, pointing. I thought I heard the word 'ghost' a few times.

Andro bit his lip. "I hate the thought of you in danger."

"I know," I said. "Can you q-lapse if we have to fight it?"

QUANTUM MAYHEM

He nodded. "I haven't done it for a while, but I think I can. Can you?"

"Yes." I resisted the urge to ask him for a kiss. Revving up the adrenaline helped with q-lapsing, and it didn't matter how you got revved up. But we didn't have time. The not-a-ghost could disappear or threaten someone any second.

"Okay, here we go. Be ready for anything." I strode right up to the not-a-ghost.

From the hall, Professor Chen said, "Campus police are on their way," as we passed the open front doorway. There was a campus police office across the street from the physics building.

Great. Like my cousin Ryan Martin and his officers could do anything. Ryan was the Chief of the university police and probably my closest relative. I'd stayed with him and his wife and daughter when I first moved to town. Unfortunately, they'd all been endangered by the quantum criminals. It was one of the reasons I'd moved out of their house.

I strode right up to the phantasm with a confidence I didn't feel.

Andro followed.

"Hi, uh, Casper," I said. "What do you want?"

It sort of moaned and bobbed. Okay, so not super communicative.

"I'm Madison," I said. "Did you ask for me?"

"Madison," it said.

"Yes," I said. "That's me. What do you want?"

I heard Ryan's voice call out from the doorway. "What is it, Madison?" He tiptoed over to me and Andro. "Is that a ghost?"

"No," Andro and I and several others in the crowd said at the same time.

"What's happening?" Professor Chen called out from the doorway. He was surrounded by a group of campus cops.

Ryan glanced at the crowd. "What is it then?"

The creature said, "Help," and then faded away.

Oh, good grief.

The people in the crowd all started talking at once. "Where'd it go?" "What the hell was that thing?" "What's going on?" "I wouldn't have believed it if I hadn't seen it myself."

Professor Chen stomped into the room, followed closely by

the officers. "Where'd it go?" he asked.

"I don't know," I said. "We should look around." We all scoured the room and the surrounding hallways but didn't see anything unusual.

So, crisis averted? I had a sinking feeling it was just crisis postponed.

Afterward, Chen said, "What did you do now, Madison?"

I felt my forehead crinkle up in annoyance. "Me? I didn't do anything. Maybe it was you. What did you do?"

"Me?" Professor Chen said. "What could I have done? This has got to be more of that quantum criminal stuff you got into last year."

Was he implying I was some kind of criminal? My blood boiled like steam in a fumarole. I may have growled.

"Let's calm down," Andro said. "No harm done."

"Yeah, whoa," Ryan said, holding up his hands now. "I'll take the miscreant Madison to the security office and get the whole story. We'll grill her as long as it takes." He winked at me with the eye not visible to Chen.

Professor Chen nodded. "Good idea. Chief Martin, get to the bottom of this and report back to me."

He nodded solemnly.

Professor Chen left.

Alyssa bounded up. "What happened? What was that thing?"

The three of us turned as one and glared at her.

"Ah, maybe I'll just go home, then," she said.

"Good idea, Alyssa," I said. "And write up a summary of the seminar." Purely for her own edification. Not so I'd know what neat discoveries I'd missed while, ah, concentrating.

She departed.

In the meantime, Ryan had been talking to his officers, and they also departed.

I looked to Ryan. "Are you really going to grill me?"

He smiled. "If I had the right encouragement, I could refrain."

"Would a beer at Boulder Brews be the right encouragement?" I asked. I knew it would be. The restaurant was one of our favorite hangouts. They had pastries and coffee in the morning and beers and burgers in the evenings. Plus, it was almost exactly midway between Ryan's house and campus.

"Yes, it would." Ryan smiled.

"Are you coming?" I asked Andro.

"I want to stop at the store and then get dinner started," he said. "Plus, I don't know anything." He pointed at me. "Tell Ryan about that Caribou thing."

I didn't know anything either. Unfortunately. "Okay, I'll see you at your place a little later."

"Sounds good." We smiled at each other. I got lost in his blue eyes for a second. Andro departed.

"Caribou?" Ryan frowned. "You saw a reindeer?"

At Boulder Brews, Ryan and I sat at one of their tiny cafe tables with our frothy beverages. I'd been adventurous and ordered one of their Thanksgiving seasonal brews, the sweet potato stout. I took a sip. It tasted like a regular stout with just a hint of sweet potato and maybe maple. Not bad. I smacked my lips.

"I can't believe you ordered that, Mad," Ryan said after taking his own sip. "Does it taste like sweet potato?"

"A little bit." I held out my mug. "You can try it if you want."

"No thanks." He mock-shuddered. "So, let the grilling commence." He waved his left hand around.

"Huh?"

"Just tell me what's going on," he said. "And don't forget the reindeer thing."

"Reindeer?" I said. "What reindeer thing? There's no reindeer thing. You must have Christmas on the brain. It's still almost two months away."

"Just talk," he said. "Are the quantum crimes starting up again?" Things had been pretty quiet on the quantum crime front for the last year or so.

"I guess so." The corners of my mouth dipped down in a frown. "You saw the ghost in the seminar room."

"I don't know what I saw." He looked alarmed. "You think it was a ghost?"

"No." I shuddered. "I think it was someone trying to q-lapse and having something go wrong." I sipped. "Have there been any weird bodies found?" I really hoped not. We'd found some bodies about a year ago. It was bad.

"Not that I know of," he said slowly. "I can check. What's the reindeer thing?"

"Ben and I caught a case up in Caribou, Colorado. The whole town had been destroyed."

"Caribou? I'm not familiar with it." Now it was his turn to frown. "Were there injuries? And how do you destroy a whole town?"

"It was an old ghost town, so no, no one was hurt. That we know of. Unfortunately, it does appear the miscreants used quantum mechanics."

"Why wreck a town?"

That was an excellent question. "I have no idea."

I needed to get some ideas. And fast.

Chapter Five

At Boulder Brews, Ryan and I discussed ghosts, ghost towns, and possible quantum criminals but did not reach any conclusions. He went home to his family, and I didn't let myself feel bad about missing them.

I purchased some beers in handy to-go bottles.

The pub was pretty close to Andro's apartment, so I strolled on over. Soon, I was knocking on his apartment door.

His nieces Maria and Theresa threw the door open. They were eight and ten, respectively, and both adorable with dancing eyes and quick smiles.

"Madison!" Maria said.

"Maddie!" Theresa said. "We thought you might be Mom."

"Hi girls," I said. "It's nice to see you again. But, nope, I'm not your mom."

Andro walked over. "We talked about this, girls," he said. "Your mom's on a date. She's not picking you up until after dinner. Please go back to your game."

They scampered off.

"Sorry," he said, opening the door wider to let me in. "Yasmin asked me to babysit last minute." I was disappointed we wouldn't have any alone time, but I understood.

A wonderful smell wafted toward me through the open door, chicken with some mysterious spices. I licked my lips. As I came through the door, I could see a large variety of foodstuffs and cooking utensils spread out over the kitchen counter. "No worries." I held up the beer and let a big smile slowly spread over my face. "Sous chef reporting for duty." The two of us had had a lot of fun times in the kitchen over the last couple of years.

Andro matched my smile and leaned in, and gave me a

quick kiss on the lips. Mmm.

The girls groaned. "Oh, gross!" Theresa said.

"Ick!" Maria said.

"Game," Andro said, looking over his shoulder at them. Giggling, they turned back to their game, and we went to the kitchen.

I took a beer out and held it out to him.

He glanced at it and shook his head. "Better not."

I said, "Save them for later?"

He nodded.

I decided to follow his lead and put the entire six-pack in the fridge.

As I surveyed the kitchen, I realized there was a lot of food there. "What all's going on here? This seems like a lot."

He rubbed his hands together. "I'm practicing for Thanksgiving."

"Thanksgiving requires practice?" The few times I'd hosted Thanksgiving had been in grad school, and it had been a kind of catch-as-you-can potluck. It worked great. Of course, that may have been because of the large quantities of beer and football.

"Wait a minute. Are you hosting?" In their family, his sister Yasmin usually hosted.

"Yes." He nodded.

"Am I invited?"

"Of course." He smiled. "But aren't you going to Ryan and Sydney's?" Since I'd moved to Boulder, I had spent all the major holidays at my cousins' place. They had a super-adorable toddler Emily, who kept us all on our toes.

"We haven't discussed it," I said. "I'll talk to them. In case of emergency, though, I could have two Thanksgiving dinners." That actually sounded fun.

He laughed a little. "In case of emergency, huh?"

I sat down on a stool at the kitchen island. "You know, if it would help you out."

He nodded exaggeratedly. "Oh, yeah. It would."

I smiled. "But seriously, let's get this show on the road." I pointed at all the food on the counter. "What would you like me to do?"

Andro surveyed his gastronomic kingdom. "Will you whip up

40

the carrots for the soufflé?"

I'd never heard of carrot soufflé, but I'd try anything once, or, okay, maybe twice. "Sure."

After about forty-five minutes of intensive culinary activities, Andro, Maria, Theresa, and I sat down for a practice-Thanksgiving feast. And 'feast' was the appropriate word. There was a whole roast chicken with some kind of marinade and spices, mashed potatoes, cheese quesadillas, some kind of corn dish, three kinds of salsa, and the aforementioned carrot soufflé.

My mouth was watering as I put a napkin on my lap. "This is kind of an odd combo." I pointed at it all. It all smelled heavenly.

The girls were already shoveling pieces of quesadilla onto their plates.

Andro laughed. "It's family tradition. We have it every Thanksgiving. Let's just say there was a time when Yasmin and I would only eat quesadillas. It drove Mom crazy." He smiled and then looked sad.

I knew his mom and his dad, for that matter, were gone, but I didn't know the details. "You miss her, huh?"

He nodded.

I paused, waiting for more. It was not forthcoming, and I didn't want to pry. I turned to the girls. "So, which salsa is the best?"

"This one." Theresa pointed at the green sauce in front of her.

"No, this one!" Maria pointed at the red sauce in front of her.

"Girls, you have to leave at least one piece of quesadilla for Madison," Andro said. The girls had bogarted it all. I was a little disappointed. Quesadillas were one of my favorites.

"No worries." I smiled. "Everything else looks delicious, too." I started spooning food onto my plate.

It turns out carrot soufflé takes like pumpkin pie. "Mmmm," I said. "This is my new favorite vegetable."

Andro chuckled. "I'm not surprised."

After that, there wasn't much talking while we all stuffed our faces.

When we couldn't eat any more, we sat back in our

chairs and chatted. I debated asking if there were any practice Thanksgiving pies.

Someone knocked on the front door.

"Come in!" Andro called out.

The door swung open, and Yasmin stood there, smiling widely. She took a step inside, her beau Hector followed, also smiling.

The girls said, "Hi, Mommy and Hector."

"Hey, Hector," I said. "Hey, Yasmin." Something was up. Yasmin didn't usually look quite this happy.

"Hello, Madison," Yasmin said.

"Hey, Madison," Hector said.

I scrutinized Yasmin's hand. Beautiful ring--check. Ah ha. I knew what was up. They must have gotten engaged. That was awesome news. She was a widow and had had a very difficult couple of years. I jumped up. "Awesome! Congratulations!" I was so happy for her. I ran over to hug her.

Yasmin beamed. "Thanks."

Andro got up, looking confused.

Yasmin and I separated.

"I think they're--" I started to say. "Oops. Not my news to tell." I waved my hand at the happy couple.

"We're engaged!" Yasmin bounced up and down.

Hector nodded enthusiastically. "Yes. I am a very lucky man."

How sweet. I teared up a little at his obvious emotion.

Andro's look of confusion morphed into happiness. "That's great! Yes, congratulations!" He ran over and hugged Yasmin and then, after hesitating for a few seconds, enthusiastically hugged Hector.

Hector chuckled as he hugged him back.

I'm sorry to admit I had a split second of heartache, seeing Andro so happy and enthusiastic about Yasmin's marriage. Why couldn't he be happy like that about the idea of marrying me? Get a grip, Mad.

The girls were still sitting at the kitchen table.

"What's happening?" Theresa asked.

"There's going to be a wedding!" Yasmin said. "And you're going to be flower girls! And Hector's going to be your new dad!"

The girls looked uncertain.

"Ooh, wait," Andro said. "I have just the thing." He darted to the kitchen, opened the refrigerator door, and pulled out a bottle. "Let's have a congratulations toast!"

Yasmin's eyes narrowed. "What's that? The girls can't have wine, Andro."

He chuckled. "Relax. It's sparkling cider."

"Let me help." I went to the kitchen and started getting out glasses. Soon all six of us had a small glass of sparkling cider.

Andro held his up. "To Yasmin and Hector." He seemed to be blinking back tears. "Two of my favorite people. I wish you all the happiness in the world."

We all yelled, "To Yasmin and Hector!" and took a sip. I was definitely blinking back tears. It was wonderful Yasmin could find love again after losing it.

"Actually," Hector said, looking a little sad. "Can we toast Armando?" Armando had been Yasmin's husband and Hector's best friend.

A tear escaped and rolled down my cheek. I wiped it unobtrusively.

Andro smiled sadly. "How about we toast 'dads'?" He glanced at the girls. "Is that okay, girls?" My heart ached again to see him acting like such a great dad himself. Sophia was a lucky little girl.

The girls nodded. I got the distinct impression they weren't sure what to make of all this.

"To dads!" we all said and then took a sip.

We all finished our cider, and Yasmin and Hector collected Theresa and Maria.

When the front door closed behind them, I said, "I've got a proposal for you."

"Yes?" Andro looked concerned. I knew he thought I was thinking about a marriage proposal. But when we'd had the marriage talk a while ago, it hadn't gone well, so I knew better than to bring it up again. At one point, I'd thought I wanted to marry Andro, but with everything we'd been through, I was less sure now. He hadn't been a hundred percent there for me in the past. But maybe that was an impossible bar?

"I propose I help you with the dishes?" I asked. This was

extra nice of me because he didn't have a dishwasher.

He laughed, relieved (probably). "Yes, you can."

We'd just finished cleaning the kitchen when he said, "Would you like some green tea?"

"That dragon fruit stuff you have?" I nodded. "Sounds good to me."

He filled the tea kettle with a little water and turned on the stove, and I sat down at the kitchen table. He took a box of tea from the cabinet and put it on the table. Almost immediately, the tea kettle started whistling. He poured hot water into two mugs and brought them over.

I dropped a tea bag into my mug. I smelled dragon fruit-- whatever that was, something fruity anyways. "Mmmm."

Andro smiled, organized his own beverage, took a sip, and then said, "Something about a hot beverage after a meal hits the spot."

"I concur."

We sipped in companionable silence for a few moments.

I was thinking about Armando and a life snuffed out too early. I was thinking about being able to pick yourself up after a tragedy and keep going. I was thinking about two little girls growing up without a dad. Until now.

"Do you want to talk?" he asked, picking up on my melancholy mood.

He probably thought I wanted to talk about the big-M (marriage), and I didn't want to talk about that. Really. "Thank you for the nice dinner, Andro." Generally, I tried to be positive.

He smiled.

I was still appreciating that carrot soufflé, aka near-pumpkin-pie. "Pumpkin!" I said, joking. "Your pet name could be pumpkin." Now that the girls were gone, I was hoping things might take a more romantic turn. I needed some fun. We both did at this point.

He snickered.

We sipped.

And then the non-ghost appeared in front of us. "Maahh. . .," it said. Dammit! So much for the possibility of some romantic times with Andro.

I didn't know if it was my melancholy mood or what, but I felt sorry for the 'ghost.' I put down my tea and stood up.

Andro jumped up and held out his hands like he was going to quantum zap the creature.

I thought it was a q-lapser. I reached for it. "Focus on solidifying! Instantiate the reality in which you're standing here!" I concentrated. Luckily that beer back at Boulder Brews was quite a while ago. I focused. "You're real! You're solid!" I tried to concentrate on helping him q-lapse.

The misty man began to coalesce into a real man. "Madison, help me!" he said.

"I'm here," I said. "Focus on me. I'll help you." I'd started all this q-lapsing after all. No one deserved to be stuck in quantum limbo.

The man solidified. I felt his hand in my hand, warm and real.

But my spirits fell as I realized who it was. This could be bad. This could be very bad.

The non-ghost had materialized into a six-foot-tall, handsome, twenty-three-ish Italian-American man. Luke Bacalli.

Standing next to me, Andro said, "Shit."

The former ghost smiled tentatively. "Thank you. Thank you for helping me."

The next thing I knew, he was wrapping his arms around me. "Thank you." His voice was full, as if he was crying. "Thank you."

I patted his back. "There, there, Luke. You're okay now. You're okay."

For the moment, we all ignored the fact that Luke Bacalli, my brilliant former student, was the biggest, most nefarious quantum criminal of all time.

Chapter Six

When Luke and I stepped apart, I was at a loss for what to do next. "Would you like some green tea?"

"I'd love some green tea," he said, flashing me an uncertain smile. His whole body shook like a molecule under Brownian motion.

"Have a seat." I pointed at the table.

Luke collapsed in a chair, still shaking.

When I looked at Andro, his mouth was hanging open like he couldn't believe I'd offer a nefarious criminal a soothing hot beverage and a seat. Then he closed his mouth, turned, got out a mug, poured hot water, and placed the mug in front of Luke. What a good sport.

But he needn't have worried; a plan was percolating.

The two of us watched as Luke put the teabag in the water and began to dunk it up and down.

Andro grabbed my arm and whispered fiercely in my ear, "Can I talk to you for a minute, please?"

I knew what he was going to say: I shouldn't be hugging or offering tea to criminals. But I just smiled at him and said, "Sure."

We stepped out of the kitchen and walked across the family room, keeping an eagle eye on Luke all the while.

"What are you doing?" Andro whispered.

"I'm getting ready to call in the cavalry," I said, cutting him off at the pass. "I know Luke killed Armando. I know he needs to pay. But we need to be cautious. He's dangerous."

"So this is you lulling him into a false sense of security?" Even though he was still whispering, I could detect the sarcasm.

"Yes. Exactly. Keep an eye on him. I'll call Ben and Agent Baker."

He nodded.

More loudly, I said, "Gosh, I have to pee," and speed-walked down the hall.

From the kitchen, I heard faintly, "Jeez. TMI."

In Andro's bedroom, I closed the door, pulled out my phone, and speed-dialed Ben. "Ben," I whispered.

"What?" he said. "Speak up. I can't hear you."

Why was I whispering? There was a hallway and a closed door between me and Luke. "Ben, it's Madison."

"I know who it is," he said.

Ack, right. I was rattled. "I'm calling on official business. Luke Bacalli just showed up at Andro's apartment. I need you to bring Boulder P.D. and arrest him for killing Armando."

"Oh no!" he yelled. His voice really carried. I was glad there were many feet and a closed door between me and Luke. I didn't want to spook him. I wasn't sure if he could q-lapse away at this point, but he could definitely run away.

"Shh!" I said. "He's a good q-lapser, so you'll need to sneak up on him. And you'll probably need to tase him immediately. Bring back up, but no sirens or anything. The front door of Andro's place is unlocked."

"I thought Luke was dead," Ben said.

"Yeah, me too," I said. "Apparently not. Hurry up and get over here. I'm calling Agent Baker next. Hopefully, she can q-lapse over here and provide backup from inside the apartment."

"This is bad," he said.

"Are you coming or not?" I asked.

"Sorry. Yeah. We're on the way." He hung up.

I speed-dialed Agent Baker.

"Baker," she answered in clipped tones.

"Luke Bacalli just showed up at Andro's apartment," I said. "Ben and Boulder P.D. are on the way. Can you q-lapse over here now and provide backup?"

She was silent for a moment, and I imagined her thinking, 'I thought he was dead.' but thankfully, she didn't say it. "Yes. Hold up your phone. Show me the apartment." It was easier to q-lapse to a place you'd been before and could clearly picture in your mind's eye. She'd only been to Andro's apartment once before.

I held up my phone, scanning the room with the camera. "Here I come," she said.

I imagined her standing next to me. I concentrated. I focused.

Poof, suddenly she was standing next to me. Even after five o'clock, she wore one of her dark power pantsuits, and her graying blonde hair was in her signature ponytail.

She looked a little wobbly. "How do you feel?" I asked.

"My head hurts." She put her phone in her pocket, unholstered her gun, and took a step towards the door. "What's Ben's ETA? Maybe I'll let him take point until my headache goes away."

I shrugged. Boulder wasn't that big. "A couple of minutes?" She nodded.

"I better go back," I said. "We don't want him to get suspicious." I opened the door and walked back down the hall to the family room.

Andro still stood on the edge of the kitchen, near the hall, staring bullets at Luke.

Luke still sat at the kitchen table, sipping tea. He looked terrible, skin grayish, hair lank like he was on death's door. I guessed being in quantum limbo for two years or so wasn't so good for your health.

Andro glared at me as I walked by him.

I approached the kitchen table and gingerly sat across from Luke. Belatedly, I realized if the cops came in shooting, I was in the line of fire. Maybe I should get up. But wouldn't that look suspicious? Ugh. Focus, Mad.

I picked up a mug and took a sip. "Good, huh?" Luke nodded.

I was afraid to ask him anything because it might set him off. He probably blamed me for everything. And, truthfully, it was my fault he'd learned to q-lapse.

Behind Luke, the front door slowly opened. Ben and some other guys in SWAT gear tiptoed into the room.

I carefully tried not to look at them or react in any other way as they crept closer and closer to us. "Uh. Supposedly this has dragon fruit in it. I don't know what dragon fruit is, do you?"

He shook his head, 'No,' right before Ben zapped him with

48

a taser. He seized, muscles spasming. When the taser shut off, he dropped his mug, and it broke. His head hit the table with a smack. Ouch.

Agent Baker ran up, gun pointing at him.

I stood, backing away from all the guns and officers.

One of Ben's colleagues injected Luke with something.

"We got him!" Ben yelled. "Yeah!"

Agent Baker holstered her weapon. "I'll come with you guys." She pulled out her phone. "I better call this in."

And as quickly as they'd arrived, they all hustled themselves and Luke out of Andro's apartment.

Suddenly, Andro and I were standing there alone.

"I can't believe you almost put Theresa and Maria in danger!" He exploded like a supernova. "Oh, my God! And what if Sophia had been here?"

"None of them were here." I didn't put anyone in danger, except maybe his mug. I held up my hands. "You need to calm down."

"Don't tell me what to do!"

"Okay, sorry." I tried to keep my voice calm--not so easy when someone was yelling at me. "I can see you're upset, but I didn't do anything wrong. It's not like I invited Luke here or anything."

He just stood there fuming, lips pressed together in a thin line. I was guessing he was stopping himself from yelling at me some more--which I appreciated.

I took a step towards the door. And then I took another one. "Thanks for the nice dinner. I appreciate it." Step. He could stop me. Step. "I guess I'll see you at work." Step. He could ask me to stay. Step. "Goodnight."

Clearly, no kisses would be forthcoming tonight. He didn't even say goodnight.

I was too angry and annoyed at the moment to feel sad about it.

As soon as I got outside, I called Ryan. "Can I come over?"

"Yeaah. . ." he said, drawing out the word. "But it's pretty late. What's up?"

The last time Luke had been around, he'd tried to kill Ryan

with a lawnmower and threatened his family. "This is more of an in-person discussion. I can be there in a few minutes." Andro's apartment and Ryan's house were both in the neighborhood due south of campus. Practically everyone who lived in that area either went to school or worked at the university.

"Okay," Ryan said.

As I walked over, I tried to calm down. Seeing Luke again brought up mixed emotions. The encounter itself was very stressful. On the other hand, I was relieved I hadn't actually killed him two years ago when I thought I had. I was worried about what would happen to him now--they wouldn't just shoot him like they did Nate, would they? My thoughts whirled round and round like a satellite in Earth's orbit.

And, yes, I was avoiding thinking about me and Andro and our relationship.

Several minutes later, I knocked softly on Ryan's front door.

He opened it right away. He was wearing his ratty old robe. Behind him stood his beautiful wife Sydney, wearing her beautiful matching ginkgo leaf pajamas and robe.

Sydney was like a tiny brunette Martha Stewart. "What's happening?" she asked with fear in her voice.

I stepped inside, and Ryan closed the door behind me. "I don't know how to say this, so I'll just say it. Luke's back. Ben took him into custody."

"Oh no!" Sydney's hand flew in front of her mouth.

"Shit," Ryan said. "I thought you said he was dead."

"I thought he was," I said. "I saw his molecules fly apart."

"But he got better?" Ryan asked.

"I guess." I nodded. "Yes."

"We have to get out of town!" Sydney said. Considering Luke had come here to this very house in the past, she had a good point.

"We shouldn't assume he'll escape," I said. "He is in custody."

"You and Emily go to your mom's place," Ryan said, ignoring me.

"We don't want to go without you," she said.

"Ryan, I think you should go, too," I said. "Luke knows where you live."

"Come on, Ry," Sydney said.

"If you go with them, you can protect them," I said.

He nodded. "All right. Let's get out of here ASAP."

There was an outside chance this might be the last time I saw them. I reached out and hugged him and then her. "Hug Emily for me," I whispered. "I love you guys. Good luck."

Back at my apartment, I waited up for Ben.

The second he walked in the front door, I basically pounced on him, like a hungry grad student grabbing the last seminar cookie. "What happened? Is he still in custody?"

Ben sighed as he saw me. "Just a second." He held up his hands. "It's been a long shift." He walked to the kitchen, emptied his pockets, got a beer from the fridge, and opened it. He sat down at the kitchen table and took a swig of beer. "Ahhh."

I sat down across from him. I resisted asking 'What happened?' infinity more times. I felt my pulse zinging through my body like electricity through high power lines.

He took another swig. Finally, he put down the now half-empty bottle. "Yes. He's still in custody. We're keeping him sedated."

"Good." But my mouth curled into a frown. "So much for his fifth and sixth amendment rights."

Ben frowned, too. "I know. But we have irrefutable evidence that he killed Andro's brother-in-law in a hit-and-run accident. And we know he's committed a lot more crimes, including bank robbery. And he's very dangerous. We can't let him escape."

"What's the plan?" I asked. "I hope you're going to at least give him a trial for the hit-and-run."

"Me?" he said. "What's this 'me'? I'm not in charge." He gestured at his form-fitting uniform. "I did my part. Now it's up to the D.A. and others to do their parts."

"The U.S. Attorney guy declined to prosecute for the bank robbery and all that other quantum stuff back then," I said. "He said there wasn't any evidence." Apparently, q-lapsing seemed pretty freaky to uninitiated people, like U.S. Attorneys. And basically every other human being.

"If I was in charge, he'd be prosecuted for the hit-and-run," he said. "Since someone died, it's a class three felony punishable by four to twelve years in prison and fines up to $750,000. Once he was in prison, we could try to collect more evidence for the other stuff."

"Four to twelve years for someone's death doesn't seem like very much," I said. Poor Armando. Poor Yasmin. Poor Theresa and Maria. Poor Andro. I was feeling melancholy again.

"No, it's not." Ben drank some more of his beer.

"I guess it would be better than nothing," I said. I didn't say they could have a hard time keeping him in prison, considering he could q-lapse out. "Are they going to pursue it?"

He shrugged. "When I left, that Agent Baker was transferring him into federal custody."

If she was taking charge of everything, her q-lapsing headache must be gone--at least that was good.

"Are they going to kill him?" Even though Luke had done a lot of bad things, I didn't think that was right--especially without a trial and the chance to defend himself.

"I don't know what they're going to do."

"Do you think this is related to the destruction of that town?"

"I don't know," he said. "You're the quantum cop. Do you think it's related?"

"I don't know," I said. "How did Luke seem? Did he seem like he could q-lapse to destroy an entire town?"

"How the hell do I know?" His voice went up a little at the end there. "Actually, he seemed like he was in bad shape. I'm not sure he could collapse a beer can, the shape he was in."

That had been my impression, too.

We sat there at the kitchen table in silence for a few moments.

"Can I ask you something, Madison?" he finally asked. The way he said it, it was like he was nervous or something.

"Yes." Where was this going?

"I have to go to that wedding this weekend. Any chance you'd go with me. . . as my date?" He looked at me with hope in his eyes.

Chapter Seven

Of course, I agreed. Ben was a good guy; I'd been to my share of weddings alone--it was no fun.

I hypothesized Andro wouldn't care if I went to a wedding with another guy. Unfortunately. This hypothesis became fact when I mentioned it to him in passing. So, date with Ben. Check.

The next day after work, I surveyed my closet. Somehow I didn't think Ben's friends would appreciate my killer suit, which I only wore for interviews, no matter how nice it was.

My collection of nerdy t-shirts--such as Maxwell's electromagnetic equations with 'And then there was light,' 'This shirt is blue if you fly fast enough,' 'Never trust an atom; they make up everything,' and the like--weren't going to cut it either.

I had no wedding-worthy clothes.

Furthermore, I had very little time, so my go-to for shopping, the internet, wouldn't work. I also wasn't psyched about shelling out a lot for an outfit I might only wear once.

I called Sydney.

"What is it, Madison?" she said, breathless. "Is Luke attacking?"

"No." I gulped. I'd been texting Ryan with Luke updates every couple of hours (still in custody) but hadn't reached out to Sydney yet. Guilty much? "Sorry I haven't called. He's still in custody and sedated. They've taken him to Denver."

"That's what Ryan said," she said. "But I'm still worried."

"Are you still at your mom's?"

"No," she said. "We're back. Ryan was going stir-crazy." In the background, I heard Ryan yell, "Is that Madison? Is Luke coming after us? What's happening with Luke?"

"Nothing's happening with Luke." I pushed aside my guilt.

"Syd, I was just calling because I was wondering if you wanted to go shopping with me for a wedding outfit."

"Oh, my God!" she shrieked. "Andro popped the question? You're getting married? Oh, my God!"

"Shit!" Ryan yelled in the background. "I can't believe it!" What the heck did that mean? On the bright side, my annoyance with Ryan's reaction pushed away the guilt for not calling Syd earlier with a Luke update.

"No," I said. "I'm not getting married. Ben asked me to go to a wedding with him. I need an outfit."

"She's going to a wedding with Ben," Sydney said in the background.

"Oh," Ryan said. "That makes more sense. Atta boy, Ben!" I was calm. I was not annoyed. I was cool and collected.

"Anyway, do you want to go shopping with me?" I asked her. She hesitated for a moment but then said, "Sure."

I met Sydney at her house. She answered her front door after the first knock. "Hi, Madison!" She fairly beamed.

"Hi. . ." I wasn't sure I'd ever seen Sydney this excited. "So, you've stopped worrying about Luke?"

She waved me inside. "Ryan convinced me. Luke's sedated, and he's down in Denver." I felt a tiny bit guilty about Luke's situation.

Personally, I didn't think we were out of the woods yet, with Luke, but Ryan was a law enforcement professional. He must know better than me.

"So, are you ready to go?" I asked. "Is Emily coming?" I glanced around but saw no sign of the adorable little girl.

"No. She had a playdate she wanted to go to," Sydney said with a smile.

Personally, I hadn't known two-and-a-half-year-olds were in charge of their own schedules, but you learn something new every day. I smiled. "Next time."

"But, look, here's a bonus Martin," she said as Ryan walked up the front walk. Sydney hadn't quite managed to close the front door yet.

"Hey, Syd." He leaned down and kissed her. "Hey, Mad." He stepped towards me.

"You better not be getting ready to give me a kiss," I said.

He grinned and leaned down. "Just for that. . ." He gave me a peck on the cheek. It was nice.

"So, you're feeling good about the Luke situation?" I asked slowly.

He shrugged.

"You don't seem too guilty about any of this," I said.

"Luke broke the law," he said. "He needs to face the consequences."

"Did you get some kind of special training to avoid guilt?" I said. "I need that training or at least some advice on how to deal with all this."

He froze for a moment. "That's a longer conversation for another day." He smiled. "Today, where are you two fine ladies going?"

"We're going shopping!" Sydney chirped. "Where should we go? Downtown? The mall? Which mall?"

"We're going to Goodwill," I said.

"Aw," she said.

"Have you ever been to Goodwill?" I asked.

She shook her head.

"It's awesome."

The Goodwill thrift shop was crammed with racks and racks of clothing. Right near the entrance, there were glass cases filled with jewelry and a few selected pieces of nice furniture. Along the edges of the huge space, dressers and other less nice furniture resided.

I made a beeline for where I thought the fancy stuff was. Sure enough, there were several racks of designer and formal or semi-formal women's clothing.

When I glanced at Sydney, following me, she seemed surprised. "This stuff is amazing," she said. "Designer." She held up a silk sleeve, examining the price tag. "This was probably several hundred bucks originally; now it's ten bucks."

I whistled. "Ten bucks? That's a lot for in here." I started pawing through the rack. "You really haven't been in here before?"

"No," she said, pawing through the rack herself. "I thought it would all be crap."

"I think you're forgetting what a rich town we live in," I said. "The median house price is like a million dollars. Plus, you get a bunch of rich college students that just leave stuff behind when they move away."

"I can't believe I've been paying retail when I could just come over here for pennies on the dollar." She pulled out a black silk blouse. "A dollar! And it's my size."

"Don't forget the cost to dry clean it."

She looked slightly less ebullient. Then, her expression changed again. "Will you let me choose for you, Madison? Please."

"What?"

"You said you were going to a wedding, right? Can I pick out your outfit?"

"Why?"

"You dress kind of crappy," she said. "No offense."

I glanced down at my jeans and t-shirt combo and then at her. Why did people always say 'no offense' right when they offend you? It was one of the mysteries of the universe.

"You're not angry, are you?" she asked.

I grinned. "No." I pulled some cash out of my pocket. "I've got sixty bucks. Do your worst."

She pulled a bunch of stuff off the rack, took me to the dressing room, and made me try it all on. Honestly, some of that stuff had to be a joke, like the lime-green bridesmaid dress. But Sydney was really enjoying herself, laughing and taking pictures.

As I stood there in lime-green polyester, I said, "Should I be concerned about blackmail?"

She giggled and wiggled her phone. "Let's just say I've got you right where I want you if I need any emergency babysitting or anything."

I couldn't argue with that. Of course, she knew she had me for emergency babysitting anyways. I was just happy she was in a good mood and not worried about a quantum criminal coming after her.

When Sydney was examining purses, I pulled out my cell and called Agent Baker.

"What now?" she answered.

"I'm just calling to check that Luke is still in custody," I said. "Or, is there something else I should be worried about?"

"No." She calmed. "Sorry. I guess I'm on edge, waiting for something to happen, now that Luke did reappear. He is still in custody. I'm looking at him right now."

I was counting my lucky stars that I hadn't gotten pulled into the FBI Luke drama yet. But Lisa knew I was available if she needed me.

"Maybe we'll get lucky, and the shit won't hit the fan," I said.

She frowned. "I don't think we're that lucky."

Yeah, I didn't think we were that lucky either.

Saturday, I got all gussied up, and Ben picked me up at my bedroom door. (Luke was still in custody.)

He whistled when he saw me. "Wow, you clean up nice." He shook his head a little. "I'm not sure I've ever seen you all dressed up before."

I wore a blue silk dress Sydney'd picked out that clung to my curves in all the right places, strappy black sandals, and had a new (to me) matching purse. I'd accessorized with sterling silver drop earrings and a pendant I'd inherited from my aunt.

"Thanks, I think." I was starting to get a little annoyed with Ben. "You make it sound like I'm dirty all the time."

He grinned. Uh oh. That grin was deadly; it said, 'Dirty sounds fun. We could make love (or at least strong like) all night long.' He'd clearly interpreted the word 'dirty' differently than I'd meant.

Phew. Resist, Mad. "So, ah, what was I saying?"

"I don't know." Grin. "What were you saying?"

"You look nice, too." He had on a nice, dark blue suit. It was kind of a shock, frankly, since I'd only ever seen him in his uniform, jeans, or casual workout-type clothes. Or naked. There was that one time I saw him naked. He looked exceptionally good naked. Phew. Don't think about that!

He held out his arm, and I took it, but only because I wasn't used to walking in high heels. That was the only reason, I swear. It wasn't because I watched to clutch the buff arm of a handsome officer of the law.

Andro and I had never been to a wedding together, and I

was starting to think we never would. But… That was a downer topic. I wasn't going to think about any downer topics. I was going to try to have fun. I deserved it.

And Ben deserved it. I glanced at him, handsome as ever. He spent all his time protecting and serving. He spent all his time trying to help other people.

The service at Boulder Presbyterian was nice. The couple wrote their own vows. I liked it when people wrote their own vows; it made it more personal.

The bride vowed never to nag him, to support his dreams, to be an awesome wife and mother to his future children. I had to blink back a couple of tears, but I wasn't the only one.

The groom vowed never to leave the toilet seat up (which got a laugh), to support her dreams, and to come home to her every single night, safe and sound.

In a room full of cops and cops' spouses, we were all blinking back tears at that point.

The reception was apparently at Folsom Field on the university campus. Considering this was where they played football games, I was quite confused as several of us wedding guests got in the elevator at the football stadium.

"I don't want to sound stupid," I whispered to Ben, "but where are we going?"

"Straight to the top!" He sounded gleeful.

We got out at someplace called the Byron R. White Club Level.

Not yet sunset, the views out the floor-to-ceiling windows were magnificent. The mountains and town of Boulder lay spread out before us. "Wow!" I said, looking at Ben. "This is amazing. I didn't know this was up here. Have you been here before?'

"Sure." He nodded, nonchalant. "Cops go everywhere. Plus, sometimes football tickets get donated to Boulder P.D. and we trade-off who gets to go. So, I've been to a game here. They had an open bar. It was pretty great."

"Hey, Ben!' One of his friends clapped him on the back.

We got busy greeting people. He introduced me to a lot of people as the quantum cop. They seemed impressed. I was having a great time. In fact, I couldn't remember the last time

I'd had so much fun. There was an open bar, and I hadn't even gotten around to getting a drink yet. And it wasn't like me to turn down free booze, so that says how much fun I was having.

People were starting to sit down to dinner, and Ben and I had just found our table when the groom approached us.

"Ben? And Madison? Right?" He looked worried, and it was disconcerting to see a groom looking so upset. He should look happy, even overjoyed.

Ben and I gave him our full attention.

"What's up, Evan?" Ben said. Oh, Evan, right; that was his name.

"We have a little problem," Evan said.

"What, buddy?" Ben said. "We're here for you, buddy, whatever you need." He gave me a pointed glance that said, 'Step up, girl!'

"Yes," I said. "We're totally here for you." My high spirits were sinking. Evan was acting like this was a matter for the quantum cop. Please don't let someone be hurt--or worse--here at the wedding. I started scanning the beautiful room for murder and mayhem.

"I'm not sure what's going on," Evan said. "But all the champagne and the wedding cake have disappeared."

Phew. "That's all!" I said. "Thank God."

The two men looked at me like I was some kind of extraterrestrial. "I mean, oh no. How awful."

"You got that right, 'oh no,'" Evan said. "We spent weeks tasting cakes. That cake cost a lot. If we don't have a cake, how will we cut the cake? How will we feed each other a piece of cake? How will we save the top layer for our first anniversary? It'll break Aria's heart; she loves all that traditional stuff. And the champagne was a gift from my parents. It was fancy. It'll break their hearts. How will we make toasts? How will--?"

Ben interrupted him. "We understand. It's bad. Show us where the stuff was."

Evan led us to a kitchen area adjacent to the reception area, filled with caterers. He pointed at a large empty table. "It was all right here. Just a minute ago."

"I assume you asked the caterers," Ben said, pointing at the staff.

"That's who told me it disappeared, the catering manager," Evan said. "I haven't told Aria yet. It'll break her heart." I was sensing a definite heart-breaking theme.

"Are you sure someone didn't just steal the stuff the regular way?" I asked.

"Yes!" Evan said. "It was here one second, and then, poof, it wasn't here!"

Ben looked at me. "It does sound quantum."

It did sound quantum. Damn. So much for my fun night off. "All right," I said. "Give me some space." In the past, I'd been able to sort of follow quantum criminals by sensing large improbabilities.

They took a step back.

I closed my eyes. I tried to empty my mind of my personal concerns (like how my feet were starting to hurt in my new shoes) and focus on improbabilities.

But I couldn't concentrate; I kept hearing the clink of utensils and quiet conversations amongst the caterers.

I opened my eyes. "Can we get the caterers to leave the room for a few minutes?"

"Yes," Evan said and darted over to them.

The caterers left the room.

I closed my eyes. I concentrated and focused on improbabilities. There. An improbability. I concentrated on it. I willed myself to be where it was. I felt myself fuzz out.

I concentrated and reappeared in some apartment with a big cake and a bunch of bottles of champagne on the kitchen table in front of me.

Where was I? I glanced around the room and saw. . . Griffin Jin--my former student and Luke's partner in quantum crime.

Chapter Eight

In some random apartment, who knows where, I stared at my former student, Griffin. Even though I hadn't seen him in about a year, he looked about the same: Asian-American, chubby, in his early twenties. Only his highlighted, spiked hair was different, giving off a surfer dude vibe.

I was getting a headache.

I finally found my voice. "Griffin, I'm disappointed in you, very disappointed." Last year I'd refrained from turning him in to the authorities on his promise that he wouldn't q-lapse ever again. He'd been involved in some nefarious deeds in the past, and his partner in crime had been summarily executed in a hail of bullets. I hadn't had the heart to do that to him.

For his part, he'd been staring at me with a look of horror. He said something that sounded like "Eep!" and then he fuzzed out and disappeared.

"Griffin, come back here!" I stamped my foot, forgetting I was wearing high heels. I almost twisted my ankle. Dammit.

Where was I? Griffin was supposed to be in California, but I had a sneaking suspicion he was not in California now. I went to the window and peeked out.

Flatirons. "Dammit!" He was back in Boulder. I did a quick limp-through of the apartment, gathering data. Judging by the furnishings: an ultra-high-end gaming system with a giant flat screen, a microwave, a pile of empty beer cans, and a futon, he, or some other single man, was living here alone.

I did spy a wallet, phone, and some cash on the floor near the bed. I checked the wallet, and it was Griffin's.

How did he even know about the wedding? And why steal from it?

Should I try to follow him, stay here and wait for him, or bring the wine and cake back to the wedding? It wasn't much of a dilemma. I voted for wine and cake.

As ransom, I took Griffin's wallet, cash, and game controller, concentrated, and q-lapsed myself back to the reception.

My headache was getting worse.

Ben and Evan jerked back when I poofed into the kitchen next to the reception area.

Ben was the first to recover. "What?"

"It's Griffin," I said, feeling my lip curl into a grimace.

Ben gasped. He knew Griffin was a quantum criminal. He didn't know I'd essentially let him go a year ago.

"What?" Evan asked. "Who's Griffin?"

"A perp," Ben said. "He's on my personal most-wanted list." Ben thought he was a quantum cop in training. I guessed he was. "Was he alone?"

I nodded. "As far as I know. But he got away. And you better make sure Luke's still in custody." I handed Ben Griffin's stuff. "Here. This should hamper him. Can you find a sticky note and write 'Call Madison ASAP' on it?" I was going to put it on Griffin's phone.

"Why?" Ben asked.

"I don't mean to sound callous, but what about the champagne and cake?" Evan asked.

"I'm going to bring it back," I said. "But I need you guys to keep this whole area clear. I'd hate to run into someone when I was holding a giant cake." It was so giant I was a little worried I'd be able to carry it. "Actually." I slipped off my fancy new (to me) shoes. "Can you put these somewhere safe?" I scooped them up and handed them to Ben.

"Sticky note?" Ben asked.

"I don't want to chase Griffin all over the galaxy. . ." I said.

Evan jerked back again as if he was surprised.

Ben smiled a little and shook his head. He knew we didn't go all over the galaxy. Although. . . Focus, Mad.

"I think he'll call me since I've got all his stuff," I said. "To summarize, take care of my shoes and Griffin's stuff, keep this area clear, get me a sticky note."

I didn't wait. I concentrated and willed myself back to the

apartment, grabbed two bottles of champagne (they were still cold), and q-lapsed myself back. I put the bottles on the sad, empty table.

Headache approaching the bad zone--but not near the hospital zone yet.

Ben gave me a sticky note.

"Actually, look for a bag or box or something for the rest of the bottles," I said. "I'm going to get the cake."

I q-lapsed back to Griffin's apartment and very, very carefully picked up the cake. It had three round layers, the bottom was about eighteen inches in diameter and seven inches thick, and they got slightly smaller from there. The whole thing was covered in ivory icing with real (yep, I touched one) white and light pink roses. I q-lapsed back to the kitchen and carefully put the cake on the table. Phew.

Ow. My head.

Evan stood there, staring, his eyes bugging out a little.

Ben handed me a large cloth bag with a sturdy shoulder strap.

"Nice," I said. "You know, I've been thinking. . ."

"How did Griffin know about the reception?" Ben asked. Huh. He was a pretty good quantum cop, or at least a good regular cop.

"Yes," I said. "Someone here must have told him. And I'd be surprised if it was a cop." Actually, now that I was thinking about it, it was pretty crazy to attack a cop wedding. . . At least half the people here were cops. Maybe he didn't know it was a cop wedding?

"I'll question the staff," Ben said.

"Yep." I nodded. "That's what I was getting at. Be right back."

I q-lapsed back to the apartment and went and picked up Griffin's phone. I texted myself the numbers already in there (only four). I stuck the sticky note on it and placed it back on the floor.

I went back to the kitchen, put the rest of the bottles in the bag, and q-lapsed back to the wedding reception. I unloaded the bottles onto the table.

Bad headache.

Ben came up to me. "One of the staff apparently took off when I started questioning the caterers."

"Friend of Griffin's?" I said.

"Probably." He shrugged. "What do you think we should do now?"

He was asking me? He was a cop. My headache was making me grumpy. "I have to drink some coffee and take some pain meds for my aching head." I felt like I was wilting. I wanted to go home and lie down but wasn't entirely sure I could even make it there at this point.

"Are you all right?" He seemed sincerely concerned.

"Probably," I said.

He looked alarmed.

"I mean, yeah," I said. "I just really need some coffee. Can you commandeer some for me?" I pointed at the caterers. I was guessing there was a hundred percent chance they had coffee here.

"What are you going to do?" he asked.

"I have to go sit down for a minute and take some pills." I pointed back in the direction of the reception.

I went back to my chair and took my special prescription strength headache capsules that I'd taken to carrying around in my purse. It felt good to sit down. I exhaled and leaned back in the chair. I wondered where my shoes had gotten to?

Most of the wedding guests were still milling around the open bar. I saw a lot of smiles. They must be happy for the bride and groom and optimistic about their future together. Nice. Or they'd already enjoyed several drinks. Anyway, the cake was returned, and the reception wasn't ruined. That was a good thing.

Ben rushed up with a steaming cup of coffee. "Here."

"Bless you." I took a big gulp. Too hot. Ouch. I blew on it and cautiously took another sip.

"What now?" he asked. Ben was attractive and a good guy, but he wouldn't become a detective, or a quantum cop, or an FBI agent for that matter if he didn't take more initiative. I resisted sighing.

"Go get me another cup of coffee and let me rest for a few minutes."

He rushed off.

I watched the crowd, sipping my coffee. My headache started receding. Huzzah. I wouldn't die of a brain aneurysm. In retrospect, it was probably stupid to risk my life for a cake and some fancy wine.

Note to self: in the future, think before q-lapsing. Sadly, I dimly recalled making that note to self in the past. Maybe I should get it tattooed?

Ben brought me another cup, setting it gently on the table in front of me and studying my face.

I finished the first cup and started in on the second. My headache was not as bad now.

Ben rushed over to Evan and said something in his ear. Evan looked instantly happier. Ben said something else. Evan pointed at the chair in front of him.

Ben scooped up my shoes and brought them over, setting them gently on the floor near my feet.

He stood. "Should I still leave you alone?"

I shook my head, cradling the cup in my hands. "Sit."

He sat in the chair next to me.

"What can you tell me about Luke?" I asked.

"I've been assured he's still in custody. They even showed me a picture." He held his phone up in front of me. "What are you thinking?" he asked.

"Griffin's back in town, in Boulder," I said. Ben knew Griffin could be anywhere on Earth and still steal from this wedding.

"In Boulder!" he said. "Where is he? We should bring him in."

Shoot. I just realized I should have already told Andro about Griffin; they had a long, unpleasant history. And Ryan. Crap. "Just a sec." I texted Andro and Ryan the info. And, yes, I was aware texting rather than talking was a bit wimpy. But at least I hadn't avoided the problem entirely, right? I was getting better.

I took a sip of coffee. "We can't bring him in right this second because we don't know where he is."

"Can't you just do that following improbabilities thing you do?"

Technically, he was right; I probably could. But I didn't want to. I didn't want a brain aneurysm. "I've already q-lapsed too much today."

I took another sip, debating what I wanted to say. I didn't think Griffin was that dangerous. I landed on, "Griffin's not much of a criminal."

Ben sputtered. "What do you mean? He escaped from federal custody! He robbed a couple of banks. He attacked people. He murdered people!"

"Griffin's a sidekick," I said. "He's not a mastermind. Luke was definitely the architect of the first set of quantum crimes. And I think the rogue FBI Agent, Nate Sawyer, coerced Griffin into helping him last year. Nate was probably the one who released him from federal custody. I know Griffin was afraid of him." We'd never actually unraveled all those threads--thanks to the hail of bullets hitting Nate. "I don't think Griffin murdered anyone. He just helped murderers."

"That still counts!" Ben said.

"I know." I nodded. "I'm not saying it doesn't count."

"What are you saying?" he asked.

What was I saying? "I think if we do. . ."

"If!" he said. "When," I said. "When we track Griffin down, I think we should try to turn him. Make him into a double agent."

"Double-agent is a spy thing, not a cop thing," Ben said, frowning. "What are you talking about? You want to make him into some kind of criminal informant?"

"Criminal informant!" I held up a finger. "Yes. That's what I'm saying! We can use him to smoke out the other quantum criminals."

"Other criminals? Isn't Luke the criminal? We have him. What do you think is going to happen?" Ben was still frowning. "Is Griffin trustworthy enough for that? Does he have the balls for it?"

Those were all good questions. "I'm not sure."

"Should we go pick him up?" he asked. "Where is he?"

I knew approximately where he was from the view outside his apartment window, but I wasn't up for picking anyone up. I was up for going home and going to bed. "I don't think we should pick him up. If he's going to be an informant, don't we have to make it look like he's on the street?"

Ben looked thoughtful.

I handed him my phone. "His number's in here. My last call.

I sent myself all the contacts on his phone. You can investigate. Please bring my phone back by the morning."

"What are you going to do?" he asked.

"I'm going home to bed," I said. "Please call me a ride."

He glanced around the room, looking disappointed. I could sympathize; I'd been looking forward to a fun evening of dining and dancing.

"You don't have to go," I said. "You should stay. How often does your buddy Evan get married, after all?" Hopefully, only once. Or twice. Or three times, tops.

"But. . ." he started to say.

As I scanned the room, I'd noticed a lot of people noticing Ben in his nice suit. "I think all three bridesmaids and maybe one of the groomsmen have been checking you out." I pointed at the group of four standing near the bar, and they all smiled broadly at Ben. I felt a split-second pang; it would be fun to spend the evening here with Ben. But I said, "You'll be fine."

"If you're sure you don't need me to come home with you to take care of you?" But he'd already taken out his phone.

Body language was a dead giveaway. I grinned a little. "I'm sure."

He made the call.

Once I'd had a lie-down, I'd be right as rain.

Hopefully.

Chapter Nine

Sunday morning, I woke as fresh as superconductivity in spin-three-half quasi-particle electronic structures. I stepped out of my bedroom. "Ben? What's the coffee sitch?"

But Ben didn't answer me. Maybe he'd gotten lucky, after all? I was not jealous of him. I was not at all jealous of the person he'd hooked up with. Not at all.

I sauntered into the kitchen. There was a note taped to the coffee machine. 'Coffee ready to go. Press button.' with a big arrow. I snickered. Even I could have figured that out. 'Call me.' There was another arrow pointing down at my phone on the counter.

I pushed the coffee button and then picked up my phone. There were a lot of missed messages and texts from Ben, Andro, Ryan, Sydney, and FBI Agent Lisa Baker. A lot of messages meant a lot of drama. A lot of drama meant bad guys. I started to feel as blah as regular conductivity.

I needed to fortify myself. I opened the fridge and found the tube of cinnamon rolls I'd bought earlier in the week. Yay! Cinnamon rolls on Sunday morning were perfect. I popped the tube and put the rolls in the oven. After I poured myself a cup of coffee, I pulled a chair over to the oven and stared through the little window, watching them bake. Yum. I sipped.

My phone rang, and I answered it, still staring into the oven. "Madison?" It was Andro.

We hadn't talked for a couple of days. "Yes."

"I'm sorry about how we left things when Luke showed up at my house," he said. "I didn't act …great."

"Thanks for saying that," I said.

"Are you all right?" he asked. "I heard you had some kind of quantum battle with Griffin and got hurt?"

I shook my head. "No. The grapevine's wrong. I just overdid the q-lapsing and gave myself a headache. I'm fine now." Sip.

"Griffin's really back, the little twerp?"

"'Fraid so."

He growled. "I could kill him. . ." Andro was there when I'd basically banished Griffin to California. Correction: I'd thought I'd banished him, but apparently, it hadn't stuck.

Andro frowned. "I guess we should have turned him in back then."

"Maybe not." I peeked in the oven. The rolls were rising and turning goldeny. "I guess you didn't hear. We're going to turn him into a double agent once we bring him in." Sip.

Andro laughed a little. "You mean a criminal informant?" Why did everyone but me know all the crime-fighting lingo?

"Yeah."

"Once you bring him in?" he asked. "I guess you didn't hear. They brought him in last night. Tasered him, tasered him hard. I don't know what they're doing to him to keep him in custody, more tasering or drugs or what, but he's still there."

"What!" I jerked my head up, narrowly missing the oven handle. "They brought him in already?"

"Don't you check your messages?" he asked.

"Not yet," I said. "I'm fortifying myself, getting ready. Can we talk later?"

"Sure." He paused. "I'm glad you're all right," he said tenderly. "Bye, babe."

I briefly wished we were snuggled up in bed together for a sexy Sunday morning. "Bye, babe." We hung up.

I looked at my long list of missed calls and texts. I decided to call Agent Baker. Lisa. After everything we'd been through, I was determined to get on a first-name basis with her. "Hey, Lisa."

"Hey, Madison." No admonishments! This was progress. "What do you want?"

"Where's Luke?" I asked.

"In custody, as far as I know," she said. "Do you know something I don't know?"

"No." I definitely didn't know as much as Lisa about bad guys. "I hear Griffin's also in custody. Do you have him?"

"I might," she said. I thought I detected a smile in her voice. "What's it worth to you?"

"What do you want?" I asked nervously. I thought Lisa and I were friends, but I also knew she had a holding cell and wasn't afraid to use it.

"I want you to start teaching FBI agents about q-lapsing classes again." She was the only agent that I'd successfully taught. Correction: the only good agent. "The brass is demanding it."

"Are you sure that's a good idea?" Honestly, I was tired of having the same argument with Lisa. Q-lapsing was too dangerous to teach people. "Absolute power corrupts absolutely," I said.

"Are you saying you're corrupt?" she asked.

"No." The rolls puffed up in the oven. I took a sip of coffee, willing them to bake faster.

"Are you saying I'm corrupt?" she asked with steel in her voice.

"No, uh, of course not," I said, backpedaling. "But we didn't think Nate was corrupt, either, did we?" Nate had been her partner, and he'd definitely been corrupt. I held up my hand. "Enough. I'm sick of debating it. I'll start the class up again. I think we should do it at the university's physics building." That was the only place I'd successfully taught people to q-lapse.

"So, what's going on with Griffin?" I asked.

"We've got him in custody at Boulder P.D. Ben and Detective Davis are trying to convince him to become our informant. I'm observing."

I was a little annoyed. How could they do all this without me? Without even consulting me? Wasn't it my idea? And I was the one with a relationship with him.

I shook my head a little. Focus, Mad. It wasn't about me.

"Is he all right?" I asked. "How many times did they tase him? Have they been giving him drugs?"

"No taser," she said. "At least not once they apprehended him. No drugs. He's been cooperating. If I didn't know better, I'd say he was depressed. Or scared. Maybe both." She paused for a moment. "He asked for you."

"Why didn't somebody call me?" I asked.

"We did," she said. "I called you. Ben called you. For all I know, other people called you. You didn't answer."

"I've, uh, been busy," I said stiffly.

"Well, it's Sunday morning," she said. "I know you're not drinking beer. I know you're not at church--"

"I could be at church," I said.

"If you're at church, you should quit talking on the phone and disrupting the service," she said very reasonably.

"Okay, I'm not at church."

"So, you're either having some kind of sex games with Andro, or you slept late, and now you're gorging yourself on coffee and cinnamon rolls."

The rolls were just about to come out of the oven, almost ready for their crown of delicious cream-cheese icing. I was annoyed that she thought she knew me so well. And clearly, I was too predictable. I needed to shake things up a bit. "You're wrong," I said. Technically, she was wrong. I hadn't started gorging. The rolls weren't ready yet.

"About which part?" she asked. I definitely heard a smile in her voice.

"I'm on my way to the station," I said. I could gorge on the way.

When I got to the police station, the desk officer called Ben without me even needing to ask.

About two minutes later, Ben jogged out from the back. "There you are. Good." He smiled. It made him look good. As in handsome and charming good. Dammit.

I'd been all ready to yell at him for going behind my back and bringing Griffin in without me and possibly hurting him, but I knew he meant well. He was pretty straight-arrow. More so than me anyway. So, I just said, "How's it going?"

"Come on back." He led the way. "I think he's open to being a CI. He knows something about what's going on now, but we haven't been able to get it out of him. He asked for you." He turned and glanced at my face. "He seems depressed." He nodded at a uniformed officer standing at attention outside a closed door.

The officer nodded back.

Ben opened the door, and we went into the interrogation room. It was a small, plain room with a table, four uncomfortable wooden chairs, and a big mirror. I'd been interrogated before in this very room. I couldn't say it was my favorite place.

When we came in, Griffin looked up and me and seemed relieved. "Thank God, Professor Martin."

The other person in the room was a plainclothes detective I did not like because he'd basically arrested me for murder last year. "Detective Davis." I nodded, but not in a friendly way. Davis was a balding, overweight, white, middle-aged man. Essentially, he looked like a stereotypical television detective. But I guessed stereotypes existed for a reason.

"Ms. Martin." Davis nodded back. Then he turned back to Griffin, curling his lip. "The perp's been asking for you. Why is that?"

I couldn't help thinking: lawyer. The kid needed a lawyer. He needed a lawyer bad.

Ben pointed at the empty chair next to Davis and stood behind him, at attention.

I sat. "It must be because of my charming personality." I smiled.

Griffin leaned over the table toward me. "Professor Martin, you have to help me. It's starting again. People are making me do things, things I don't want to do. Bad things."

Davis snorted. "Going for an insanity plea, kid? Don't bother."

I gave him a dirty look and reached out for Griffin's hand and squeezed it gently. "I'm here for you, Griffin. I'm sorry you're having a tough time." Considering he could q-lapse out of here any time he wanted, he was being surprisingly cooperative.

Davis was scowling. "No touching."

Griffin and I stopped touching.

I leaned back a little. "Did they tell you what they want? They want you to go along with the quantum criminals and help us take them down."

He nodded. "But can you protect me from them?"

"Yes," I said. I hoped so. "We need your help. Can we count on you?"

He nodded again.

This situation wasn't really fair. Or legal. I couldn't help myself; I had to say it. "Lawyer."

Davis scowled some more. It seemed to be his go-to expression.

"He needs a lawyer," I said, pointing at Griffin. "Did you ask for a lawyer, Griffin?"

He stared at me for a moment. Then he said, "Lawyer."

Davis got up. "Can I speak with you for a moment, Ms. Martin?" He pointed at the door. "In the hall."

Outside, he grabbed my arm. Ow. "What the fuck do you think you're doing?" he said.

I shook him off. "I think I'm protecting the sixth amendment rights of a young man, who, as far as I know, hasn't been charged with any crimes. He has a right to counsel."

Another door opened. Lisa stepped out.

"Technically, she's right, sir," Ben said. He'd followed us out of the interrogation room. Yay, straight arrow.

"You all know this is an unusual situation." Davis clipped his words like he was trying to keep from shouting.

Lisa approached us. "Freedom act."

"Ugh!" I said. "I'm sick of debating the same things with you people. That kid is not a terrorist. I thought we were supposed to be the good guys? The good guys follow the rules; they don't break the rules. They follow the United States Constitution."

Ben was nodding.

"The kid is a significant security threat," Davis said.

"He's a U.S. citizen," I said. "He has rights."

"I disagree," Davis said.

I stopped myself from saying, 'Well, screw you,' or worse.

The four of us stared at one another. No one said anything. I was trying to resist cussing out Davis. I don't know what the rest of them were resisting.

"I guess we can take over," Lisa said. "FBI jurisdiction. You won't have to worry about him, Davis."

Davis threw up his hands. "Fine." He turned and stalked away.

"Griffin's a bad guy, Madison," Ben said. "He needs to face the consequences of his actions."

"I agree he's done bad things," I said. "And I agree he needs to face consequences. I just think we should follow the rules."

Lisa was shaking her head, but she didn't look upset. "I guess we're taking him down to Denver to the field office."

"Can I come?" Ben asked.

I wanted to ask, 'Can I not come?' but I knew I was stuck. I had to go.

"Sure, Ben," she said. "You've been involved in all this stuff since the beginning, haven't you?"

He nodded, and the two of them entered the interrogation room together.

"How did it start for you?" she asked inside the room. The door was still open.

Cooling my heels in the hall, I debated q-lapsing some more baked goods or coffee into my hands but decided against it. Unfortunately. I might need to save my q-lapsing for something more dire.

Inside the interrogation room, I heard Ben say, "I went to break up a party on The Hill, and my clothes disappeared. There I was buck naked--"

"Never mind." She held up her hand. "I don't want to know."

The two of them brought Griffin out, handcuffed. When he saw me, he relaxed a little. "Oh, good, Dr. Martin." He glanced back at the law enforcement officials on either side of him and said, "Lawyer."

I could call my lawyer, Tom, but I was already too embroiled in Griffin's problems. "If you're going to be in Denver, you might be better off with a Denver lawyer," I said.

As the four of us stood there in the hall of the Boulder P.D. station, a ghost materialized next to Griffin. The misty man-shaped figure became more and more solid.

Griffin cried out, "Oh no. He's coming for me!" He turned and looked at me, clearly terrified. "Help!"

Ben jerked back and said something like, "Shit."

Lisa jerked back almost imperceptibly, gaping.

The ghost grabbed Griffin, and they both wisped away.

Chapter Ten

I gathered my courage in the hallway of the Boulder P.D.

Ben and Lisa both gave me looks that said, 'Go after him!'

I knew it wasn't truly a ghost who'd stolen Griffin. It must be Luke. He must be out of custody. I also knew I had to go after them. I couldn't procrastinate--at least not more than these few seconds.

I focused, seeking improbabilities. I concentrated on the resulting found improbabilities and q-lapsed.

I reappeared in a cloud. Misty white nothingness surrounded me, closing in on all sides. I couldn't see anything but whiteness; I couldn't feel or hear anything. It felt a little like being dead and buried in a cloud.

Was this quantum limbo? I'd been in quantum limbo before. It seemed to be a misty cloud of nothingness, of possibilities, rather than reality. Where exactly it was in the universe, I did not know.

I wasn't sure it actually was in the universe.

Quantum limbo terrified me. Was this where Luke had been stuck? Despite his evilness, I felt sorry for him.

"Hello?" I said. "Luke? Griffin?"

No answer.

"Anyone? Is anyone there?"

No one answered.

Well, crap. They must have moved on. I needed to follow them.

I focused, seeking improbabilities. I concentrated. All the white nothingness was scaring me. I squeezed my eyes tight, concentrating harder, looking for improbabilities.

Unfortunately, I was surrounded by improbabilities. I was

cocooned in a white misty cloud of improbabilities. All I could sense were improbabilities. I couldn't sense Luke or Griffin or where they might have gone at all.

"Shit!" I'd lost them. Luke had figured out a way to stop me from following him.

It wasn't going to work.

I didn't want to be here any longer than I had to. I focused, concentrating on being back in that hallway at Boulder P.D., and a moment later, I appeared back in that hallway at Boulder P.D. with a headache.

No one was standing there. Had Luke done something to them?

"Hey! Hello? Anyone?" I called.

A woman in uniform poked her head around the corner and frowned at me. "Who--?"

"It's okay." Ben touched her shoulder and then jogged past her to me. "Oh, good. There you are. What happened? The ghost took Griffin, and then you disappeared, too."

"It wasn't a ghost," I said. "It was Luke. He took Griffin. I followed them."

"Did you get them?" He looked behind me. "Where are they?" He seemed puzzled.

"I lost them," I said, starting to seriously feel the pain in my head.

Lisa appeared and walked toward us. "Where are they?" She must have realized what was going on.

Ben pointed at me. "She lost them."

Her eyebrows rose. "You lost them?"

"How many times do I have to say it?" I said. "Yes. I lost them. They got away."

"How'd they manage that?" she asked.

"It was pretty brilliant, er, I mean dastardly," I said. "They went through quantum limbo."

Lisa shuddered and looked sick. And with good reason. She'd been to quantum limbo before. Once. For a couple of minutes. And that had been more than enough.

"I don't get it," Ben said.

"I used q-lapsing to follow Luke and Griffin's strong improbabilities, right?" I said.

He shrugged.

"Well, I did," I said. "I followed them to quantum limbo--which is made of improbabilities. Going through there blocks their improbability signal because the whole place is improbabilities. Like I said, as escape plans go, it was pretty brilliant."

Lisa frowned.

"Of course, I meant brilliant in a bad villainy kind of way." I suppressed a groan. Luke had been one of my best students of all time. Okay, if I was being honest, he was the best. He might have accomplished amazing things if he'd stayed on the straight and narrow.

"Aw," Ben said. "So, they foiled you? Your following thing was your neatest quantum power."

Now I felt worse, and I hadn't thought that was possible.

"Let's regroup," Lisa said.

I said, "Is there any chance I could get some--"

"Coffee?" Ben asked. "Yeah. I was just brewing a new pot."

My hero.

I sat in Boulder P.D.'s bland, boring conference room, sipping coffee with Ben and Lisa. The furniture quality was a step up from that in the interrogation room. The table was polished wood, or at least looked like it, and the chairs had padding.

Lisa was looking at her phone. "So, to summarize, Luke Bacalli's back, stronger than ever, he escaped from custody, and now he's got his sidekick Griffin Jin with him."

I sipped. Mmm. Coffee. That was about the only good thing about this day. And those cinnamon rolls I'd scarfed down.

Lisa looked up at me and gave me her evil eye stare. It was pretty scary, but I was learning to ignore it. Mostly. "I still can't believe this Luke kid is back? I thought you killed him?"

"Yeah, Madison." Ben chimed in. "You said he was dead."

"I thought he was dead," I said slowly. "I made his molecules and protons and neutrons fly apart. He should be dead."

Ben looked confused.

Lisa was still giving me her evil eye.

I cleared my throat. "If you recall, I also thought I spotted Luke last year. Maybe he was gathering his molecules. . ."

"How come I didn't hear about this before?" Ben asked.

"I thought you decided Nate was impersonating Luke?" Lisa asked at the same time.

"I thought so," I said, replying to Lisa and ignoring Ben. "But maybe Nate was only impersonating Luke part of the time."

"Part of the time?" Lisa said.

"We don't know for sure since Nate, ah. . ." Since the FBI took him out. "Since we didn't get to interrogate him. I would have liked to ask him some questions."

Now Lisa looked angry. Her way of dealing with betrayal? She and Nate had been partners for quite a while, and she'd thought they were close. She'd thought he was a good guy. Ryan thought he was a good guy. Heck, even I thought Nate was a good guy. Until I'd learned otherwise.

"The FBI was the one who ordered shoot to kill," Ben said. He'd been there. "Generally, it is better to bring people in for trial."

"Rehashing the past isn't getting us anywhere," Lisa said, with her evil eye now directed at Ben. "What are we going to do moving forward?"

"We need to find Luke and Griffin," I said. "I can try to train more FBI agents to q-lapse."

"I'd like to get in on that action," Ben said.

I shrugged. It was surprisingly difficult to teach law enforcement officers to q-lapse. They didn't seem to have the imagination for it. But the more, the merrier--assuming they didn't turn evil. "Fine with me." I looked at Lisa.

"Okay." She sipped her own coffee. "Where should we look for the q-criminals?"

"We could use regular law enforcement techniques." I wanted to avoid q-lapsing if I could. "Someone could go to all their old haunts and look for them." I sipped. "Maybe we could set up some kind of surveillance?"

"We do have one lead on Griffin," Ben said. "His new apartment here in town."

Lisa nodded.

"And the wedding," I said, nodding as well. "Someone had to have told him about the wedding." My brow furrowed. "Maybe Luke was trying to draw him out?"

QUANTUM MAYHEM

"It doesn't make sense to hit a cop wedding," Ben said.

"We're missing something here," Lisa said.

Detective Davis burst into the room. "I demand Madison Martin be taken off the case."

"Which case?" Ben asked.

"All cases," Davis said, still standing in the doorway. "Whatever's going on in here."

"You don't have jurisdiction," Lisa said. "This is an FBI matter."

"She's a menace," Davis said.

"Hey!" I said.

My phone rang. 'Unknown number.' I answered.

"Professor Martin?" Griffin whispered.

I held my hand over the phone. "It's Griffin."

The folks in the room with me shut up, straining to listen.

"Yes, Griffin," I said quietly. "Are you okay? Are you in danger?" I put my phone on speaker.

"I don't think I'm in danger right now," he whispered. "Did you mean what you said about protecting me if I helped you?"

"Yes," I said. "If you help us take down the q-criminals, I'll help you. You help us, I help you. I promise."

"But. . ." Davis said.

Lisa gave him her evil eye, and he shut up.

"Where--" I said.

At the same time, Griffin said, "Okay. Oops. Luke's coming. Gotta go." He hung up.

I hung up. "Well, finally, some good news." I smiled a little.

Davis grimaced.

"Should we fill out the C.I. paperwork?" Ben looked at me and added, "Criminal Informant."

"No," Davis said.

While they were fighting for turf, I texted Andro and Ryan that both Luke and Griffin were out and about.

Lisa smiled her scary smile. "You're right, Davis. I'll fill it out at the FBI."

Davis scowled as he turned and left.

"You better be right about this, Madison," Lisa said, turning her attention to me. "I'm going out on a limb for you and this Griffin kid."

I gulped. "I'm right."

Ben met my eyes. He gulped, too.

After all the interrogating and conferencing, I needed some lunch and some more coffee. I called Andro. "Want to meet me at Boulder Brews for lunch? My treat." It was right near his apartment, and how could he resist my charms and free food?

"I was going to go meet Sophia, but I guess it can wait an hour or so," he said. "I'll meet you there in a few. Bye." As he signed off, I thought I heard a smile in his voice.

At lunchtime on a November Sunday, the restaurant seemed to be filled with a lot of students studying. Nice ambiance.

I got their largest coffee and two cinnamon rolls and went to one of their tiny bistro tables to wait for Andro.

He was there momentarily and sat down at my table. "Thanks for the texts. Is one of those rolls for me?" He pointed.

No. "Of course!" I said, smiling. "I wasn't sure what kind of beverage you were in the mood for."

He went up to the counter and came back with some kind of coffee. He sat down and took a sip. "What are you drinking?"

"Some special sweet potato brew." It pretty much tasted like pumpkin spice latte. I grinned.

"So, I wanted to apologize," he said. "I sort of ghosted you the last couple of days. No pun intended." He smiled a little.

I smiled a little back. "Yeah, you did." I nodded.

"I got worried about the Luke situation," he said. "But whatever Luke does isn't your fault."

I wished I could believe that. "You think?"

"Yes, definitely," he said. "You're a good person. And you don't deserve to be ghosted."

"Thanks," I said. "I appreciate you saying all that." I did.

We sipped our coffees and ate my cinnamon rolls. He didn't ask me how the wedding with Ben went, and I didn't tell him. I didn't sigh in exasperation or ask, 'What was up with us?' or anything else I didn't want to know the answer to.

"So, what's on tap this afternoon?" he finally asked.

"Q-lapsing class with the FBI," I said. "You want to help?" I grinned to let him know I didn't actually think he would want to help."

"Sophia, remember?" He glanced at his phone. "I should probably go."

I nodded. "Probably."

He stood and leaned down, wrapping me in a hug. "Stay safe, Mad. I love you." His arms around me were wonderful. I choked up for a moment.

"You, too," I said quietly when he released me.

Sunday afternoon found me at Gamow Tower outside my office with Lisa, Ben, a bunch of FBI agents, and some physics equipment.

Lisa said, "Professor Martin, this is Agent Wood, Agent Barnes, Agent Ross, Agent Henderson." She pointed at each agent in turn. "Agent Coleman, Agent Jenkins, Special Agent Perry, and Special Agent Gonzales." They all wore dark suits. The men all had short hair. The only woman, Special Agent Perry, also had short hair.

I had no hope of keeping them all straight. I nodded. "Thanks, Lisa, er, Agent Baker. Nice to meet you all. Thanks for coming."

I faced them. "Quantum physics is the physics of extremely small particles. It's a science of probabilities. Almost anything could happen."

Ben wiped his hands on his pants. "Like gambling, poker probabilities?"

I nodded. "Basically."

"I like gambling." He smiled, then, glancing around, he lost his smile. "Legal gambling, of course."

The agents just looked at him. This was going to be a long afternoon. "Each particle is represented by a mathematical thing called a wavefunction with a particular probability. Quantum physics says it takes a human consciousness to pick amongst all these possibilities, all these wavefunctions, to make one come true. This is called collapsing the wavefunction."

"That's so cool," Ben said.

"This piece of physics equipment can help you concentrate and learn to collapse the wavefunction." I pointed at the apparatus in front of us.

81

We all stood in the hall around the double-slit experiment apparatus. I had lined up the electron gun with the condenser lens, aperture, objective lens, another aperture, intermediate lens, electron biprism, and the two-dimensional detection apparatus. I also pointed one digital video camera at the detection apparatus and one at me. I turned everything on.

"This is the electron double-slit experiment," I said, pointing at it. "I'm shooting electrons, particles, from one end. Look at the detection screen on the other end."

Slowly a series of lines appeared on the detection screen due to the wave nature of the electrons interfering with each other.

"The lines show up because the particles are also waves, and they interfere with each other."

"Is that like waves on the beach?" Ben asked, rubbing his face, which I knew he did when he was trying to think.

"Yes, good, waves. It's like waves on a beach." I nodded. "Now Lisa's going to collapse the wavefunction, or q-lapse, and change the lines to blobs. Right, Lisa?" I stepped away from the apparatus.

She nodded and walked closer to it. She narrowed her eyes and stared at the equipment.

The screen refreshed, and for a few moments, a series of lines and two blobs were superimposed on the screen resulting in much fuzziness.

I turned my full attention to Lisa. Was she getting blurry?

"Yeah," she said. "I did it." She was a pretty good q-lapser.

When I turned back to the screen, the two blobs had won out.

"How do you feel?" I asked her.

"Not bad," she said, smiling. She took a step back. "Now, you guys do it."

They seemed restless, muttering and shuffling their feet.

Ben finally said, "Who cares about blobs?"

"She q-lapsed," I said. "This is the most effective way I've learned to teach people. Do you want to q-lapse or not?"

"Yeah," he said.

"You agents care about blobs," Lisa said," because I say you care about blobs. Let's get started."

As I suspected, it was a long afternoon.

Lisa did get better and better at q-lapsing, and she said she didn't feel bad.

A couple of the other agents made blobs once or twice but couldn't seem to duplicate it reliably. I was just glad they'd done it at all.

Ben was not successful, and he was not happy about it. "I don't get it. Why can't I do it?"

"It's difficult," I said. "But I can work with you some more if you want."

One of the agents snickered and said something that sounded like 'teacher's pet' but couldn't have been. FBI agents didn't act like that, did they?

Dinnertime was approaching. Lisa said, "Let's knock off for the day. You guys did well. Thank you for trying. Come on. Let's go back to Denver. Thanks, Madison."

The agents shuffled off to Denver, leaving me and depressed-Ben standing in the hallway.

"Buck up, Ben," I said. "Let me buy you dinner."

"Boulder Brews?" he asked, face lighting up.

"You know it." My own face was no-doubt lighting up. I wondered if they had any cinnamon rolls left. I still had some work to do to get ready for my class on Monday, but I could do it at home tonight. "Just give me a sec. I have to get some papers from my office."

He nodded. "Okay."

I walked into my office.

In the hall, I heard his phone ring. Then, he said, "What? The Boulder Turnpike? Oh no!" The turnpike was the major highway between Boulder and Denver.

I ran back into the hall. "What's wrong with Highway 36?"

He looked at me, eyes wide. "It's gone."

"Gone?" I asked. "What do you mean gone?"

"It just disappeared."

Chapter Eleven

I was still gaping and standing in the Gamow Tower hall with Ben when Lisa called me. "Did you hear?" she demanded.

"Yes," I said, feeling suddenly exhausted. How had Luke done it? The Boulder Turnpike was huge. And it was quite improbable that a highway would just disappear.

"It must be Luke, the little bastard," she said.

"Yes." I had an even worse thought. "Were people hurt?"

"I don't know yet," she said.

"What about the overpasses and ramps and stuff?" I asked. "Wouldn't the cars crash down?"

"Just a sec," she said. I heard talking in the background. "We're not sure. It just happened. Emergency services are having trouble getting to them; you know, since the highway's gone."

My heart sunk. So, mayhem, and also possibly, murder, was afoot.

"You need to pop over there and fix it," she said. "I don't need to tell you how bad it'll be tomorrow morning with no turnpike. Traffic will be crippled."

"That was probably his plan," I said. It was a good plan as far as mayhem went.

"So?" she asked.

"So?" I asked.

"Aren't you going to pop over there and fix it?"

I wasn't entirely sure I could fix it. "How about you come pick me up and drive me over there, and I'll give it a try. I need to save my quantum mojo for fixing."

"We're turning around now." They couldn't have gotten too far. "Meet us at the south door."

"Okay. Good. You can help me q-lapse."

We hung up.

"What's happening?" Ben asked.

"Lisa's coming back to pick me up. We're going over to the turnpike, or, I guess, the turnpike's former location."

"Can I come?" he asked.

I nodded. "Yes, please." I had a feeling I'd need all the help I could get. "If it's okay with Lisa."

I quickly called Andro. He didn't answer, so I left a voicemail telling him what was going on.

When Ben and I emerged from the south door of the tower, Lisa was already there waiting for us, sitting in the passenger seat of a black SUV. She rolled down the window. "Come on then."

Ben and I ran around and got in the back seat. We raced across campus and started toward the highway--and almost immediately got stuck in a massive traffic jam. No wonder. The traffic didn't have anywhere to go.

"Can you go around?" Lisa asked.

"I can try," the agent driving said (Wood? Barnes? Henderson? I had no idea), turning the wheel to the shoulder.

"Sounds dangerous," Ben said. "You don't have lights or a siren or anything?"

"No," Lisa said, turning around and scowling.

"Wait," Ben said. "Let me see if I can get a patrol car." He got on his phone.

I suppressed a sigh. We were practically close enough to walk to Highway 36 from here.

Within a couple of minutes, a patrol car zoomed up next to us on the shoulder, lights flashing, siren blaring. It stopped on a dime. The officer got out of the driver's seat and walked toward us. "I got a message to meet an officer named Ben Willis. Are you Ben?"

Ben yelled, "Yes."

Ben and I and Lisa got out of the car.

"What about me?" the driver of Lisa's vehicle said.

Lisa said, "Stay with the car."

Ben was approaching the officer. "Yeah, hi, I'm Ben Willis."

The officer said, "I got orders to pick you up and whoever

was with you." He turned to me. "Hey, are you the Quantum Cop?" It was hard to hear him over the blare of the siren.

"Yes." I made myself smile. Now wasn't the time for autographs, but he meant well.

He furrowed his brow. "I heard something freaky happened to the turnpike. Did you do it?"

So much for my accolades. How could he think I would disappear a highway? "Of course not!" It was difficult conversing with the siren sounding. Why didn't he turn it off?

"Anyway, officer?" Lisa said. "I'm Special Agent Butler, FBI."

"Sorry, ma'am." He snapped to attention. "I'm Officer Moore."

"Officer Moore," she said. "Please take us to the closest entrance to Highway 36. Now."

"Yes, ma'am." He saluted her.

She smiled. Wow. So, that was the way to make her smile, saluting her. Who knew?

I got in the back of the patrol car. It wasn't pleasant being in the perp seat.

Lisa and Ben seemed to be having some kind of contest of wills to see who would get the front seat. Finally, Ben shrugged and smiled and got in next to me. Lisa got in front.

We zoomed off along the shoulder, siren blaring, lights flashing, jerking away from obstacles. Surprisingly, the siren wasn't quite as loud inside.

I was sitting on the side nearest the road. Mistake; it was nerve-wracking. There were scant inches between us and the stopped vehicles. Every once in a while, we'd have to dodge around one that had inched into the shoulder.

In town, the street that would turn into Highway 36 appeared to be intact.

Officer Moore was muttering and shaking his head. "Stupid. Don't they know they're not allowed on the shoulder?"

After one very near miss, when my heart very nearly missed beating, I turned away from the window. "So, Ben. How's it going?"

He expelled a burst of grim laughter. "What? What do you mean, how's it going? You know how it's going. Bad."

Lisa gave me her milder baleful eye from the front seat.

"Just talk to me," I said. "Distract me."

"Talk about what?" he asked.

"I don't care. Whatever!"

"Okay. Do you think we'll ever have sex?" he asked, looking at me out of the corner of his eye.

Lisa and Officer Moore made noises that sounded suspiciously like quickly quashed laughter.

"Not that!" I said. "Let's not talk about that. Something else."

"Uh," he said.

Officer Moore said, "I don't get how the quantum cop stuff works. Explain that."

I exhaled. I was sick of explaining that. With the siren sirening and all the swerving and stopping and starting, I was in a bad mood.

Ben took in my expression. "I think I get it. Sort of. Q-lapsing is like making a wish, isn't it?" he asked.

"Yeah, sort of," I said. Once you knew how to q-lapse, using the skill was a little like wishing. I frowned. But it was the Arthur C. Clarke 'Any sufficiently advanced technology is indistinguishable from magic.' kind of wishing--it was advanced physics, not magic.

"I wished I could q-lapse, but it didn't do anything," Ben said. He had gone to several of my q-lapsing classes in the Gamow Tower.

"Why don't you wish he can q-lapse, Quantum Cop?" Officer Moore asked.

Lisa turned around. "Can you do that?"

"I'm not sure," I said. "I mean, I can wish it, but I don't think it'll do anything. The point of q-lapsing is human consciousness has a special ability. Human consciousnesses are special. But my consciousness shouldn't be any stronger than your consciousness."

"Try," Ben said.

"All right." I closed my eyes and concentrated. Ben can q-lapse. Ben can q-lapse. I opened my eyes. "Do you feel any different?"

He held up his hand and flexed his fingers. "No. Did it work?"

"I don't know." I was betting the odds were that it did not

work. "Try to q-lapse something."

"What?" he asked.

"Nothing dangerous," Lisa said. "Or drastic. You don't want to hurt yourself."

"Get me a cup of coffee," I said.

"I wish I had a cup of coffee for the Quantum Cop," he said.

No coffee appeared, but my phone buzzed. It was Andro calling me back.

"What's up, babe?" he asked. "An emergency with the turnpike? Why are you involved?"

"Supposedly, Luke q-lapsed Highway 36 away," I said. "I'm on my way there. I'm not sure what's going on yet."

"Highway 36?" he asked. "I'll get there as soon as I can." That was a little relief, at least.

"Good luck," I said. "Traffic's hellacious."

"Okay," he said. "Good luck to you, too." We ended the call.

My attention back in the car, I didn't see any new cups of coffee anywhere.

"Close your eyes," Lisa said. "Madison usually closes her eyes."

He closed his eyes. "I wish I had a--"

We screeched to a stop.

"Sorry," Officer Moore said. "The shoulder's blocked ahead."

In front of us, the road was even more chaotic than it was behind us. All the vehicles were stopped and slewed all over the road and the shoulder. We were right where the exit to Highway 36 should be.

"What a mess," Lisa said, grimacing. "We can get out here. Moore, you should go help with traffic control." Traffic wasn't her responsibility, but no one else seemed to be taking charge.

Shaking his head, Officer Moore turned off the siren and engine. The lights still flashed, reflecting off every smooth surface, becoming more and more dramatic as the sun started to set.

Phew. The sudden near-silence was delightful.

"Thanks for the ride, Officer Moore," Ben said, opening his door.

Moore nodded. "You're welcome."

The area where the highway had been stretched in front of

us, full of crunched vehicles, surrounded by wide open space. To our west, the beautiful Rocky Mountains rose into the sky, bright in the setting sun.

The cars weren't moving. Nothing seemed to be moving. That was a little odd. Why hadn't people at least gotten out of their vehicles? It had been less than an hour since the event occurred. There should be plenty of people around.

Lisa, Ben, and I walked to where the highway was supposed to be.

I stared at the ground. At first glance, it looked smooth and dark, just like a highway should look

Officer Moore drove off to deal with the traffic jam, going back the way we'd come, lights flashing.

"Let's do it!" Ben said. "Let's save the day."

I liked his enthusiasm. I knelt. Upon closer inspection, it seemed like the hard asphalt had turned into a soft, dark powder. Bizarre. I raised my head and glanced around more.

I now realized the cars in the distance weren't just stopped. Several vehicles had crashed into each other. And there were no emergency vehicles in sight. "Look!"

"Shit!" Ben started running through the powdery remains of the asphalt toward the cars.

Further down the former road, there were more clumps of wrecked vehicles. How many crashes were there? How many people had been hurt? I broke into a sweat.

Lisa had pulled out her phone and started talking. "Multiple injuries, dozens or even hundreds. Mass casualty event. I'm not sure. . ." She leaned down and touched the ground where the highway used to be. "All-terrain vehicles should be able to get access. But no standard ambulances or other regular vehicles."

My pulse raced, and I felt woozy.

In the distance, Ben had reached the first grouping of cars. He poked his head inside one of the car windows.

Lisa listened for a few moments, nodding. "Yeah, emergency. Give it everything we've got. Helicopters, everything. This is the worst emergency we've ever seen in Denver-metro." She listened. "I'm busy." She shook her head. "I can't." She glanced at me. "I don't know. I'll call you back in a little while."

She hung up and ran over to me. "Why are you just

standing there?'

I slowly turned to face her. "What?"

She grabbed my arm. "I think you're in shock. But you need to get over it. The people of Boulder and Denver need you. They need the Quantum Cop."

I looked at her some more.

"Get it together, Madison!" She shook my arm.

"But I don't know what to do first," I said. "There's so many people hurt. We should try to help them, get them to a hospital. Shouldn't we? What if we can't get to them in time?"

Lisa put her face right in my face and screamed, "Madison!"

I jerked back away from her. "What?"

"You're not a first responder," she said. "Quit trying to be what you're not. You just need to be the Quantum Cop." She pointed at the ground. "Figure out what the hell is going on here and hopefully how to fix it."

She was right. I tried to calm my nerves. Calm. I was calm. What was that breathing thing? In through the nose, out through the mouth? I tried that for a few moments. Calm, I was calm.

Feeling slightly more calm, I leaned down and studied the ground. It resembled black sand. I scraped up a handful and examined it more closely. It reminded me of what I'd seen up in Caribou.

The light dimmed as the sun started to go down behind the mountains. And, then, poof, it dimmed significantly as the sun disappeared.

"Well?" Lisa said.

"It's like the asphalt was dissolved or ground up," I said. It was the consistency of flour. It was creepy. I dropped it. "Let me look around a little more."

I stalked around, staring at the ground. Unfortunately, it was starting to get dark. One section looked different. It looked like goo. I leaned down and poked the goo gingerly. Yep, it was gooey. I straightened.

"Well?" Lisa asked again.

Whup, whup, whup Black flour-like substance was blown in our faces as a helicopter touched down. People in uniforms jumped out. Ben waved some of them over to him at the wreck.

Good. At least some of the people would get help.

"Madison!" Lisa said.

"You're right. It's q-lapsing," I said. "And I've seen this before. In Caribou. A few days ago. The whole town was destroyed."

She paled and looked nauseated. "A whole town?"

I nodded.

"You mean this could spread?"

Chapter Twelve

I stood, immobile, at the former location of the highway to Denver. Ben was helping a couple of first responders carry a bloody someone to the helicopter. Lisa was giving me one of her patented dirty looks.

I needed to get my act together, but it was all too overwhelming. There were so many people hurt. I couldn't concentrate on a stupid road right now. I needed to help people.

"Well?" Lisa said. "Can you fix the road or not?"

I shook my head. "I--I can't, I can't do it right now. They're hurt--I have to try to help them." I took a step towards the nearest group of mangled cars, where Ben was working. "Are you going to help?" I asked her.

She joined me. "You want to try to use q-lapsing to help injured people?"

I nodded. "Yeah."

"How would that even work?"

"We'll just have to play it by ear."

I ran through the black sand to one of the cars. After a moment, she ran after me.

Inside the crunched car, a middle-aged man in business attire looked at us through the broken driver-side window. The door on the driver-side was crunched in. "What's happening?"

I didn't see any injuries. "Are you injured?"

He shook his head slowly. "I don't think so. But I can't open the door." He tried to open it again. Unsuccessfully.

"Just a sec." I ran around to the passenger side and tried opening the door. It opened. "Come on over here and get out of the car."

So far, Lisa was still just standing there, gawking in the

dimming light.

The man slid across the front seat and got out. He stood next to his car. "What happened to the road? It, like, dissolved."

Lisa finally moved, stepping over to the two of us. "We need to do triage."

I nodded. "How do you feel now, sir?" I asked. "Are you injured?"

He looked down at himself. "No."

Lisa whispered, "I think he's in shock."

"Too bad," I said. "We need him." I turned back to the man. "Sir, my name's Madison. What's your name?"

"I'm Jose," he said.

In the meantime, Ben poked his head inside another car near us.

"Hi, Jose. It's nice to meet you," I said. "I'm deputizing you."

"Uh, okay," he said.

I pointed at a grassy hill next to the on-ramp. "Please go over to the hill. I'm going to send people over to you. Get their names and get them to sit down."

"Uh, okay," he said.

"What are you doing?" Lisa whispered. It was getting darker and darker, the only illumination from some of the cars' headlights.

"Like you said, triage," I said. "We'll send him the people that are less injured."

"He's gonna need some supplies," she said.

"Yes." That, I could do. I imagined the car contained a bunch of bottles of water, blankets, and a pen and pad of paper. I concentrated. Poof. They appeared on the seat. I grabbed them up and shoved them at Jose.

He took them, looking kind of boggled again. "What just happened?"

"Don't worry about it," Lisa said, putting her arm around him and leading him off towards the hill. "Please walk over there and sit down. We'll send people over. Give them a blanket and some water if they want and get their names. You're helping us out a lot, Jose."

Jose stumbled off, and I joined Ben at the next car as the helicopter took off. Black dust flew into the air.

"Try to remain calm, ma'am," Ben was saying to a skinny older woman with blood flowing down her face.

For her part, the woman just looked at us.

"I wish I had some bandages," Ben said.

I could do that, too. I imagined a big pile of bandages. I concentrated, focusing on the reality where that was true. And then it was.

So far, I hadn't done anything improbable, so my head wasn't even hurting.

Lisa joined us. "Do you want me to try stuff like that?"

Nodding, I handed Ben a bandage, and he started blotting the woman's head. "Ma'am, it's important that you tell me your name and how you feel. Does anything besides your head hurt?"

"I'm Taneesha. My chest hurts," she finally said in a gravelly voice.

"Uh oh," Ben said, looking at me. "Uh, try to remain calm, Taneesha."

Inside the car, the airbag had gone off. "Ma'am, is it all over your chest, or is it more of a piercing pain on your left side?" I said.

"It hurts all over," she said.

I pointed. "She probably got bruised by the airbag."

Ben nodded and said quietly. "I don't think this head injury is too bad. Head lacs just bleed a lot."

Lisa stepped up. "We're sending the ambulatory people over there." She pointed over to the hill.

"All right, Taneesha," Ben said. "I'm going to help you out of the car."

Another helicopter landed near us with a cloud of dust. Lisa ran over to them as Ben directed Taneesha to the hill.

I ran through the dark to the next clump of crashed cars. At least there were few obstacles on the former road, nothing to trip over except random car parts.

A younger couple, a man and woman, were already out of their car. I didn't see any injuries. "Are you guys okay?"

"Yeah," the man said, pointing. "But I don't think this guy is doing so well."

As I approached the car, I heard moaning.

Turning to the young couple, I said, "Do you guys have first aid training?"

"No," the man said. The woman shook her head.

"Please go over to that group of people on the hill." I pointed at Jose and company, and the couple hurried off.

Inside the car, the moaning man was clutching his red arm to his chest. There was a kind of odd nonlinearity to it, as if the bone was broken.

"Sir? Is your arm broken?"

He moaned and nodded.

"Does anything else hurt?"

Ben joined me. "How is he?"

"I think it's just a broken arm," I said quietly.

"Can't you q-lapse up a temporary cast or something?" he asked.

"Yes. But I'm not sure what kind of break it is." I was vaguely aware that different kinds of breaks called for different treatments. "It's safer if we just bandage it." I focused and concentrated on the reality in which I had more bandages.

Then, I had more bandages.

"I wish I could do that," Ben said. Did he look blurry for a second? I couldn't tell it was too dark out.

"Wait," he said. "What's that look?"

"The more improbable something is, the more difficult it is to instantiate and the more likely it is to hurt my head."

"Maybe you should stop doing improbable things, then," he said.

"You're probably right." But these things weren't that improbable.

More interestingly, did he q-lapse? I leaned toward him. "How do you feel?"

He shrugged. "Fine. Why?"

Lisa joined us. "What's going on here?"

"Broken arm," I said.

"We're supposed to be triaging," she said. "The new medevac guys are looking for seriously-injured people."

"Do you want me to run ahead and check all the cars and see who's the most injured?" Ben asked.

"That's a good idea," she said.

95

"Yeah," I said. "You guys go ahead. I got this."

They ran off.

I tried opening the car door, and it opened right up. "Sir, if you exit the car, I can wrap your arm."

He nodded. "Okay." Very gingerly, keeping his arm clutched, he swung his legs around and got out of the car.

I closed the door behind him.

He stood next to me, leaning against the car.

I held out the bandage. "This is probably going to hurt, but we're going to put your arm in here."

He nodded, wincing, as he held out his arm, breaking into a sweat as I carefully wound the bandage around it.

"That seems a little better," he said when I secured the bandage as a sling around his neck.

"Please go join the group on the hill over there." I pointed at the group, illuminated now only by cell phones.

And so it went. I helped people with minor injuries. Lisa and Ben triaged and then helped the first responders. Somewhere in there, Andro texted that he'd arrived and was helping first responders.

By the time the sky started turning a beautiful orange-red-pink, I'd made it down to Cherryvale Road, where the last people near me were getting on buses. I didn't think I'd ever been so tired.

My headache was only medium.

I stared at the sunrise. It was pretty as if there was a layer of molten gold along the eastern horizon.

"Miss?" Someone in a uniform touched my arm. "Come on. Get on the bus. You're safe now."

For a moment, I just looked at the first responder. What was he talking about? Then I understood. "Oh. I wasn't in the accident," I said. "I just stopped to help." I glanced around. I'd totally lost track of Lisa and Ben. And Andro. I never even seen Andro.

Nearer to the bus, another first responder on the phone called out, "Are you Madison Martin?"

"Yeah," I said.

He talked into his phone and then turned it off and put it

in his pocket. He marched over to us and started talking to his colleague. "They're coming to pick her up on some ATVs. I think we're ready to head out. Come on." The two of them got on the bus and drove off, leaving me in the middle of the now-deserted former highway.

I sat down in the black asphalt dust. I just wanted to rest my eyes for a minute. . .

I heard a sound like a herd of lawnmowers approaching. I opened my eyes. The sun was over the horizon, and I faced a group of people on ATVs.

"Madison!" Ben called out from the front vehicle.

I scrambled up off the ground. "Ben." I didn't have the energy to shout. "Please tell me we get to go home."

He roared right up to me. Lisa followed close behind, stopping next to Ben.

I didn't recognize any of the other three men. "Is Andro with you?"

Lisa shook her head and turned off her machine. "He was falling asleep on his feet. We sent him home a couple of hours ago. What about you? I thought you were going to try to fix the road."

I just stared at her. I was too tired to fix anything.

Ben got off his machine and walked over to me. "Madison? Can you fix the road?"

I stared at him for a few moments. Finally, I shrugged and said, "Sure." I was too tired to argue.

Lisa got off her vehicle and approached us. "What do you want us to do?"

"Us?" I asked.

She pointed behind her. "These agents know all about q-lapsing. They've been to your q-lapsing class."

"Okay," I said. "Everyone gather around me. I'm going to say, uh, the road is fixed and concentrate really hard on fixing the road, and I want you all to do the same."

Ben was nodding like that all made total sense. Yay, Ben.

I grabbed his hand. The human warmth felt delightful. "And we're all going to hold hands while we do it."

Lisa walked right up to me. "Why are we holding hands?"

"We're combining our consciousnesses," I said. "The more improbable something is, the harder it is to do, and the more human consciousnesses we have working together on it, the better." It sounded plausible, at least. "Now everyone repeat after me and concentrate." I grabbed Lisa's hand in my other hand.

"The road is fixed," I said. None of the rest of them said it. "I'm serious. Everyone say it: the road is fixed. And concentrate."

"The road is fixed." They joined in. "The road is fixed." I closed my eyes, concentrating with all my might. "The road is fixed." My headache started getting worse.

"Hey, it's working!" someone said.

Everything went black.

Chapter Thirteen

I awoke to a zooming noise, but this time it surrounded me, and my cheek was pressed to warm leather. Everything was jostling, and my head hurt like someone had driven over it. "Ow."

"Madison?" Ben said from in front of me. "Are you all right?" I was leaning against his back. I tried to move away from it but couldn't go very far.

"Are we tied together?" On an ATV. Kinky. I briefly considered asking him if he was a fan of E.L. James.

"Yeah," he said. "We were afraid you were going to fall off."

"Say what now?" I asked, looking around. We zoomed along what appeared to be a deserted dirt road. Ah. We were on the former Boulder Turnpike. Darn it. So, we didn't fix the road.

"You passed out," he said. "I'm taking you to an ambulance."

"How long was I out?" My head didn't hurt as much as it used to.

"Just a few minutes."

"I don't want an ambulance," I said. "Can't you just take me home?" I rested my cheek against his back again. It was nice. If not for my medium headache and the loud zooming noise, I would be enjoying this. I yawned. Correction: if not for my headache and the noise and my fatigue, I'd be enjoying this.

He zoomed towards Boulder. After several minutes he stopped and turned off the machine. Ah. Silence. Nice.

It was still just after dawn, and there didn't appear to be any traffic. I stayed nestled up against his back. My headache was diminishing a little.

"Madison?" Ben asked.

"What?" I mumbled.

"What are you doing?" he asked.

"Resting," I said. "Shhhh." I may have dozed off there for a second.

Then, I heard Lisa's voice. "Is she still passed out?"

"No," Ben said. "I think she's asleep."

I opened my eyes and lifted my head. "Nope. She's not." I glanced around and spied Lisa and the other ATVs and agents from earlier. I also spied an SUV and an ambulance parked there, waiting.

"She says she doesn't want an ambulance," Ben said.

Lisa stared at me for a few minutes, looking the worse for wear herself. Her hair was half in-half out of its trademark ponytail. Her blazer was missing. Her pants and shirt were blotched with black dust and possibly spots of blood.

Ugh. Blood. My relatively good mood evaporated. "Are all the injured people okay?" I paused and then screwed up my courage. "Did anyone die?"

"I don't think the stats are all in yet," she said. She glanced back at the ambo. "Are we doing this thing or what?"

"Or what," I said. "Is that your car?" I pointed at the SUV.

"Yeah," she said. "It's the bureau's; I drove it to Boulder yesterday. Yesterday?" She looked confused for a second. "Yeah, yesterday." She rubbed her temple.

"Do you have a headache?" I asked her.

"Yeah," she said.

"Me, too," said Ben, still sitting in front of me.

I called over to the other agents, "Raise your hand if you have a headache."

The men, in disheveled black suits, all raised their hands.

"Interesting," I said quietly. Did that mean they'd all q-lapsed? Had my idea of linking consciousnesses worked? But then why wasn't the road fixed here?

"What?" Ben asked.

Reluctantly, I started disentangling the bungee cords tying us together. "Lisa's gonna take us home in her fancy government SUV, and we're all gonna clean up, take painkillers and naps and then regroup."

So that's what we did. And somewhere in there, I even managed to text Andro and ask him to take my Monday morning quantum mechanics class.

Much later that day, Lisa, Ben, and I sat at our kitchen table, wearing sweats and drinking coffee. Ben looked very good in his gray sweatpants and hoody.

Lisa had checked in with the FBI and told us there had been no fatalities, but Luke and Griffin were still missing. She'd slept on the pull-out couch, and I'd (a little maliciously) loaned her my pretty pink sweats. With her hair down and no makeup, she looked different from the tough FBI agent I'd gotten to know. "Were you a cheerleader in high school?" I asked her.

"No." She practiced giving me her baleful stare over her coffee mug. Then she grinned. "I was a pom-pom girl. Captain of the poms."

"Cheerleaders and pom-pom girls are different things?" I asked. Who knew?

Ben snorted.

"Of course, cheers and poms are different," Lisa said like that was as obvious as the difference between hadrons and leptons.

"What did you do with yourself in high school, anyway?" Ben asked.

Mostly studied. "Ah, I did school work and hung out with my friends and stuff."

"So no sports or extracurriculars?" Ben asked.

Somehow, I didn't think he wanted to hear about my adventures with the mathletes. "I think we're digressing." I sipped my coffee. Ah, coffee. "What happened when we tried to fix the road?"

"You don't remember?" she asked.

I shook my head.

"We fixed a section of the road," she said. "A patch of asphalt rematerialized."

Fixing sounded good.

"And all got headaches," Ben added.

Headaches sounded less good. "Lisa, did anyone get blurry?" Were we all q-lapsing?

She shook her head. "I don't know. But I wasn't paying attention to the people; I was concentrating on the road."

"I don't understand how a person could get blurry," Ben

said.

I scrunched my nose up a bit. "It may be a side-effect of q-lapsing. A person might phase out of definite reality and get caught up in infinite possibilities in indefinite reality."

"What!" he yelled and jumped up, knocking his mug of coffee over. A small brown pond of coffee spread over the table. "Did I know about this side-effect?"

"Madison says it's not dangerous," Lisa said, looking at me over the top of her mug again.

"It's not," I said. "Not super dangerous. Probably."

Lisa frowned and put down her cup.

"Probably!" he yelled again.

"What are you worried about?" she asked him. "You can't q-lapse anyway."

"Unless he can," I said.

Ben stared at me.

"You did ask me to q-lapse to wish you could," I said. "And we did work together to try to fix a section of road. Did we fix it?"

"And you did get a headache. The data supports my hypothesis." Wow. I was convincing myself. I bet I had enabled Ben to q-lapse.

Ben and Lisa nodded.

"But, it's all circumstantial," Lisa said.

Ben sat down and then frowned at his empty coffee mug, righting it. He started to get up, presumably to refill said mug.

"Wait," I said. "Try to q-lapse to fill up your mug. I think you can do it."

"What do I do?" he asked.

"Concentrate on the possibility where your coffee mug is full of coffee," I said. "It's very probable. It should be easy. Instantiate the coffee reality."

I glanced at Lisa, and she was hiding her expression behind her mug.

"Lisa can do it," I said. "I think you can do it."

He still looked confused.

"Just try," I said. "Lisa and I will try, too. We'll back you up."

Ben closed his eyes. "Okay."

Lisa had raised her eyebrows as if questioning me: would we really back him up?

I shook my head at her and turned my attention back to Ben.

He had his eyes pressed tightly together and was muttering something.

He may have been starting to get a little blurry around the edges. I put down my mug and rubbed my eyes. When I opened them again, he was definitely blurry.

Lisa's eyes were wide open.

Suddenly, Ben's mug was filled with coffee.

Did that mean my wish that he could q-lapse had worked? No. More likely, my instruction paid off, and he finally understood how to do it.

He opened his eyes as his blurriness disappeared. "It worked!" He stared at the mug and then glanced over at Lisa and me. "Tell the truth, did you guys do that?"

"I can honestly say I did not do that," Lisa said.

"You did it, Ben," I said. "Congratulations. How do you feel?"

"I feel pretty good," he said.

"Do you have a headache?" I asked.

"No," he said. "I don't think so. Should I?"

"Of course not," I said.

But Lisa's expression spoke volumes. She looked skeptical.

Ben pointed at her. "What's that look? Why does she have that look?"

Her phone beeped, and she picked it up to read a text.

Ben turned his attention to me. "What's going on?"

"Nothing," I said. "You did not get blurry. Not blurry at all. No blurriness."

"I got blurry!" His voice got yell-y again.

"No," I said. "I said you didn't get blurry. At all."

"That means I got blurry," he said. Jeez. Cops were tricky to lie to.

"Okay," I said. "You got a little blurry. But you got better. And you just said you felt pretty good, so calm down."

He looked like he wanted to yell some more and/or jump up and pace around the room. But after a moment, he picked up his mug and took a sip of coffee.

"Huh," Lisa said, still scrolling on her phone.

"Huh, what?" I asked, thankful for the distraction.

"There's a lot about the missing Boulder Turnpike in the news. . ."

No surprise there.

She continued. "Including they're suing the paving contractor for incompetence." She glanced up at me.

"That's. . . good, isn't it?" I blew out a slow breath. We dodged a bullet. "A non-quantum reason for the mayhem is outstanding. I mean, I feel bad for the company, but. . ."

"The paving company isn't going to take that lying down," Ben said.

"Are we going to try to fix the rest of the road?" Lisa asked. "Soon?"

"Yes--" I said.

My phone rang, and I answered even though I didn't recognize the number. "This is Sandra Jones from the Denver Post. Is this the Quantum Cop?"

Eek. I ended the call.

"What?" Lisa asked.

"Reporter," I said.

My phone rang again.

"Don't answer," Ben said.

And then someone knocked on our apartment door. Loudly.

"Quantum Cop?" someone yelled from the hall. "Quantum Cop, are you in there?"

More people started yelling. I could hear them through the door.

"Officer Willis?"

"Hey, open up!"

"Professor Martin, are you the Quantum Cop?"

"Mr. Willis? Are you home?"

Lisa had picked up her phone again and was scrolling again. She grimaced. "I think there's a live feed outside."

"Are you two living in sin?"

"Did you wreck Highway 36?"

"Are you using physics to commit crimes?"

Yikes.

Chapter Fourteen

Ben, Lisa, and I were basically barricaded in the apartment, surrounded by reporters. Who knew reporters even still existed? I would have guessed they were as rare as functional cold fusion.

I exhaled. Whatever was on deck next, I was guessing it would be better if I was dressed for it. "I'm getting dressed." I chugged the last of my mug of coffee, ran back to my room, and threw on some pseudo-respectable clothes, including my 'Science is not an alternative fact' t-shirt. I even combed my hair and put on some mascara. Yes, being on the five o'clock news did cross my mind, so sue me.

The reporters were still clamoring in the hall.

"Madison!" one called through the door.

"Ben, are you in there?" another one yelled.

When I came out of my room, Ben was neatly dressed in clean jeans, a wrinkle-free t-shirt, and a leather jacket. For her part, Lisa was back in her no-nonsense FBI uniform, a dark suit, white blouse, and hair back in its ponytail. I couldn't figure it out; she looked totally put together. Hadn't we all come straight from the same bloody, dirty mayhem at the crack of dawn?

"What do you want to do?" Lisa asked. "We could probably q-lapse out of here."

I shook my head. "We need to save our quantum mojo for fixing the road."

"The hallway is private property," Ben said. "They aren't supposed to be inside the building." He grabbed his phone. "I can call some buddies. But first. . ." He walked to the front door and stopped right next to it. "You're on private property!" he yelled through the door. "Get off! Now!"

The reporters quieted immediately.

In the meantime, Lisa was talking on her phone, her voice low.

Ben raised his eyebrows like he was surprised that had worked. He opened the door a crack and peeked through.

Instantly, his face was bathed in flashes of light. "Ben!" someone yelled.

"Officer Willis!" someone else yelled.

"Is Madison your girlfriend?"

"What'd you do to the road?"

He quickly shoved the door closed. "Okay. That didn't work."

He pulled out his phone, dialing as he came back over to where Lisa and I sat at the kitchen table. "John, buddy? How's it going? Uh-huh."

I felt left out with all this phone action and went back to my room to get my cell phone. When I picked it up, there were several texts from Unknown Number: 'Help! Madison, where are you? Luke left for a few minutes. Text me back.' and the like. Unfortunately, the most recent one was from a couple of hours ago.

I quickly texted him back: 'You okay?'

He didn't reply.

When I looked up, Ben and Lisa were both still on their phones.

Ben said, "Seriously? You can't help me out, dude?" He shook his head.

Lisa ended her call. "Luke and Griffin are still in the wind. We can't afford to stay here any longer."

"Well, Boulder P.D. says reporters aren't their jurisdiction," Ben said.

"All right." She grabbed her grungy-looking (for her) coat, with a few spots of dirt and blood, and put it on. "Let's get this over with."

"Just a sec." I ran to my room for a coat.

When I got back to the kitchen, Ben had his on, too.

Lisa strode for the front door. "Your statements should be 'no comment.' Nothing more. Walk through as quickly as possible. The Bureau's SUV is down in the parking lot." Without asking for or waiting for any input, she threw open the door and strode out.

"Who are you?" someone yelled.

I heard some muttering that sounded like 'Law Enforcement.'

Ben quickly followed her. "No comment. No comment."

"Is that your girlfriend, Ben?"

I approached the door. It looked like there were about twenty reporters crammed there in the hallway, most pointing their phones my way. There were even a few professional video cameras. Again, who knew those still existed in the wild?

"Professor Martin!"

"Quantum Cop!"

"Madison, over here!"

I stepped out into the hallway, pressing my lips firmly together, determined not to say anything. I turned around to lock the door.

"Are you guys a polyamorous triple?"

"What!" I said, starting to get annoyed.

"What's going on in that apartment? Some kind of orgy?"

Now I was totally annoyed. Where were they even getting this stuff? Few things could get me fired as a university professor, but moral turpitude was one of them. "What's wrong with you people?" I asked. "Why are you talking about orgies?"

Lisa ran back to me. "We have no comment!" She talked at a normal volume, but her voice was somehow very commanding. In a much quieter voice, she said, "Be quiet. They're just trying to get a response out of you."

"I'm a police officer," Ben said. "Not a degenerate. And Agent Baker's in the FBI." He pointed at Lisa as he walked back to us in front of the apartment door. "We're trying to protect and serve the people of Colorado."

Lisa muttered something under her breath I couldn't make out.

"Agent Baker, over here!"

"Agent Baker, what's the FBI doing in Boulder?"

"No comment," she said with steel in her voice.

"What is a quantum cop?" a man asked. His voice sounded familiar…

"Yeah. Quantum what?"

"What's quantum?"

"What does quantum have to do with the turnpike?"

I panned the group. Who'd asked what a quantum cop was?

My eyes met the eyes of Luke Bacalli, quantum criminal. He grinned at me like he hadn't a care in the world. He still resembled a tall, handsome twenty-two-year-old Italian-American.

I pulled on the arm of Lisa's coat and pointed. I did not yell. At least not a lot. Not a huge amount.

When she saw him, she pulled her weapon and pointed it at him. "Luke Bacalli, you're under arrest." The reporters moved away from her gun like magnetic north moved near magnetic north.

Luke just smiled.

Lisa's gun got blurry. That got the reporters' attention.

"What the hell?" someone said.

"Oh my God!" someone else said.

Lisa just stared at it for a moment; then, she let it fall. It wisped away before it hit the floor.

The hallway was silent for a few instants as we all stared at the empty space where the gun should be. Then Ben yelled and charged at Luke.

Everyone turned to watch Ben.

Luke looked surprised for a moment, and then his cocky look came back. Ben started to blur. It was as if Luke was q-lapsing Ben away. But Luke's consciousness shouldn't be able to override Ben's consciousness.

"Ben!" I ran after him and grabbed his shoulders. "Ben, look at me. You're real. You're substantial. You're right here with me in the hall."

"Madison, what are you doing?" He was looking more and more insubstantial. "Luke's right there. Get him!" His ghostly arm pointed at Luke.

"Lisa, come here!" I yelled.

Lisa ran over to us. "What?"

"Touch Ben," I said to her.

She grabbed what was left of his hand.

"Ben, focus on being here with us," I said, staring into his fading eyes. "Focus!"

Without looking at her, I said to Lisa, "Concentrate on Ben being here with us."

"Ben! Stay with us!" I said.

The crowd of reporters was being quiet for the moment, no doubt confused.

"Ben, stay with us!" Lisa said.

I glanced around the hallway, and, yes, the reporters looked confused. "Ben Willis is here. Ben Willis is here. You say it, too, Ben. Ben Willis is here."

Lisa joined in immediately. "Ben Willis is here."

I glanced back at Ben. He looked a little more substantial. He said, "Ben Willis is here."

Some of the reporters joined in. "Ben Willis is here. Ben Willis is here."

Ben was looking more and more substantial. We kept chanting for a few minutes.

Ben looked down at himself, patting his chest with his hand. "I think I'm back. Thank God. I'm all here!" He grabbed me for a hug. "Thank you, Madison! He looked past me to the reporters. "Thank you, everyone!"

I didn't *think* the non-q-lapsers had actually done anything. . . But I needed to investigate. But now was not the time.

I moved away from Ben and scanned the crowd but couldn't see Luke anywhere now. Dammit. He had been right here.

The people in the hall cheered and clapped. "Woo hoo!"

"All right!"

"Yeah!"

And then, the tide turned again. "What the hell just happened?"

"What was wrong with him?"

"Why did he get all ghosty?"

Jeez, reporters had a short attention span.

"And that's our cue to leave," Lisa said. She grabbed my sleeve and Ben's and practically dragged us through the crowd and down the hall.

Once free of the group, the three of us started running. We ran down the hall, down the stairs, down the ground floor hall, right out the back door, and across the parking lot to an idling SUV. We all climbed in as the swarm of reporters flowed into the parking lot, yelling and holding up their phones. With the SUV door closed, I couldn't hear what they were saying.

"What took so long?" asked the driver

"Go," Lisa said. "We need to get out of here."

"Where are we going?"

"Just go!"

We pulled out, leaving the swarm to eat our dust.

Lisa glanced back at us, face wry. "Well, that could have gone better."

I couldn't disagree. "But maybe it's not so bad…."

Ben had his phone out. "Oh crap. They recorded it, and it's already posted. I look like a ghost!" He stared at the little screen. "Did that happen?" He glanced over at me. "Did I almost die?"

"Uh…" I said cleverly.

"I don't understand," he said.

"Neither do I," Lisa said. "Explain." She pointed at me.

"I'm, uh, not exactly sure…." I said.

"Guess," Lisa said.

"So, q-lapsing is based on quantum mechanics," I said.

"Quit stalling," she said. Yikes. She knew me too well.

"The point is human minds, human consciousnesses, play a special part in the universe. Q-lapsing makes use of this fact. Every person exists because of their consciousness. We each know and believe we exist; it's the fiber of our being. Luke's will, his consciousness, seems very strong. I think he tried to overpower your consciousness with his. He tried to q-lapse you to quantum limbo, or, maybe, out of existence."

"Is that a guess?" Lisa asked.

"Yeah," I said. "It shouldn't have worked. A person's existence is their most strongly held belief. It's powerful. It's the core of their being."

"How come it almost worked?" Ben asked, voice fluttering.

"I'm not sure," I said. "Maybe because you can q-lapse?" My nose had scrunched up as if it didn't want me to say it.

"So, to be clear, you're saying q-lapsers are in extra danger from Luke?" Lisa said.

This was not a good development.

"Uh, yeah?" I said.

Chapter Fifteen

Lisa and Ben and I, along with another FBI agent, were zooming away from my apartment and a bunch of reporters. We hadn't narrowly escaped being ambushed--we'd been ambushed. And we were all over the news. Already. My phone was blowing up with texts and messages. I didn't know what the consequences of this would be, but I was guessing they wouldn't be good.

When Andro called, I answered. "Hey."

"Hey, Madison," he said. "Are you all right? What's going on? I heard something about Ben turning into a ghost? Is he all right?"

Wow. Information definitely flowed fast and free in the information age.

"I'm okay. Thanks for asking. And Ben's all right, too."

"What happened?" Andro asked.

"Just a typical case of quantum-villainy," I said. "Luke tried to dissolve Ben." I glanced at Ben sitting next to me in the back seat and saw he was looking at me, wincing.

"What?" Andro said. "I don't understand."

"I don't really understand either," I said. Sadly, mysteriousness was pretty typical when it came to quantum villainy. "I'm still processing. We can discuss it in more detail later. But, in the meantime, if you see Luke be extremely careful."

"Okay," he said. "Where are you? Are you coming in to work?"

I leaned towards the front seat. "Where are we going?" I asked Lisa.

"I thought you wanted to try to fix the turnpike again," she said. "We're going to the turnpike."

"We're going back to the turnpike to try to fix it again," I said to Andro on the phone.

"Again?" Andro asked. "Did you try before? What happened? For that matter, what happened to the turnpike in the first place? It was freaky."

Now, I was wincing. "Luke happened."

"Wha--" he started to say.

This was getting us nowhere. I cut him off. "I know you're confused. I'm confused, too."

"Are you going to q-lapse?" he asked. "Do you want my help?"

"Can you help?" I asked. "Did you get any sleep last night?" Q-lapsing depended on brainpower, and a tired brain was not a powerful brain.

"I got an hour or two," he said. "I want to help."

"Thanks for the offer," I said. "Not this time. But I will find you later, and we can hash everything out. And, oh yeah, thanks for covering my class."

"You're welcome," he said. "Okay, babe. Love you."

"Love you." I quickly ended the call.

"Is Rivas joining us?" Lisa said.

I eyeballed her. If she heard enough to deduce I was talking to Andro, she probably heard the whole conversation. "Did you hear me ask him to join us?"

"No," she said. "Why didn't you?"

"I don't think he can help. He's too tired; he didn't get a nice nap like we did. Besides, we don't need him."

Lisa seemed like she wanted to argue with me, but she didn't. "So, what's the plan?"

Good question. "Ah. . ." I tried to jumpstart my brain. "How long is the turnpike?" At least we knew the road wasn't destroyed in Boulder--because we'd driven on it.

Lisa scrutinized her phone. "About forty miles, from Boulder to Denver."

Shit. "Is it all wrecked?"

She scrolled on her phone. "Yeah." She focused on me.

Craptastic. Forty miles of highway? How had he done it? I refused to believe my student could be a better q-lapser than me. I was the one who'd invented it, after all!

There was one person I could ask--Griffin. Among the calls and messages I'd missed, there'd been a bunch from him.

Did he know how Luke achieved his dastardly goals? I quickly texted him, then sat and stared at my phone. Griffin did not immediately text me back. Apparently, like a pot, a watched cell phone didn't boil.

"Remind me what happened last night when we fixed the part of the road?" I asked.

"You don't remember?" Ben asked.

I tried to remember. . . We'd all stayed up all night helping folks in car crashes. We were all covered in black former-road dust and blood. . ."Just remind me, please," I said.

"We held hands."

Ben gently picked up my hand and smiled at me, tiny lines crinkling at the edges of his eyes. It felt nice to be smiled at. My hand in his also felt nice.

The driver said, "Why hold hands?" It was the first peep we'd heard out of him in a while.

Lisa threw him a glance I was assuming was baleful. I couldn't see it from the back seat.

"We were combining our consciousnesses," I said. "Q-lapsing depends on human consciousness to collapse the wavefunction and instantiate a reality. We all said, 'The road is fixed.' and concentrated. And I guess it worked. Somewhat. Right?" In the light of day, with a rested brain, I was doubting the effectiveness of the hand-holding and chanting together, but I didn't say that.

"Yeah," Ben said.

"To a limited extent," Lisa said. "Ten square feet got fixed."

"And we all got headaches," Ben said.

Uh oh. Too much q-lapsing was bad for the brain. If the others got headaches, too, it stood to reason that they might have q-lapsed. If so, did I somehow enable them to do it?

"Why?" the driver asked.

"I don't understand," I said. More mysteriousness. "Q-lapsing's based on probabilities. It seems like more probable things are easier to instantiate. Less probable things are more difficult, and they take more brainpower. I think."

"Do you think we q-lapsed last night? How dangerous is

q-lapsing?" Ben asked.

I met Lisa's eyes in the mirror. She'd ended up in the hospital at one point. Q-lapsing was dangerous.

"It's pretty dangerous," I said. "I think. . ."

"What?" the driver asked. Jeez, he was a regular twenty questions.

"I think q-lapsing puts a person in danger of a brain aneurysm if they do it too much," I said.

Ben frowned and let go of my hand. Aw. "Did I know this?" I shrugged.

"I'm not sure I want to learn how to q-lapse," he said. Now he said this? It might be too late.

As we approached the exit to the turnpike, there were a bunch of temporary traffic signs along the road. 'Highway 36 closed until further notice. Alternative routes suggested.'

We drove right up to the entrance ramp and stopped. Traffic slowly moved past us to the detour. We were surrounded by flat prairie covered in dried grasses. In the distance, back towards Boulder, there were some rolling hills, and behind them, the Rockies.

The four of us got out. Despite the bright sunshine, it was November cool. I shivered and zipped up my coat. Reluctantly, I walked down the ramp to the former location of the turnpike. Ben and Lisa followed right behind me.

It was still covered in black dust. There were still several mangled cars--but not as many as there would have been at rush hour. "We're lucky Luke did it when he did." I walked along in the dust, staring down.

"What?" Lisa asked.

"I mean, we're lucky he didn't do it at rush hour," I said. "He did it Sunday night when there was relatively little traffic."

"That's true," Ben said.

Lisa grunted.

"What should we do?" he asked.

"Where's the part we fixed?" My eyebrows raised, I took my hands out of my pockets and waved at the road. Brr. Now my hands were cold. I put them back in my pockets.

"South of here," Lisa said. "But like I said, it's only about ten feet square."

"That's it? That's all we managed to fix?" I glanced up at my companions. "There were a whole bunch of people here trying to fix it."

"We were tired," Ben said.

This did not bode well. But I didn't say that.

"Okay. Let's give it a try." I knew Ben and Lisa knew how to q-lapse.

I pointed at the driver. "Have you been to my q-lapsing class?"

He nodded. "Yeah."

"Okay." I grabbed one of Ben's hands and one of Lisa's. She grabbed one of the driver's hands. "So, repeat after me and concentrate. 'The road is fixed. The road is fixed.'" I stared down at the ground.

They did repeat after me. Presumably, they concentrated.

"The road is fixed," we all said. "The road is fixed."

The ground beneath our feet shimmered and got cloudy-looking.

"The road is fixed. The road is fixed." I started getting a small headache.

A five-foot by five-foot section of road got misty and then solidified to resemble normal road.

We stopped chanting.

I leaned down and touched it. It felt like a normal road. "Well, the good news is we did fix a piece of the road."

Ben was squatting down, patting it.

"I have a headache," Lisa said.

Ben stood up. "Me too, but it's not a huge headache."

"Okay, I'll say it," I said. "Q-lapsing is an impractical way to repair the road. There's no point in putting our brains in jeopardy when they can just repave the road, the usual way."

"I agree," Lisa said, pulling her phone out of her coat pocket. She stepped away from us, punched in a number, then started talking.

I pulled my own phone out. Had Griffin texted me back yet? No. Why not? Was he okay? Had Luke discovered Griffin was working against him?

Ben was also looking at his phone.

Lisa hung up and walked over to us. "The normal

resurfacing is working fine."

"Good," I said. "So, we can turn our attention back to catching Luke."

She nodded.

A little later, they dropped me off at school. I was supposed to go meet up with Andro, and right now, he was teaching his big Physics One lecture. I went to the big auditorium classroom, slipped inside, and sat down in the back row.

He stood far away, down in the front of the room, wearing black pants, a maroon shirt, and a black suit blazer. "Conservation of angular momentum is one of the fundamentals." He seemed animated, excited about what he was talking about, but tired, as well. "The big three are conservation of momentum and conservation of energy--both of which we studied earlier in the semester, and now, conservation of angular momentum." He had a 'Conservation of Angular Momentum' slide projected on the giant screen on the front wall.

I glanced around the large room, filled with students, but there seemed to be a lot of empty seats. The missing road must be having an impact.

The students there seemed to be waiting on his every word--a good trick in a freshman physics class.

"Next time, we review chapter eight and start chapter nine," he said. "Recall the midterm before fall break will include chapters eight and nine."

A few students groaned.

"And, now. . ." he said, "it's clicker time. Get in your clicker groups." Clickers were sort of like little garage openers the students used to electronically send teachers data. They generally had five buttons marked 'A' through 'E,' and teachers used them to collect answers to multiple-choice questions.

A few more students groaned, but they moved around to sit in groups.

Andro put up a slide of multiple-choice questions. Once they weren't watching him, he sank on a stool there in the front of the room.

The students immediately started talking to each other. What was going on? I wasn't familiar with 'clicker groups.' I had to investigate, so I got up and walked around and eavesdropped. The students were all discussing the multiple-choice questions. It was like a group quiz. I'd never used clickers like this--but then again, I hadn't taught a big lecture class like this in a few years.

The discussion dropped off as the students started clicking.

Andro was watching his computer. After a few moments, he said, "It looks like most people are done. . . Just in time. Class dismissed."

A few stragglers kept clicking while most students gathered their stuff together and started exiting through the back.

I walked against the tide down to the front of the classroom.

Andro was getting his stuff together.

"Nice job, Professor Rivas," I said, smiling.

"Madison? What are you doing here?" he asked, also smiling.

"I wanted to see the master at work."

"Thanks, I think." He smiled a little. "So, does the fact you're here mean you fixed the turnpike?"

My smile slipped off my face. "No. It was too hard. They're going to have to repave it the regular way."

Zipping up his computer bag, he nodded.

"So. . ." I plastered my smile back on. "I need to talk to another physicist about what's been going on." There had been a lot of q-lapsing developments I didn't understand.

Chief among them: how had Luke gotten so good at q-lapsing?

Chapter Sixteen

"Professor Rivas?" a young man behind me said.

I jumped. After I got a hold of myself, I turned around.

"Yes?" Andro said to the student. Then, he turned to me and said, "I'll meet you at your office, Madison."

Ah ha. He didn't want to say anything quantum in front of a student. The word might be out about q-lapsing, but there was no need to stoke the fires.

That reminded me. . . I needed to check on a few former quantum mechanics students who might know how to q-lapse. I mentally slapped my forehead. I was out of Luke-leads for the moment, but I could investigate other possible q-lapsers.

"Sounds good, Andro." I hurried off.

When I got to the physics department office, I walked right up to the department secretary, Nancy, and smiled broadly.

"What now?" she asked.

"Have I told you lately what a good job I think you're doing?" I said, still smiling.

"No." She frowned. "What do you want?" Jeez. Tough crowd.

Okay. Clearly, Nancy was not susceptible to my charms. "I need contact information for some former students of mine."

Her eyes narrowed. "Is this about official university business?"

"Uh, yeah. I smiled again. "Yes, totally."

She looked skeptical, but she started typing on her computer. I gave her the names, and she gave me contact info.

Just as I was about to go back to my office to meet Andro, he texted me. 'Too tired to go up to office. Can we meet somewhere else?' Poor guy. He'd been up all night responding to quantum emergencies and all day doing physics.

I put my former student investigation on hold and texted him back. 'Meet you at your apartment.' He probably needed some comfort food. 'I'll bring quesadillas.' No doubt he was too tired to make himself dinner.

He texted me back: 'Yay.'

Yay was right. I needed to discuss the latest developments with someone who understood q-lapsing, and doing it over cheese and tortillas and the like was perfect.

I got double orders of quesadillas and nachos, all with extra guac, and went over to Andro's.

When he answered the door in late afternoon, in his sweats and a plain t-shirt, he'd never seemed more tired. "Babe."

"Babe." I entered, trying out the new hypocoristic. "Thanks again for taking my class. How'd it go?"

He closed the door behind me. "Fine." He pointed at his briefcase on the couch. "That reminds me. I've got their homework assignment for you."

"Thanks, babe." Nah. It wasn't working for me. I held up the food bags. "Let's eat."

He nodded and led the way to the kitchen table.

As I unloaded the food onto the table, he laughed a little, getting out the plates. "Think you got enough?"

I smiled. "Better safe than sorry."

"What do you want to drink?" He opened the refrigerator.

What was I in the mood for? "Milk." I'd gotten a variety of sauces and suspected some of them might be a little h-o-t for me.

He shrugged and poured us both glasses of milk, came to the table, and sat down.

"Thanks for helping out at the road last night," I said, taking a big bite of guac- and sour cream-slathered cheese quesadilla.

"I thought we were going to do some q-lapsing together to try to fix the road," he said, taking a big bite himself.

"I got too freaked out," I said. "I couldn't concentrate on q-lapsing when I was surrounded by people in pain and bleeding."

"That's what Lisa said." He nodded. "She said you were

using q-lapsing to help the injured, so that's what I did. My first aid training ended up being helpful."

I stopped eating for a moment. "You had first aid training?"

"I got it when I first started teaching, you know, in case there was ever an emergency in class."

"That's an awesome idea. I'm going to do that." I really needed to do that.

He nodded.

We were silent for a moment, eating. I needed to pick his brain about q-lapsing but wasn't sure this was the right moment. He'd basically been up for, like, a day and a half, and I'd had a nice long nap this morning. How could I ask him for help? I sighed.

He put down his food and reached for my hand, squeezing it gently. "What's wrong, *mi amor*? Are you worried about Luke? About those reporters?"

Wow. I'd forgotten about the reporters! I had so many problems, being exposed on camera as having a near superpower wasn't even my biggest problem.

I nodded. "Luke. And something else...."

He stared at me. "Tell me."

"I think Ben and maybe some of the other FBI agents q-lapsed," I said.

"That's good news, isn't it?" He took a drink of milk.

"It's the way it happened," I said. "I sort of wished they could q-lapse, and then it seemed like they did."

"Are you wondering if you did something to make them able to q-lapse?" Wow. He understood me so well.

"Yes."

"I don't think that's possible," he said. "Ben took your q-lapsing class, right? Did the other agents?"

"Yeah." I nodded. "I think so."

"Well, then, it finally clicked," he said. "You can teach people, even non-physicists. You taught Lisa and Nate. You should be able to teach other law enforcement folks."

I was feeling much better. "Right. You're right. Of course."

"Besides, your mind can't overpower someone else's mind." He paused. "Unless..."

"Unless what?" I asked, feeling less better. "What are you

thinking?"

"No." He shook his head. "It's probably stupid."

"Tell me," I said.

"Like some people are smarter, and some are more creative, maybe some brains are more powerful than others?"

"More powerful at q-lapsing?" Now, I felt a little queasy. This made a certain amount of sense. What if Luke's brain was extra powerful?

Andro shrugged. "I guess. I mean, how would we know? We're using our brains in a way that hasn't been used before, aren't we?"

"Yes." I didn't want to ask this next bit, but I had to. "Do you think Luke might be the best q-lapser?"

Andro just stared at me for a moment. Finally, he said, "Based on recent events, he's been inconsistent. But I hate to say it, maybe…."

Ugh. I had to agree.

We turned our attention back to the food for a few minutes.

I tried to rally. "So, the gist is: Ben and the agents probably figured out how to q-lapse on their own. That's good, right?"

Andro nodded.

"And it seems like maybe multiple q-lapsers working together can be more effective than one." I was starting to get an inkling of how we might stop Luke no matter how powerful his brain was.

"Makes sense, as much as any of this stuff does." He nodded while yawning. "Sorry. So, what next?"

"If you're done eating, you should go to bed." I grinned. "Let me tuck you in."

He grinned back.

Just after sunset, I stood outside Andro's apartment building in the crisp fall evening, clutching my students' homework.

While I'd been with Andro, I'd gotten a text from Ben: 'Don't go home. More reporters than ever.'

I shivered.

Where to go was a no-brainer. I should go to my cousin Ryan's place and see if I could crash. It was close by, and I'd stayed there before.

On the other hand, I'd stayed there before. Would reporters know that? Luke did.

That decided it. I needed to go to Ryan's to protect him and his family in case Luke attacked.

Soon, I was standing on Ryan's front porch, staring at the front door. I felt bad about putting Ryan and Sydney and adorable Emily in danger in the past. If I stayed here now, would I be doing so again? Well, I could see what they thought.

I rang the doorbell.

A wary-looking Ryan answered the door. He was over six feet tall and built like a football player. His little metal-rimmed glasses sort of ruined his intimidating image, though. "Oh, Mad, it's you." His expression morphed to relief.

"Hi, Ry." I waved. "What would you think of me crashing on the couch tonight?"

"I think it would be great!" He smiled and opened the door wide.

As I walked in, he yelled, "It's Madison. She wants to stay on the couch to protect us."

Sydney appeared from the bedroom, holding Emily. They had on matching organic cotton t-shirts with pink and orange flowers and stripes. "Oh, thank goodness," Sydney said.

Now I felt bad I hadn't rushed over here immediately to protect them. "Hi, Syd. Hi, Emily. You look adorable."

Sydney smiled. "Thanks, but how does Emily look?"

I snickered. "Good one." Joking when they might be in danger was impressive. A cop's wife was apparently as tough as a cop.

"Come on, Sweetie," Sydney said, looking down at Emily. "Time for your bath."

Grinning, Ryan said, "Thanks, Syd, but I think I'll take a shower later."

Sydney looked up at him and smiled.

"You guys are hilarious," I said. "You should take this show on the road."

Ryan snickered, went to the kitchen, got a bottle of beer from the fridge, and handed it to me. Another person who knew me well. It was nice.

He handed me the opener and got out his own beer.

I opened the bottle and took a swig.

"So, Ben says you made him into a q-lapser." He took his own swig. The buddy-network strikes again. Ryan had an impressive array of law-enforcement friends in the area, and they all seemed to share info.

"No," I said. "I don't think so. I think he finally figured it out on his own."

He pointed at the couch.

I followed him, and we both eased onto it.

"Ben also says you are a superhero, and it's on camera."

I grimaced. "Well, obviously, I'm not a superhero. That's just stupid."

He shrugged and took another swig. "What happened to the Boulder Turnpike?"

I grimaced some more. "Luke."

"I don't get it," he said.

"Me neither." I decided not to mention Andro's hypothesis that Luke might have a more powerful brain than the rest of us.

We drank in companionable silence for a few moments. From the bathroom, we could faintly hear the sounds of splashing and laughing.

I had a loose thread I wanted to follow up. "I need to find out everything I can about some former university students. Do you think you can help me?"

"I'm sure the FBI is all over Luke and his background."

"Not him," I said. "Some other students."

"Do I want to know what they've done?"

"You probably already do," I said. "Just minor q-crimes. I thought I should follow up on what happened to them. See if any of them are out and about in town."

"I know a guy." He nodded slowly. "Text me the names and what you have on them."

I got out my phone and started texting.

"I'm sincerely sorry about all this, Ryan," I finally said when I'd finished. Q-lapsing had been my invention, after all.

"It's not your fault what criminals do."

"But I taught Luke how to q-lapse."

"You didn't make him a bad guy," he said.

I didn't say that I didn't think Luke was a bad guy when all this started.

And then my cell phone rang. It was 'Unknown Number.'

I answered, heart pounding. It better not be Luke threatening people. "Hello?" I didn't have a big quiver in my voice.

"Oh, thank God you answered! Finally!" It was Griffin.

Chapter Seventeen

"Griffin! Are you in danger?" I asked.

"Yes," he said. "Luke, he's, well, I don't know what's wrong with him, but he's not the same guy."

"Can you q-lapse away?"

"No," he said. "My head hurts. He's been making me help him."

"What kind of danger are you in?" I asked. "Can you call 9-1-1?"

"Oh, no," he said.

"Did you have anything to do with the Boulder Turnpike disappearing?" I asked.

"I think he's coming!" He hung up.

On the couch, Ryan leaned toward me. "What did Griffin want? What's happening? Is Luke attacking?"

I stared at my phone. What had I gotten Griffin into? "I don't think Luke's attacking, but I have no idea what's happening. I think Griffin might be in danger."

"Well, take a breath," Ryan said. "Tell me what he said."

I was still staring at my phone.

"Take a sip of your beer," he said.

I looked away from my phone. Oh, right, I had a beer. I took a sip. I leaned back on the couch. That was better. I was not actually in immediate danger.

I glanced at Ryan. He was a good guy.

I heard splashing sounds from the bathroom. That jumpstarted my brain for some reason--maybe it was the normalcy. "Griffin said he was in danger, but he wasn't specific. He said Luke was making him help him, and he, quote, wasn't the same guy as before. And he said he had a headache. That was about it."

"How is Luke not the same guy?" Ryan asked.

I shook my head. Good question. Originally, Luke had been a college student, very smart, but he'd always had shall-we-say flexible morals. After he started q-lapsing, he'd seemed to be a murdering villain. But when I saw him as the non-ghost only a few days ago, he'd seemed to be a man broken by quantum limbo.

"Griffin wasn't specific, so I have no idea," I said. "He also didn't say what they were doing or where they were. How am I supposed to help him if I can't find him?"

Ryan smiled.

"What are you smiling about?"

"Griffin called you," he said. "We have his phone number. We can track his cell phone." I must have looked clueless because he added: "You know, police work. We can find him using regular police methods. Should I call Ben?"

Apparently, I needed some kind of instruction on regular police methods. "Sure."

Ryan got out his phone and had an extensive conversation with Ben as I leaned back, sipping and chilling.

When he finally ended the call, I said, "Do you have any tips for me on regular police methods? They didn't cover that in physics graduate school."

He took a sip of his own beer, considering. He held up his bottle. "I think I have some of my old criminology textbooks from grad school." He stood up. "Now, where did they get to?"

A little later, he gave me a book, and I started reading.

Police procedures put me right to sleep.

Tuesday morning, I texted Ben when I got up. 'What's the reporter sitch?' He said he didn't know; he was on a stakeout.

I called him up. "Who or what are you staking out?"

"We think we found Griffin's location," he said.

"Way to bury the lead. Did you see him?" I asked. "Or Luke?"

"We haven't seen anything; that's why we're still staking it out," he said.

"So. . . you're at the location of Griffin's cell phone?"

126

"Technically, yes." He sounded unhappy to admit that. "I'm not supposed to be chatting while I'm on a stakeout."

It almost sounded like he was telling me to shut up. I exhaled slowly, trying to keep my cool. "You know if Griffin and Luke are there, they could q-lapse away, and you'd never see them, right?"

"Uh. . ." Then, he said, "I need to go."

"No," I said. "You need my help. Where is this stakeout?"

"Wait. Are you volunteering for a stakeout?" he asked.

It was basically an emergency. It was also Tuesday, so I didn't have to teach today. "I guess after I take a shower and stuff. Text me your location."

In fear of reporters, I decided against going home via the bus or q-lapsing. Sydney kindly offered to let me use their shower, and I'd left a few t-shirts here. Soon, I was dressed and raring to go, ready to fight crime.

Supposedly, Griffin was in downtown Boulder at the St. Julien, the fanciest hotel in town. Lucky for me, the St. Julien was on the bus route. Ben said I would find him in the lobby.

I sauntered into the St. Julien lobby with a big cup of coffee (necessary, in case of q-lapsing). I did not see Ben there. I very casually sauntered from one end of the lobby to the other. It was large, filled with plants and rich-looking beige couches and chairs, with lots of big windows and a vast, beautiful gas fireplace. It smelled like chlorine. The only people I saw were two female employees behind the counter and an old man sitting in a plush armchair. Where was Ben?

I pulled out my phone and texted him: 'I'm in the lobby. Where are you?'

He texted back: 'I'm in the lobby. Get a clue.'

I glanced around the room. Once you eliminate the impossible, whatever remains, no matter how improbable, must be the truth. I couldn't believe it, but the old man must be Ben. I casually sauntered over to the plush chair next to him and sat down.

I opened my mouth and received a text: 'Don't talk to me. I'm undercover.' I closed my mouth. It seemed weird to me that he was in disguise in the hotel lobby. Clearly, there was still a lot I didn't know about police work.

On the other hand, Griffin definitely did know what Ben looked like, so the disguise made a certain amount of sense.

On yet another hand, he also definitely knew what I looked like--as did Luke. Did I need a disguise? I texted old-man Ben: 'Do I need a disguise?'

'Yes.'

Now he told me! 'I don't have a disguise.'

'Sit behind a plant.'

I moved to a different chair, behind a big plant. Now I couldn't see the elevators, front desk, or stairs. 'I can't see anything.'

'Quit texting me. I'm undercover.'

I did not understand what was going on here. Where was the FBI? And since when did police officers dress up in disguises and stakeout hotel lobbies? If the police needed to talk to a witness or suspect, wouldn't they just go up to the front desk, flash the person's name and/or picture and ask for their room number? I stared at my phone. Did I dare text all that after Ben asked me to quit texting him?

I got another text: 'He's coming.' Who was 'he'? Griffin?

I very carefully peeked through the plant and spied Griffin. He was wearing a black tracksuit and a t-shirt.

Ben stood up. "Keep back," he whispered. "Don't let him see you."

Griffin walked through the lobby and exited. Ben followed him. I followed Ben. The three of us walked west down Walnut Street, with me far behind. It had clouded up, and the temp seemed much lower.

They crossed Ninth Street, and then I lost track of them. I hurried to catch up, crossing Ninth. Darn. I didn't see either one of them anywhere. The sky spat a few flakes of snow at me.

If I was Griffin, where would I go? I scanned the nearby buildings. In the window of what looked like a house-turned-shop, I saw a green cross and a small sign that said 'The Dandelion.' Something about that made me think of Griffin. I walked up to the house and entered. Ah ha.

From the smell--and the glass cases filled mostly with jars of dried green leaves--it was clearly a marijuana dispensary. Griffin was at the counter, turning to see who had just come in.

His nervous expression morphed to fear and then to relief when he realized it was me.

"Dr. Martin!" he yelled across the shop.

Ben, still in disguise, browsed at the other end of the store, keeping an eye on us but otherwise not reacting.

"Shh!" I said, rushing over to Griffin. I put my arms out for a hug but stopped myself before contact. We probably weren't on hugging terms. I'd just been so worried about him.

"How did you find me?" he asked.

"Uh…" I glanced around. Even I knew telling Griffin we were following his cell phone would not be a good thing. "I, uh, shop here. They've got good buds."

I may have heard a faint snicker from old-man Ben.

"Never mind that, Griffin," I said. "Are you all right?"

He nodded. "Yeah. Pot helps a lot with the headaches."

Interesting.

"But Luke gets mad if I do too much because then I can't q-lapse." He looked scared.

Interesting.

"So, Luke hasn't hurt you?" I asked.

"No." He shook his head.

"How are you in danger?" I asked.

"He keeps making me q-lapse," he said.

"What has he made you do?"

"He made me help him wreck the Boulder Turnpike."

I took a step closer to him. "How did you guys do that?"

He shook his head. "I don't know. It's like Luke's a crazy strong q-lapser now. I don't know how he does it."

"Can you ask him?" I asked him.

Griffin shook his head no, looking jumpy again.

My mind was racing. "What else does he have planned?"

He shrugged. "I don't know."

"How is he not the same guy?" I asked.

"He was my best friend, a good guy." Clearly, 'good' was a subjective term.

"Are you guys going to buy something or not?" the woman standing behind the counter asked. "It sounds like you've already smoked plenty."

Griffin still looked scared. "I have to." He started talking a mile a minute. "I told Luke I was going to buy something. He'll be suspicious if I don't. I need to get back. I don't know what he'll do to me if he thinks I betrayed him." Did that mean Luke was back at the St. Julien?

I held up my hand. Jeez. If anyone ever needed some pot, it was this guy. "Try and calm down, Griffin. I've got your back." I glanced over at old-man Ben.

Ben nodded at me. I took that to mean me and Ben both had Griffin's back.

"Do your business," I told Griffin and took a step away, taking out my phone.

I texted Ben: 'What else?'

He texted back: 'We need a reliable way to meet up with him.'

Griffin finished up his transaction.

"I have to get back," he said to me when he was done.

"I understand," I said. "But I need you to find out more info. How is Luke so strong? What does he have planned? You said you would help us."

"I know," he whispered. "But I'm so scared."

"I know you are." I felt sorry for him. "We need a reliable way to communicate." I couldn't think of anything at the moment. "Come here tomorrow at the same time, and me or my agent will give you more info."

"Your agent?" he asked. "What agent?"

I nodded my head at old-man Ben.

Old-man-Ben nodded his head back.

When Griffin saw it, he screeched. "Ack!"

"Calm down," I said. "He's a friend."

Ben joined us.

"I have to get out of here!" Griffin said. He was shaking so much he almost dropped his pot.

"Okay," I said. "But try to calm down."

He opened the front door.

"You don't want to make Luke suspicious," I added as he hurried out, leaving us behind.

"Well, that could have gone better," I said to Ben. "We didn't really get any info."

"It could have gone worse, too," he said.

The proprietress said, "Are you guys buying something?" For a pot shop lady, she wasn't very mellow.

"Sorry." I shook my head.

Ben and I left. We stood outside. It was still trying to snow.

"You realize if you had an 'agent' with you, you didn't accidentally bump into him, right?" he said with a small grin.

In his old man getup, it seemed condescending. "I don't understand what's going on here. Why are you in disguise? What kind of stakeout was this? What about probable cause and all that stuff? For that matter, why did you quit following him now?" I definitely felt confused.

He appeared taken aback by all my questions. "I'm just trying to do my job, Madison. Give me a break."

"Your legal Boulder P.D. cop job? Or some weird vigilante job?"

He examined me silently.

"I'm calling Lisa to see what she has to say about this." I pulled out my phone.

"No," he said, pushing my phone down. "Don't call her. Please."

I stared at him with an expression of horror on my face, no doubt. Ben had finally learned how to q-lapse, and now he was operating outside the law? That was too much like Nate Sawyer, former FBI agent, former quantum criminal, current corpse.

Ben couldn't be turning bad, could he?

I shivered.

Chapter Eighteen

I stood outside, shivering, in downtown Boulder with Ben.

"You look cold," he said. In his old-man getup, including the beard, he did not look cold. "Let me buy you a coffee, and we can talk. Inside."

He led me over to the local Boulder Brews. It was pretty crowded in the middle of the day. I let him buy me a latte. I was generous that way. Once we were sitting at a tiny bistro table, I said, "Okay, talk." I took a sip and started to warm up from the inside. "What have you been up to? You're not a detective. And why aren't Lisa and the FBI involved?"

"I just wanted to have some actual intel before we reported in to Lisa or my bosses," he said. "What would a person even say at this point? We talked to Griffin? It's not exactly thrilling or even helpful." Still wearing the trim white beard, he took a sip of his coffee. He was really pulling off the old-man thing. He sort of looked like, not a silver fox, but maybe a white fox? Was that a thing?

I shook my head. For a brilliant professional woman, I had a bad habit of acting like a teenage girl.

His phone rang, and he answered it. I needed to quit staring at Ben. Evidently, my objectivity about him was flailing. What did I really know about him, anyway? He was a cop. That was about it, besides mundane roommate stuff, like he folded his socks and underpants after doing laundry.

I glanced at the table crammed in next to ours. On the laptop there I saw what looked like some interesting mathematical equations. "Is that quantum field theory?" I looked up at the person sitting there, working on the laptop. It was a man in his late twenties, looking very Boulder with shoulder-length light brown hair and a fuzzy, hand-knit hat.

He grinned at me and our eyes met. Wow. He had nice eyes and an especially nice grin. "Yep. I'm working on the Yang-Mills existence and mass gap problem." Yang-Mills theory was the math underlying the Standard Model of particle physics, so I had studied it quite a bit when I was a grad student.

I was not recalling the mass gap problem, though. "Remind me, mass gap problem?"

He laughed. He had a nice laugh. "So a random person I sit next to in a coffee shop knows about Yang-Mills theory?"

Ben was engrossed in his phone conversation.

I nodded.

The stranger snickered some more. "Only in Boulder. Yeah. I'm trying to prove the mass of the least massive particle predicted by the theory is greater than zero. It's one of the Millennium Prize Problems."

I'd heard of that; it was an international math competition. "Million dollar prizes? Nice." I nodded. "Good luck."

Ben jumped up, punching his phone off. "Madison. We have to go. There's been a murder."

For a moment longer, I looked at the beautiful equations on the computer, not wanting to leave the world of esoteric thoughts and theories.

"Madison!" Ben said.

I reluctantly stood up and followed him as he ran out. For some reason, people in the coffee shop were staring at us.

Math-man called after me, "Who are you?"

I didn't answer.

Back at the St. Julien hotel, the cops were swarming in the lobby like objects in a physiocomimetics study.

Ben rushed inside and went right up to Detective Davis. Logically, I knew Davis was a dedicated law enforcement officer trying to keep the public safe. But we'd tangled in the past, and I knew he thought I was a danger to the public.

"I'm sorry, sir," Detective Davis said to Ben. "This is a police matter. Please vacate the area." He saw me and frowned. "Martin. I should have known." Our dislike was mutual.

Ben ripped off his beard. "Ouch!"

Davis looked at him like he wanted to say, 'What the hell?' but he just pointed at the stairs and said, "Your FBI buddies are upstairs."

I was getting a very bad feeling about this. Had Luke figured out we'd met with Griffin? Had Luke killed him?

Ben ran up the stairs, and I followed, my chest feeling like it was inside a massive black hole.

On the top floor, there was another swarm of cop-types. Ben elbowed his way through the crowd, and I followed him, feeling a little bit like a quarterback running the ball--I was guessing.

Finally, I saw a twenty-ish man lying still on the fancy carpet in the hallway. I didn't see any injuries, but he was clearly dead. It was odd how that was always so obvious. It was tragic that I'd seen more than one dead body. I sniffed.

The victim wasn't Griffin, or Luke, for that matter. My feeling of relief was immediately followed by sadness. Poor man. Whoever he was, he'd had his whole life ahead of him. He didn't deserve to have it cut short.

"There you are, Madison," Lisa said, picking her way through the crowd from the other end of the hall. She had on her usual black-power-suit blonde-ponytail combo.

Someone was taking pictures of everything with an actual camera. Its flashes of light were a little surreal.

"How do you know it's murder?" I asked. "Maybe he died of natural causes."

Ben sidled up next to us.

"And why do you think it's quantum murder?" I asked.

Lisa pointed behind her. "Luke and Griffin were staying here. It's too big of a coincidence." Yeah. That was too big of a coincidence.

"I take it they're gone?" I asked.

"Yes." She nodded definitively. "Their suite is empty."

"Are we sure they were staying here?" I was pretty sure, myself, but it didn't hurt to be super sure.

"Yes," she said. "We showed several employees their photos, and they all identified them. They paid cash for their room." Well, that was suspicious. Who used cash anymore?

I stared at the dead man. He looked slightly familiar. I knelt.

"What?" Ben asked.

"I feel like I've seen him somewhere before?" I said.

"Hhm," Ben said. "Me, too."

Still staring at the victim, I mentally ran over every place I'd been in the last few days with Ben: just now in downtown Boulder, here in the lobby earlier, at our apartment with the reporters, at the turnpike after the q-catastrophe, at the Boulder police department. Nope. It wasn't any of those.

What else? The wedding. Ah ha. "Was it at the wedding?" I thought it was the wedding.

"Oh, yeah. I think so," Ben said, nodding.

"You two were at a wedding together?" Lisa said. "Wait. I don't care. We don't have an ID yet, so this wedding tip is helpful. Whose wedding? Can I get the guest list?"

"It was my buddy Evan," Ben said. "He's a cop. He's on his honeymoon, but I'm sure he'll want to help." He got out his phone and started giving Lisa Evan's contact info.

I looked the victim up and down. I did not see any injuries. How did he die? At this point, it was a mystery.

In my opinion, he looked a little too young to be one of Evan's friends. As I recalled, there was an unresolved connection between Griffin and the wedding. . . "Check the caterers, too," I said.

"Oh right," Ben said. "I bet this is the catering employee who ran off when we started investigating the q-lapsing!"

"So, he was in Luke's quantum gang?" Lisa's brow was furrowed.

"Or a patsy?" I said.

The elevator dinged, and a man rolled out a gurney. "Move it!" he called out. The crowd parted for him like he was Moses, and they were the Red Sea.

"Did you know the Red Sea is one of the saltiest bodies of water in the world?" I said. "It's four percent saltier than the world average." It was weird how some facts stuck with you.

"What?" Lisa asked.

"What are you talking about?" Ben asked.

"Never mind," I said. What was wrong with me? Dire events were unfolding, and I was not appropriately freaked out. Could q-lapsing be having a deleterious effect on my brain? I pulled out my phone and started looking for the contact info for my primary care physician.

The gurney-guy was putting the victim onto his gurney. The vic's appendages were flopping around. It was sickening. I needed to think about something other than flopping.

I swallowed. "I thought bodies had that rigor mortis."

Lisa and Ben glanced at the gurney as it rolled back down the hall towards the elevator.

"He hasn't been dead long enough," she said.

"How long do you think it's been?" Ben asked.

"We've only been here a few minutes," she said. "But it took us about an hour to get here from Denver." She frowned. "The road situation is a problem." She grabbed one of the uniformed officers. "When was it called in?"

"A little over an hour ago," he said. "We were under orders to wait for the FBI before clearing the scene."

I glanced at Ben. He looked guilty. "We might have an alibi for Griffin," I said. "We were following him."

"Please tell me that's not why you're wearing that white wig," she said to Ben.

"Okay," he said. "That's not why I'm wearing the wig." He gave her a tentative smile.

She glared at each of us in turn. I shrugged it off. I was used to her evil looks by now.

I tried smiling innocently at her.

Lisa exhaled. "Well, come on, Madison. I think we're going to need your help with the autopsy."

My smile evaporated. "Please, no. I don't know anything about autopsies. And I don't want to know anything about autopsies."

"How do you expect to be a cop if you can't deal with autopsies?" Ben asked.

"I never wanted to be a cop!" I said. "In fact, I need to go. I have stuff to do for my actual job." Please let me go.

Now Lisa was frowning at me. "All right. You can go."

I took a step towards the stairs.

"But if we come across anything quantum, I'm calling you, and you're coming in," she said.

"Fine." I turned on a dime and speed-walked down the hall to the stairs before she could change her mind.

Outside I took in a cleansing lungful of fresh air. Ah.

I turned towards the bus stop and started walking.

At the bus stop, there were several other people loitering about: three sorority-looking girls and a man behind them. The girls were all laughing and talking fast and looking at their phones. I was not in a laughing mood. I gave them a wide berth and moved to the other side of them, closer to the bus stop sign. There I got a good look at the man. It was the math guy from the cafe. Of course.

"Hey, it's murder-woman," he said, grinning. "What are the odds." Apparently, with my luck, quite high.

The three women froze, staring at us.

I smiled politely. "Haha, good joke."

The women unfroze and turned their attentions back to their phones.

"I wasn't--" he said.

"Please don't call me that," I said. "I'm a physics professor at CU. Sometimes local law enforcement calls me in to consult."

"Okay." He looked abashed. "Sorry." He smiled. "Consulting for the cops sounds--" He quit talking and gaped.

The three young women started screaming and pawing at each other. "Oh, my God!"

I turned around.

There, flickering in and out exactly like a ghost, stood Luke. "Mad. . . elp. Please. . ."

"It's a ghost!" math-man said. "I can't believe it."

The women had quieted, just staring now.

I also stared at the apparition. He looked almost normal for a second, and then he fuzzed out, just forming the outline of a person. Almost absentmindedly, I said, "There's no such thing as ghosts." Luke solidified a little more, then flickered. And then faded out. And so on, and so forth.

It was as if he was at the mercy of the quantum possibilities rather than controlling them. Had he been in quantum limbo too long? Or maybe he was q-lapsing too much? Flicker, flicker.

Finally, I said, "I'm not helping you. You're a murderer!"

"But I'm not. . ." He flickered a final time, and then he was gone.

Chapter Nineteen

On the bus driving south to campus, I sat in the back, far, far away from the other passengers, and called my physician's office. "Hi, this is Madison Martin. I'd like to make an appointment."

"Sure," the receptionist said. "Just let me find your file." I heard typing noises. "There is it. What's the issue?"

I watched the other passengers and debated what to say. The three sorority girls had recovered from their fright. Math-guy was staring at me. I sank down in the seat and turned away from him.

"I'm not sure," I finally said. "There might be something wrong with my brain."

"Your brain?" She sounded surprised. "Why do you say that?"

"A lot of dramatic stuff has been happening, and I haven't been freaked out enough."

"That doesn't sound--" she said.

I interrupted her. "And I've had some really bad headaches. Really bad. And, ah, I might be in danger of an aneurysm. And I'm sort of in a confusing love triangle." I risked a peek at math-guy. He'd turned his attention back to his computer.

The receptionist didn't say anything.

"Well?" I said. "Can you check my brain?"

"Yes," she said. "Please come in ASAP." Now, that was more like it. It just so happened that my doctor's office was at the other end of the bus line. I got off at the next stop and got on the next bus headed north.

My doctor's office was on the top floor of the small medical building. I walked up to the counter. "Hi. I'm Madison Martin. I called a little while ago." The waiting room was empty. Somehow all the ancient magazines, old chairs, and battered toys seemed lonely in the large space.

All three women in scrubs at the front desk glanced at each other.

The woman sitting in front of the phone stood up. "Madison. Yes. Come right this way." She came around the counter and led me through the door to the back. "This is Madison," she said to a seated woman in a long white coat. I didn't recognize her. I was starting to get a bad feeling. Maybe I should have been a little more suspicious about getting right in to see the doctor?

The woman jumped up. "I'll take it from here. Thanks. I'm Dr. Hasanov." She put her hand on my back and led me to a small treatment room. It was about twelve feet square with some medical advice posters on the wall, a small desk and stool, a chair, and an examination table.

"Is Dr. Khatri on vacation or something?" I asked. "Or are you some kind of brain doctor?"

"Please take a seat, Madison." She smiled as I sat down in the chair, avoiding the examination table. "Yes, I am a brain doctor of sorts. I'm a psychiatrist."

Considering all this talk of brains, mine was having a little trouble keeping up. "What? A psychiatrist? Why did Dr. Khatri send you?"

"You called and said you were experiencing a flat affect," she said. "And you're afraid of an aneurysm? I have to say that's an unusual fear. Have you been under an unusual amount of stress lately?"

"Ha!" I laughed bitterly. "That's putting it mildly."

"A flat affect can be a symptom of depression or," she paused, "of schizophrenia. Tell me a little about what's been going on with you. Have you ever thought someone was spying on you? Or maybe you're famous? Or have special powers? Hallucinations? Disordered thinking?"

I froze. I had a bunch of those so-called symptoms. Suddenly, I was terrified to say anything. What if she threw me in the loony bin--or whatever the current politically correct term for that was?

"Madison?" She stared at me.

I was afraid to say anything.

"What's wrong?" she asked. "Madison, answer me, please."

Calm, Mad, be calm. "I have been under some stress lately," I said deliberately calmly. "Partly because I've had some bad headaches. And my mom told me I might have inherited a tendency to form aneurysms." That all sounded totally reasonable, right? "I was hoping to get some medicine or something for the headaches." My self-medicating was not cutting it.

My phone buzzed with a text from Ben. I ignored it.

I got a call from Lisa. I turned my phone off.

"Get that if you need to," Dr. Hasanov said.

"No, thanks," I said. After her comments, I was not about to say the cops and the FBI needed me. "Can I see Dr. Khatri?"

"Of course." She nodded. "Are you sure you don't want to talk to me about anything?"

Griffin's comments about Luke not being the same had stuck with me. "I do have a question about a ...friend. He went through a trauma, and he doesn't seem the same. What's going on there? Can anything be done to help him?"

"Without meeting the. . . friend." She stared at me.

I nodded.

"Without meeting the friend, I can't say," she said. "What kind of trauma are we talking about? Was it something serious?"

"Yes." How to put this? "He, ah, was in a serious fight and seriously injured. We thought he was dead."

"An assault and battery?" she asked with raised eyebrows. "Can you tell me anything more?"

Like I was the one who attacked him--but I was defending myself and defending reality itself? "Ah, no."

"And, dead? It was attempted murder?"

Ugh. I considered. Maybe, from Luke's perspective, it seemed like that. "I guess. . ."

Dr. Hasanov exhaled. "Poor guy. Yes. Such an extreme trauma would have significant effects on a person. He could be suffering from post-traumatic stress disorder or any number of things. He absolutely should be under the care of a therapist." She paused. "Are you sure this is really about your friend?" She gave me a look like she thought I was talking about myself.

I realized I'd been through almost as much as Luke over the last couple of years. I probably needed to be under the care of a therapist. But I did not trust this Dr. Hasanov. "Yes," I said. "I'm talking about my friend."

She stared at me some more. We sat there in silence for a few moments.

"So, Dr. Khatri?"

"Okay." She stood up. "Come on."

She led me back to the nurse's station. "Can we fit Madison in with Dr. Khatri? She wants some medicine for headaches?" She studied me.

I nodded.

The nurse started typing on the computer. "We can slip her in before Dr. Khatri's next appointment. It'll just be a few minutes."

"Okay," I said.

"I guess I'll leave you to it, then," Dr. Hasanov said. "Nice meeting you, Madison. You'll let me know if you ever want to talk about anything?"

I smiled. "Of course." Don't hold your breath.

She walked away from the counter, back towards the hallway.

The nurse in front of the computer said, "What'd you think of Dr. Hasanov?"

I noticed the nurse's name tag said, 'Sue.' I smiled. "Well, Sue. I think you guys sort of ambushed me with Dr. Hasanov." I was still unreasonably(?) worried she might hold me against my will somehow.

Her expression blanched.

"But I know you thought you were doing your job and trying to help me." The other two nurses also looked uncomfortable.

I had an idea that might help me. "I'm just glad you didn't hold my recent notoriety against me. That was so embarrassing how I was all over the news. I didn't have anything to do with the Boulder Turnpike disappearing or that whole ghost thing." If they knew about the effects of q-lapsing, they'd be less likely to think I was schizophrenic, right? What's the old aphorism, 'You're not paranoid if they're really out to get you?'

Sue's eyebrows rose.

Dr. Khatri walked up behind Sue. "Who's next?"

Behind me, a mom and a little boy emerged from the closed door.

Sue pointed at me. "Madison wanted a few minutes."

Dr. Khatri smiled at me. "Hi, Dr. Martin. Nice to see you. Come on back." I relaxed a little.

"Cute t-shirt," she said. I had on my 'A Day without Fusion is a Day without Sunshine' shirt. She led me to the same little examination room I'd just been in. My stress level rose again. "You saw Dr. Hasanov? How did that go?"

"Not well. I wasn't looking for a psychiatrist." I shook my head. "I came in because I wanted some meds for these bad headaches I've been having. And, uh, some general recommendations for brain health."

"I better do a physical exam," she said. "Tell me more. . ."

Later I was riding the bus south again after a thorough head exam with my lovely new prescription meds in my pocket. Dr. Khatri had even snuck in an MRI. I tried not to be worried that she thought I needed an MRI.

I took out my phone to check it. There were a bunch of missed texts and messages, including several from Ben. I called him. "Hey, Ben." I watched the scenery pass by outside the bus window.

"Hey, Madison," he said. "So, I got in trouble for going rogue. My boss read me the riot act. Why did you let me do all that?"

"Let you!" I said. "You were in disguise staking out Griffin's hotel before I got there! You--"

"Okay," he said, sounding chagrinned. "You're right. I was too gung-ho. I just want to get promoted. And maybe even join the bureau someday."

The bus drove past our building. "Well, the good news is I don't see any news vans outside our apartment."

"That is good news," he said.

"I thought you were going to update me on the murder," I said.

"Oh, yeah," he said. "You were right. The vic was working

for the caterer. The catering manager identified him. We're sending some officers over to his apartment now."

Something was nagging me, something I hadn't told him yet. . . Oh, right, Luke. "I saw Luke at the bus stop about an hour ago."

"You saw him!" Ben said. "Did you fight him? Did you stop him?"

"No." My nose scrunched up. I should have tried to stop him, but I didn't want to. I couldn't say that. "It was too quick. He was gone before I could react." It wasn't too quick for me to chastise him. "Do you think I have a flat affect?"

"I don't know. What does that mean?" he asked.

"You know, I don't freak out enough about all this freaky stuff." The bus passed the pedestrian Pearl Street Mall. A lot of folks were out and about, enjoying the fall day.

"You seem like a cop to me," he said.

Maybe that was it. I wasn't suffering from mental illness. I was like a cop. Focus, Mad. "Luke did not seem to be in control of his q-lapsing. Like he's not all here, in reality."

"Weird."

"Yeah." I didn't add 'poor guy' even though I was thinking it.

"You should tell Agent Baker," he said.

I glanced at my phone. One of the messages was from Lisa.

"I know." The bus approached the campus. "So, maybe I'll see you at home tonight?"

"Yeah. Let's give it a try. Maybe we can go home and not be inundated by reporters." We ended the call.

I hopped off the bus at my usual stop and walked through campus, trying to stay alert and aware of my surroundings. If Luke popped up again, I'd be ready for him.

I made my way all the way over to the physics building without incident and trudged up the many, many stairs to my eleventh-floor office. I stopped by Andro's office, but he wasn't there.

I finally got to my office and sat down to work.

My office phone actually rang.

Who could that be?

Chapter Twenty

Nancy, the physics department administrative assistant, was on the phone. She told me Professor Chen (my boss) had been looking for me and, in addition, she was sending up a mysterious someone to my office. She wouldn't say who was coming, but she sounded happy about it.

I turned and watched my open doorway, waiting for him/her/it to appear.

I heard footsteps walking down the hall.

I held my breath.

My grad student, Alyssa, appeared in my doorway. She had on a t-shirt that showed a spilled beaker and said, 'Forget lab safety, I want superpowers.'

I released my breath.

"What?" She also wore a cute light green jacket with a faux-fur-trimmed hood, darker green leggings, and gorgeous tall brown leather boots. Her outfit, while super-attractive, reminded me a little of Robin Hood.

"Nothing," I said, smiling. "It's nice to see you." Why had Nancy been so mysterious about Alyssa? I needed to do some fence-mending with Nancy. But she was the one who'd turned to a life of q-crime. Why did I have to apologize for catching her?

"Did you forget our appointment?" Alyssa asked, walking inside, taking off her messenger bag and placing it on the chair opposite my desk.

Yes. "No," I said. "Of course not."

She grunted and pulled out a large sheaf of papers. "Here it is, as requested. The first five chapters of my Ph.D. dissertation."

I took the heavy pile of actual paper. Talk about old-school. I vaguely recalled asking her to print it out and give copies to everyone on her Ph.D. committee. I put it down on my desk.

"My general intro, a history of neutrinos and their discovery, existing neutrino theory, my new proposed neutrino theory, and my experimental method." She smiled. "It's pretty awesome if I do say so myself."

"It sounds great," I said. "What about those additional experiments on the computer?"

She dipped her head once. "I'm still doing the analysis. I'll drop off the rest of the chapters later today."

"Sounds good," I said.

Someone knocked on my open office door. An unfamiliar twenty-something man stood there. "Madison Martin?"

I nodded, mortified. I knew my memory wasn't great but was this a student I didn't recognize? I only had like thirty students. How could I not recognize this guy at all? "Yes. . . Are you here for office hours?"

He snorted and just walked in, uninvited. "No." He thrust a thick manila envelope at me.

I stood up and took it. "Thanks?"

"Hey, buddy," Alyssa said, "We're in the middle of something here." She pointed at her dissertation on my desk.

My phone chirped, indicating a new text.

"You've been served," the man said and then turned and walked off.

Alyssa moved her bag and plopped down in the chair. "Served? What's that? Some legal thing?"

No doubt. I stared at the envelope. No doubt it was some unpleasant at best, terrifying at worst, no doubt expensive, legal thing. *This* must have been what Nancy had been foreshadowing. Ugh.

"Aren't you going to open it?" Alyssa asked.

Well, I didn't think it was from my boss or the university. The last time I'd gotten in trouble, they hadn't served me any legal papers. So, it could wait.

I looked at her. I sat down in my chair. I put the envelope down on my desk next to her dissertation. "Nope. You are more important. Thank you for bringing me the paper copy so punctually. Did you deliver the other copies to the rest of your committee?"

"No. You're the first." She leaned forward. "Do you want to take a quick look to see if it looks okay?"

Ah ha. She was nervous. I started paging through the document. "Nice title page. Nice acknowledgments. I'm not trying to boss you around, but you might consider including your committee members here." I pointed at the page.

She stared at me for a few seconds. "You want me to acknowledge you?" she finally said.

I touched my chest. "I don't care. I'm just saying the other members of your committee might like feeling appreciated. . ."

"So, I should suck up?" she asked.

I just smiled at her.

My phone chirped. I ignored it.

"Yeah. Okay," I said. "Suck up. Couldn't hurt." I pointed at the papers. "Why do you think I asked you to print it out? You got some old men on your committee. They like paper. And acknowledgment."

"Okay," she said. "I can redo the acknowledgments page."

I quickly looked through some more pages. "Nice table of contents. Nice formatting of the text. Your formulas look good." I scanned the rest of the pages. "Everything looks good. Except I see citations in the text, but you didn't include any references in the end."

"I haven't finished the refs," she said. "I'm still adding to them since I'm still writing up my methods and results and conclusions and stuff."

"That makes sense." I nodded and pointed at the pages. "Leave the updated pages and the new chapters on my desk if I'm not here."

She sighed and stood up. "Okay."

"Please deliver the complete first draft to the other committee members," I said. "In fact, I would say put it in their hands and smile and be polite."

"Okay." Now she was frowning.

"Overall, really nice job, Alyssa," I said. "I'm impressed. You should be proud."

She genuinely smiled. Now that was more like it. "Thanks," she said. She got her stuff together and walked out of my office. In the doorway, she said, "Oh, hi, Professor Rivas."

I heard Andro say something unintelligible in return, and then he appeared in the doorway. "Hi there, Madison. You seem to be having a busy day." He smiled, and it felt like I was standing in sunshine.

I jumped up from behind my desk and went over to him. "It's so nice to see you, my little baklava," I said.

He laughed while we hugged. "I thought we'd given up on the pastries."

"My little *bizcocho*?" Yes, I'd looked up kinds of pastries on my phone while I was on the bus.

He leaned down, and we shared a quick kiss. It was not passionate. I was confused. What was going on between me and Andro? I stared into his eyes and decided. . . not to bring it up.

I stepped away from him and sat on the edge of my desk. "Did you hear we found a body?"

"What!" Looking surprised, he took a step back. "Who? Where?"

My phone chirped. I couldn't see it from where I was sitting.

"I'll take that as a 'no,'" I said. "You didn't hear. Me and Ben were on a stakeout downtown at the St. Julien. We followed Griffin to a pot shop, and when we got back to the hotel, there was a body upstairs in the hall outside his and Luke's room."

"Who was it?" Now he looked sad.

"One of the caterers from the wedding," I said. "Lisa and the FBI were there--at the crime scene, not the wedding. They think Luke murdered the guy."

Andro shook his head. "Isn't that kind of a step up for him? He doesn't generally go around blatantly murdering people, does he? He wrecked the turnpike, but it wasn't a direct attack on anyone. in the heat of an argument, and there was that security guard who had a heart attack, and. . ." He trailed off, and I knew instantly he was thinking about his late brother-in-law, who Luke had killed via vehicular manslaughter.

I held out my arms for a hug.

He smiled sadly, and we shared a quick hug. "Are you all right?"

"I'm all right," I said. "Are you?"

He pulled his phone out of his pocket and glanced at the time. "I think I'll go home and play with Sophia. Do you want to come?"

"I can't. But it sounds good for you," I said. It sounded like just what the doctor ordered. For a split second, I wished I had a toddler at home to play with. "Have fun."

"Call you later," he said, and after I nodded, he turned and walked out.

My phone chirped. What was going on with that thing anyway? It was blowing up. I went back around to the other side of my desk. I'd missed a bunch of texts. Nancy said Chen was looking for me again. There were a bunch of reporters asking for comments--how did they get my number? Ben texted the name of the murder victim. Lisa texted that the autopsy was 'inconclusive' and was I sure I didn't want to come check it out? Lisa texted that the FBI was opening a field office in Boulder to deal with the quantum crime menace.

My phone rang--an actual voice call was coming in. It was Lisa. I answered it and started opening the mysterious manila envelope.

"Didn't you get my texts?" she said without preamble.

"Nice to talk to you, too, Agent Baker," I said. "How are you doing? Gee, I'm doing okay, thanks for asking."

"I need you to come to the morgue--"

I'd opened the envelope and slid out the papers. I was being sued. By AAA Paving in Denver, Colorado. They wanted expenses for repaving plus five hundred thousand dollars in damages. "*Aaurggh*!"

"Are you being attacked?" she asked. "Should I q-lapse there?"

"No!" I said. "Don't q-lapse." Q-lapsing was bad for everyone. "I'm being sued by some paving company."

"Oh, right," she said. "Because of the Boulder Turnpike."

"You knew about this?" I asked. "Why didn't you warn me?"

"I heard some rumblings," she said. "Not my jurisdiction." It was as if I could hear her shrug. "Anyway, I need you to come to the morgue. The coroner can't figure out the cause of death. There doesn't seem to be anything wrong with the man."

"Except for the whole being dead thing." I knew the Boulder coroner was not as experienced with murder as some--but, jeez, that sounded ridiculous.

"Right."

"Why are you asking me? I don't know anything about murder or bodies or anything. Bring in some super-duper FBI expert."

"I'm asking you because you're the expert. You're the quantum cop," she said in a level tone. "We need your expertise." She was thoroughly annoying me.

"No," I said. "I'm busy. And next time, if you want my help, you should ask me nicely." I hung up on her.

She didn't call back, so I guess: point made.

I was still staring at my phone when Ryan called. Filled with dread, I answered it. "Hi, Ryan. How are you?"

"Hi, Mad," he said. "I'm okay. You sound weird. Are you sure you're okay?"

"Close enough," I said. "What's up?"

My landline rang. Too many calls!

"Just a sec, Ry." I put down my cell.

I answered the landline. "Professor Chen wants you down in his office ASAP." It was Nancy.

"Okay, Nancy," I said. "Tell him I'll be right there." I hung up.

I picked up my cell phone. "What's up, Ryan?"

"The CU computer system was hacked," he said. "Some grades were changed. I started investigating, and I think it might be a quantum crime."

Could this day get any worse? It had been too much. I was out of energy. "I'm sorry, Ryan. I can't help you."

"What do you mean you can't help me?" he asked. "I just said it was probably a quantum crime. You have to help me."

"Sorry," I said. "You know I love you, but I can't help you with this. I've got too much on my plate. I have to prioritize. Good luck." I ended the call. I felt horrible about not helping him, but I couldn't--at least not this second.

I sat in my office for a quiet moment, my pulse racing. Calm, I was calm. I breathed in. I breathed out.

First things, first. What did I need to do?

Calm, I was calm.

I needed to go talk to my boss--while I still had one.

Chapter Twenty-One

Down in Professor Chen's office, I let him yell at me for a while.

I must admit my attention did wander a bit. That paving company couldn't truly make me pay them money, could they? My next task was clearly to call my lawyer, Tom. Tom's legal fees were why I was still renting a room from Ben, despite my professor's salary. I was lucky Ben had been so generous--not requiring a security deposit and the like.

What was going on with me and Ben? Should something go on? That raised the question again: what was going on with me and Andro?

"Madison!" Professor Chen said. "Are you even listening to me?"

"Yes, sir," I said. "I'm sincerely sorry my actions may have caused you and/or the university any problems."

"You are?" His eyebrows raised up his forehead. I don't know what it was, but he always reminded me of the early Beatles. It must be his bowl haircut.

"Yes, sir," I said. "And I promise to try not to get into any trouble in the future."

"You do?" he asked. "Well, that's all I wanted." He seemed to relax a little. "So, how's your class going?"

I nodded. "Good."

"And your research?"

"Good." I nodded some more. "I finished two grant proposals last month, you know."

"I did not know that," he said. "That sounds good. And your grad student? How's she doing?"

"Excellent," I said. "She gave me the first five chapters of her dissertation just a little while ago."

"I'm impressed with your work with Alyssa," he said. "I thought she was a problem student, but I guess not."

I refrained from saying something like, 'Yeah, women are trouble, with their human emotions and all.' Maybe someday I'd have a female boss. Or, maybe I should try to be the department chairperson someday.

But I just said, "She's doing great. Thanks for your faith in me, sir." Alyssa wasn't the only one who knew how to suck up.

My phone indicated a new text, and I made the mistake of looking at it. Lisa still wanted me to come to the morgue.

I must have been frowning because Professor Chen said, "What's wrong?"

"Nothing." I forced a smile. "FBI Agent Baker just wanted my advice on something. But she's fine on her own."

"You're not going to help her?" He looked aghast.

"Do you think I should?" I knew people liked to think their advice was valued.

"Of course!" he said.

Well, now, I'd put my foot in it. I didn't see how I could get out of it now. "Then, if you think I should, sir, I guess I will." I stood up. "I should get going then."

"You do that." He pointed at me.

I made myself smile and nod as I walked out the door.

Back in the main office area, Nancy sat at her desk near the window, glaring at me.

I smiled at her as I called Lisa. "Okay, you wore me down. Where's the morgue?"

"It's in the justice complex near Pearl Street mall," she said. "How long will you be?"

"Long," I said. "I'm taking the bus. I'll text you when I'm close."

"All right." She sounded annoyed but ended the call.

Nancy and I were still staring at each other. I took a step towards her.

She gave me an evil smile. "How'd you like that process server?"

Shit. The process server. I still needed to contact Tom. I texted him: 'I'm being sued in civil court for $500,000. Can you help? If not, do you have a referral?'

I took another step toward Nancy. We needed to clear the air. . ."I'm sensing you're angry with me," I said.

"Well, duh," she said.

"Any crimes you committed were your own fault," I said. "I'm not sorry I helped catch you. What you did was wrong."

"But I thought my boyfriend was back from the dead," she said. "That was your fault. That rogue FBI agent wouldn't have been able to impersonate Barry if you hadn't taught him that quantum stuff."

"Nate's crimes were his responsibility, and he paid the price." We both quieted. Nate was d-e-a-d. Finally, I added, "And people don't come back from the dead. You should have known better. You knew better."

She just frowned at me.

Well, I don't think that cleared any air or made anyone feel better, but at least we knew where we stood.

I headed for the bus stop

Well, it turns out the morgue is exactly as creepy as you'd think. It's cold. It smells like chemicals and worse.

Lisa walked in just as I was walking in. "Took you long enough," she said.

"I told you I didn't want to come," I said. "I don't know anything about bodies or. . . body-stuff."

The employee, a middle-aged, balding guy, snickered. "Hi. I'm Dr. Park. You want to see Brad Gaciometti again?"

"Yeah," Lisa said.

"Gaciometti?" I said. "Is that an Italian name?"

Dr. Park went to a large metal door and opened it. He went inside the freezer, or whatever it was.

"Probably," Lisa said. "Who cares?"

"Luke Bacalli is Italian," I said. "It just struck me."

"So, all Italian-Americans know each other?" she asked, disbelief on her face.

"I don't know," I said. "They're a similar age. They live in the same town. They're both associated with CU. They're both Italian-American. They both seem to know Griffin? There has to be some connection between this Brad guy and our villains. Maybe they went to the same Catholic church? Had first communion together? I don't know."

"So, you're saying all Italian-Americans are Catholic?" she asked. "That sounds racist to me."

Dr. Park reappeared from the freezer, rolling a young man on a metal table our way.

I blew out a big breath. This day was hideous. "Whatever. I was just trying to help."

Dr. Park stopped at the table next to me and Lisa. The young man looked peaceful; there were no blatant wounds or anything. But at the same time, it was abundantly clear he was dead. I didn't know what it was, but there was no mistaking it. No one was home.

"So?" Lisa asked.

"So, what?" I asked, staring down at the poor young man. He'd had his whole life ahead of him. And now it was gone. I glanced up at Dr. Park. "What about his family?"

"They've been notified." He looked grave. "Worst part of my job, dealing with the bereaved."

I could imagine.

"Do you detect anything?" Lisa asked.

"What? With my spidey-sense?"

"Well, yeah."

I exhaled again. Calm. I was calm. I was a calm crime-fighter. If I could find something out, it would help bring this man's killer to justice. I needed to try.

"So?" Lisa asked.

"You know what?" I said. "You're distracting me. I need to be alone with Brad. Both of you, please leave."

Dr. Park shrugged and walked out. Lisa looked annoyed, but she followed him. Possibly, she was having a bad day, as well. I closed the door after them.

I went back over to the young man. "All right, Brad. I'm sorry this happened to you. Do you have anything to tell me?" I stared at him for a few moments, but nothing happened. I didn't detect anything.

I pulled a stool over and sat down, then closed my eyes and tried to concentrate. Did I detect any weird quantum stuff? I concentrated. Did anything seem out of the ordinary? Or odd? Or downright weird? I focused on the quantum possibilities.

There. Was that a thread of improbability? I definitely detected a thread of low possibilities. I concentrated and gathered my thoughts. I needed to follow that thread.

I focused and q-lapsed. . .

I found myself in a misty quantum fog of possibilities.

My pulse started racing. This was what I called quantum limbo, where reality was in flux, where many, many quantum possibilities were all in play. I did not like quantum limbo. My pulse ratcheted up.

Calm, Madison. Stay calm. You're the quantum cop. You can best some flimsy quantum possibilities.

I tried to focus. Could I detect the improbability thread I'd followed here? Where did it go from here? I sent out my senses. I concentrated.

I thought I caught a whiff, a sense of the essence of someone familiar, but it was faint.

I concentrated some more, but I couldn't differentiate one grouping of possibilities from another. The mystery essence, soul(?), whatever it was, did not come into focus.

Enough of this. I needed to go back.

I focused, concentrating on the probability where I was back in the morgue. My head hurt a little.

And then I was. I was back in the cool antiseptic room.

Dr. Park shrieked and fell back against a cabinet. "Where did you come from?"

Lisa said, "So, Madison?"

"What's happening here?" Dr. Park asked.

"It's above your pay grade, don't worry about it," she said.

"I did detect q-lapsing associated with poor Brad here," I said.

"I knew it," she said.

"Detected what?" Dr. Park said.

"But I lost the trail in quantum limbo," I said.

"Quantum what?" he asked. We ignored him.

"Are you sure you lost the trail?" she asked. "No chance of picking it up?"

"I tried."

"So, it's Luke," she said.

"That would be my guess," I said. "I sensed someone. But,

try to prove it in court. . ."

Lisa scowled like she was disappointed at this turn of events.

"I don't understand," Dr. Park said. "What's going on here?"

"She'll explain." I pointed at Lisa and retreated, exiting the morgue.

"Hey!" she called after me. "Where do you think you're going?" I ignored her.

Walking through the government building, I now had a small headache due to my q-lapsing, no doubt. The best fix for a quantum headache was coffee--especially since I didn't have my new prescription meds with me. I stepped outside into the cold air.

Since I was downtown, I decided to go back to the coffee shop from. . . earlier in the day. Had that been earlier this same day? A lot had happened today.

Inside Boulder Brews, I breathed in deeply, savoring the smell of coffee and pastries, and beer. *Ahh.* Nice. At the counter, I procured a double espresso and took an immediate sip. *Ahh.*

There was one empty table. I elbowed my way to it through the crowd and sat down just as my phone started to ring. It was Tom.

"What's going on now?" he asked. "You're being sued?"

"Thanks for calling me back," I said. "Yeah. I'm being sued for five hundred thousand dollars."

I glanced around and realized math-guy was sitting at the table next to mine. He'd taken off his sweater and wore a t-shirt that said, 'My pin number is the last four digits of pi.' He gaped at me.

"By who?" Tom asked. "Why?"

"Some Denver paving company," I said. "I guess they blame me for the turnpike mayhem, not that I had anything to do with it. Directly."

"You better come to my office," Tom said.

"It just so happens I'm pretty near there right now," I said. "I was just at the morgue."

"Why?" Tom asked. "Wait. I don't want to know. See you soon." He ended the call.

Math-guy was still staring at me. Finally, he said, "Are you stalking me?"

"Of course not," I said. "Are you stalking me?"

"Of course not," he said.

"Well, there you go." I stood up to go. I started for the exit.

"Did you say suing? And morgue? Who are you?" math-guy called after me.

Tom's office looked the same as ever, like a classy, expensive office. Sadly, I was one of the folks who'd helped pay for it. The receptionist nodded me right on through to the back.

I knew the way. At Tom's open door, I knocked. "Hey, Tom."

He stopped typing and nodded. "Hey, Madison."

I took a sip of coffee. Look at me, all calm.

"What's up?" he asked.

"I got served. AAA Paving in Denver is suing me for $500,000," I said, walking into his office.

"It's a civil suit?" he asked. "The burden of proof is much lower in civil suits."

I sat down in the chair opposite his desk. "I guess so."

He blew out a breath.

"What?" I asked.

"I think this is blow-back from your stint on the news the other day," he said.

I knew that wouldn't end well. "What should I do?"

"Give me the papers, and I'll start investigating."

I took a sip of coffee. "I didn't actually bring the papers with me."

He looked exasperated. Jeez. Everyone was grumpy today. "Please email or fax me a copy as soon as you can."

"Okay," I said. "Should I be worried?"

"Yes, Madison," he said. "You should be worried."

As if I needed something else to be worried about.

Chapter Twenty-Two

As I was leaving Tom's office, I got a text from Ben saying the reporters were back at our apartment. Somehow they'd heard I was being sued. So I messaged Ryan and asked if I could stay with his family again. He kindly agreed. It was especially kind since I hadn't helped him with his quantum-computer-hacking problem earlier.

After stopping at my office to get some work stuff, including Alyssa's chapters, I stood on their front stoop and knocked on the door.

Sydney answered adorable Emily on her hip. Both of them smiled when they saw me standing there. "Madison, welcome!" Sydney said.

It was awesome seeing some friendly faces. I stepped into their home gratefully. I smiled back at her. "Sydney, I think you might be my favorite person--besides Emily, of course."

"Ryan isn't home from work yet," she said. "I'm excited for some grown-up talk. Can I offer you some wine?"

I didn't have much wine expertise. I just knew I liked it. I glanced at my bulging bag of work. I could get to it later. I needed some good relaxing. Besides, sleep was overrated, right? "Sure!"

She put Emily in her playpen and then stepped into her pretty, Tuscan-style kitchen. Soon, she joined me in the family room with stemless glasses of white wine. The glasses were frosted where the liquid was. She pointed at the couch with her elbow.

I took a glass and sat down. "Pretty glasses. Are these new?"

She smiled some more and nodded.

I took a sip. *Mmm*. It tasted winey. "So, how's it going?" I asked. "Emily seems good."

"Emily's great," Sydney said. "I must admit...." She trailed off. We sat in silence for a few moments.

"What?" I asked, starting to get worried. Was Sydney okay? Was Emily okay? "You can tell me anything."

"I need more mental stimulation," she said.

Phew. That didn't sound serious. "Okay," I said, not sure where she was going. "I'm all in favor of mental stimulation. How do you plan to get this stimulation?"

"I'm thinking about going back to work." She examined me over the top of her glass.

"That sounds good to me," I said. I was loving this totally normal conversation about a totally normal problem. "What's the issue?"

She frowned. "Ryan and I had an agreement. I was going to stay home until Emily went to kindergarten."

Uh oh. I didn't want to get in the middle of agreements between married people. "I support whatever you and Ryan decide to do."

She stared at me for a moment, then said, "Okay. You don't want to get involved. Fair enough."

"What's your degree in, again?" I asked.

"Psychology," she said.

After my meeting with Dr. Hasanov, I had to work not to shudder. "Neat."

We sipped quietly for a few more moments.

"So, what's up with you?" she asked.

I'd just started relaxing after a long week. I didn't want to get into murder or being sued for five-hundred-thousand plus dollars. What could I talk about that wasn't non-relaxing? "I sort of met an interesting new guy...." I didn't know math-man's name, so I hadn't truly met him.

She snorted. "Another guy? Why would you need another guy? And how do you sort of meet someone?"

"What are you saying?" I asked. "I shouldn't get into a love quadrangle?" I smiled.

"Only you would want to be in a love quadrangle," she said. "And what's a 'quadrangle,' anyway? Some kind of square?" She paused, peering at me. "What's going on with you and Andro?"

I took a sip, considering Andro. He was great, but our relationship wasn't. And I wasn't getting any younger. "I'm not sure," I said slowly. "I think. . ."

"What?" she asked.

"I think maybe …."

"What?"

"I think maybe we should call it," I said slowly. "Andro and I should break up."

"Whoa," she said. "Are you sure?"

No. I nodded.

"So you're hot for Ben?" she asked.

Yes. I shook my head. If I went out with Ben and it didn't work out, I'd have to find a new place to live, and I was sick of moving around.

"I gotta say, you're not super convincing, Mad," she said. "So, who's this new quadrangle guy?"

Ryan burst in the front door. Yay. Saved by the cousin. "Ryan!" I said. "So nice to see you."

As he took in the scene in his family room, he grinned and said, "Greetings, lovely ladies."

"This conversation isn't over, Mad," Sydney whispered. Then in a normal voice, she said, "Nice to see you, Ry. Greetings, back."

"Thanks, honey." Ryan leaned over the couch and kissed her.

She flushed a little. Jeez. That was so not me and Andro. I was envious of what Sydney and Ryan had. I wanted true love.

"I'm going to get comfortable." He walked back to his bedroom.

"What do you want to do for dinner, Madison?" Sydney asked.

"I can take care of it," I said. "Please, let me handle dinner."

"By which you mean, order in?" she asked with a smile.

"Yeah," I said, smiling back. "I am a really good orderer. I'm a gourmet orderer."

A little later, Ryan, in sweatpants and a t-shirt ('Be Safe: Sleep with an Officer of the Law'), had joined us on the couch.

"Would you like some wine, honey?" Sydney asked.

"Sure," he said.

"Really?" she asked, eyebrows raised in surprise.

"Sure," he said. "I'd like some wine." He stood. "But let me get it." He walked into the kitchen and poured himself a glass of wine, and brought the bottle back to the family room. "Would anyone else like some more? Sydney? Madison?"

I was enjoying my wine adventure, but not as much as I enjoyed beer. Plus, the considerable pile of work that was waiting for me was weighing on my mind even though I was trying to ignore it. "No thanks."

Sydney held out her glass. "I'll take a splash."

About an hour later, after we'd ordered and consumed a nice Thai dinner, Ryan and I were back on the couch. I even did the dishes, i.e., I threw the containers in the trash.

"I'm giving Emily her bath," Sydney said.

"Sounds good, honey," Ryan said.

She stared at him like she expected something more from him.

"I need to talk with Madison about something," he said.

Uh oh. Was I in trouble with him now?

"Okay," she said and walked back to the bathroom with Emily.

"So, what's up?" I asked.

"I have a bone to pick with you," he said. "You asked me to help you find those previous students--which I did. But then, when I asked you for help today, you wouldn't help me."

All the blood had rushed to my stomach for digestion, so I wasn't thinking as quickly as I might have. What was he talking about? "Uh, sorry?"

"Don't say 'sorry,'" he said. "Say you'll help me."

"Okay, I'll help. It could be related to Luke and his machinations," I said, with no idea what I was about to get myself into.

"Good." He jumped up off the couch, grabbed his bag, and took out his laptop. "So, I think these kids hacked the university's computer system and changed their grades." He set up the computer on the breakfast bar. "And our system is very secure, so I think it was a quantum crime."

Ah ha. He had mentioned this before. And I'd wriggled out of it before. I was a bad cousin.

He turned it on and logged in.

"I'm not a computer security expert," I said. "I'm not sure I can help."

"Just let me show you something," he said, navigating around some computer system. "So here were the grades." He pointed at a spreadsheet.

"Is this legal?" I asked. "For me to be looking at this? For you to be looking at this?" I thought student grades were confidential. The administration emailed us a bunch of legalese every semester about precisely this.

Ryan frowned. "And, then, magically, the grades turned into this." He pressed some keys, and the spreadsheet changed.

That didn't sound like Luke. "Couldn't it be regular hacking? What am I supposed to do about it?"

"Do your quantum cop thing." He pointed at the computer. "Do you detect any q-lapsing?"

Instead of arguing, I tried concentrating. Did I detect any q-lapsing? I concentrated. I focused. Did I detect any tendrils of quantum weirdness? Focus, Mad.

Nothing. But the wine I'd drank earlier wasn't helping.

"Sorry," I said. "I don't detect anything. If it was q-lapsing, maybe if I was in the same physical place that the miscreants had done their misdeeds… But no."

"Darn." The corners of his mouth and his eyes drooped down.

"But why do you need me? If you know these particular students changed their grades, can't you interview them and punish them appropriately?"

"I guess," he said. "We were just having a heck of a time figuring out how they did it."

"Well, I would definitely encourage faculty to keep paper copies of their grades." Did I have paper copies of my grades? I'd have to print some out the next time I was in my office.

Something he'd said earlier was important. What was it?

Oh yeah. My previous students that had been suspected of q-lapsing. "What did you find out about those students I asked you about?"

"I think I found the addresses of all three students," he said. "Arjun Chatterjee ran afoul of Agent Baker, so ICE got involved, and he was deported back to India. He's living with his parents in Mumbai--at least as far as I know." Yeah. I was guessing it's not so easy to check up on a young man in Mumbai.

"Drew Robinson and Brandon Lewis are still here in Boulder, still at their fraternity house, and still enrolled at the university."

"Seriously?"

"Well, no charges were brought against them," he said. "Nothing was ever proved against them, right?"

"Right," I said reluctantly. The two of them might explain the potential hotbed of fraternity-based q-lapsing. I'd seen some odd things over the last two years: never-ending beers, girls losing their tops, cop cars malfunctioning, stolen liquor, naked Ben. Grade changes might be right up their alley. "Hey, I wonder if these two might be involved in the grade changes?"

He nodded his head once. "It's worth investigating."

We chatted about the students a little while longer, but I had to read Alyssa's chapters and get ready for my class in the morning.

Wednesday morning, I had a heck of a time getting up.

Ryan shook the guest room bed like an 8.0-Richter earthquake. "Wake up, sleepyhead." He sat down on the bed.

"Ugh." I looked at the time on my phone. It was only a half-hour until my class. "Why didn't you wake me earlier?"

"I tried." He shrugged. "What's up with you?"

"I stayed up too late grading papers and stuff," I rubbed my eyes and sat up.

"Well, at this point, you can either take a shower *or* stop at Boulder Brews for goodies," he said.

"You know how much I love goodies," I said. "But, I better take a shower." It was a tragedy, but maybe I could get a pastry later in the day.

"Okay." He stood. "Suit yourself. Will I see you tonight?"

I shook my head. "I don't know."

I managed to step into my basement toothpaste-green

classroom with two minutes to spare.

The students were in more disarray than usual, standing in clusters on one side of the room and talking excitedly.

"Take your seats, please," I said. "I have graded homework."

A few people moved to sit down.

There seemed to be too many people in the room. The crowd parted more, and I saw someone who shouldn't be there, someone who was supposed to be on another continent.

"Arjun?" I asked. "What are you doing here?"

He disappeared.

Chapter Twenty-Three

Standing in my quantum mechanics classroom, I was pretty freaked out. My former student and q-lapser, Arjun, had appeared and disappeared. Was he involved in the current quantum-crime spree?

I'd just been talking and thinking about him last night with Ryan. Did thinking about people make them appear? Like I said, freaky.

My students were also freaking out, talking and gesticulating loudly, pointing at the now-empty space.

"Did that guy just disappear?"

"Shit!"

"He's gone, like, gone! He was just here, and now he's gone."

Damn. It was hard to keep quantum mechanics students from learning about q-lapsing when people q-lapsed right in front of them.

The best offense was ignoring the situation. "Please take your seats, people."

They continued standing around and muttering.

"I'm not joking. Sit. Be quiet. Or your participation grade for today will be zero." I always made class participation part of the students' grades so I'd have some leverage over them in class.

That shut them up. They sat down at their desks.

I got their graded homework out of my bag. "Pass your new homework up to the front." They started passing homework up, and I walked around, passing out graded homework. On my way back to the front table, I picked up the new homework.

"Okay." I smiled. I hooked up my computer to the projector. I brought up today's lecture. "Today, we're discussing the

Schrodinger equation." I projected the equation.

"I have a question," a young woman said.

I turned around. "Yes, Grace?" Today she had on a t-shirt that said, 'distance-raptor over time-raptor equals veloci-raptor,' with a picture of a velociraptor. Cute. I almost complimented her on it but decided to stay in teacher mode.

"Are you seriously going to ignore that a guy disappeared into thin air?" she asked.

I had been planning on ignoring that a guy disappeared into thin air.

The students started muttering again.

"Theoretically speaking," I said loudly, "if something weird happened, I don't know what it was--but I do know it won't be on the test. So can we focus on actual quantum mechanics?"

She frowned at me. Everyone else frowned at me.

"Great." I smiled. "So, Schrodinger's equation. It's basically derivatives of wavefunctions. Recall a derivative describes how something changes. Thus the Schrodinger equation describes how wavefunctions change. . ." I turned back to the screen.

We successfully made it through class. Phew. I waited until everyone left the classroom, then closed the door behind them and sank into an empty chair.

How could Arjun be here? I wasn't sure how, or more importantly, why he was here. But since he'd used q-lapsing, I might be able to follow him.

I suddenly realized I should have tried to follow Luke when he'd been all ghost-style at the bus stop. I could try it later. In the meantime, I had another mystery right here.

I stood up and walked over to where he'd been standing. I closed my eyes and focused. Did I detect any unusual quantum possibilities? Yes. There was a small one. . .

I concentrated and collapsed the wavefunction, instantiating the reality in which I'd followed this particular improbability to its source. I could be anywhere in the world. I felt cold wind on my face and heard a muffled bass beat thumping--as if through a closed door.

I opened my eyes. I stood on a sidewalk outside a large house. Judging by the familiar foothills to the west, I was in Boulder, Colorado, in the neighborhood called The Hill, surrounded by fraternity houses. Huh. I had a mild headache.

"Psst!" someone whispered.

I jerked in surprise.

"Hey, Madison!" someone else whispered.

I looked around and spied Ryan and Ben crouching in the street behind a parked car. They both had their uniforms on.

I walked over and crouched down next to them. "What are you two doing here?"

"What are you doing here?" Ryan asked. "I thought you wouldn't help with this. I'm investigating the possible quantum grade changers."

"And I followed Griffin's phone here," Ben said. "Ryan and I just ran into each other just now. It's a little freaky." Freaky was apparently the word of the day.

This fraternity house looked familiar. "Ben, isn't this where you were naked two years ago?"

He didn't answer me, but his face did turn red. So that was a yes.

Ryan didn't answer either; his face seemed to be struggling not to break into a smile.

I didn't like coincidences. I wasn't sure coincidences were even a real thing. "I followed Arjun Chatterjee here," I said slowly.

"Arjun!" Ryan said. "He's supposed to be in India."

"I know," I said.

"I don't like coincidences," Ben said.

"Yeah," Ryan said.

"Yeah," I said at the same time. I looked at him. That was not a coincidence.

"How do you want to handle this?" Ryan asked me.

"I think. . ." I said. The wind blew through my light sweater. Brr. I was getting cold. I rubbed my arms.

"Yeah?" Ryan said. He had on a nice warm-looking jacket.

"Yeah?" Ben, also wearing a jacket, said at the same time. Also, not a coincidence.

"I think we should put this place under surveillance," I finally said. It wasn't because I was chickening out. It was because it was dangerous.

"Really?" Ryan asked. "Just surveillance?"

"I don't believe in coincidences," I said. "I think there are multiple q-lapsers inside this fraternity house. And, sorry, but I don't think the three of us can handle it. We need backup."

"But I can q-lapse now," Ben said.

"Have you ever used q-lapsing to fight?" I asked.

"Well, no." He grimaced and looked at the pavement.

"What are you all doing here?" a woman asked.

Still crouching and focused on the two men, I jumped. They jumped as well (not a coincidence).

It was Lisa in all her ponytailed glory. She stood next to us, wearing a no-doubt toasty coat.

The thick plottens.

"Uh. . ." I said. What did she know? "What are you doing here?"

"We followed Griffin's phone to this location," she said.

"Who's we?" me and Ryan and Ben all asked at the same time. Not a coincidence.

"The Boulder FBI field office, of course," she said.

The three of us looked at her and then at each other. I mean, I knew there was now a Boulder field office, but I didn't realize these guys knew. But, since they didn't say 'What Boulder field office?' I was guessing they knew.

"So, we're going in," she said. "Are you helping?"

"Going in? Isn't that sudden?" I asked. "Don't we need a plan?" When we'd taken down Luke and Griffin two years ago, it had been a huge operation. "Don't you need to watch the place for a while first?"

"We've been here for hours," she said. "We were going to go in a little while ago but then you. . . guys all showed up." I got the distinct impression she'd been going to say something besides guys. Interlopers? Jokers?

"In or out?" she asked.

"In, of course," Ben said, standing up straight.

"In," Ryan said, also standing.

I suppressed a groan. If they were all in, I had to be in to protect them. "In. But can you guys at least try to be objective? Don't go in guns blazing." I stood up straight, squared my shoulders, and put my hands on my waist in superhero-stance. Huh. I did feel more superhero-like.

Lisa held up her radio to her mouth. "It's a go. Now! All agents approach target."

Four giant black SUVs squealed up and stopped, two from one direction, two from the other, disgorging multiple black-clad agents wearing flak vests, equipment-laden belts including stun guns, and holding very large guns.

Lisa was already running towards the house with her sidearm drawn.

Ben and Ryan drew their guns and ran after her.

I ran after them. The bass-heavy music still sounded from somewhere inside the house.

By the time I got to the front door (last), a bunch of officers had already entered the front, back, and side doors. Wow. They were quick.

"FBI, show yourselves," Lisa yelled in the front foyer.

And the floor moved. It rolled like an ocean wave and not like a solid floor at all.

Suddenly all the gun-toting agents had to work to keep their balance. They had their arms spread out (luckily, their guns were supported by straps around their necks) and moved their feet apart. And they all looked unhappy.

Lisa's ponytail rose into the air right before the rest of her did. She managed to keep hold of her weapon. She closed her mouth firmly as if biting back a scream. She reholstered her gun. "FBI. You're under arrest. You need to surrender."

The other agents started floating, too. Now they looked freaked out. A few of them were not successful in squelching little screams or sounds of dismay.

Inside the house, the bizarreness had all happened very quickly, within a matter of seconds.

Out on the front porch where I was, things were still normal.

I needed to get in the game! I closed my eyes and concentrated. Where was the quantum freakiness centered? I focused. I found multiple tendrils of high improbability inside the house. I concentrated, trying to damp them down or dismantle them.

I concentrated on the closest one. Everything's totally normal here. Nothing's weird. The acceleration of gravity is nine point eight meters per second squared.

The improbability seemed to be dissipating.

I opened my eyes to sneak a peek. The agent closest to the front door was floating to the ground, looking relieved.

I took a step toward him. "Everything's normal," I said.

"But--" he sputtered.

"You need to think everything's normal!" I said loudly. This had worked in the past. "Everyone! Normal! Think normal!"

Still floating, Lisa immediately pressed her eyes closed and started muttering, "Normal, normal, normal."

All the guns disappeared. Shit. The agents didn't seem to notice with everything else going on.

"Everything's normal," I said.

Ryan and some of the other agents joined in. "Everything's normal. Everything's normal."

I heard a laugh from someone I couldn't see further back in the house.

And then all of Ben's clothing got blurry and then slowly disappeared. He seemed embarrassed, but he had nothing to be embarrassed about. Nothing.

The other officers' clothing got blurry and started disappearing.

I glanced down, and my clothes were fine.

Lisa's clothing got blurry.

"Lisa!" I yelled. "Concentrate."

She looked down at herself and immediately closed her eyes tight and started muttering something else. Her clothing solidified.

Wow, we were getting distracted by the clothing situation. At least I was.

We needed to focus on the bad guys. I took a step back onto the porch.

In the house, someone put on some loud annoying music, which sounded like cheesy porno music. The main room lights dimmed, replaced by some kind of colored lights, which flashed on and off on a schedule I couldn't discern. Was this all part of their plan? Or. . . could it be some kind of side effect of q-lapsing?

I took another step back.

Most of the agents were now nude, floating in mid-air. And,

yes, they all seemed freaked out.

On the bright side, the floor had stopped moving quite so much.

"Everything's normal!" I yelled. "Normal!"

Unfortunately, no one believed me. And if they didn't believe it, they couldn't instantiate it.

I ran into the foyer and grabbed the two closest floating agents by the arms, and ran back out to the porch.

As we reached the porch, they fell and stumbled. "Everything's normal," I said to them. "Come on. Concentrate." I couldn't recall if these were agents I'd taught to q-lapse or not. In any case, their clothes did not materialize.

But they stood up straight. "What next?" one asked.

"Let's get the other agents out of there," I said. "Come on. Follow me. Step where I step." I didn't really think it mattered where I stepped, but they needed to think I had things under control. Psychology was important when it came to q-lapsing.

The three of us ran inside, and each grabbed two agents and ran back out to the porch.

Lisa grabbed onto my head and held on as I passed her.

I heard laughing from further inside the house.

The ten of us regrouped on the porch.

"Normal," I said. "It's normal. Come on. Let's get the rest."

The ten of us managed to retrieve all the other officers/agents and ran back outside.

So, within minutes, the whole huge attack force stood on the front lawn, nude--except me and Lisa. (And, yep, there were no other women.)

I took off my sweater, ran over to Ryan, and handed it to him. I immediately started shivering.

He managed to tie it around his waist like an apron.

Lisa handed Ben her coat, and he did the same.

The men looked extremely cold. And with just my shirt, I was cold.

We needed to get out of here ASAP. What if the q-criminals attacked again? What about the guns? What if the bad guys had the guns?

"Back to the SUVs, men!" Lisa said. "Hustle! On the double!"

They all ran to the SUVs. I followed them across the yard.

They'd lost their keys with their pants. I closed my eyes and concentrated. "The SUVs are unlocked. The SUVs are unlocked." I focused on instantiating the possibility in which the SUVs were unlocked.

I opened my eyes. The men opened the doors and jumped right inside.

I closed my eyes and concentrated again. "The SUVs start. The SUVs start." I collapsed the wave functions and made the SUVs start. My mild headache was approaching bad territory.

So, Ryan, Ben, Lisa, and I were standing on the curb next to four huge roaring SUVs. It was probably around thirty-five degrees or so, and Ryan and Ben looked like they were seriously suffering from the cold

"You guys need to get inside," I said to Ryan and Ben. They weren't talking. They were just shivering.

Lisa nodded and opened the back door of the closest car. Heat blossomed out. They must be running the heater at full blast. Good.

The guys got in immediately and closed the door behind them.

Now, Lisa and I were standing on the curb. I debated what to say.

'I told you so,' would not be appreciated. But score one for the quantum criminals. They were getting very good at q-lapsing. I shivered, and I didn't think it was entirely because of the cold. "Well, at least there were no fatalities."

She grimaced. "We lost our weapons." She seemed upset, clenching and unclenching her jaw and her fists. Her face was red. I'd never seen her lose her cool like this.

"That is bad." I frowned. "But they didn't shoot us. So, no injuries." Why hadn't there been injuries? It was as if the different q-lapsers had different MOs. How many different q-lapsers were there? We still had a lot to learn about what was going on.

"We were ineffective," she said.

We needed more information. "You should probably keep the house under surveillance in case they try to move the guns-- if they have the guns." I might be able to q-lapse the guns out of there, but I didn't want to say anything in case it didn't work. Did we even know where the guns were? No.

"Duh," she said and scowled. "That was a fucking disaster."

Duh. I shivered.

Chapter Twenty-Four

Once the quantum mayhem at the fraternity had mostly settled down, I realized I'd left my computer and other stuff unattended in my classroom in the physics building. I q-lapsed back. The toothpaste-green room was empty. Everything looked the same as I'd left it, and my stuff was still there. Phew.

I put my computer in my bag and started tramping up the stairs to my office.

I reached my office with a minimum of huffing and puffing. I noticed Andro's office door was closed. Phew again. That could mean he wasn't there, or he was busy working. Either way, I didn't have to talk to him. I was dreading our breakup conversation. What if I broke his heart? Or, worse, what if I didn't break his heart? My heart was feeling a little achy-breaky just thinking about it all.

I grabbed a bottle of water from my mini-fridge, sat down in my chair, put my bag on the desk, and took a pain pill for my headache.

I exhaled. Things were strangely quiet here. Or, maybe, I just wasn't used to quiet anymore. I inhaled deeply.

Okay. First things first: what was up with the agents' guns? Where were they now?

Second things second: Where were Luke and Griffin? Were they at the fraternity house? What exactly was up with that place? How many men there could q-lapse?

Considering everything, I was surprised my phone hadn't been blowing up.

I pulled it out of my pocket. It was turned off. Oh. Right. I turned it off for class.

I turned it on. Immediately all the missed texts and calls

started pinging.

Before I could check any of them, Lisa called. "Where are you?"

"I'm in my office," I said. "Where are you?"

"Still in the car, driving to our new Boulder office," she said. "Listen, I'm worried about the guns."

Great minds think alike. "Me, too."

"What happened to them?"

"I don't know," I said. "They disappeared?"

"But what does that mean?"

"I don't know."

She was quiet for a moment. Then she said, "I don't like it. I don't like any of this."

"Me, either," I said. "I'm tempted to go back to the frat and have a look-see?"

"Can you go back there?" she asked.

"Yeah, but as soon as they see me, won't the result be the same? Attack? Mayhem?" I asked.

"So, don't let them see you," she said.

"I'm pretty sure even I don't have the ability to become invisible." Right? My mind raced. Q-lapsing only worked for possible events. I couldn't imagine a real scenario where I could be invisible. So, no. I couldn't be invisible. Darn.

"I meant go as a fraternity guy," she said.

"You mean in disguise? Like Nate?" Her old partner, Nate, who turned evil, had impersonated Luke surprisingly well. I didn't know how to do that. "I don't know how to do that."

She was quiet for another moment. I imagined her thinking, 'Figure it out.' Finally, she said, "Figure it out."

"All right," I said, suppressing a groan. "Next steps, I think we need to get all the good-guy q-lapsers together and practice quantum fighting. Maybe later this afternoon?"

"I think you're right," she said. "Can you teach quantum fighting?"

"It looks like I'm about to find out."

"I'll find a place," she said.

We ended the call.

I sat quietly at my desk for a moment and sipped at my water. My physical headache was going away. My metaphorical headache was getting bigger.

How had evil FBI agent Nate impersonated people? One element was a physical disguise. He used makeup and wigs and stuff like that. So, it stood to reason that I needed a physical disguise.

Mind whirring, I rummaged around in the back of my biggest desk drawer for a t-shirt; I was pretty sure I'd secreted some there for emergencies. I found one. "Ha." I pulled it out. It said, 'I like Science, but I Love Be Er'--where the last part showed the chemical symbols for Beryllium (Be) and Erbium (Er). Possibly the chemistry was a little too nerdy, but the beer message should even it out. Part one of my disguise: check.

When I'd been investigating Nate, I'd gone to the theater department and learned all about theater makeup and prosthetics. . .

At the university theater, I walked around backstage. In the middle of the day, there were a lot of people back there, mostly students. I finally found a gray-haired woman who looked older than the others. "Are you a professor?"

She giggled. So, maybe not so old. "No. I'm in costume."

"I need to look like a twenty-ish man," I said. "Can you help me out?"

"Sure." She nodded. "Easy-peasy."

She led me over to a stool in front of an expansive lighted mirror. "Sit." She took a nose-sized piece of rubber out of a large makeup case there on the counter. "I think you need a big nose." She giggled again.

"Uh, how big?" I asked as she held up what appeared to be a giant nose.

She started dabbing some kind of glue on my not-giant nose. It smelled gluey. "Uh, are you sure about this?"

She nodded and giggled.

I tried to breathe through my mouth.

Soon I had a giant nose, big bushy eyebrows, and short-ish curly brown hair. And she'd done something to hide the seams. On the bright side, I looked nothing like myself. On the dark side, I looked a bit like a hobbit.

She dibbed and dabbed more makeup. Finally, she leaned

back and smiled. "Hello there, Frodo."

I knew it! I did look like a hobbit. I also looked like a twenty-ish man, pretty much. "Uh, thank you." I guessed I shouldn't complain. She'd done me a favor with no questions asked. "Why didn't you ask why I wanted a disguise?"

"*Why then 'tis none to you, for there is nothing either good or bad, but thinking makes it so,*" she said. Was that an answer?

"Uh, okay," I said and stood up.

She examined me from head to toe. "One more thing." She stepped over to a clothes rack crammed with all sorts of coats. She grabbed a large olive-green army-surplus jacket. "Here."

I put it on and looked at myself in the mirror. *Hhm.* I looked like Madison dressed up as a hobbit.

What if I tried q-lapsing to make it better? I closed my eyes and focused. I look like a hobbit, a male hobbit. I opened my eyes and looked into the mirror again.

A hobbit in the U.S. Army looked back at me. Wow. No way would anyone recognize me. "Thanks! I'll drop the stuff back here after my, uh, scene."

She stared at me. "Wow, I'm good."

I was a little worried when I got outside the theater people would point and say, 'Look at the hobbit!' but no one gave me a second glance. I started walking to the fraternity house.

When I got to the house, I threw back my shoulders and just walked in like I had every right to be there. The main foyer area was empty as it had been before.

I quickly walked through all the rooms on the first floor: a living room with a bunch of couches and a huge TV, a dining room, a study room, and a large kitchen. Every time I passed someone, I nodded and kept walking like I knew where I was going. A few guys were lounging around or studying, and an older woman was working in the kitchen, but no one seemed to care about me.

I opened every door and checked every closet. Bottom line: no guns on the ground floor.

I gazed at the large staircase. Upstairs, here I come. The second floor was uneventful: a long hallway with a sequence of closed doors.

I tried the door closest to the stairs. Locked.

QUANTUM MAYHEM

What were the chances this door would be unlocked? Nonzero. I closed my eyes and concentrated, trying to instantiate the reality in which this door was not locked. I collapsed the wavefunction, opened my eyes, and tried the doorknob. Unlocked. Sweet! And my head only hurt a little.

I slowly opened the door a little and peeked inside. It looked like a typical dorm room with two dressers, two desks, two chairs, two closets, and two beds. The coast was clear. I crept inside, closing the door behind me, and carefully searched the closets and under the beds. There were only so many places to hide a large cache of large guns. Okay. So one bedroom down, about a million bedrooms to go.

I went to the door and opened it, getting ready to dash into the hall.

"What are you doing in Jackson's and Liam's room?" a guy standing in the hall said. "Who are you?"

Shit. My mind raced. "Hi." I tried to pitch my voice lower. "I'm, uh, Fr, Frank Smith," I held out my hand as if I wanted to shake. "I'm interested in rushing. I've heard a lot of awesome stuff about you guys, and, I admit, I wanted to see the house. I hope that's okay." I smiled broadly. "My, uh, dad and grandfather and uncle were members--but back east. They're always going on and on about the brotherhood. Well, you know."

The man's expression had been morphing from suspicious to pleased as I talked. He shook my proffered hand, smiling a little, himself. "I'm Liam, the other Liam. I'm Rush Chair this year."

"Any chance you could give me a tour?"

"A legacy?" He glanced at his phone. "Yeah. I think I've got a little time. Sure." He was as good as his word and showed me the whole house.

Of course, he did not let me look in all the bedrooms, so there were a lot of closets and under-bed regions I didn't get to check.

Back in the front foyer, I smiled broadly. "Thanks so much. I really appreciate this, Liam. I'll tell my dad to put in a good word about you with National."

Now he smiled broadly.

"So, what's the partying sitch here?"

He smiled. "We like to party, but *of course,* we obey all relevant laws."

"*Of course.*" I smiled like I was in on the joke. "Speaking of, er, partying, one of my buddies said he saw a bunch of naked dudes running out of here this morning. What's up with that?"

"I wasn't here for that. I was in class." He snickered. "But, yeah, some dudes lost their clothes. I didn't get the whole story because the two brothers involved went to the health center after." Now he frowned. "It was kind of weird. They got, like, these killer headaches."

Not so weird. "Weird. Bummer." I nodded. "Any other weird stuff I should know about?"

He gave me a sharp look. "Like what?" Uh oh. Was I ruining my excellent cover?

I held up my hands. "I don't know. Just asking."

He frowned and shook his head. "I don't think so."

I debated asking if Drew and Brandon were members here. And what about Arjun?

"Any chance I could get a list of your members?" I asked. "So, I can see if I, uh, already know any?"

Now other-Liam scowled at me. "No."

"Uh, no worries." What would an actual college guy do in this situation? "So, you guys got any parties coming up any time soon?" I grinned.

He grinned back. "Oh yeah. We got one this weekend. You wanna come?"

I nodded. "Awesome."

My phone buzzed with a new text. It was Lisa: 'Where are you? Get over here.' No doubt she wanted to start the quantum fight training.

"Gotta go!" I said to Liam. "I appreciate the tour."

As I exited, I thought I heard Liam say, 'Legacy,' and someone else say something like, 'Dude needs a nose job.' But that couldn't be right.

Lisa'd texted me the location of the new Boulder FBI field office, and luckily it was downtown. The bus dropped me off right near the address Lisa had indicated. The whole ride over, I'd been pondering how to train someone to do quantum fighting.

When I caught a glimpse of myself in the bus's review mirror, it was clear any q-lapsing I'd invoked to make my costume better had worn off. I was back to looking like Madison in a hobbit costume. Oh, well.

Standing outside the building, Lisa told me about it, and I stared up at it. It looked like a generic office building, exactly like all the other generic office buildings in the area. I went inside, and the lobby also looked like a generic office building. The directory on the wall did not say 'FBI,' but Lisa had told me they were on the top floor. I got in the elevator and rode up.

The doors opened onto a large open space with no interior walls. There were a few desks with computers clustered by the elevator. There was also a large locked, empty locker near the elevator. For weapons?

"Finally," Lisa said, glancing at me. She stood up from one of the desks and gestured me to follow her. She led me over to the open area where about a dozen men loitered, all dressed in black. Were these the guys from this morning? I thought so, but they looked different with clothes on. They all looked to be in their twenties, clean-cut, and very fit. I didn't see any tats or distinguishing marks. Was that intentional?

Ben broke from the pack and ambled up, pointing at me. "Something's different."

I resisted the urge to say, 'Yeah. You're dressed.' If the tables had been turned, I didn't think I'd appreciate being teased about being naked.

Lisa nodded and said solemnly. "New jacket?" I was still wearing the army surplus jacket from the theater department.

"Oh, yeah," Ben said. "That's it." He grinned.

Okay. Clearly, they weren't going to comment more explicitly about my disguise. Fine. I could play that game, too.

The other guys walking toward us couldn't help snickering or grinning. Me neither; I joined in.

I didn't see Ryan. "No, Ryan?"

"No," Lisa said. "He said he couldn't make it." More quietly, she said, "Any sign of the weapons?"

At a normal volume, I said, "I was just looking around the fraternity house. There was no sign of your weapons. If they're there, they are secured well out of sight."

The guys didn't seem to know how to react to that.

"Two of the frat guys had to go to the health center with 'killer' headaches," I said.

"That's the first good thing I've heard all day," Lisa said with a grim smile. Badass. Check.

"Are you going over there to investigate?" I asked.

"No," she said. "There's a little thing called doctor-patient confidentiality. They won't tell me anything."

We all stood there in silence for a few moments. Okay, that's the end of that conversational topic.

Finally, I said, "So, you guys want to learn quantum fighting?"

They all nodded and said some variant of 'Yeah.'

"Have you all taken my informal q-lapsing class over at the university?" I'd attempted to teach several sets of agents over in Gamow Tower, using the double-slit apparatus.

Again, nods all around.

"And did you do it?" I'd tried to teach at least twenty agents how to q-lapse over the last couple of years. As I recalled, however, none of them had mastered it--besides Lisa and Nate.

Ben held up his hand. "I think I did." He'd q-lapsed, but I wouldn't say he'd mastered it.

The agents just muttered and shifted from foot to foot.

"Q-lapsing is based on probabilities." I started getting into professor mode. "It is much easier to q-lapse something that has a high probability. It's harder to q-lapse something that has a low probability."

"I think we should start by using q-lapsing to enhance your considerable existing fighting skills." On the way over here, I'd pondered my quantum disguise. It seemed like q-lapsing had enhanced something real, something physical. What if we could do that with fighting? What if we could use q-lapsing to enhance real fighting abilities? "It's highly probable that you guys are good fighters."

They nodded.

"So, let's warm up with some usual hand-to-hand combat exercises, and then we'll add in q-lapsing," I said.

Lisa snorted. "You say that like you know some usual hand-to-hand combat exercises."

I shrugged.

She pointed at a particularly burly agent. "Max. You're in charge."

They started pairing off.

I took off my borrowed jacket and wig and started pulling off the bits of rubber from my face.

I really hoped this would work.

Chapter Twenty-Five

I was doing hand-to-hand combat drills with a bunch of black-clad federal agents on the top floor of a generic office building. Yeah, my life was weird.

Lisa sidled up to me. "Where's the quantum stuff? Are you done procrastinating yet? "

I drew myself up to my full height. "I'm sure I don't know what you mean."

She seemed to snicker for the briefest of seconds. "I thought you were supposed to be some kind of genius."

"I never said that." I narrowed my eyes. Had I said that? I didn't think so. "Anyway. . ." I stepped towards the grappling men. "Nice job, guys."

They stopped moving around and walked calmly toward me. Soon I was surrounded by assorted fit twenty-somethings with a variety of skin tones. Ben fit in seamlessly with the rest of them. Lisa, the only woman, a little older, did stand out.

"Now, let's bring in some q-lapsing," I said. "The most important thing to remember about q-lapsing is it involves your mind."

Lisa made that snickery sound again. I did not glance at her.

My mind was racing. How to teach this? What did I do when I q-lapsed? I vocalized. "So, the best way to focus your mind is to speak."

"No, it isn't," Lisa said.

I ignored her. "So, now I want you to repeat your combat drills, but yell what you're doing, and keep it positive."

They all looked at me like I was a crazy hobbit.

Lisa said, "I think I understand what she's getting at." She stepped up next to me. "Madison and I will spar." She gestured to me, and the two of us walked into the middle of the empty space.

I knew I didn't stand a chance sparring against Lisa unless I cheated. I immediately yelled, "My right jab is world-class!" and threw a right jab at her head.

She moved away quickly, but I still managed to catch her cheek with a glancing blow. Hurray. Her head jerked back. She looked surprised.

The guys, clustered closer to us, looked a little impressed.

"I can kick Madison on the shoulder!" she yelled, and then she got fuzzy and seemed to float in the air for a moment as her foot approached my shoulder.

I barely stepped back in time. It was definitely easier to defend oneself when you knew what was coming.

The guys seemed impressed with Lisa's actions. With mine, not so much.

Ben said, "Correct me if I'm wrong, but doesn't telling your opponent what you're about to do to them sort of defeat the purpose of fighting?"

"Yes." I nodded. "But we're training now. Once you get some q-lapsing moves under your belt--so to speak--you can yell mentally rather than out loud, and your opponents won't know what hit them."

The men stood there for a second as if not believing all of this.

"Remember," I said, "you need to believe in q-lapsing. You need to focus your mind to collapse the wavefunction and instantiate the reality you want."

"You have your orders, men," Lisa said in her no-nonsense voice.

They got to work.

"You too, Madison," she said. "You need practice fighting even more than the rest of us."

Darn it. She was right. I got to work.

After an afternoon of quantum fighting, I was dragging, no doubt about it. And my headache was back. I took an Uber back to my office.

At the physics building, I trudged up the stairs on the way to my office.

On my floor, Andro poked his head out of his office. When he saw me, he jerked back. What was that about?

"Hi, Madison." He seemed to force himself to smile. "How's it, ah, going?"

I nodded. "Pretty good. I have a headache, though."

Now he looked concerned. "Have you been q-lapsing? I hope nothing's wrong."

What wasn't wrong? I couldn't recall what Andro knew and what he didn't.

I started getting a little panicky. Exactly how bad was q-lapsing for your brain? "Uh. . . No current emergencies. I'd like to take a pill and sit down on my couch." I wished I had some coffee.

"Can I get you some coffee?" When he smiled genuinely, it was like the warm sun peeking out from behind the clouds on a dreary winter day, bathing everything in its radiance.

What were the rules on asking people for favors right before you were going to dump them? I was guessing it was frowned upon. "That would be great, Andro. Thanks." I went into my office, got a water out of my mini-fridge, took a pill, and sat down on the couch.

In the meantime, he went on a coffee quest.

I leaned back on my couch.

The next thing I knew, Andro was saying quietly, "Madison? Do you still want coffee?"

I opened my eyes. "Sure." I reached for the cup and took it. Sip. Ah. The caffeine jumpstarted my brain. "Thanks a lot. I appreciate this."

He sat next to me on the couch. "So, what's going on?"

Since I didn't know exactly what he knew, I figured I could start now and work my way back. He'd stop me when I got to stuff he knew. "I was just at the new Boulder FBI field office, training the agents in quantum fighting."

"There's a Boulder FBI office? And, wait, you know how to do quantum fighting?" Now he definitely looked surprised.

Truth be told, in the past, when Andro and I had gotten into quantum fights, it had been a little haphazard. "What, you don't think throwing lawn furniture at someone is a good tactic anymore?" he said and laughed a little.

Yeah, that happened. I joined in.

Once we settled down a bit and I drank more coffee, I said, "This morning, we traced some quantum criminals to a fraternity house on the hill. The FBI raided it, but it didn't go well. Their guns disappeared and. . ." Maybe I didn't need to get into the details of a bunch of good-looking, naked agents all around me. "So, uh, it wasn't a success. No one was arrested."

Andro was frowning. "What happened with the guns?"

"We don't know," I said. "To find out, I went back to the fraternity house, in disguise. . ." Uh oh. What did I look like now? I grabbed my phone and accessed my mirror app. "Oh, my God!" I looked hideous. I had wig-hair (like hat-hair but even worse) and little bits of rubber stuck randomly to my face. It looked like I had leprosy or something.

I glanced at Andro. "Why didn't you say something?"

He seemed to be suppressing laughter. "I figured it was quantum cop business."

I didn't think I was a vain woman, but this was a bit much even for me.

Focus, Mad. What else was going on? I was being sued. I didn't need to talk about that. What else? "So, you know about the murder, right?" I started picking off the pieces of rubber.

"Yeah." He nodded. "I heard it through the grapevine." He shifted on the couch, leaning towards me. "Listen, Madison. I've been waiting for you. I think we need to have a difficult conversation. You know I care about you. But this isn't working anymore. I don't think we have a future. I think we should stop seeing each other."

Suddenly I felt hot and sweaty all over. I couldn't believe this was happening. This couldn't be happening. He couldn't dump me. I was going to dump him! I took a sip of coffee.

And why? I waited for more of an explanation.

"Say something," he said.

My phone rang. Saved by the bell. It was Ben. I answered.

"You'll never guess, Madison!" he said. "My gun's back in my lock-box! The sidearm I had with me at the raid this morning! It magically reappeared in the box sometime today."

I didn't immediately answer him.

"Madison?" he asked.

Finally, I said, "That's good news, Ben. I'll be home in a little while. Let's talk then." I ended the call.

"Madison?" Andro asked. "Are you all right?"

I took a sip of the--apparently--pity coffee. Finally, I said, "I hear you. I'm all right. And you're right about us breaking up. I was going to say something. We haven't been connecting."

"I'm so relieved." He exhaled, leaning back a little. "And of course, I'll help with any q-lapsing you need. And we're still colleagues. Friends." He patted my knee in a platonic way and then stood up. "We'll still see each other all the time. Our offices are right next door."

Ugh. We'll still have to see each other all the time. Our offices were right next to each other.

He smiled and started walking away. At the door, he turned and smiled gently. "You're a remarkable person, Madison. I'm glad we went out. Thanks." And then he beat a hasty retreat.

On the couch, I took another sip of coffee. On the bright side, my headache was going away.

On the dark side. . .

No. I wasn't going to go to the dark side. I was staying in the light. I was awesome. If Andro didn't want to date me, it was his loss. I was great. Andro wasn't. Andro was. . . Whoops, almost went over to the dark side again. I was great. I was great. Maybe if I kept thinking it, I'd feel it.

Or, maybe I should vocalize. "I'm great. I'm awesome. I'm super awesome."

I went to the ladies' room and primped a bit. A girl needs some dramatic red lipstick in this type of situation. And no rubber on her face. And no wig-hair. "I'm awesome," I whispered to myself in the mirror.

I got my stuff together and caught the bus back to Ben's neighborhood. In the strip mall across the street from Ben's place, I stopped at the little Chinese restaurant and ordered a bunch of food from egg rolls to crab rangoons, to dumplings, to fried rice, to sweet and sour pork and General Tso's chicken. While I waited for them to get it together, I drank a Tsingtao at the bar. Quickly.

I was remarkable. I was awesome. I was the quantum cop,

after all. "Awesome."

It was for the best that Andro and I broke up. I'd already decided. It was for the best. Now I was available for new romantic adventures. With math-man, or whoever.

I was remarkable. "Remarkable."

"Order up, Madison!" the man behind the counter said.

I picked up the two large paper sacks.

When I got to the apartment, I was carrying too much stuff to unlock or knock on the door. I stood outside. "Ben! It's Madison! I'm outside. My hands are full. Open up."

I heard someone clomp up to the door. And then the door flew open, Ben smiling widely when he saw me. "Madison! Finally. I've been waiting for you."

And then I don't know what happened; we were kissing. It was even hotter than I'd imagined.

He pulled me inside the apartment. I dropped my messenger bag and the sacks of food. My hands explored his body, and, yep, I was right: not an ounce of fat on him. Soon, his hands were all over my body. He pushed the front door closed and then led me to the couch. Still clothed, our bodies fit together perfectly.

He gently pushed me away, looking into my eyes. "Are you sure, Madison?"

I reached for him. "Oh, I'm sure. I'm definitely sure."

Later, we were both lying naked and exhausted on the couch.

Ben sat up. "Well, I didn't see that coming."

I hadn't seen it coming either.

"Not that I'm complaining," he quickly added. "I think you're awesome."

That was more like it. "I am awesome! So are you. You're awesome!"

I was also famished. I got up and went over to the paper sacks of food on the floor. The bags were stained with sauce, but most of the food had remained in their little cardboard containers. "I didn't realize how awesome these little cardboard containers are. Look." I held a container out. "Hardly anything spilled."

He stood up. "I'll get plates. And beers."

So, the two of us had a naked Chinese food feast on the couch.

An auspicious beginning.

An awesome beginning.

Chapter Twenty-Six

I woke up in my bed, alone. I looked around my bedroom, but there was no sign of Ben, aka my roommate, aka hot-cop, aka my lover. "Ben?"

No answer. I also didn't have any missed texts or anything on my phone.

I wasn't sure how I felt about that. Was it rude? Or was it super easy and convenient? The jury was out.

I got up and took a shower. After looking like a leprous hobbit yesterday, I took my time getting ready for work. I put on makeup, including lots of mascara and lip gloss, a slightly-too-tight sweater, a flouncy skirt, and cute short boots. I looked really good. "Yay, me." That was more like it.

When I finally made it into the kitchen, I found Ben had left a note on the coffee maker. 'I bought you some fancy coffee. The coffee maker's ready to go. Just press button.--B'

I pressed the button, and the coffee maker started gurgling. So, score one for super easy and convenient. I drank a giant mug as soon as it was ready. Mmm. It tasted extra good, rich, and full of Thanksgiving-era pie flavors.

Then I filled my giant travel mug, grabbed my coat, and headed for the bus stop.

At work, I didn't run into anyone I knew before getting to my office. Darn. I wanted someone to see me looking fine.

But I strutted confidently past Andro's closed office door. Your loss, buddy!

In my office, I got busy accessing email. One of my grant proposals had made it to the final round. Yay! Two of Alyssa's Ph.D. committee members had emailed me questions about her dissertation, and I wrote them back. I shot Alyssa an encouraging email and asked when she might have more chapters for me. My former boss at Wash. U. in St. Louis emailed me and invited me to give a talk at my alma mater.

"Hey, Mad," Ryan said, grinning, from my doorway. "You look pretty today."

"Hey, Ry." I grinned back at him. Since he was wearing his uniform, he looked official today. "Thanks. Nice to see you. What brings you by?" I gestured at one of my office chairs.

He came in and sat down. Then he just smiled at me. Finally, he said, "So, anything you want to tell me?"

"Like what?" I asked. "We found the murderer? I would've told you that right away. Do you know something about the murder investigation? Or the sabotage of Highway 36?"

He blinked, and his smile slipped. "No," he said, sober now.

"Can you check with your buddy law enforcement network and see if there've been any developments on the crimes?" I asked.

"Sure." He nodded. "But I meant about Ben. Do you have anything to tell me about Ben?"

My brow wrinkled. Surely Ben wasn't bragging to my relatives that we had sex. That would not be gentlemanly.

"So, why would I have something to tell you about Ben?" I asked slowly.

"He texted me this morning that the two of you had a date last night," he said. "Chinese food?"

"Yeah." My forehead relaxed. "We did. It was nice."

Ryan leaned forward over the desk. "What about Andro?" he said softly.

"We broke up," I said. "It was mutual, totally mutual. In fact, it was my idea, totally my idea." I was not defensive. "I'm awesome, you know."

"I know." He smiled and leaned back. "Okay." Then, he grinned a little. "Are you going out with Ben again?"

"I don't know," I said. "It's a bit complicated since we're roommates." Jeez. It was complicated since we were roommates. What had I been thinking?"

I'd been thinking he was hot, was what I'd been thinking. But hooking up with him was a very bad idea. Plus, he seemed to have relationship potential, so I didn't want to wreck that by hooking up. And I'd have to be crazy to try to jump into a new relationship right away.

And I might have been feeling a little sorry for myself that Andro didn't want to go out with me anymore, that he didn't love me. . .

"Did you hear me?" Ryan said. "Earth to Madison."

"Uh. . ."

The landline telephone on my desk rang, and both of us jumped. I answered it.

"Madison?" It was Lisa.

"Lisa?" I said. "Why are you calling me on this number?"

"I texted and called you on your cell, but you didn't respond," she said.

I glanced at my phone. "I don't see any texts or--"

She interrupted me. "We picked up the president of that fraternity from yesterday. Can you come to the office to help interrogate him?"

Why did it seem like I was always involved with interrogations these days? "I guess," I said. "You know I don't have any training in interrogation, right?"

"Oh, I know," she said. "I know full well." She sounded tired. "But this is about q-lapsing. It's imperative we find out what those miscreants did with our guns."

"Did Ben tell you his sidearm appeared back in his lockbox at home?" I asked.

"No, I did not hear that." Now she sounded annoyed. "Why didn't you mention that before?"

When would that have happened? "You seem to be forgetting I don't actually work for you," I said. "I have a real job. I do need to pay some attention to it." I glanced at my quantum mechanics textbook. Was I ready for class tomorrow morning? No. Ugh. I needed to do some grading.

"Madison?" she asked. "Are you listening to me?"

Not really. "Yes," I said. "I'll come down to your office to help, but I can't spend all day on this stuff."

"I need you here ASAP," she said.

"Fine. I'll be right there." I ended the call.

"Trouble in paradise?" Ryan asked.

"What paradise?" I frowned. "I have to go down to the Boulder FBI field office. Sorry. We should cut this short."

He stood up and pointed at me. "I'll let you know what I hear about the q-crimes, and you do the same for me, okay?"

I nodded. "Sounds good."

He ambled out of my office.

I took a big gulp of coffee. I hadn't q-lapsed yet today. I didn't have a headache. I could q-lapse over to the field office. . .

Lisa jerked back when I appeared out of thin air next to her. "I thought you said q-lapsing was bad for your health."

I did say that, didn't I? "It's a hypothesis. And, anyway, this'll be the last time I q-lapse today." I unzipped my coat.

She looked me up and down, and I had a premonition she was about to say 'Famous last words.' She opened her mouth. I started feeling a little shivery. "What are you wearing? You look pretty." She seemed surprised.

I resisted the powerful urge to say something snarky back. Instead, I said, "What about the guns? Did you check your lockbox for your gun? What about the Denver FBI armory?"

"The guns aren't here in the new office." She looked thoughtful. "I haven't had a chance to check my lock-box. And I didn't think of checking the Denver armory. That's a good idea." She sent a text.

"So, where's this president guy?" I said. "Let's get this show on the road. I've got stuff to do."

"Since when?" she asked, looking up from her phone.

"Since always. I'm an extremely busy person."

She led me into a brand-new interrogation room. It still smelled like wet paint.

The twenty-two-ish-year-old man sitting there definitely looked nervous. And stylish. How'd he get his hair to stick up just the right amount? He glanced at us as we came in, then glanced away and wiped his (sweaty?) palms on his jeans. I didn't recognize him, thank goodness. I'd had too many students turn to a life of crime.

Lisa sat down, throwing a closed manila folder on the table. "Mr. Lopez."

The young man, Mr. Lopez, apparently, stared at the folder

like he really wanted to know what was in it.

I couldn't blame him. I really wanted to know what was in the file folder, too. I sat down in the chair next to Lisa.

Finally, he tore his eyes away from the folder. "What am I doing here? Are you really FBI?" His eyes slid to me and my sweater. "I, uh, didn't do anything."

"Account for your whereabouts yesterday morning, Mr. Lopez," Lisa said with super-strong nanospheres in her voice.

"I was in chemistry lab all morning," he said and then swallowed. "Er, I mean, I demand you let me go. I want a lawyer."

"Which is it, Mr. Lopez?" Lisa's posture seemed less erect. "You demand to be let go, or you demand a lawyer? Or you're a chemist?"

"Both." He swallowed again. Yeah, he was clearly nervous. Guilty conscience? Or, maybe just not accustomed to FBI interrogations.

If he was in chemistry lab all morning, he couldn't have been involved in the FBI raid. He might not even know much about it.

The three of us sat in the room for a few moments without talking. I was guessing Lisa was trying to make him sweat. For my part, I wasn't sweating, but I was impatient to get back to physics work.

We sat there in silence for a while longer.

Suddenly, he blurted out, "My dad's a lawyer! My dad's a big lawyer. Out in California. You guys are screwed if you don't let me leave right now."

Lisa must have given him one of her patented baleful looks because he shrank back in his chair.

Then she said, "USA Freedom Act."

His dad must have truly been a lawyer because he made a little 'eep' noise. If he looked nervous before, now he looked terrified.

He must have known the USA Freedom Act was an anti-terrorism tool. I'd seen Lisa use it before to keep people for questioning. I didn't like it. This kid was obviously not a terrorist. She was just trying to intimidate him. It didn't seem fair to me.

I leaned over the table. "What did you hear about the FBI

raid on your fraternity yesterday?"

"Uh. . ." He glanced from me to Lisa. He shrank back. "The Feds stormed in, and then they ran away like little bitches?" He lost his nerve partway through that sentence and, instead of trash-talking, ended up asking a question.

"Aw," I said. "That's not nice."

"Where are the guns?" Lisa asked.

"Guns?" He gulped. "What guns? I didn't hear about any guns?"

I believed him. "Do you know what q-lapsing is?"

Lisa gave me some irritated side-eye.

"Queue-what?" he asked, clearly baffled.

"Who went to the health center yesterday?" Lisa asked.

"I don't know." Shaking his head, he looked miserable.

Lisa stood up and pointed at the door. She walked over and opened it.

I followed her. Once I closed the door behind us, I said, "He doesn't know anything."

"Or he's lying," she said.

"Well, then, he deserves an Academy Award because I've never seen anyone act so innocent and ignorant. Get him to ask his brothers--" My cell rang. I glanced down at it. It was Griffin.

"You didn't turn your phone off before an interrogation?" She looked disgusted.

"No," I said. "And good thing, too. It's Griffin." I quickly answered.

"Madison?" he whispered. "Er, I mean, Professor Martin?"

"Yes, I'm here," I said. "Are you all right? Is Luke there? Is it safe to talk?" I put my phone on speaker mode.

"Yeah, Luke's taking a nap," he said. "He said he had a headache. I need to tell you some stuff. Can we meet?"

Lisa was staring intently at my phone. She glanced up at me and nodded.

"Yes," I said, suppressing a sigh. So much for getting back to work. "Where? What about that pot shop where we met before?"

"Yeah. Sounds good," he said. "But no one else. I don't want to see any cops or agents or anything. And hurry up."

My phone suddenly lost the signal.

"Did he hang up?" Lisa asked.

"I don't think so," I said. "My cell just stopped working."

"Gee," she said. "Maybe you should have charged it."

"That's not it--"

"You better get going," she said. "I have to finish here." She reached for the doorknob of the interrogation room.

"Backup?" I started to ask, but she was already back inside the room.

Gee, I got to meet with a nefarious quantum criminal with no backup or anything at a place that sold drugs.

What could possibly go wrong?

Chapter Twenty-Seven

On my way to meet a quantum criminal informant, I q-lapsed to the sidewalk outside the Boulder Brews, across the street from the pot shop in downtown Boulder. A gust of wind hit me, brr, and I zipped up my coat.

I heard a low-pitched scream from inside the coffee shop. When I looked through the large plate glass window, math-man stood there in front of a laptop on a little table, staring at me, his eyes as round as high precision gage balls, his lap soaking wet.

"Sorry," I called out. Hopefully, that coffee hadn't been too hot.

Without waiting to see if he'd heard me, I turned away and speed-walked across the street to The Dandelion. When I reached the shop, I rushed inside, but then I stopped, uncertain what to do. I was the only customer in there.

The grumpy woman behind the counter said, "Oh, look, it's the lookie-lou again, the woman who doesn't buy anything."

I could empathize with her; if people came into a shop, you'd think it would be to buy something. And I did stand out, just standing around. If I was supposed to be undercover, I was doing a poor job of it.

What had Griffin said? Pot helped with the q-lapsing headaches? I was starting to get a small headache. I stepped up to the counter. "What do you have for pain management?"

She smiled and waved her hand at the whole counter. "What don't we have? Do you want psychoactive effects or not?"

I just looked at her. Finally, I said, "Huh?"

"Do you want to feel high or not?"

I wouldn't mind feeling high, but somehow I didn't think it would help with catching criminals or doing physics. "Not."

"How do you want to ingest it?"

"Not smoking," I said. "That seems hazardous to your health, like cigarettes."

"There are no studies that show smoking marijuana is hazardous to your health," she said quickly.

"How could there be? Up until recently, no one admitted to smoking it," I said. "Anyway, I'm pretty sure inhaling burned organic materials isn't good for you. People living near coal-burning power plants, and people--"

"I don't want to get into a debate with you," she said, grumpy again. "Do you want to buy some pot or not?"

"All right," I said. "Sorry. What about edibles?"

"Yes." She studied the containers in front of her and then picked up a bunch of bright-colored gummy candies with a pair of tongs. "How much?"

I pointed at the tongs. "That looks fine."

She put the candy in a plastic bag inside a plain brown paper bag. "Now, only take one of these at a time until you see how it affects you. And do not let kids or animals eat them. They might look like candy, but they're not." She gave me a sharp look. "Okay?"

I nodded. "Okay."

She rang me up and handed me the bag.

"Thanks," I said, opening the bag and peeking inside. I stood there for a few moments. My first legal pot--it was kind of exciting.

"Anything else?" she asked.

"No, thanks," I said.

She gave me an expectant look.

"What?" I asked.

"If you don't want something else, why are you still here?"

"I'm, uh, meeting a" criminal informant, "friend here."

She frowned and exhaled loudly.

I didn't know why she was so grumpy. You'd think the proprietress of a pot shop would be mellow. I was the one who should be grumpy since my headache was getting worse. I opened the little plastic bag and popped one of the candies in my mouth, chewed, and swallowed. It tasted like sugar and red.

The proprietress started sputtering. "Wha-- How-- Why--

You can't eat those in here!"

I shrugged. "Sorry."

"Oh my God!" She turned abruptly and walked through the doorway to the back of the shop.

I didn't feel any different. I sat down on the couch. I was starting to think Griffin was standing me up.

Or, what if Luke found out he was planning to meet me? I really hoped that hadn't happened. Maybe Griffin couldn't come.

Go away, headache. I leaned back on the couch. I rested my eyes for a few minutes.

"Dr. Martin!" Griffin jostled my elbow. "I think Luke might have followed me! Help!"

I opened my eyes to see Griffin looking terrified, eyes round, sweat on his face.

Poor guy. But I did not feel terrified. "Hey, Griffin."

"What's wrong with you?" he said. "I think Luke's on his way here, and he might be pissed. You have to help me."

I stood up. "Okay." I realized my headache was gone. Yay. "Sure, I'll help."

The open space in the middle of the pot shop filled with white mist.

"Oh no!" Griffin screamed.

The white fog coalesced into a Luke-shaped object and then a solid Luke.

I felt like I should be all worked up by the appearance of Luke, aka the quantum supervillain, but I wasn't.

"What are you doing here, Griffin?" Luke asked. Then he saw me and frowned. "Madison! What are you doing here?" His solidity wavered, and he looked more like a ghost. "Oh no." He grew very insubstantial, almost fading out completely.

I heard faintly, "Help." What was going on with him?

Then he solidified again. "Betrayed!" He held out his hands and pointed at us. The artwork and shelving units behind us flew off the wall.

Griffin and I ducked. I got hit with a small woven tapestry. Some glass containers smashed on the floor.

The proprietress came out from the backroom, saying, "What is going on out here?"

Luke turned to face her and held out his hands again. Oh no! I needed to q-lapse and stop him before he hurt her! I closed my eyes and concentrated, focusing on the possibility that Luke tripped on the tapestry and fell on the floor. I concentrated on collapsing the wavefunction and instantiating the reality I wanted. "I'm concentrating. Luke trips."

But nothing was happening. I couldn't seem to concentrate the way I usually did.

I heard crashing, glass breaking, and the proprietress yelling. I opened my eyes.

Luke, not tripped, was smashing up the glass display case without touching it. "Argh!" He seemed frustrated or something. The woman raced to the back, slamming the door closed behind her.

I tried to q-lapse some more, but it wasn't working. "Trip." I giggled.

Luke continued smashing things.

Then, some black-clad FBI agents ran through the front doors, weapons raised.

"Freeze!" one yelled. "Bacalli, Jin, you're under arrest!"

Griffin immediately q-lapsed out. Luke faded, blinked in and out and in and out, but then finally disappeared.

The officer in charge approached me. "Are you all right, ma'am?"

"How did you know to come?" I asked.

"Agent Baker sent us," he said, holstering his weapon. "We're your backup. Why didn't you q-lapse to stop them?"

Because I couldn't seem to q-lapse anymore.

"Ah, I was trying to interrogate them," I said. "Yeah, that's it. I was questioning them."

His eyes scanned the destroyed shop. But all he said was, "Okay."

A little while later, I left the agents to calm the understandably-upset proprietress.

Coffee usually helped me q-lapse. I walked into Boulder Brews and ordered a pecan-pumpkin-pie latte. When it came up, I sat down at one of the tables near where math-guy had been. There was no sign of him now. Darn. One of these times, we should have an actual conversation.

I took a sip. It tasted like a pecan pie and a pumpkin pie had had a baby together. Yum. But I was too upset to enjoy it.

Could I really have lost the ability to q-lapse? That would be bad. Who would stop the quantum criminals then? I needed to make sure I'd lost my ability.

The floor near my table was wet.

Drying it should be simple. I closed my eyes. I concentrated. The floor is dry. I focused and picked out the possibility I wanted. I tried to collapse the wavefunction. "Dry. It's dry. I'm concentrating."

I could tell it wasn't working. I opened my eyes. The floor was still wet.

Damn.

Well, it had to be because of the pot. What else was the pot doing to me? Would my inability to q-lapse wear off once the pot wore off? How long would that take?

I took my phone out of my pocket. Who would know the answer to that question? I looked through my contacts list, but they were all pretty straight arrows. I knew Ryan had done pot in the past, but since he was a responsible law-enforcement officer, husband, and father, he probably hadn't done any lately. But it was worth a try.

I punched the screen to call him. Nothing happened.

What was with my phone today? It was powered up, but I couldn't make any calls. I tried to send Ryan a text. No go.

The woman sitting next to me pounded her tiny table. "Dammit!"

"What?" I asked.

"My phone's screwed up," she said.

I started getting a tingly feeling like my spidey-sense was going off--if I'd had a spidey-sense. I had some kind of sense, but I wasn't sure what to call it. "Oh?" I said. "How so?"

"I can't seem to send any texts--"

Ryan, in his full university police uniform, burst into the shop. "Madison! There you are! Come with me." Since I'd just been trying to call him, this seemed like a weird coincidence.

"I'm glad to see you, Ryan," I said. "Why are you looking for me? Is it about your phone?"

At the same time, he said, "The mayor wants to see you and your boss, Professor Chen, in her office. I've got him in my car. Come on."

I grimaced. Being summoned somewhere never seemed to work out well. "Fine." I stood up, grabbed my coffee, and started walking toward him. "What's this about?"

"She's pissed about Highway 36," he said quietly as we exited the coffee shop. "I guess she finally figured out it was a physics thing, your fault."

"My fault?" I said. "I didn't do it. It's not my fault. Plus, what's the mayor going to do?"

Nevertheless, Ryan had me and Professor Chen sitting in the back of his university police car like we were some kind of perps.

"So, ah, Professor Chen," I said, "it's nice to see you, sir."

He just scowled at me. I guessed that was better than yelling. Or firing me.

Within minutes we pulled up in front of Boulder's art deco City Hall. It looked like it belonged in Gotham City. Professor Chen opened his door as soon as the car stopped and burst out.

"Good luck, Mad," Ryan said quietly.

I trailed behind Chen. Somehow I was having trouble getting too worked up about this latest problem. Being called on the carpet by the mayor wasn't even the worst thing that had happened to me today. Maybe I was feeling the effects of the pot.

I followed Chen all the way to the mayor's office. When we got there, the administrative assistant was standing behind her desk. She just pointed through the open doorway to the inner office.

The mayor, an older Latina, looked beautiful and tough. "Sit down, Professor Chen, Professor Martin." She indicated the empty chairs in front of her desk.

As soon as my butt hit the seat, she said, "It's come to my attention that Highway 36 was destroyed by some kind of physics."

As opposed to being destroyed by what? Fairy-dust? I had to suppress the urge to giggle.

Professor Chen turned to face me. If looks could kill, I'd be writhing on the floor about now. I concentrated on keeping my face impassive and looked back at him.

"Well?" the mayor said. I couldn't remember her name. Why hadn't someone introduced us? I glanced around the room, trying to find something with her name on it.

"I can assure you, Madame Mayor, the university physics department had nothing to do with it," Professor Chen finally said.

I stared at the framed diploma behind her head. I could almost make out the name, L-something M-something. I tried to focus. I finally made out Lorena Martinez.

Wait. Did I q-lapse to read that? Did I have my q-lapsing ability back?

"Say something, Madison," Professor Chen said."

The problem was I wasn't sure what to say. What was the official story on the highway? "I understand your concern, Mayor Martinez. Highway 36 is an important part of our local infrastructure. I understand the repairs are underway and will be completed soon--"

From behind us, the administrative assistant said, "My phone isn't working right. Is yours?" When I turned around, I saw she'd taken a few steps into the room.

Mayor Martinez glanced at her cell phone on the desk in front of her. She pressed the screen and, apparently, didn't get the desired result because she frowned. She picked it up and pressed the screen some more. "Shit."

She glanced at me and Chen. "Are your phones working?"

I pulled mine out and tried it. Still not working. "No."

Chen was pressing stuff on his phone. "My phone's not working!"

My whatever-sense had stopped tingling and had moved on to doing an energetic samba.

"Ah, Madame Mayor, maybe you should call the police or the FBI. This might be an attack," I said.

"An attack?" Her anger morphed into fear. "Like a terrorist attack? On the cell phone system? That could be bad, very bad. But if my cell's not working, how do I even call--"

Her roving eyes landed on the dusty landline, partially covered by papers, on the edge of her desk. "Angie, get me the number for the FBI," she said.

"Yes, ma'am," Angie rushed back to her desk.

"Hold on a minute," Professor Chen said. "How do we know this isn't a coincidence? Maybe it's just your office."

But I knew. Where q-lapsing was concerned, there was no such thing as coincidence.

Chapter Twenty-Eight

A short time later, Professor Chen and I found ourselves standing outside City Hall in downtown Boulder. It had clouded over, and I caught the distinctive waft of cow manure which meant the wind was coming from the North. Usually, when I literally smelled manure, it meant it was going to snow. I zipped my coat up all the way and pulled up the hood.

When I glanced over at him, Professor Chen was staring forlornly at his phone. "Where do you think Officer Martin went? He was my ride."

Downtown was uncharacteristically empty.

I shrugged. "Dunno." I was about to add, 'Why don't you text him?' but stopped myself in time. I pulled my phone out and tried it. Still didn't work.

"How are you going to get back to work?" he asked me.

I still felt weird--from the pot, presumably. "Uber? Oh, shoot." I couldn't call Uber, Lyft, Z-Trip, or anything else. So, I could q-lapse, walk--and I didn't want to walk--or take the bus. I took a couple of steps over to a bench and sat.

"Madison?" Professor Chen followed me.

I held up a finger. "Give me a minute." I closed my eyes and concentrated on q-lapsing. I focused on being back in my office in the physics building. I concentrated, picking among all the possibilities and collapsing the wavefunction. "I'm concentrating. I'm in my office." Absolutely nothing happened. I opened my eyes.

"Madison?" he asked again, looking lost. You wouldn't think a department chair would be so helpless.

"Come on," I said. "We're taking the bus."

I led him the short distance to the nearest bus stop. As we

stood there, it started snowing. Luckily, the bus showed up right away. I quickly got on and flashed my EcoPass. It was nice and toasty inside.

The driver nodded.

Chen stood out in the snow in front of the door, not getting on.

"Come on," I called down the stairs to him.

"I don't have any cash," he said.

"Don't you have an EcoPass?" I asked. "They're free from the university--unlimited bus rides."

He shook his head. "I never picked one up."

"I got you." I dug in my pocket and found a couple of dollars and shoved them into the machine.

"It's two-sixty," the driver said.

"He's a senior citizen." I pointed back at Chen, now on the stairs. I didn't know for sure if he was, but with his wrinkles and gray hair, it seemed plausible.

The driver nodded. "Okay." He closed the door behind Chen.

The two of us found seats near the front.

Feeling odd, I wasn't in the mood to talk. I just looked straight ahead out the front window. As we drove away, I realized Lisa would probably want me to come to the FBI office to help with this latest catastrophe. But with the phones down, she couldn't reach me. Oh well, too bad, so sad. Without my special power, I wasn't much good to her anyway.

"Madison." Chen interrupted my reverie.

I braced myself for more accusations and negative what-not.

"Thanks for your help," he said. "I'm not sure what I would have done with the phones down."

Wow. He was being nice. "You're welcome, sir." I pulled down my hood and smiled at him.

"It occurs to me that I may have been too harsh with you over these last couple of years," he said. "You try to help people, don't you?"

My mouth fell open. Could it be I'd finally won over Chen? I nodded, humble. "Well, I try, sir. I try."

A little later, he said, "If this cell phone outage continues, I'm thinking classes will be canceled tomorrow."

Back at my office, the message light was lit on my landline telephone. I hadn't ever seen that light on before. I didn't even know it could light up. I picked up the handset and pressed the message button.

It said, 'Input mailbox,' in a robotic voice. I guessed it wanted my extension number and typed it in. Nothing happened.

Then it said, 'Input mailbox, followed by the pound sign.' I did so.

It said, 'Input password.' Well, there, my robotic overlords had me. I had no idea what my landline phone password was. I gave up on the phone.

My plan for q-lapsing followed the a-watched-pot-doesn't-boil maxim. Maybe if I ignored the problem, my power would come back when I wasn't looking.

I accessed my university email (at least the internet wasn't completely down). I answered and wrote some emails and even wrote some reminders down on sticky notes in case my cell phone didn't come back up today or tomorrow or. . .

Think about something else, Mad.

I turned to the pile of papers I needed to grade.

After several hours I was interrupted by a knock on my door. I looked up to see uniformed Ben with a big grin on his face, holding a paper fast food bag. "Madison?"

My stomach rumbled, reminding me that I'd missed lunch. I grinned back at him, hoping he was about to share his bounty. "Hi, Ben. Come on in." I waved at my visitor chair. "To what do I owe this pleasure?"

He put the bag on my desk, along with a large paper coffee cup. "These are for you. Coffee, cheeseburger, fries."

I'd gotten a text after a hookup. I'd even gotten flowers before. But never coffee, cheeseburger, and fries. "Wow!" I grabbed the food immediately. "You are quickly becoming one of my favorite people."

He blushed. A tough-ass cop in his uniform actually blushed. It was adorable.

I took a sip of coffee and opened the bag. I snagged some

fries--still piping hot. Nice!

"Do you want some?" I asked politely--because that was how I rolled, polite. And, oh yeah, humble, too.

He shook his head. "No, thanks."

I shrugged and dug in.

He watched me eat and drink, seemingly amused.

"What?" I asked.

"I love," he said. My heart skipped a beat. Surely we weren't at the I-word already? I wasn't ready for that. "That you eat real food."

Phew. I glanced over at the wall that stood between mine and Andro's offices. He was pretty scarce today. What was up with that? I glanced at my cell, sitting on my desk. Of course, it wasn't like he could text me.

"What do you hear about the cell phone outage?" I asked.

"Ah, that's why I'm here," he said. "Agent Baker sent me to pick you up."

A pickup? A giggle escaped my mouth.

"Er, I mean," he said, blushing again. "Give you a ride, er. . ." He trailed off.

Giggle. Possibly, the pot wasn't totally out of my system. Focus, Mad. "What does Agent Baker want?"

"She said to tell you the Quantum Task Force is back, and they need you ASAP."

I finished the last of the burger. "So, the snack is a bribe?" Aw. I thought Ben brought it to be nice.

"Er, no," he said. "I knew you'd enjoy it. I--" He was obviously uncomfortable.

I stared at him. He must really like me. Maybe our hook-up wasn't just a hook-up for him. What did I feel about Ben? Well, he was super hot and a good guy, but I'd thought our hook-up was just a hook-up. Could there be something more there?

"Madison?" he asked.

There was no point in fighting the inevitable. If there was going to be a Quantum Task Force, I had to step up and participate. "Okay," I said. "Give me a minute to finish the coffee and get some work together for later, and we'll go."

I was still uneasy about losing my q-lapsing power, but surely it would come back? Soon? I mean, how long could the pot's effects last?

At the Boulder FBI office, there was no one near the elevator. All the desks and chairs in the main room were empty. I did notice the big locked weapons locker was full of weapons. I pointed at it with raised eyebrows.

"Yeah, Lisa said their weapons magically appeared back in the Denver armory," Ben said. At least that was one less thing to worry about. It made sense--the guns had reappeared where they were the most likely to be.

"Where is everyone?" I asked.

"Agent Baker said they'd be here," he said.

We kept walking through the empty space. I started to worry that something had happened to the FBI agents. Where were they? Had Luke attacked? Were we too late? Were they all dead? My heart started racing. They must be dead. And we were next.

My heart was racing so fast; that I started feeling dizzy. I stopped walking and reached out to a chair to steady myself. "Just out of curiosity, do you know if paranoia is a side-effect of marijuana, Ben?" I asked.

"I think so." He gave me a sharp look. "Why?"

"No reason," I said.

"I hear something," Ben said, pointing ahead of us.

I followed him to a conference room. We stepped inside, and I smelled wet paint. Lisa stood in front of a large map of the U.S. projected on the white wall. There was a giant red blob centered over Colorado, encompassing most of Wyoming, Utah, Arizona, New Mexico, Kansas, Nebraska, part of Texas, and Oklahoma and encroaching into all the surrounding states.

About twenty agents sat around a large conference table, all in dark suits (even the women).

"Finally," Lisa said. "What took so long, Willis?"

I knew what took so long, stopping to get me food and then chatting with me.

Ben glanced at me for a couple of seconds and then held out his hands, palms up. "It took as long as it took, ma'am."

I walked up to the map. "Don't tell me this red section is where the cell phones have failed?" I turned and glanced at Lisa.

"Yeah." She nodded, looking grim. "And I don't have to tell you, no cell phones means people can't call emergency services." Apparently, she did have to tell me. But I'm sure my expression matched hers at this point.

While we watched, the red blob grew into Nevada, Idaho, South Dakota, etc. Uh oh.

The agents at the table shifted in their seats. I heard a little muffled cussing.

One of the agents said, "It's spreading faster."

"Okay," Lisa said. "Let's fix it. What should we do, Madison?" She stared at me.

When I scanned the room, I realized everyone was staring at me. I wanted to say, 'Why are you looking at me?' but I knew why. They needed the Quantum Cop. They expected the Quantum Cop to make everything better. My heart started racing.

I took a couple of steps closer to Lisa. I whispered, "Can I talk to you?" I jerked my head toward the open doorway. "Outside."

Looking mystified, she said, "Okay."

I turned and walked out of the conference room. Lisa followed me. Ben followed her.

"What?" she said.

I wasn't keen on telling law enforcement officers I was high--even if it was legal. "I ate a marijuana edible for my headache, and now I can't seem to q-lapse," I whispered.

"What?" Ben said.

"What?" she said. "Speak up."

"I ate a marijuana edible, and now I can't seem to q-lapse," I said a little louder.

They both just stared at me for a few moments, looking disgusted--or maybe that was my imagination?

"On the bright side, now I know how to deal with quantum villains after we catch them," I said.

They stared, not impressed.

"Are you sure you can't q-lapse?" Lisa asked.

"Pretty sure. I haven't been able to q-lapse all day," I said. "Can you guys still q-lapse?"

"I think so," Ben said, nodding.

"Yes," Lisa said. "But none of the rest of us are very

effective compared to you."

"You haven't done it all day?" he asked. "When did you eat the edible?"

"This morning."

"What time?" he asked.

"How many did you eat?" she asked.

"It was like ten o'clock," I said. "And I ate one."

"Was it some super-powerful one?" he asked.

I shook my head. "As far as I know, it was a regular one."

Lisa exhaled. "Madison, that was over six hours ago. It should have worn off by now."

I looked at Ben.

He nodded. "Yes. Definitely."

"Really?" I asked. I hadn't tried to q-lapse for a while. . .

"Yes," she said.

An agent stepped into the open conference room doorway. "The area's moved into California and Illinois. It's spreading faster." That did not sound good. My heart started racing again.

"Go back inside," Lisa said to the agent. "Give us a minute." She turned her attention back to me. "Madison?"

"Okay," I said. "I believe you. I will q-lapse." I pulled out a chair and sat down. "I will." Yes, I was trying to convince myself.

But even if I could q-lapse, I didn't know how to fix the cell phone network. "Do we know exactly what's wrong? Is he taking out the cell phone towers physically, or is it some kind of software thing or what?"

"I'm not sure," Lisa said. "Let me call the Denver office. I'm just glad we set up some landline phones." She stepped to a desk and picked up a telephone handset, and started punching numbers.

"Maybe you should try to q-lapse something simple in the meantime," Ben said quietly, leaning over me.

"I agree. Please be quiet." What would be something simple? I could try to get a cup of coffee. Yes. That was it. I'd q-lapsed to do that a bunch of times in the past. Surely, I'd ignored my power long enough for it to recharge.

I closed my eyes. I thought about coffee, dark, rich, piping hot, delicious coffee. Energizing coffee. I concentrated on picking amongst all the many possibilities in the universe, seeking the one where I held a cup of coffee in my hands. I concentrated. I focused. I really concentrated. I really focused. I pressed my eyes closed. Coffee. Coffee. Coffee. "Coffee."

Nothing happened.

I concentrated. I focused. Still, nothing happened.

"What's happening?" Ben asked slightly. "You look like you're having a stroke or something."

I opened my eyes. "I can't q-lapse."

An agent inside the conference room yelled out, "It's hitting Canada and Mexico, now!"

I couldn't q-lapse.

Chapter Twenty-Nine

Lisa made me stay at her FBI office for a couple more hours, but I couldn't q-lapse no matter how many times she told me to concentrate. I did discover someone telling me to concentrate did not help me concentrate. It just stressed me out.

Finally, I lost my temper with her. "Stop telling me what to do! I don't work for you!"

She took a step back from me. "I know you're under a lot of pressure, Madison, but this is a dire situation. The entire world cell phone network is going down. Get a grip."

"You get a grip! In fact, screw you!" I jumped up from my chair. "I'm going home!" I'd had it.

"What brought this on?" she asked.

"You could stand to be nicer to me," I said. "I'm basically doing you a favor here. Do you ever say 'thanks' or 'nice job' or even treat me with basic respect?"

"But it's an emergency. We need you. . ." She trailed off.

She was right; it was an emergency. I tried to calm down. But I was right, too. She should be nicer to me.

Ben approached us. "What's going on over here? I heard yelling. Is something wrong?"

Lisa pointed at me and opened her mouth, and then closed her mouth. It was like she was afraid to say anything. Lisa, afraid, I didn't think I'd ever seen that before.

"I'm going home," I said. "This isn't working." My stomach rumbled. Loudly.

"Let me take you home for dinner, Madison," Ben said, smiling gently.

I nodded. "That's more like it." I grabbed my bag, and we headed for the door.

On the way home, we stopped at Pizza Pi and ordered a large carnivore pizza with extra cheese. Pizza Pi was in the strip mall across from our apartment. They seemed glad for the business, complaining vociferously about cell phones being down. I tried not to let it stress me out any more than I already was. They said they'd deliver it in thirty minutes or less.

At our apartment, I sank onto the couch.

Ben handed me a cold frosty beer from Boulder Beer.

I popped the can and took a long slug. "Ah." Then, I recalled beer interfered with q-lapsing. "Shoot."

He sat down next to me with his own beer. "What?"

I waggled the can. "Beer interferes with q-lapsing."

"I think you should give yourself a break," he said. "Take the rest of the night off."

"But it's an emergency," I said softly. "The cell phone network's down." By the time we'd left the FBI field office, it had spread all the way around the world. The moments of slight relaxation I'd just experienced evaporated. "Without cell phones, people are probably in trouble, even dying." How could I just sit here, drinking, when people were dying? I put the beer on the coffee table next to my phone--which was just a paperweight at this point.

Frowning, he took a sip. "Yeah. In third-world countries, many households never had landlines. And most people in the US got rid of their landlines. We don't have one here in the apartment." That was true. We were basically off the grid here.

Ben focused on his beer.

I closed my eyes and focused on q-lapsing again. Nothing.

"Madison?" he asked.

I tried to squelch down the panic rising in my gut, bury it.

On the other hand, if I couldn't q-lapse, I wouldn't have to deal with quantum criminals anymore. Plus, Ben was a cop. And people were supposed to do what cops told them to do, right?

I picked up my beer. "My office at the university has a landline," I said and took a sip. "I think all the offices at the university have them."

"Yeah," he said. "The police station still has a lot of landlines, too."

I sat up straight. How many people needed help right now and couldn't ask for it? "How are people going to call 9-1-1 if they need the police? Or an ambulance?" My panic surged again, overflowing the barrier I'd tried to create.

"Madison, you need to calm down," he said. "Whatever happens, it's not your responsibility. You aren't the one hurting people."

Was it my responsibility? I was the one who taught Luke how to q-lapse, but I hadn't believed he was capable of this level of evil. Wow, I was a bad judge of character. It was all too much pressure. I couldn't take it anymore. I wanted to feel numb. I slammed the rest of my beer, then waggled my now-empty can. "Got any more?"

I woke up quite early, lying on the couch with the afghan tucked around me. "Ben?"

He didn't answer.

I tried out the flat rectangular paperweight covered with sticky notes resting near me on the coffee table. It was still a paperweight. Darn.

I had a headache, but I thought it was a beer-induced ache rather than a quantum-induced ache. I got up and got aspirin and a glass of water. "Ben?"

He wasn't in the apartment. I went back to the couch and closed my eyes.

Sometime later, someone jostled my arm. "Madison? Wake up, please."

I opened my eyes. It was Ben. He was in his uniform. He'd shaved his face and his head. He looked good. He looked kissable. I felt confused. "Morning?"

"Good morning. How are you feeling?" he asked with a small grin--as if he knew I wasn't feeling great.

I took a survey. My hangover was mostly gone. "Okay."

"Good. I'm supposed to take you over to the FBI office."

Hello, pressure. It returned with a vengeance, weighing me down like I was carrying Mount Elbert on my back. I'd forgotten about it for a blissful minute.

"Do I have time to take a shower?" I asked.

He smiled slowly, and somehow I got the distinct impression

that he wanted to ask if he could join in. But he only said, "I'll make coffee."

When Ben and I got to the FBI office, I was surprised to see Andro there, standing in the open space with a bunch of black-clad officers. "Close your eyes and concentrate," he said. "Think of the reality you wish to instantiate." Andro's eyes were closed. He hadn't seen me yet.

I shouldn't have been surprised to see him. After me, he was the best q-lapser in the world.

He looked handsome if a bit rumpled. His hair was mussed, and his blazer was wrinkled. He looked pretty adorable. Too bad I hated him now. If he didn't appreciate how awesome I was, it was his loss. He was a big 'ole loser. Yep. A loser. A loser that I hated.

"Earth to Madison?" Ben asked.

"Yes. Hi." I turned to him and smiled. "What?"

"I thought you broke up with Andro?"

"Yup. Totally." I nodded. "Dump-er-roo. Dump city."

"Why are you staring at him like that, then?"

I didn't ask him what he meant by 'like that.' I didn't want to know. "I'm staring at all of them to determine if they can q-lapse."

Both of us turned back to the group of agents. A few of them did look blurry.

Andro got misty, disappeared, and then reappeared about ten feet from his previous location. He started to turn my way.

I grabbed Ben's arm. "So where's Lisa anyway? Didn't she want to see me?"

Ben led me into the conference room where Lisa sat alone, eyes closed, looking pretty blurry herself.

He cleared his throat.

She opened her eyes and looked right at us. Very carefully, she said, "It's nice to see you, Dr. Martin. As you've no doubt deciphered, the university is closed today."

Oops. I should have deciphered that. I fingered my cell phone in my pocket. The back had several paper sticky notes stuck to it. No doubt one said 'Quantum Mechanics Class Friday!'

She continued, "Thanks for coming in."

"Did you guys decipher what happened to the cell phone network?" I asked.

"Yes," she said. "Can you q-lapse?"

Evidently, she wasn't going to explain what happened to the cell phones at this moment. "I'm, uh, not a hundred percent sure about the q-lapsing," I said. "Can you q-lapse?"

"Yes," she said. "Would you, perhaps, like to try it out?"

Ben was watching us converse like it was some kind of new invention.

"Okay." I sat down in one of the chairs. I closed my eyes. I focused on having a nice cup of coffee right in front of me on the conference table. (I did drink a big cup in Ben's squad car, but it was gone now.) I concentrated on all the myriad possibilities. I tried to select the one I wanted. I focused. I concentrated. I really concentrated.

Nothing happened.

I opened my eyes. Oh, my God. I still couldn't q-lapse.

Why not? Had Luke done something to me? Why couldn't I q-lapse?

Lisa's expression of hope morphed into disappointment. "Keep trying." She waved her hand at Ben, and the two of them walked out of the conference room.

I tried to q-lapse all morning with no success.

At lunchtime, Lisa came back into the room. "Andro wants to talk to you--"

I cut her off. "No."

"He said he might be able to help," she said.

Andro, thinking I was powerless and pathetic, unable to do what I needed to do, was almost more than I could stand. "No," I said. "He won't help. I promise you he won't help."

She frowned but left the room, and Andro did not enter.

I resumed trying to q-lapse.

A little while later, Ben came into the room. "Ryan's here. He said he wants to take you out to lunch."

What a relief. I needed to get out of this conference room and away from all these expectations. And I was super hungry. I jumped up out of my chair. "Yes."

Ryan entered the conference room. "Hey, Madison. How's it going?" he said slowly like I was some kind of invalid. Or imbecile.

"It's about to be going much better," I said. "Let's get out of here."

As we walked through the FBI office, one agent near the elevator had his computer turned to the news. The newscaster was saying, "Casualties are rising due to the worldwide cell phone outage."

I quickly ducked into the stairway. Ryan followed.

Outside, it had started snowing. Brr. I zipped up my jacket.

"Where to?" Ryan asked, faking joviality. "Burritos and Beers? Boulder Brews? My treat, of course. The Rio Grande?"

I shook my head. "Let's avoid places where I might be tempted to drink."

"Where to, then?"

"What's that new sushi place down the block?" I pointed. Japanese beers and/or sake were not my favorites.

"Let's go find out," he said.

Ryan and I had a nice lunch at Sushi-a-go-go. They had some weird stuff like jicama in their rolls. The restaurant reminded me of Nobu.

We were drinking some delicious hot green jasmine tea when he leaned back in his chair. "So. . .q-lapsing. What's up?" he asked. I admired his restraint, waiting all the way until after lunch.

I shook my head. "I don't know, Ryan. I just can't seem to do it anymore. And I know it's an emergency. I know I need to do it. I need to fix the cell phones. I know people all over the world are in danger. People are getting hurt, dying. And it's all my fault. People are dying, and it's my fault--"

He put his hand over my hand. "You've got to calm down, Madison. I've never seen you like this."

"We've never had an emergency like this."

He leaned back again. "You know what this reminds me of?"

"No, what?" I sipped my tea.

"When I played in the football championship."

I knew for a fact that despite his physique, Ryan hadn't played football in many years. "When you were a little kid? And your team was in the peewee championship?"

"Yes."

I vaguely recalled being jealous that girls didn't get to play football. "But you didn't play in that game, did you?" I definitely recalled he was whiny and upset about it when his team won the championship, and he'd ridden the bench the entire game.

"Exactly," he said. "I freaked out, cracked under pressure, and Coach refused to put me in."

"But my situation is different. My coach, Lisa, isn't refusing to put me in," I said. "My coach won't leave me alone."

"I think you're suffering from performance anxiety," he said.

"Oh, come on, Ryan," I said. "Peewee football has nothing in common with our current situation."

"I think it does," he said.

I started to say, 'I think it doesn't,' but clearly, something was going on with me. I couldn't blame the pot edible anymore. I could only blame myself. "Hypothetically speaking, if I did have performance anxiety, what would I do about it?"

"You need to relax," he said.

"I already tried that," I said. "I relaxed last night."

He looked pensive. "Well, Sydney's always talking about 'talking it out.' Maybe you need to talk to a counselor? Do you know any counselors?"

In point of fact, I had been ambushed by a counselor at my doctor's office. Did I dare ask her for help?

"Yes, I do," I said. "Unfortunately."

Chapter Thirty

I couldn't believe I'd voluntarily agreed to talk to that psychiatrist, Dr. Hasanov, after she'd basically ambushed me last time. But there I was, walking into the medical building and up the stairs to my doctor's office. The small building was pretty deserted. I guessed the cell phone outage was affecting business? In any case, it was eerie. Often this place was jam-packed full of people.

I pushed my rising panic way down deep.

At my doctor's practice, only one scrub-clad nurse, Sue, sat at the front desk. She smiled when she saw me, "Madison! Nice to see you." I relaxed a little for a second. It was nice to be appreciated. "Er, did you have an appointment?" she asked.

"No," I said, walking right up to the counter. "I was hoping to get in to talk to Dr. Hasanov."

"Dr. Hasanov?" Sue threw me a furtive glance. "Sure, sure. I think she's here. Just a sec." She picked up the handset and pressed a button on the landline. "Hi, Dr. Hasanov. Madison Martin is here to see you. Are you available?" She paused and then nodded. "Okay." She hung up, stood up, and then walked quickly over to the door. She opened the door, saying, "Right this way, Madison."

Dr. Hasanov popped her head out of an examination room. "Madison. Nice to see you. Come on in." She stepped back into the small room, and I followed.

The nurse whispered, "Good luck," before heading back to the front desk.

"So, Madison. . ." Dr. Hasanov sat down on the rolling stool. I sat down on the chair.

"What can I do for you?"

What could she do for me? If I told her the cell phone outage was my fault, she'd send me to the mental hospital. If I told her I had a superpower, she'd send me to the mental hospital.

"Madison?" she asked. "Are you ready to consider you might have PTSD?"

Was I? Did I have PTSD? "I'm not sure," I finally said. "What is that again? And what would be my symptoms if I had it?"

She smiled a little. "I guess 'not sure' is an improvement over 'no way.' So, as we discussed before, PTSD, post-traumatic stress disorder, is a disorder that can occur in people who have experienced a traumatic event." She paused and became more serious. "Have you experienced a traumatic event?"

Gee. I'd been violently attacked multiple times, defended people I loved from attack, was in a duel to the death (or so I thought), saw an FBI agent being shot to death by dozens of bullets. . .

"Madison?" she asked.

"Uh, yes," I said quietly. "I guess."

"Thank you for admitting that. It was brave. How long ago was it?"

"The first one was like two years ago."

She frowned. "How many events have there been?"

"A lot," I said.

She frowned some more. "And have you been experiencing any symptoms of PTSD?"

I shrugged. "What are they?"

"Intrusive thoughts? Those are unwanted memories, dreams, or flashbacks of the trauma--"

I pictured Luke's molecules flying apart, dissolving into a cloud of particles. I shuddered.

"Madison?" she asked. "Are you listening?"

"Uh, yeah."

"Have you been avoiding things? Reminders of the trauma?" she said.

I nodded. "Yeah." Even I realized I was the current Queen of Avoiding Things.

"Have you been having negative thoughts or feelings? Blaming yourself for things that are out of your control?"

Shit. I had that, too.

"What about arousal and reactive symptoms?" she asked.

"Arousal?" I asked, startled. "What? Like sex?" Surely sex wasn't part of PTSD.

"No," she said. Phew. That was a relief.

She smiled. "Not sex. Angry outbursts. Behaving recklessly. More like that."

I did have that. But I had reasons to be angry, so it wasn't necessarily a symptom, right?

"I'm not saying I have PTSD, but if I did, how would one treat it?"

"Psychotherapy and medication are what I recommend," she said.

Psychotherapy sounded like it would take a long time. Medication sounded like it would interfere with q-lapsing. "I'm not sure either of those would work for me. There's a timing issue. I need to get better, like, right now."

"Well, there's no quick fix." She shook her head. "Why right now? What's going on right now?"

"I need to do some stuff, perform, and I can't seem to do it," I said.

"If you have PTSD, and I believe that you do, you need psychotherapy and medication," she said. "And you're right. It's a long road to a cure."

"I don't have time for a long road," I said. "What can you do to help me perform right now?"

"Generally for performance anxiety, like for an athlete or a musician. . ." She raised her eyebrows at me.

I nodded. "Close enough."

"I recommend plenty of rest, a solid eight hours of sleep a night, minimal stress, healthy eating, plenty of practice, and some mental exercises."

"What kind of exercises?"

"Shift the focus off yourself. You aren't the point of the exercise. Don't focus on what could go wrong, Don't have self-doubts. Often, positive affirmations help."

"Like what?"

"I will succeed," she said. "I will hit the baseball with my bat."

I will q-lapse. A little panic started to burble up. I pushed it back down.

"It doesn't work immediately," she said. "You need a low-stress environment and then a lot of affirmations. You can't rush it."

Low stress. That was a good one. There was no way any place in Boulder would be low stress.

"What are you thinking?" she asked. "I can tell you're thinking something."

"I was thinking no place in town is low stress right now."

"So, get out of town." She held up her finger. "But this doesn't address your larger issue: PTSD."

Get out of town. That was an amazing idea. But we were right in the middle of an emergency; I couldn't just leave town. Could I? No. Could I? No.

"What are you thinking?" she asked.

"I'm thinking I'll think about it," I said.

On my way out, I ran into Dr. Khatri in the hall. "Madison," she said. "I'm glad I caught you. I tried to call you in for a meeting, but with the cell phone situation. . ." She frowned. "Anyway, I've consulted with a neurologist, and she says the results of your functional magnetic resonance imaging are surprising."

I stopped dead. "Oh? How so?" Was my brain broken?

"It appears your neural activity is off the charts," she said. "I have concerns. We'd like you to come in for more tests, such as a positron emission tomography test."

Concerns? That didn't sound good. "What does that measure?" I asked.

"It measures the levels of the sugar glucose in your brain," she said. "It shows where neural firing is taking place."

"So, what are you saying?" I asked. "There's something wrong with my brain?" My worst fears were realized. I started hyperventilating.

"Madison, calm down." Dr. Khatri touched my arm. "I'm not saying there's something wrong with your brain. Please come into my office for a few moments."

"I don't have time!" It's hard to yell when you're hyperventilating.

"Yes, you do," she said. "I can give you something to help you calm down if you'd like."

I let her lead me into her office, a fairly large room with shelves of books, a big wooden desk, and several comfortable-looking chairs. On the wall behind the desk, several diplomas and awards hung in fancy frames. I'd been her patient for over two years, and I'd never been in here before.

"Please sit down." She pointed at one of the comfortable-looking chairs.

I sat. It was comfortable.

She sat in the chair next to me. "Please try to calm down. Try breathing in through your nose and out through your mouth."

I did so and soon stopped hyperventilating. "Why does that breathing thing work?"

"It makes you focus on your breathing, so it takes focus away from whatever's upsetting you." She smiled gently. "What is up with you, Madison? I've never seen you like this."

"Oh, you know," I said. "The usual." I waved my hand around. "Maybe a little more so."

"More so, how?" she asked. "How's Andro? Can he help you?"

Suddenly, I started crying. Tears flowed down my cheeks like a flash flood. I tried to suppress the sobs. I leaned over and cradled my head in my hands.

"Madison?" Dr. Khatri said. "Please tell me what's going on. I only want to help you." She stood up and grabbed a box of tissues from her desk. "Here."

I took a tissue and tried to get my act together. I was embarrassed; I'd never cried like that before. I wiped my face and tried that breathing thing again.

"Madison, talk to me," she said.

"Andro dumped me," I said in a small voice.

"You guys were together for quite a while, over two years, right?" she said.

I nodded.

"But I didn't get the impression that he was the love of your life," she said.

How could she know that? I didn't even know that, for sure.

"But if he did dump you, you need to take time to deal with

it, to grieve," she said.

Well, I definitely hadn't dealt with it. That was clear. I frowned.

"Are the headaches continuing?" she asked. "Getting worse? What's going on?"

I paused. I hadn't had a headache since I'd eaten the pot. Huh. Of course, I hadn't q-lapsed since then either. Huh. "I haven't had a headache recently."

"That's good." She looked at me.

I looked at her. The silence grew.

"Ah, how did your meeting with Dr. Hasanov go?" she asked.

"I don't know," I said. It's hard to get good advice from a therapist when you can't tell them what's going on.

"What did she say?"

"She essentially said I needed a vacation."

"That sounds like a great idea," she said. "I was going to push for more tests, but if you haven't had a headache recently, relaxing sounds like it might be rather helpful."

"I'll think about it." I stood up.

"This is important," she said. "You shouldn't ignore this. You need to take care of yourself. Can we schedule more tests next week?"

"I'll think about it."

As I walked up to my apartment building, Ben, wearing tight jeans and an awesome leather jacket, rode up on his motorcycle. He parked and took off his helmet, and smiled at me, little lines crinkling at the edges of his eyes. His smile was so friendly and warm that I couldn't help smiling back.

I realized one of the last times I'd had truly had fun was when Ben and I had ridden his bike up the mountain roads to Caribou.

"A Madison smile," he said, coming up to me. "Now that's what I like to see. So the meeting with the counselor must have helped?"

Quit looking at the jeans, Mad. "How do you know I went to a counselor?" I asked. Ben wasn't the hottest guy in the world.

"Ryan told me," he said. The buddy-network was alive and

well, despite the cell phone outage.

We went inside.

"So what did the counselor say?" he asked as he unlocked the front door. I stared at the back of his jacket. The leather looked silky smooth.

"Hhm," I said. "Uh, basically, the medical profession seems to think I'm a hot mess and need to relax."

He laughed. "Hot mess? Is that a medical term?"

"Yes." I laughed a little, too. It felt good. I looked at Ben as he walked into the apartment. He was a good guy. It was good to remember that not everyone was a criminal or a dumper-for-no-reason.

"So?" He put his stuff down on the coffee table. "Where are you going to relax?"

"I don't know." I glanced around the room. I'd tried relaxing here, but obviously, it wasn't enough. "Dr. Hasanov thinks I should get out of town, but how can I with everything that's going on?"

"Don't take this the wrong way, Madison," he said, "but you haven't been super helpful lately. We might all be better off if you got out of town and got your mojo back."

"Do you think so?" I wanted to go out of town, but it felt like running away.

"I do think so." He grinned. "And I'm a cop, so you have to do what I say."

I grinned back at him for a second. What would he tell me to do next? What did I want him to tell me to do? "If you say so, officer."

I tried to focus on the matter at hand. "Er, I did get invited to give a talk in St. Louis, but that seems too far away."

"Come to think of it," he said. "I have a buddy with a cabin in the mountains! I bet we could borrow it. We could take my bike up."

"We?" My heart started pitter-patting. "I'm not sure that would be relaxing, with you and me, and you know." I pointed at the couch. "I think we should take a break from all that. I'm confused about you and me. Sorry."

He held up his hands in front of him. "What about if we promise it's a completely platonic trip? We are focusing only on relaxing. No funny business."

Aw. A part of me was disappointed with no funny business. "Platonic. Yeah, that's what I meant. Uh, sure. Sounds great."

The ride through the mountains on the motorcycle was as wonderful as I remembered, although colder. We pulled up to a cozy cabin, seemingly in the middle of nowhere, surrounded by snowbanks. There was a surprising amount of snow for so early in the season.

Ben turned off the bike.

I still vibrated for a few moments. "Wow. There's so much more snow here than down in town." I got off the bike.

He got off and opened the storage compartment. "That's Colorado for you." He smiled at me. "I keep forgetting you're a pretty new transplant."

"How long have you lived in Colorado?"

"All my life, so far," he said.

We walked up to the front door, and he retrieved the key from under the front mat. He unlocked the front door, and we walked in.

Inside, it was the perfect picture of a Colorado cabin, every wall covered in wood paneling, with a massive fireplace with firewood, and a tidy kitchen.

And one bed.

Uh oh.

Chapter Thirty-One

In an isolated cabin in the Colorado mountains, officer Ben and I finished up the sandwiches we'd picked up on the road.

The roaring fire in the fireplace crackled; our conversation did not.

"What was it like growing up in Colorado?" I asked.

"Good," he said.

Ben wadded up his paper bag with the napkin and food wrapper inside. "I volunteer to do the dishes." He threw his bag into the fire. It immediately flared up.

I snickered and handed him my trash. "By all means."

He repeated the gesture.

"So, now we relax," I said. Ordering yourself to relax didn't seem so relaxing.

"Technically, you're supposed to relax," he said. "Not me."

"How does one relax, again?" As I looked at him, all I could think of was sex, which was not consistent with platonic. From the top of his smooth head to his sexy boots, he looked like he was in perfect shape, with not a microgram of fat on him. I didn't drool.

Why was I against sex, again?

I wasn't over Andro. Right. I needed to focus on getting my power back and catching bad guys.

And I liked Ben a lot. I shouldn't rush into anything and potentially wreck it.

He grinned at me, and I knew he was thinking of sex, too.

Don't think about sex, Mad. Ugh. All I could think of was sex.

To distract myself, I looked around the cabin. It was essentially one giant wood-floored, wood-paneled room. We were surrounded by knotty pine (or whatever), from the kitchen to the bedroom area, to the family room area in front of the huge stone fireplace. It was a quintessential Colorado cabin. I felt like I was inside a giant tree

"Well, since you nixed the beer. . ." he said.

After the pot debacle, I thought I should stay substance-free.

He continued, "And a certain other type of activity. . ." Sex. "How about a massage?"

My expression must have indicated confusion because he added, "A non-sexual, platonic massage. I put myself through college as a masseur."

My jaw dropped open.

"Seriously," he said. "I know what I'm doing. It's nonsexual--at least it can be." He gave me a long, slow smile practically flashing: carnal delights here! Get your carnal delights right here!

For a second, I wondered what a sexual massage would be like from Ben. Not helping!

I had had plenty of massages in the past. They had been relaxing. And nonsexual. "Okay."

"Good. I think this will help." He walked over to the closet door and opened it, pulling out a sheet. "Please go in the bathroom and undress." He handed me the sheet, all business. "I think this coffee table will work as a massage table. I can put some cushions on it."

I glanced down at the wooden coffee table that sat in front of the fire. It was at least seven long and three feet wide and seemed sturdy enough to support neutronium. "Okay."

A few minutes later, wrapped in a sheet, I eased myself face-down onto the coffee table.

Ben rearranged the sheet. "So I'm going to start with your arms, shoulders, and neck and work my way down to your upper back, lower back, glutes, and legs. Is that all right?"

I nodded. "Sure." I felt more relaxed already. It must be something about the whole massage process.

He started kneading my neck. As his strong fingers dug into my muscles, it felt heavenly. I started relaxing even more.

"Is this all right?" he asked.

"Yes. Good," I said into the pillow.

228

"Madison?" Ben asked.

I awoke, cold, lying on the coffee table in front of the fireplace, the fire burned down to glowing embers. They provided the sole light in the cabin. I looked around. In the dimness, I could just make out Ben sitting up in the bed.

"What?" I asked.

"I think something's happening." He got out of the bed, wearing only some tracksuit pants, and walked towards me, staring at a spot next to me.

I heard a noise: ". . .elp. . ." I started getting a bad feeling.

I sat up, holding the sheet in front of me.

"Close your eyes," I said to Ben, now standing next to me. I did not check out his bare chest.

"What?" he asked, glancing at me.

"Quick. Close your eyes, please," I said. There was no way I was fighting a quantum duel naked or wearing a sheet.

I pushed away the question of *if* I could fight a quantum duel.

Ben closed his eyes.

I jumped off the coffee table, grabbed my long winter coat, and zipped it up. "Okay."

Ben opened his eyes, took in my outfit without comment, and continued peering around the room. "I heard something."

"Me, too," I said and joined him in peering.

Then, next to Ben, I saw what appeared to be a small cloud. I knew it wasn't a cloud.

It got bigger. I pointed at it. "Look."

Ben took a step back.

The cloud coalesced into a ghost shape. Then, it said, "..elp me. . ." It sounded like Luke.

"I think it's Luke," I said.

"What's wrong with him?" he asked.

"He's. . ." I wasn't a hundred percent sure what was wrong with him. "Something's wrong, something quantum."

The ghost started bobbing towards the door. Yeah, I was tired of calling it a non-ghost. So sue me, the ghosty thing wore me down.

Ben and I stared.

229

And then the ghost went right through the door.

"Shit!" Ben ran to the front door and threw it open.

I ran up to the open doorway.

Outside with the full moon shining on the snow, it was brighter than inside the cabin. It was also much, much colder. Brrr.

We watched the ghost float down the front steps, across the parking area, and towards the large hill next to us.

Ben turned to me. "What do we do?"

The ghost floated right up the hill.

The whole thing had only taken a few moments.

"We need to follow him!" I said. "Capture him." But there was no way I was running outside, barefoot, into the snow.

The ghost reached the crest of the hill.

"Shit!" Ben said.

I looked for my boots.

"He's getting away!" he said.

"Put on your boots," I said. "And your jacket. We're going after him."

It only took us a few moments to get ready, but by the time we burst outside onto the front porch, there was no sign of the ghost.

I eyed the snow-covered hill dubiously. I didn't want to charge up some random snowy hill in the middle of the night, insufficiently dressed, chasing after a ghost.

"Are we going?" Ben asked.

"I don't know," I said slowly. "Does this feel like a trap to you?"

He paused for a moment, considering. "Yeah."

I couldn't quite wrap my head around all this. Why here? Why now? "Are we near anything?" I asked.

He shook his head. "Nah."

"Anything at all?"

He froze. "Well. . ." He pointed at the hill. "That old ghost town, Caribou, is over that hill."

"The ghost town that was destroyed?" Good grief! I wished he'd mentioned earlier we were near Caribou.

"Yeah," he said.

"That can't be a coincidence!" I said. "Let's really get

dressed and then take your bike over there!"

Within a few minutes, we'd taken the road the long way around and were driving into Caribou, or I guess it was former-Caribou, Colorado. With everything covered in a layer of snow, you couldn't even tell there had ever been a ghost town here. There was a nice flat, snow-covered stretch that was the road, and then just a bunch of snow-covered lumps, which could have been rocks. (Some of them probably were rocks.)

I didn't see any ghosts.

"Do you see anything?" I asked.

"Nothing," he said, frowning.

"Well, he came this way," I said. "It can't be a coincidence."

"No," Ben said. "That's a big cop rule: coincidences are suspicious."

Yay. I knew a big cop rule.

I realized I didn't have a plan for if we did find Luke. What if I still couldn't q-lapse? "Do you have a gun?"

"No," he said. Ben could q-lapse, but as far as I knew, he hadn't done anything useful with it.

He turned off the bike.

The two of us straddled the bike in the clearing under the moonlight. The wind blew little wisps of snow around. Above us, the stars twinkled in the cold night air.

I scanned our surroundings. Presumably, Ben also scanned our surroundings.

"I wish we could call for backup," Ben said. With the cell phone outage, we'd never even taken our phones out of the bike's storage compartment.

I tried to make sense of things. Ghost-Luke must have come over here for a reason. He must have destroyed what was left of the ghost town for a reason. "What if this was practice?" I pointed at the now-empty space.

"What do you mean?"

"What if Luke destroyed the town as practice for Highway 36?"

"Okay." He nodded. "But why come back?"

My brain raced. Q-lapsing was all about quantum probabilities. "If Luke came here, it must be likely that he's here."

"What?" Ben said.

"There must be a high probability that Luke is here," I said.

"What are you saying?" he asked. "Luke's got a lair here? I don't see anything."

I didn't see anything, either. Darn. But, there was something important going on here. I could feel it. "What about that mine we saw before?"

"It's worth checking out." He turned the bike back on, and we slowly and quietly drove over to the ginormous hole in the ground.

Getting off the bike, we crept over to the hole. It was at least fifteen feet in diameter and appeared as if a meteorite had punched a perfectly round opening in the rocky soil.

I peered inside. The bottom of the hole resembled nothing so much as an apartment with furniture and stuff--but that couldn't be right. That wasn't what we saw when we were here before. My pulse started thundering in my ears like a vacuum pump.

"I see lights," he whispered.

"There's definitely something down there," I said, adding softly, "Dammit." I didn't want to go down into an old mine.

"Luke Bacalli, come out with your hands up," Ben shouted. "You're under arrest."

"Ben!" I whispered. "What are you doing?"

"Getting him to come out," he said. "I don't want to go down there."

A loud *crash* emanated from farther down in the mine, followed closely by a scream.

Was it a Luke-sounding scream?

"Oh no! Argh! Help!" Whoever was yelling--maybe Griffin?-- sounded upset.

A second voice screamed incoherently. Each loud noise ratcheted up my pulse more and more.

There was another crash and scream and 'Help!' from down below. Whatever was going on down there, it wasn't good. I couldn't just stand here and do nothing.

We couldn't wait. We needed to go down in the mine.

I ran over to the ladder leaning against the edge of the hole and started climbing down. "Come on, Ben!"

He groaned but followed me.

It got warmer and darker as I climbed down. When I reached the bottom of the ladder, I was aware of a musty smell. I looked around. Despite having open sky above me, I was in what appeared to be a fancy bachelor pad that extended further underground.

Ben jumped down next to me. "This is not what I expected."

The uneven floor was covered in expensive-looking throw rugs. There were two couches set up in front of a cutting-edge TV/stereo/game console. I didn't see any people, but I did see several tunnels leading deeper into the mine.

Then the whole place seemed to gyrate. There were loud groaning, cracking noises. A bunch of rocks fell from the ceiling, some crashing into the electronics gear and furniture. I flinched at each loud noise, my heart beating faster and faster.

From two different tunnels, I heard yelling.

Then, the floor gyrated some more. What was this supposed to be? An earthquake?

"What the hell?" Ben said, spreading his legs and holding out his arms to keep his balance like he was on a snowboard.

I followed his lead and did find it easier to keep my balance.

"We shouldn't be down here!" he said. "This whole place could collapse."

"You're right!" As soon as the ground stopped rocking and rolling, I was so out of here.

The ground quieted as a chubby ghostly figure appeared in front of us. It quickly solidified into a normal-looking Griffin. His clothing was smudged with dust, and his normally-carefully-coiffed hair was all over the place. "Thank God!" he said. "Get me out of here!"

I heard a noise from one of the tunnels. "Where's Luke?" I started getting a very bad feeling.

My emotions were too volatile. I needed to try to calm down. I was the quantum cop! I needed to start acting like it.

Calm, I'm calm. I tried the breathing in through the nose and out through the mouth thing.

Griffin stepped closer to me. "Look at me. I'm in danger. Get me out of here."

"You're under arrest, kid," Ben said, joining us.

I felt a little calmer. In through the nose, out through the mouth.

Griffin frowned and glanced behind me.

I knew that wasn't good.

I whirled around and saw a fuzzy angry-looking Luke raising his hands, pointing them at Ben.

Oh no! Ben was in danger! "Look out, Ben!" I cried.

Luke shot what looked like lightning bolts straight at Ben.

He'd hurt Ben over my dead body.

"Away!" I yelled, throwing my hands out in front of me and concentrating. 'Away. Away. Get away from Ben.' My arms and hands got blurry, and then Luke and his lightning bolts flew five feet through the air.

It worked! I q-lapsed!

Luke landed in a pile on the ground. "Bitch." He immediately pushed himself back up.

"You got your power back!" Ben said behind me.

"Yeah." My racing pulse now felt like racing energy I could tap. I kept my eyes on Luke as he scowled and walked toward us.

Behind me, I heard, "Take this, loser," in Griffin's voice, and then a sound like 'Oof.'

I glanced behind me, and Ben was on the ground, clutching his stomach.

When he saw me looking at him, he smiled weakly and got off the ground. "I'm okay."

I looked at Griffin, and he fuzzed out. So, we were officially dealing with two quantum criminals. Damn. But I couldn't say I was surprised.

"Look out!" Ben yelled and pointed behind me.

I grabbed his outstretched hand and turned to stand next to him.

Luke and Griffin both looked like they were getting ready to shoot lightning bolts at us.

I kept hold of Ben's hand and said, "We're going to q-lapse together. Concentrate. Think of a shield, an energy shield."

"What?" he asked. "Like in science fiction?"

"Just do it!" I closed my eyes and concentrated, focusing on the possibilities, picking out the reality I wanted. "Shield. Shield.

We're surrounded by a shield. Shield." Holding Ben's hand, my power did feel stronger. I opened my eyes, still concentrating.

A bunch of lightning bolts slammed into what appeared to be an energy shield and reflected toward Luke and Griffin. Some of them smashed into the stone ceiling, and rocks started crashing down.

The two bad guys got slammed with rocks from the ceiling. They flickered and disappeared.

"Dammit!" I couldn't believe it: they got away. Again.

And to top it off, now I had a stabbing headache.

As we turned back towards the ladder, I heard groaning. Both Luke and Griffin had rematerialized. We ran over to them. The two of them lay on the ground, groaning, covered in dust, with multiple cuts and gashes. Griffin's eyes were closed, his face covered in blood.

"They're still alive?" Ben asked.

I nodded. "Apparently."

From the ground, Luke raised his hands and pointed at us.

"Look out, Ben!" I said, readying myself to fight some more.

But Luke dropped his hands and collapsed. Blood trickled out his ears.

"Well, that doesn't look good," Ben said and then glanced at me. "You can probably let go of my hand now."

I let go and suddenly felt less powerful and more scared and tired.

Ben leaned down and grabbed Luke's wrist. "He's still got a pulse." He felt Griffin's pulse. "Him, too." He stood.

I stared at the three men in front of me with a huge mix of emotions. I was responsible for all of this. I'd gotten all of them into q-lapsing. I felt sad and guilty and also relieved that Luke and Griffin were out of commission.

I was so tired of fighting them.

I was also relieved Ben was okay. But I was worried that q-lapsing would end up hurting him. My pulse raced in time with my roiling emotions. There was so much: anger, guilt, fear, sadness, worry, and on and on.

And I had a rather large headache.

"Are you okay, Mad?" Ben asked softly, walking up to me.

I did not know.

Chapter Thirty-Two

Standing in a giant hole in the ground in the middle of the night, with an equally giant headache and two disabled, bleeding quantum criminals, was not ideal.

"What now?" Ben asked. Standing in that giant hole in the ground next to a hot cop who was also a good guy was a little ideal.

I tried to get my act together. I glanced over at the ladder out of the giant hole. "They need medical assistance."

"They need jail," he said.

But in the background, I heard something. Music? "Wait. Do you hear music?" I said.

We listened. I definitely heard music. I couldn't quite make out the song, but it was music, and it was coming from outside the hole.

"It's my ringtone!" Ben ran for the ladder, scaling it quickly.

I followed him, albeit less quickly. By the time I exited the hole, he was jabbering on his cell phone. When he saw me, he yelled, "My cell phone's working!" and then he went back to his conversation.

I ran (as well as I could with my head aching) to the bike and fished around in the storage compartment. Come to me, little cell phone, little marvel of technology. Please be working, little cell phone.

I pulled it out and turned it on. So far, so good. I tried calling 9-1-1. It started ringing!

"9-1-1. What is the nature of your emergency?" the cheerful female operator said.

"Hi. I'm at the old mine in Caribou, Colorado, and there are two injured men down in the mine. They need medical assistance." I glanced at Ben. "And the police."

"They fell in the mine?" she asked.

"Uh, okay," I said. "Sure. They fell in the mine."

"Oh no!" she said, cheerfulness gone. "Are you in need of assistance, as well?"

Not like they did. "No," I said.

"I'll dispatch emergency services at once," she said.

"Please hurry," I said. "They're in a bad way."

"We'll hurry," she said. "I'm going to put you on hold, but please stay on the line."

Ben finally ended his call and walked over to me. "That was my boss at Boulder PD. The cell phone network is fixed! Isn't that awesome!"

I nodded. "Awesome."

"What's wrong?" he asked. "You're not acting like it's awesome."

"My head hurts," I said. "And I don't want Luke and Griffin to die."

"No." He frowned. "Dying is bad. Did you call an ambulance?"

"Yeah." I pointed at the phone, still at my ear. "They're coming. I'm on hold."

"Let me take that." He took my phone and put it in the top pocket of his cool leather jacket. The speaker end stuck out. "How bad does your head hurt?"

"Pretty bad," I said. "Doesn't yours?"

"Yeah," he said. "I should have some water in here." He opened the storage compartment and fished out a bottle of water. It was partially frozen. He handed it to me. "Ooh. I think I saw some aspirin." He dug around.

In the meantime, I opened the water and took a swig. It was like drinking liquid ice. I shivered.

He found the aspirin, took out two pills, and handed them to me.

I washed them down with another large swallow of supercooled water.

I handed him the bottle and stamped my feet in the snow, trying to keep them from getting numb.

Ben took a couple of aspirin with some water. "Shit! That's

some cold water!"

"Yeah." My teeth were chattering. "I'm freezing."

"It's too cold out here," he said. "Maybe we should go back down in the mine."

"It was warmer down there," I said. "And there are couches. I vote yes." I quickly walked over to the ladder and descended. Ben was right behind me.

I checked on Luke and Griffin. They seemed the same as before, both unconscious but breathing. Luke had blood coming out of both ears. Definitely not good. Griffin had blood coming out of his nose. Not good.

I needed more first aid training.

I went to the couch nearest Luke and Griffin, cleared the debris off, and sat. I watched Luke and Griffin.

Ben seemed to be pacing around the bachelor cave. "So that was pretty interesting timing, huh?" he said. "The cell phones came back right when Luke went down?" He pointed at Luke lying on the ground.

Where was that ambulance? I closed my eyes and leaned back on the couch.

"Huh?" he said. "Interesting timing?"

Without opening my eyes, I said, "Yeah. Interesting." My headache was fading. Yay. And, yay, this latest chapter of quantum mayhem was finally over.

Ben must have taken pity on me because he quieted down.

Time passed--I'm not sure how much.

I heard a strange noise. My headache was almost gone. I opened my eyes. Ben was sitting on the other couch, eyes closed, and Griffin was leaning over him.

I jumped up. "Griffin! What are you doing?"

Griffin startled and stood up straight. He still had a smear of blood under his nose.

Ben startled, opening his eyes wide. "Get away from me!" He jumped to his feet.

"Thank God you saved me!" Griffin said. "Did you kill Luke? Why are you just sitting here?"

"We called for help," I said. "It's taking the authorities a while."

"Help?" Griffin asked. "Authorities?"

Just then, I heard a siren approaching from the distance. Gotta love that Doppler Effect. Did Griffin look disappointed?

I walked past him over to Ben. "Watch him," I whispered.

Ben nodded. A small voice was coming out of his top pocket. I grabbed my phone and held it to my ear. "Ma'am? Ma'am? The ambulance should be there now."

"Yes, it is. Thanks." I ended the call.

The siren was getting closer and closer.

I climbed up the ladder and emerged from the hole just as the ambulance stopped in front of Ben's bike. One of the EMTs, a young Chicano, jumped out of the passenger side. "Where are the injured people?"

"This way!" I pointed at the hole and turned, and climbed back down.

On the bottom, Ben and Griffin were standing near Luke, who was still lying on the ground. Both EMTs ran to Luke as soon as they reached the bottom and knelt over him without even getting out their gear.

The Chicano said, "Sorry. He's gone."

I stepped closer and stared down at Luke. He did look really and truly dead, more like an empty statue of a man than a man. When did that happen? I couldn't breathe. Was this my fault? Was it my fault that a mother and father somewhere had lost their baby? I'm sure Luke's parents expected his teachers to look out for him when they sent him off to college. They did not expect his teachers to help kill him.

The younger EMT put his hand on my arm. "Are you all right?"

I shrugged him off. "Yeah." Luke made his bed. He was an adult. He was responsible for his actions. I needed to keep telling myself that.

The other EMT, a gray-haired woman still kneeling, leaned back. "What happened here?"

Another siren approached. The cops?

"These two," I pointed at Luke and Griffin, "were apparently, ah, camping out here, and there was some kind of earthquake or something that caused a cave collapse."

The younger EMT approached Griffin. "Are you all right, sir? Is that blood?"

"You should check him out," Ben said. "But be careful. They're also wanted for questioning in a series of crimes."

"Yeah," I said.

The other siren stopped moving. "Are you all right down there?" someone called down from outside. Griffin looked disappointed at this turn of events.

I walked over to the ladder and peered up. "We're okay (most of us). There's a guy down here who's wanted by the police."

"Well, bring him up!" the older male cop yelled. It was our old friend Chief Goodwin. "Is that you, Dr. Martin?"

"Yeah," I yelled. "And I'm with Officer Willis. We caught the quantum criminals."

In the meantime, the EMTs had checked out Griffin and declared him okay. Griffin wanted to be taken into the hospital for observation, but they weren't going for it. As soon as he got to the surface, one of the officers started reading him his Miranda rights.

Soon, all five of us were standing outside the mine, the wind whipping the snow around us while the EMTs went over to their rig to get some kind of portable gurney to bring up Luke's body.

"I can't believe I get the collar for the quantum criminals," Chief Goodwin said, smiling. Was it a smiling occasion? Someone was dead. Personally, I thought the FBI was going to have something to say about Goodwin's collar, but he could enjoy his good mood for the time being.

Another squad car drove up, lights flashing, siren sirening.

Goodwin directed one of the officers to help the EMTs with the body. The second was instructed to take Griffin into custody.

"But I'm a CI!" Griffin said as they started cuffing him. "Madison, er, I mean Professor Martin, you have to help me! I was Luke's pawn."

"I'm sure it will all get sorted out, Griffin," I said. "In the meantime, go with these nice people."

Ben stepped up right next to me. "What do you make of all this?" He waved his hands around. "Didn't Luke hide out in a mansion before?" he said in my ear.

"Yes." Was a hole in the ground the best Luke could do? If so, he was not the man he'd once been.

Of course, now he wasn't anything.

I glanced around the barren landscape. "What if destroying the ghost town was practice for Highway 36? Or what if destroying the town and the highway were accidents?"

Ben stared at me. After a few moments, he said, "Hopefully, Griffin can shed some light. Speaking of which, what's to stop him from q-lapsing away?"

That was a good question. The wind picked up again. I shoved my hands in my pockets and detected the pot edibles I'd bought earlier. I fished the baggie out. "Here. Give these to Goodwin to give to Griffin. I don't think he'll be able to q-lapse with pot in his system."

"Irregular," Ben said. But then he grabbed the bag. "But these are irregular times." He went over and conversed with Goodwin, handing him the bag.

There was a short lull when everyone was busy with something else, and I stood alone in the cold, cold air. No doubt all of this would involve a lot of explanations and paperwork, *et cetera*. I wished I was home in my nice warm bed.

At the risk of another big headache, I closed my eyes, concentrated, and focused on the high probability that I was home in my nice warm bed.

And then I was. I reveled in the warmth of an actual heater hard at work.

Immediately my phone rang. "Where did you go?" Ben asked.

"I'm home," I said in a small voice.

He paused.

"Sorry," I added.

Finally, he said, "Goodwin won't get it. Here, you have to tell him you're okay and not at the bottom of the mine."

He must have handed Goodwin the phone because I heard him say, "Hello?"

"Hi, Chief Goodwin," I said. "This is Madison Martin. I'm sorry I left the scene, but I had, uh, FBI business. I'll be happy to answer any questions and do paperwork tomorrow."

"But how did you leave the scene?" he asked. "It's like you disappeared."

"I used quantum physics," I said.

"Huh?"

"I know you're busy, sir," I said. "I don't want to distract you from your important work. I can explain everything to you tomorrow, or in a day or two, if you want to know how it works."

In the background, I heard Ben say, "We should get the prisoner back to the station. And your wife would skin me alive if I made you stand outside here any longer than necessary. Let's go, sir." Yay, Ben.

The call ended.

I took off my jacket and boots and leaned back on my bed. I was too wired to sleep.

I couldn't believe everything that had happened. I couldn't believe Luke was dead. I couldn't believe it was all over. . .

I didn't stir until one p.m. Saturday. So much for being too wired to sleep. I rolled out of bed, feeling like I could sleep several more hours. "Ben? Ben?" I walked through the apartment. No sign of Ben.

I felt guilty for sleeping so long. But I tried not to. My doctors had both said I needed to take care of myself. Sleeping was taking care of myself, right? I couldn't fight future quantum crimes if I dropped dead. . .

Ugh. Poor Luke.

I started a pot of coffee and hovered over the machine, waiting for it to finish. I scrolled through my phone. There were a lot of missed messages and texts. A lot.

Ryan and, surprisingly, Andro had called and texted a bunch of times asking where I was and if I was all right. I sent them a quick text that I was fine and would be in touch later.

Professor Chen left a voicemail that the university would be back to normal operations on Monday.

Alyssa texted me that we needed to reschedule her Ph.D. committee meeting that had been canceled on Friday. (Oops. I hadn't even remembered we had a meeting scheduled.)

There were a few messages from Tom, my lawyer. I didn't have the heart to listen to them.

There were a few from Ben from this morning along the lines of, 'Come up to the Nederland Police Station.' and, then, later, variations on, 'Meet us at the Boulder FBI Office.'

By far, the most messages and texts were from FBI Agent Lisa Butler. They were along the lines of 'Where are you?' 'We need you.' 'Contact me as soon as you get this.'

The coffee maker finally finished, and I poured myself a giant mug and took a large sip. Ahh. I took my big mug of coffee and my phone and got back in bed. I wanted to go back to sleep, but I knew I couldn't.

Instead, I called Lisa. "What now?"

Chapter Thirty-Three

Saturday afternoon, Saturday night, and all day Sunday were a never-ending sequence of meetings at the Boulder FBI field office.

We questioned Griffin, like, infinity times. His story was consistent: Luke was the quantum criminal. Griffin didn't do anything wrong. He was a criminal informant. He helped us. We should let him go.

We met with Chief Goodwin, who was pissed that he wasn't getting credit for the collar after all.

We met with the Boulder DA, who didn't know what to do about all this.

Lisa brought a bunch of men in from the fraternity the FBI tried to raid, but they seemed too scared to be much help and barely said anything. How did they know about q-lapsing? How were they associated with Luke and Griffin?

And on and on. As far as police work went, as much as I didn't like confronting bad guys, the tedious aftermath was even worse. The only good part was I didn't have to q-lapse at all, so I was headache-free.

I finally begged off Sunday at dinnertime. "Come on, Lisa," I said. "I have to get ready for work tomorrow."

She pressed her lips into a thin line, and I knew she was thinking, 'What do you think this is?' But she didn't say it--which I appreciated.

I quickly snuck out.

I stopped in at my office. On a Sunday evening, the physics building was deserted. I double-checked that I'd finished grading my quantum mechanics students' homework. I double-checked that my QM lecture notes were ready to go. I double-checked my email, and the most noticeable thing there was I had a meeting with Alyssa and her Ph.D. committee tomorrow.

I pondered staying and getting some research done, but my growling stomach dissuaded me.

When I got off the bus near my apartment, I spied a taco truck, 'Tacos Deliciosos,' and bought six tacos, figuring I could share them with Ben. If he came home. I hadn't seen him in person since the quantum duel back at the mine. Since that massage. Suffice it to say, things were confusing between us. At least on my part. I didn't know how things were on his part.

At home, I ate three tacos and drank a beer and watched some TV, 'America's Got Dancing Idols.' or some such. And then I ate the other three tacos and fell asleep in front of the TV. At some point in the night, I woke up, turned off the TV, and went to bed.

When the alarm on my phone rang bright and early Monday morning, I felt great. No surprise there; I'd gotten almost twelve hours of sleep. I jumped out of bed.

Still no sign of Ben. Now, I vaguely recalled he'd said something about working overnight.

But, yay, the quantum mayhem was over. Everything was normal. Now I could focus on my students and my research. I sang in the shower. I put on my nicest jeans, t-shirt ('May the F=m dv/dt be with you'), and a blazer. I hummed as I walked to the bus stop with my travel mug full of coffee. The weather was cold, but I had a nice warm coat, hat, scarf, gloves, and boots. Life was good.

When I got on the bus, it wasn't crowded. Sweet.

The campus was practically empty. I started getting a bad feeling. . . I got to the physics building ten minutes before my class and went straight down to my classroom. I set up the PowerPoint and wrote some review stuff on the whiteboard. I checked my phone. It was nine o'clock. That was okay. They were just running late.

All of them.

I sat down at the front table. I checked my phone. I alphabetized the graded homework. I checked my phone.

I knew I had signed up for that university emergency alert thing on my phone, and it had definitely not gone off. I checked the local news. No emergencies. I checked Denver news. No emergencies.

It was now 9:15. No students.

I still had that bad feeling, but I was trying to ignore it.

Professor Chen must have been wrong; things must not be back to normal. The cell phone network was back up, though, so I didn't know what would be 'abnormal.'

I gathered my stuff together and trudged up the stairs to the physics office.

I glided right in--so that was normal at least.

Nancy sat at her desk, working on something. She turned to look at me when I walked in. She was wearing jeans and a sweater instead of her usual--some kind of beautiful, stylish dress. "What?" she asked.

She clearly seemed to think things were normal.

"Hi," I said. "How's it going?"

"Fine," she said. "I should be able to get a lot of work done today with the students gone."

So, students supposed to be gone, check. I nodded, furtively checking my phone. It was Monday, November twenty-fifth. Why were the students gone?

I sidled over to the bulletin board where an actual paper university calendar was tacked up. I scanned the sheet. 'Nov. 25-Nov. 27 Fall Break (No Classes; University Remains Open).'

Jeez. Mental head slap.

"What's up with you?" she asked.

"I just needed some coffee." Quickly I put my now-empty mug under the spout. I turned and flashed her an awesome smile. "Have a great day!"

When I got off the elevator, I walked with a cheerful, confident stride as I approached Andro's office. But his door was closed, so no Andro. I was a little relieved.

In my office, I downloaded a calendar app and input all the dates from the university calendar. And then I turned to my own research. Alyssa showed up a little before eleven o'clock. "Oh. You're wearing a blazer; you must have remembered our meeting."

In point of fact, she was also wearing a blazer. "You look nice," I said. "Professional."

She tugged at her jacket. "Yeah. I took your advice to heart: act like the old white guys. Suck up to the old white guys."

I opened my mouth to protest. I didn't tell her to suck up to the old white guys, had I? Well, sort of. I held up a forefinger. "Only metaphorically. If anyone does or says anything inappropriate, please tell me immediately." I was legally required to report all such things.

She nodded.

"Anyway." I smiled. "You ready for the meeting?"

"I was ready Friday," she said. "This screws up my fall break. I was going to go snowboarding."

I gathered my stuff and stood up. "Technically, as a university employee, you are supposed to work this week Monday through Wednesday."

She snorted. "Yeah, right. Like anyone does that."

We exited my office. "Everyone does that."

She pointed at Andro's closed office door. "Where's Professor Rivas, then?"

"He's, ah, working from home," I said. It sounded plausible.

But where was he, really? He was usually quite industrious. We had that in common.

My bad feeling started to come back. When was the last time I'd heard from him? It had been a while--what with the dumpage, and all.

In the elevator, I texted him. 'Happy Fall Break.'

He texted me back a smiley face immediately. So, he was okay.

I grinned. He probably thought I'd forgotten about Fall Break.

"Who are you texting?" Alyssa asked, trying to get a look at my phone.

I put it away. "No one."

In the conference room, the old white guys and one youngish white guy seemed grumpy. The youngish one had shoulder-length light brown hair and looked familiar. He should look familiar if he was on Alyssa's committee, but that wasn't it.

Alyssa and I joined them at the large conference table.

Professor Chen pointed at the stranger. "Professor Kim had to drop out of the committee. This is his replacement, Professor

Cruz." The name was not ringing any bells, but I nodded in a friendly manner at the stranger.

"So, thanks for coming, everyone," I said, smiling cheerfully. We got to work.

Alyssa's Ph.D. committee was pretty complimentary overall. No one had any big issues with her dissertation. Yay. And now they all felt like they'd been listened to, so they'd be that much more likely to pass her. Yay.

"Thanks for your input, everyone," I said. "And I guess that's it unless Alyssa has any questions for us?" I glanced at her.

"What about the questions at my defense? What can those include?" she asked. Part of a Ph.D. defense was about the dissertation, but the candidate also was quizzed about any and all aspects of their field.

"I've got a question," Professor Cruz said. "What's this q-lapsing I've heard about?"

Alyssa started to talk, but I held up my hand. "That is not within the scope of Alyssa's degree."

"It's not," Professor Chen said, pushing his chair out from the table. "And I'm ready for lunch. Let's go. I say meeting adjourned."

The other men pushed away from the table as well.

"Thanks for coming, everyone. I appreciate it," I said.

"Yeah, thanks," Alyssa said.

They started walking out the door. I ran after Cruz. "Ah, Professor Cruz, wait a sec."

He stopped. "What?" He was wearing a suit coat and a tie--a sure sign of someone new in town. He wasn't bad-looking. Some women might think he was attractive in a slightly nerdy sort of way.

Alyssa and the rest of the committee all walked away.

It was bugging me that I couldn't recall where I knew him from. "Have we met before?"

"You don't remember?" He frowned. "Not officially. We've run into each other a few times. Among other things, you made me spill coffee on myself downtown at Boulder Brews."

I was slow on the uptake this morning. I pictured Professor Cruz in a knit cap, and it hit me. He was math-man!

Oh no. I'd hate it if my bad first, second, and third impressions had a negative effect on Alyssa. "I apologize," I said quickly. "I'm happy to pay for any dry cleaning. And to buy you another coffee. Many more coffees." I couldn't believe I'd even joked about being in a love quadrangle with him. "Please don't let my actions have a negative impact on a student."

He looked offended. "I would never do that." Then, he flashed me a fleeting smile. "I forgive you for everything if you answer my question: what's q-lapsing?"

"Er, uh, where did you hear about q-lapsing?" I asked.

"One of my students mentioned he changed his grade using q-lapsing," he said. "It was odd, almost like he was bragging."

"How do you know it was q-lapsing?" I asked.

"He told me it was," he said.

Ah. This must be one of the kids Ryan was investigating. Now that the whole Luke debacle was over, I should check into it. "Don't worry. Ryan Martin, the CU Chief of Police, is on it."

"Really?" Cruz looked surprised. "That was fast."

"Fast?" As I recalled, all this had happened a while ago.

"It just happened this morning," he said. "How did this Ryan guy hear about it already? I didn't even report it yet."

"It just happened?" I asked. My bad feeling was back. "You better tell me the student's name and give me the contact info if you have it."

He nodded and texted me some info. "He's probably still on campus. He has a student job over in the admin building."

"Thanks," I said.

"You didn't answer my question," he said.

I knew that. I held up my forefinger. "I can send you a paper." Yay. My new paper was finally getting some traction.

He nodded. "Sounds good. Is that it, then? I'm going boarding." He loosened his tie.

"Yep. Thanks again. And let me know what I owe you." I walked quickly over to my office to get my coat.

The administration building was as quiet as the rest of campus. I walked into the Registrar's office. No one was visible. "Liam? Liam Jones?" I was meeting a lot of Liam's lately.

A twenty-something man appeared from the back. "Yeah.

I'm Liam. Stuck here while everyone else is boarding. What do you want?"

"Professor Cruz told me you used q-lapsing to change your grade," I said. "How exactly?"

"How did I what?" he asked.

"How did you q-lapse?" I asked.

"I didn't q-lapse," he said, gesturing at his chest. "I sort of know a guy who said he could do this q-lapsing shit. The guy wanted me to get something for him, so I asked for a favor in return." He shrugged. "I don't know what happened. He said my prof wouldn't find out about the grade. He was wrong." He frowned.

"This is very important, Liam," I said. "Who was the q-lapsing guy?"

"Uh, Luke. Luke Bacalli," he said.

My pulse started racing. "And when exactly did you interact with him?"

"This morning," he said, looking slightly alarmed. "What's the big deal?"

"This morning! Oh, my God!" I stalked away from Liam, dialing Ben.

He answered right away. "What, Madison?"

"Luke's not dead!"

Chapter Thirty-Four

I was speed-walking away from the university's administration building, still on the phone with Ben.

He said, "I'm sure Luke is dead."

I stopped. "How do you know?"

"I'm staring at his dead body right now," he said. "They did the autopsy. His brain is sitting in a jar in front of me."

"Really?" I couldn't believe it. I'd thought Luke died before, and he'd basically gotten better.

"Come see for yourself," he said. "You know where the morgue. . ."

I closed my eyes and focused, concentrating on the possibility where I was in the morgue. I focused on Ben, being near Ben. I collapsed the wavefunctions, and then I smelled chemicals.

I opened my eyes. It was almost as cold as outside.

"..is," Ben said and then shook his head a little and turned off his phone. "Hi."

There was a cut-up body on a metal table. There was a brain in a jar. Was it Luke? I grimaced and walked closer.

I looked into Luke's face, his dead frozen face, his empty eyes, his empty skull.

I felt sick. I ran over to a trash can and leaned over it. I breathed in through my nose and out through my mouth. The smells of the morgue were not helping things.

"Are you all right, Madison?" Ben put a hand gently on my shoulder.

I straightened. "Yeah."

"What's going on?" he asked.

"I don't know," I said. "I just talked to a university student who said he interacted with Luke this morning."

He shook his head. "He's lying. Or, I guess, someone could have tricked him."

My mind was racing. "Where's Griffin?" I asked.

Ben turned on his phone. "The FBI transferred him to the Denver field office. They have holding cells there."

"Were they giving him the pot edibles?" That should stop him from q-lapsing.

"Yes," he said. "At least Lisa and I gave instructions to do so." He punched a number. "Lisa?" He listened. "Yeah. I'm here with Madison. Yeah. She says someone talked to Luke this morning. And that's not possible. No. I'm sure." He listened. "I'm one hundred percent sure. I'm looking at his body, his brain right now." He held out the phone. "She wants to talk to you."

I took Ben's phone. "Hi."

"What's going on?" she asked.

"I'm not sure," I said. "I just talked to a student who said he interacted with Luke this morning."

She exhaled loudly. "Where is this kid?"

"On campus, Registrar's office," I said. "I'll meet you there." I handed Ben back his phone.

I closed my eyes and concentrated, focusing on being in the lobby of the administration building. And then I was, albeit with a small headache. The Registrar's office looked exactly the same. I opened the glass doors and strode inside. "Liam?"

Nothing happened.

"Liam?" I started walking deeper inside the office area. While walking, I texted Ryan, 'Re. q-lapsing cheaters, I'm at the Registrar's office. Come ASAP.'

Liam finally ambled out. "You're not supposed to be back here in this part of the offices. They're private."

"I need to ask you a question," I said. My phone rang. It was Ben.

"What?" I asked him.

"You left before I could show you Luke's brain," he said.

I curled my lip. "Luke's brain? Why would I want to see that?"

Liam jerked back.

"The coroner said it was destroyed by a huge aneurysm,"

Ben said. "He showed me. It was amazing." He paused. "I'm not q-lapsing anymore. And you shouldn't either."

"Now you tell me! Bye!" I hung up on him. I was mad, but I knew it was at myself. I already suspected q-lapsing was bad for the brain, and I'd done it twice this morning. Ugh.

Liam stepped back from me, his eyes wide. "Are you some kind of zombie?"

"What the hell are you talking about?" I asked.

"Braaiinns. . ." He held his arms out in front of him and mimicked shambling.

"No," I said. "I'm not a zombie. This is serious." I started scrolling through the pictures on my phone. What I needed was a picture of Luke. Or Griffin. But I only had pictures of friends and family and neat stuff like Higgs boson collision events recorded by ATLAS and CMS.

"Describe this Luke guy you saw," I said. "Was he tall, good-looking, Italian-American?"

"No." Liam snickered a little. "He wishes."

I quit scrolling and gave him my full attention. "Describe him."

"Asian-American, kind of short and chubby, with bleached-blond hair in short spikes," he said.

Griffin! That was definitely Griffin.

I had an impulse to q-lapse to where Griffin was. But I resisted. Instead, I walked over to a couple of chairs, sat in one, and pointed at the other. "Tell me everything that happened. Please."

He sat down, back to the door, and shrugged. "If I help you, can you put a good word in with Professor Cruz? He seemed pretty pissed."

"Sure." I had no idea if it would help, but I'd do what I could. "Start talking."

"So, this morning before work, I met with this guy Luke--"

"What time?"

"It was like, eight-ish," he said. "It was a bear to get up this morning because I was partying last night. I tried to hook up with this sweet--"

"I don't need to hear about last night," I said. "Tell me about Luke."

He relayed a boring story of a short meet-up with Griffin, posing as Luke, who wanted Liam to get him something from the fraternity house. Liam had asked for something in return, and Griffin offered to change his grade.

"How did you meet this Luke guy?" I asked.

I saw Ryan silently open the door to the office and tiptoe inside. Who knew such a big guy could be so quiet?

"He's, he was, a friend of my fraternity brother. . ." Liam stopped talking and looked at the carpeted floor. He seemed sad.

Wait a minute. I'd already met a Liam at a fraternity house, and I'd seen the bedroom of another Liam who roomed with a Jackson. Maybe there weren't quite as many Liams in town as I thought. "Is your roommate named Jackson?"

He lifted his gaze. "How'd you know that?"

"That's not important." Why was he so sad? I said more softly, "What's wrong? You can tell me, Liam. I will try to help you."

"One of my fraternity brothers, Brad Gaciometti, died this semester," Liam said. "That's why my grades went down. I've been having trouble concentrating. He was downtown at that fancy new hotel. I guess they found him in the hall. . ."

Behind Liam, Ryan's eyes had gotten big. I'm sure mine had, as well.

"Which hotel?" I asked softly.

"Saint something," Liam said.

"Saint Julien?" I asked.

"Yeah." Liam nodded.

"I'm sorry for your loss," I said. "He worked for a caterer?" He was the young man either Griffin or Luke had killed. It hadn't been that long, but it seemed like months ago now.

Liam nodded. "How'd you know?"

"I know this is hard," I said, "but anything you can tell me about Brad and this Luke guy might be very helpful."

My phone chirped. It was a text from Lisa: 'Almost there. Denver field office says Griffin is in custody now. Not sure about earlier. Unguarded during shift change.'

"Uh, okay," Liam was saying. "Brad and Luke were buddies. Luke said Brad was holding something for him, a computer drive.

I think Brad might have gone to high school with him? Out in California?"

Lisa had slipped into the Registrar's office and stood silently next to Ryan.

"Can you tell me the name of the high school?" I asked.

Liam shook his head.

"Which fraternity?" I held my breath. Was it the same frat we'd been having so much trouble with?

"Alpha Chi Theta," he said.

That was it! I breathed. Finally, all the pieces were coming together. The student q-lapsers seemed to be associated with one particular fraternity. And Griffin was friends with at least one of the members.

"What's on the drive?" I asked.

"I'm not sure," Liam said. "But Luke really, really wanted it. If I had to guess, maybe it was bitcoin. . ." Ah ha.

"Was Luke friends with anyone else there?" I asked.

"Not sure," he said.

"Do you know who Brad's friends were in the frat?" I asked. "Any names at all would be helpful."

Behind Liam, Lisa was nodding.

Ryan was texting someone quietly.

"There's a ton of brothers," Liam said.

Lisa took a step forward.

I shook my head slightly. "How about Drew and Brandon?"

Liam nodded. "Sure. Drew Robinson and Brandon Lewis are roommates. They're seniors." Jackpot! All the student q-lapsers were in the fraternity.

"How about Arjun?" I asked.

"No, Arjun's a tutor--" he said.

Lisa apparently couldn't restrain herself. She interrupted, walking right up to Liam and saying, "FBI." She flashed her badge.

Liam looked surprised.

"I'm taking you in for questioning, young man," she continued. "Since this is a university matter, you're helping me, Ryan." I knew better than to try to oppose her when she got like this.

Liam looked surprised to see Ryan, too. "Wait. What's going

on?" he said. "I'm working. I can't just leave."

But she ignored him.

"Why does the FBI care about me changing my grade?" he asked as she quickly led him away. Ryan followed the two of them.

I was left standing alone in the middle of the Registrar's office. "Hello? Is anyone here?" No one answered. We couldn't just leave it unlocked. I darted through the office space. No one was there.

I went back to the main lobby area and started searching for someone, anyone, who worked in administration. I finally found an administrative assistant in the Financial Aid office. She was not happy when I told her she was in charge of the Registrar's office today.

As soon as I got outside, I texted Lisa. 'What about Griffin?'

She called me back immediately. "We're going to Denver to interrogate Griffin."

"Where are you?" I asked.

"I'm outside," she said. "Where are you?"

"I couldn't just leave the Registrar's office unlocked with no one there," I said, heading for the doors nearest the street.

Lisa stood on the curb next to a black SUV. She saw me and punched a button on her phone, and put it in her pocket.

"Where's Liam?" I asked.

"On his way to be interrogated in the Boulder office," she said. "And we're picking up his frat brothers, Drew and Brandon."

I knew better than to object. "If they haven't committed any felonies, you'll let them go, right?"

She gave me a baleful look. "If."

I knew I was as likely to change her mind as I was likely to pluck a tachyon out of the air. Pick your battles, Mad. "So, are we getting in?" I pointed at the SUV.

"No," she said. "I think we should q-lapse."

That sounded like a really bad idea to me. "You get that Luke died from q-lapsing, right?"

"It's an emergency," she said.

I just looked at her.

"What?" she finally said. "What do you propose?"

"Can't we drive?" I said.

"Too slow," she said. "Especially with part of Highway 36 still missing."

I scrambled, trying to come up with a q-lapsing alternative. "You know we need to save our quantum mojo in case Griffin tries q-lapsing."

"So you admit there will be q-lapsing?"

"Maybe. Probably." I had a brainstorm. "What about we get Ben to drive us there on the side streets in a squad car, with the siren and lights and whole nine yards. Plus," I held up my forefinger. "He can help. He can help us q-lapse if we need to."

"That does make a certain amount of sense," she said.

"And what about all those agents we trained in quantum combat?" I asked.

"Most of them are already in Denver," she said. "I can call them in. You call Ben."

We both reached for our phones.

Soon, a Boulder PD squad car screeched up, siren sirening, lights strobing. Ben stuck his head out of the front passenger window. "Come on!"

As soon as Lisa and I jumped into the back seat, the car took off.

Ben said, "You remember Officer Moore." He pointed at the driver. I couldn't hear him very well over the siren.

Lisa said, "Sure. Nice to see you, officer."

I had no idea who the guy was. "Sure," I said. "Nice to see you again."

From the front seat, Ben threw me a look that said, 'I'm on to you.' I ignored it.

The siren made conversation impossible, which was fine with me. I tried to block it out. I had to prepare for a possible quantum duel.

Chapter Thirty-Five

Moore turned off the siren as we pulled up to the FBI office where they were holding Griffin. The sudden quiet was a blessed relief. I sat for a moment reveling in it.

On the drive, I'd been pondering what exactly had been revealed so far. I had no evidence that Luke had done anything nefarious since he'd been back from quantum limbo. Basically, every time I'd seen him, he'd just said 'help' and faded away.

A ghost town had been obliterated, poor Brad had been murdered, Highway 36 had been demolished, and the global cell phone network had been destroyed. The increasing complications almost reminded me of some kind of experiment: start with something simple and work up to more. In any case, the q-crimes implied an evil mastermind. I wasn't convinced Luke had been physically up for it.

But I thought I knew Griffin, and he was not a mastermind; he was a follower, a sidekick. He'd followed Luke years ago when this all started, and he'd followed Nate last year. He was never the boss.

Was it possible there was someone else involved?

I'd also been pondering how to fight a quantum duel without getting an aneurysm and concluded it was: very carefully. A better idea was to avoid quantum duels.

In the meantime, Lisa and Ben had gotten out of the car.

Ben opened the back car door. "Madison?"

"I'm coming," I said.

The three of us marched inside, where we were met with a dozen familiar-looking FBI agents.

"This is only an interrogation. We don't want a repeat of what happened with Nate," Lisa said. Nate had been her partner.

He'd been riddled with bullets in this exact building, so, yeah, repeating that would be bad.

"So, no guns?" I asked.

"Only in an emergency." Lisa nodded and addressed the agents. That was a relief.

"But if he q-lapses, are you guys ready to q-lapse to stop him?" Lisa asked them. "Do you understand the risks?"

They all nodded. Huh. How could they understand the risks? I barely understood the risks. "Be careful," I said.

"Hey, what about non-lethal means?" I asked. "Anybody have a taser or anything?"

They all looked at me like I was an extraterrestrial.

"Pepper spray?" I asked. "Seriously, anything?"

One guy held up a canister of pepper spray, and Lisa grabbed it and handed it to me. I put it in my pocket.

Together the fifteen of us marched down various and sundry halls to a familiar-looking small auditorium.

"Why did we come here?" I asked Lisa.

"We wouldn't all fit in the interrogation room," she said. Her attention turned to the chubby Asian American man being led into the room in restraints.

Griffin looked surprisingly calm. "Hey, Professor Martin, they tell me I have you to thank for the edibles." He grinned.

I nodded at him.

"Lisa, what exactly is going on here?" I asked her quietly. "What are all these agents for?" I pointed at Griffin. "On pot, he can't even q-lapse right now. He's been helping us. He's a criminal informant. Don't we owe him fair treatment?"

Two agents shoved Griffin into a chair in the front of the room. He smirked. What was up with him? Was it just the pot or something else?

Ben stepped up on the other side of Lisa. "Rules for CIs are clear."

She quieted Ben with a glance. "Relax. We're just interrogating him. The extra agents are just in case he tries something."

"He can't try anything," I said. "He's drugged. He can't q-lapse."

"Well, then, we won't have any problems, will we?" She

walked up to Griffin, and another agent brought over a chair for her. She sat down across from him.

The other agents arranged themselves in a semi-circle behind her. They all had their weapons buttoned up in their holsters.

Ben and I were left standing near the doorway.

"This is all rather irregular," he said.

"At least no one has their weapon out," I said. I tried not to think about what had happened to agent Nate, blood spewing out everywhere. . . I shuddered.

"Should we move closer?" Ben asked.

"I think I'm okay right here," I said. "You can move closer if you want."

He didn't move.

"Did you interact with someone named 'Liam' this morning?" Lisa asked Griffin. I couldn't see her face, but I was guessing she was giving him one of her trademark intimidating looks.

He smirked. So, Lisa's expressions did not intimidate everyone--good to know. "How could I?" He held up his handcuffed hands. "I'm in custody."

Something was going on here. Griffin was in too good a mood. "Something's going on here," I whispered to Ben.

"Yeah," he whispered back.

In the meantime, Lisa and Griffin stared at each other for a few moments.

Finally, Lisa exhaled and said, "Griffin Yin, we're going to charge you with first-degree murder of Brad Gaciometti."

Griffin looked a little rattled for the first time. "You can't do that."

"We have you on camera murdering him," Lisa said.

"Do we have him on camera murdering Brad?" I whispered to Ben.

"I don't think so," he whispered back.

"But that wasn't my fault," Griffin said. "This is unfair! I'm sick of this!" He held up his cuffed hands again, and then his cuffs got all misty and disappeared. "And, FYI, I have high pot tolerance." He stood up.

Uh oh. This was not a good development. "Don't q-lapse. It's bad for you!" I yelled.

Lisa stood, yelling, "Get ready, agents! If he makes another move, take him down!"

Griffin held his hands out in front of himself and shot lightning bolts toward Lisa. Sadly, I'd sort of taught him that trick years ago.

Lisa ducked.

The lightning bolts hit the agent behind her. He said, "Oof," and fell to the ground.

Immediately, all the agents tried to hit Griffin with lightning bolts of their own, but their bolts were teeny-tiny and judging by the way Griffin laughed and said, "That tickles," they weren't too effective. Then the agents were all frowning, and some were rubbing their foreheads.

Not good at all. The agents were hurting themselves more by q-lapsing than Griffin was hurting them. "Stop q-lapsing!" I said. "It's dangerous!"

Several of the agents fell to their knees. A couple started bleeding from their noses.

"Come on!" I ran to Griffin.

Ben was right behind me.

Griffin looked like he had a large headache. "You said you'd protect me if I helped you."

Out of the corner of my eye, I saw Lisa get to her feet. The other agents were mostly moaning and rolling around on the floor.

"I will," I said. "But you have to stop attacking people. You have to stop q-lapsing. It's dangerous."

"If you broke the law," Ben said, "you have to face the consequences." Did Griffin break the law?

Griffin's attention was drawn to Lisa. "Ack!"

Closing her eyes, Lisa pointed her hands at Griffin. A bolt of lightning shot out of them. Griffin ducked Lisa's attack. Then he brought his hands to bear on her. She stumbled.

"Enough!" I sprayed the pepper spray at his face. He screamed and rubbed his eyes. His face turned red as tears and snot streamed out. Ben tackled him to the floor.

Griffin moaned and said, "I'm out of here!" He got blurry. But instead of popping away, he screamed, rubbing his head as he solidified. Blood streamed out his ears.

"Griffin?" I shouted. "Are you okay?"

Lisa, Ben, and I all knelt around him.

Ben felt for a pulse. "I think he's dead."

Oh no. My heart felt like it was being squeezed through a micro-wormhole. "Dead? Really?" I felt his neck. It was warm but still. I couldn't find a pulse.

"I'm calling an ambulance." I pulled out my phone and dialed 9-1-1.

"Shit," Lisa said quietly. I was impressed with her compassion. "Now, we'll never get the full story on what happened," she added. Okay, maybe she wasn't quite as full of compassion as I thought.

She sat down heavily on the floor, shaking, and gazing over the scene.

I stared at Griffin. I couldn't believe how quickly the whole thing had happened.

All the agents were on the floor, moaning, with blood on their faces. I felt like I should be doing something. CPR? I didn't know CPR. "Does anyone know CPR?"

Ben went to the closest agent and leaned over him. "Are you all right?"

"What happened?" I asked Lisa, pointing at the agents. "How did they get so good at q-lapsing all of a sudden?"

"We all dosed ourselves with adrenaline," she said. We'd learned before that adrenaline seemed to facilitate q-lapsing.

Lisa punched a button on her phone. "Agents need medical assistance in the conference room ASAP." She put down her phone.

"You know," she said, "I could ask you something similar. What happened? Why were you so bad at q-lapsing? Why didn't you help more?"

I didn't want to get an aneurysm? I didn't want to murder my former student? "I helped--"

Some men and women carrying medical supplies ran into the conference room. Two ran immediately to Griffin and started trying to revive him.

One approached Lisa and me. "Are you all right? Do you need medical assistance?"

"I'm okay." Physically, I was okay, mostly. Mentally was

another question.

I pointed at Lisa. "She needs to be checked out." I stood up and took a step away.

"Do not leave, Madison," she called after me. "We need to talk."

"Fine. I'm not leaving." But I needed to get out of this room. "Give me a couple of minutes. Text me when you're ready."

Even with the minimal q-lapsing I'd done, I had a headache. I needed caffeine. I went in search of coffee or a soda machine.

In one of the break rooms in the Denver FBI office, I slammed diet Cokes while I texted Ryan and Andro the news that Griffin was dead.

Then, since my phone was out, I checked my texts and messages.

It turned out Tom, had gotten all the lawsuits against me dropped. He'd even calmed down the Boulder mayor. He'd also sent me a five-figure bill. Ugh. Just when I thought I might start getting out of my financial hole, something happened.

Ryan had left a message that the university was 'handling' all the student cases of student misconduct, but they only had hard evidence on Liam.

I called him. "Hey."

"Hey, bad news about Griffin," he said.

"Yeah," I said. "It was a bad business." We were both quiet for several moments.

"You're lucky you caught me," he said. "We're about to hit the road."

"Say, what, now?"

"We're going to Sydney's mom's place for Thanksgiving," he said. "I told you."

I definitely did not remember that. "Right! Have fun."

"What did you want?" he asked.

"To wish you guys a happy Thanksgiving," I said.

"No, really," he said. I thought I heard a trace of a grin in his voice.

"I was wondering about the student q-lapsers," I said. "Drew, Brandon, and any of their co-conspirators."

He exhaled loudly. "I don't think much is going to happen to

them," he said. "We have to have hard evidence of laws broken.
. ."

Not much happening meant I should remain vigilant. "Okay."

"Are you okay?" he asked quietly.

"Close enough," I said. "Have a great trip! Bye!"

He hesitated but then said, "Bye."

I sipped and pondered things. . . The more I thought about it, the more I didn't think Griffin could have destroyed the cell phone network. The more I thought about it, the more I thought Griffin must have been working with someone else. Maybe a scientist, maybe. . . Yes, probably a physicist.

So, definitely vigilant, it was.

Once I was very full of thoughts and diet Cokes, Lisa and Ben made an appearance.

She grimaced as she sat down at the little round break room table.

"Pop," Ben said. "I could use a pop." He went over to the machine.

"My head hurts," she said.

"Ben, please get Lisa a soda as well, something with caffeine," I called over to him.

"Diet Coke," Lisa said. We had something in common, after all, a favorite soda.

"Yes, ma'ams," Ben said. Soon he brought three Cokes--two diets and one regular--to the table and sat down with us.

Lisa opened hers and took a big gulp, and then put the can down on the table. "So, Madison, explain that shit show."

It was her show, but I didn't say that. "I miscalculated how effective the pot would be with Griffin," I said. "That's on me. I knew he smoked a lot of pot, should have figured he'd be more tolerant of its effects. But you FBI guys all attacking him, that's on you."

She took another swig of soda.

"Is everyone okay, by the way?" I asked.

She nodded. "A couple of agents went to the hospital, but their prognosis is okay."

"I'm sorry they got hurt," I said. I was sorry Griffin got dead. "I think we underestimated how dangerous q-lapsing is." I pointed at Ben. "Tell her about Luke's brain."

"Yeah. Luke's brain was destroyed. It was like it exploded." He frowned.

I joined him, frowning. Exploding brains sounded bad. "I wonder what Griffin's brain looks like?"

"We'll have to wait and see," Lisa said grimly.

I needed to seriously consider if I would ever q-lapse again. "I'm not sure anyone should q-lapse," I said. "Ever." I resolved to play to my strengths and investigate the issue using the scientific method.

They didn't answer me. I didn't know if that was because they agreed or because they disagreed. We all drank some soda.

"So, the, uh, investigation?" I asked. "What's the status? Brad's murder? Highway 36? The cell phone outage?"

Lisa exhaled loudly and rubbed her forehead. "We'll never know what truly happened. For my report, I'm blaming Luke and Griffin."

"I'm not sure Luke and Griffin deserve the blame." I held my palms up. "What was their motivation? It doesn't make sense."

Lisa stared at me for a few moments with her patented evil eye. Then she sighed and rubbed her forehead. "I have to put something in the report. Do you know something else I could put in it? Something concrete?"

I shook my head.

"Sounds like a plan, then," Ben said. "Can we leave?"

"Yeah," she said. "But if I call or text, answer me."

The oven timer went off.

Our apartment erupted in cheers. "Woo!" "Yeah!" "Oh, yeah!" I was reminded of the bachelor party. But there was no stripper here. Instead, a large contingent of Ben's cop friends was crowded around the TV watching football.

Ben appeared at my elbow in the kitchen. "Was that the timer? Is it ready?" He grinned.

I grinned back. "I think so. " I opened the oven door, and the delicious scent of golden brown turkey wafted out. "Will you help me get it out?"

He gave me a strange look. "I think that's the kind of thing a guy likes to hear from a beautiful woman." He laughed.

I laughed a little, too.

Someone knocked at the door.

Ben yelled, "Door!"

One of the guys got off the couch and answered the door.

"Just let me get it," Ben said, pointing at the very large pan containing the very large turkey.

"Thanks." I tried not to snicker.

He took the potholders from me.

Alyssa appeared in the kitchen, carrying two pies. "I couldn't decide on pecan or pumpkin, so I made both. I hope that's okay?"

"I give you an A for Thanksgiving," I said, taking the pies from her and placing them on the kitchen table next to the pile of plates and silverware.

Her attention was drawn to the family room and not because of the game. "I've never seen so many hot cops in one place before."

I also beheld the beautiful scenery in my family room, eight twenty-something-year-old guys, very fit and energetic, with a good sense of right and wrong. "That's not respectful, Alyssa. These are officers of the law; they put their lives on the line to protect and serve us."

"I'd like them to serve me. . ." she whispered.

I agreed, but I was mature enough not to say it. Barely.

"I think we're ready to eat," Ben called.

The guys jumped up.

"Hey, everyone," I said. "This is Alyssa." I pointed at her. "Alyssa, this is everyone."

"Hi, everyone." She waved at them. "Thank you, Madison." She glanced at the table. "What's on the menu? I see turkey, five kinds of chips, and my pies."

"That's the menu." I smiled. "And six kinds of beer. Happy Thanksgiving."

As the guys started crowding around her and the table, picking up plates, she said, "Sounds perfect."

I took a step back to let the guests help themselves and took in the pleasant scene.

The quantum mayhem was over, at least for now.

All over the country, families were enjoying Thanksgiving at gatherings like this one, full of football and turkey, safe and sound.

Thankfully, all my friends and family were safe.

I looked at Ben.

He saw me staring and smiled at me.

I smiled back.

Science Fact: Neutrinos

Neutrinos are very small electrically-neutral elementary particles. The word 'neutrino' is Italian for 'little neutral one.' They're called elementary particles because they cannot be broken down into smaller particles. Sometimes, they're called subatomic particles because of their small size, but they aren't actually found inside atoms.

Neutrinos were first predicted back in 1930 by physicist Wolfgang Pauli to explain what happened in radioactive beta decays. A beta particle is an old-fashioned name for an electron (or its antiparticle, the positron). Thus, radioactive beta decay is when an atomic nucleus emits an energetic electron or positron. From this, you might deduce that 'radioactive' just means prone to emitting things such as particles--and you would be correct. So, anyway, Pauli realized radioactive beta decay violated conservation of energy because some of the energy involved seemed to disappear. He hypothesized there must be a hard-to-detect particle there that carried away the seemingly-missing energy. Other physicists liked this idea because it saved one of their favorite laws, namely, conservation of energy.

It wasn't until 1956 that scientists Clyde L. Cowan and Frederick Reines discovered neutrinos by setting up detectors inside a large water tank near a nuclear reactor. Their experiment worked despite the fact that neutrinos are hard to detect because the reactor produced thousands and thousands of neutrinos. Since there were so many neutrinos, once in a while, one would smash into one of the many protons in the water, creating a neutron and a positron. They detected the light energy given off when the resulting positron annihilated an electron in the water. So, mission accomplished! This point is worth emphasizing: scientists know neutrinos exist because they have seen evidence of them in experiments.

Why are neutrinos hard to detect? One reason is they're electrically neutral, so they're not affected by electromagnetism. Another way to say this is: they don't interact with, or feel, electromagnetic radiation. Originally, neutrinos were also thought to have zero mass, and if so, they wouldn't be affected by gravity. To put this in more familiar terms: something with zero mass weighs zero pounds.

Practically the only thing neutrinos do feel is a force called the Weak Force. As the name implies, the Weak Force is well, weak. It's not as powerful as electromagnetism, and it only operates over very short distances. In fact, it was beta decay that led physicists to hypothesize the existence of this Weak Force; no other forces could explain beta decay. The Weak Force is important in nuclear fusion. Because of the mathematics behind the Weak Force, physicists hypothesized that there were three different kinds, or flavors, of neutrinos, called electron neutrinos, muon neutrinos, and tau neutrinos.

Neutrinos are created in supernovas, and a lot were created in the Big Bang (the giant explosion that started our universe). It turns out the greatest local source of neutrinos is our Sun. Neutrinos are produced in the core of the sun via nuclear fusion reactions. The most important of these is when the Weak Force enables two protons to interact to form a deuteron (a proton combined with a neutron), an anti-electron called a positron, and a corresponding electron neutrino.

When scientists did experiments to detect these electron neutrinos coming from the Sun, it seemed like a bunch of them were missing. For a while, this mystery was called the Solar Neutrino Problem. The great thing about a scientific mystery is it enables us to learn new stuff. The solution to the Solar Neutrino Problem was: the Sun did emit the expected number of electron neutrinos, but some of them changed into the other kinds of neutrinos on the way to Earth. This is called neutrino oscillation, and it had a further consequence: neutrinos must have a non-zero mass. Therefore, neutrinos do feel the gravity force. This discovery of neutrino oscillations and consequent neutrino mass was awarded the Nobel Prize in Physics in 2015.

You might be wondering why you should care about neutrinos. Fun fact: tens of thousands of neutrinos are passing through your body right now! Do you feel them? Probably not. You don't feel them because neutrinos hardly interact at all with the regular matter that makes up your body.

Neutrinos are still a very active area of research in physics.

Thank you for reading *Quantum Mayhem*. I hope you enjoyed it!

- For more info about me or my work, please go to my author website, http://www.lesleylsmith.com/. Sometimes, I post links for free fiction downloads!
- Please check out the Physics Is Fun website www.physicsisfun.net for lots of information about fun physics topics.
- Reviews help other readers find books. I appreciate any and all reviews.
- A sneak peek at my new novel *Neutrino Warning* follows.

−Lesley L. Smith

Neutrino Warning Chapter One

Sometimes, it seemed like Mother Nature, Gaia, was out to get us…

"Snow!" I stopped dead in my tracks inside the physics building's glass front doors, astonished to see a blanket of white outside. Colorado's Front Range rarely got snow anymore. And we never got snow on the Gulf Coast of Missouri, where I grew up.

"Whoa, Kathy. Lookout. Sorry." Jake Moretti, a new physics grad student, almost ran into me. We awkwardly stepped away from one another. My initial impression was that he was adorable with his swimmer's physique and his earnestness. "Yeah, it was a huge blizzard!" He chuckled, looking out the glass doors. "It's cool. Haha. Pun intended." He pushed his wire-rimmed glasses up the bridge of his nose. "Why didn't you notice it when you came into work?"

I'd wondered why everyone was suddenly wearing jackets. I'd hardly seen any coats this past winter, so I didn't expect to see any now that March was here. "I didn't come into work this morning." I couldn't even remember the last time I'd left the physics building--but I was not a workaholic. Definitely not. It was just that graduate students had a lot to do.

Jake stopped chuckling. "It was all over the news, too."

"Ellen, what's in the news?" Ellen was the digital personal assistant app on my fon, currently in my pocket. I'd had her since I was a girl. I'd named her after the awesome astronaut, Ellen Ochoa, from way back in the 1990s.

"March 4, 2098: Blizzard Blankets Colorado," she said.

I interrupted her. "New directive: Give me a news report every morning." I reached for the front doors as if under a spell.

Snow! I needed to frolic outside immediately.

Gopal Khan, my Ph.D. advisor, jostled me as he sped past us on the ground floor landing. "Kathy, what are you doing? The physics department meeting is about to start." He checked his worn watch and glared. "It's mandatory. You too, Jake."

When Gopal got cross with me, which was often for some reason, he reminded me of a bear with his bulky physique and shaggy brown beard and hair. Of course, I'd never actually seen a bear, so I could have been way off.

"But, look." I pointed out the doors. "It snowed."

"I know." He gazed outside for a moment, rubbing his beard. "It's remarkable and pretty. But we still have to go to the meeting."

Ellen said, "The physics department meeting starts in ten seconds."

Gopal flinched. "Now, we're going to be late." He shot me a dark look. "Tell me Lars is already in the meeting room."

I shrugged. "I can tell you that, but I'm pretty sure he went out for a toke, so it would be a lie." I pointed out the door. Lars Karlsson, Gopal's purported second-in-command in the neutrino physics group, had a problem with authority. And marijuana. It had to be because of his overbearing physicist father, Hans. If Hans had been my father, I'd have problems, too.

"Kathy, go outside and see if you can find Lars," Gopal said. "It makes me look bad as the group leader when he doesn't show up for meetings."

I rubbed my hands together. Snow, here I come! "Gosh, Gopal, if you really want me to, I will."

"Hurry up," he said.

I threw open the doors, stepped outside, and squinted. The sunlight reflecting off the snow was blinding; it was like being caught inside a very sparkly diamond. My eyes started watering profusely. A cold diamond; it was definitely cold out here. I shivered. I leaned down, grabbed a handful of (cold!) snow, and made a snowball. I threw it at a red sandstone boulder peeking through the sea of white, and it splattered into a million pieces. It smelled cold and clean out here. Everything seemed fresh and new. I took a deep breath.

"Gopal says, 'Hurry up,'" Ellen interrupted my adventure.

I sighed but started down the path through the snow away from the building: stomp, squish, stomp, squish. I couldn't help grinning; this was fun.

I heard a distant crack of thunder and looked away from my snowy path. I didn't see any clouds. Huh. The snow-covered foothills less than a half kilometer west looked beautiful as they rose majestically into the blue sky.

Focus, Kath! Now, where had Lars gone?

Following footsteps in the snow and the sweet tang of pot smoke, I found Lars behind a big red boulder. "You know smoking will kill you," I said as I approached.

He held the joint carefully with his thumb and forefinger. "I should live so long." He inhaled and held in the smoke.

"C'mon," I said. "Gopal sent me out here to get you. The department meeting isn't optional."

Lars brushed his shoulder-length blond hair out of his green eyes and let out his breath. "Tell Gopal I'll be there in a couple of minutes. This Colorado Gold I got at the farmers' market is excellent. Do you want some?"

"No, I don't want some. And tell Gopal yourself. I'm a physicist, not your errand girl." I stomped my boots in the snow as my feet started to chill.

"Kathy, you haven't finished your dissertation, so you're not a physicist yet." He flashed his perfect white teeth at me. "But you could be my errand girl if you played your cards right."

I snorted. "In your dreams, Lars." I had mixed feelings about Lars. Based on a disastrous relationship in my past, I'd vowed never again to date a fellow physicist. But Lars was unusually good-looking for a scientist. Unfortunately, that also meant his ego was unusually large.

I heard snow squishing under another pair of shoes as Jake appeared around the boulder. When he saw us, he smiled.

Caught in Jake's smile, I got a sense of the sweet gangly teenager he used to be.

"What are you guys doing?" Jake said. "Gopal sent me out to get you."

In the bright sunlight, Jake's intense blue eyes were the color of a pristine alpine lake.

Uh oh. Focus, Kath! "Uh, nothing. We're not doing anything.

We're on our way back to the meeting." I waved my hand around. "Jake, this is Lars; Lars, this is Jake. He's thinking of joining our group." I shivered. My lumpy brown handmade sweater wasn't doing its job, but then how often did it drop below 45 degrees these days?

Jake noticed. "It's chilly out here. Do you want to borrow my coat, Kathy?" He slipped it off and put it around my shoulders. It was cavernous on my tiny frame.

Lars smirked and took another toke.

"Thanks, Jake." I snuggled into it. It smelled faintly of sweat and some kind of cologne. I took a deep breath. "What a gentleman." I shot a glare at Lars, but he didn't notice.

"I don't understand how the blizzard of the last few days could have been because of global warming." Jake pushed a lock of brown wavy hair away from his eyes.

"Easy." I felt a smile take over my face. I loved talking science. "Global warming means there's more moisture in the atmosphere and more energy available for weather systems, so storms have increased precipitation, which can be snow." My nose started to run. I resisted the urge to wipe it on the sleeve of Jake's coat.

Lars stubbed out his now-tiny joint.

Another loud crack of thunder made us look up.

"That's weird." Jake searched the sky. "There aren't any clouds. How can there be thunder?"

The thunder continued to rumble.

Lars stood up and looked to the west, over the boulder. "I think it's from over there."

The rumbling got louder. "What's that?" I pointed west. A massive cloud of white moved down the mountain slope towards us. It was huge, awe-inspiring. Terrifying. "Look!"

"Huh." Lars giggled. "Pretty."

"What?" Jake asked. "Where?"

"There!" I said. "There! West! I'm telling you, there's a huge white mass of something headed right for us!" My extended finger trembled.

"Is it possible?" Jake asked. "Gaia! I've never seen a what-do-you-call-it, an avalanche, before. Shouldn't we get back to the building?" He turned.

275

An avalanche! It had been snowing for days and days in the mountains to the west of us, and now all that snow was heading our way.

I felt a sudden strong gust of cold air. And it was coming straight for us! "There's no time! Take cover!" I grabbed Jake and Lars and pulled them down behind the boulder just as the first icy tendrils of snow kissed my bare neck.

I scrunched up against the boulder and held Jake's coat above my head as the snow started to cascade over it. I couldn't catch a breath and felt as if I was suffocating. The snow fell in bigger and bigger chunks, and the patter of snow landing on the jacket turned into pounding. I tried to angle my impromptu tent so the snow would slide off me and away from the others. Wispy streams of snowflakes drifted down in the slight gap between the jacket and the rock. My ankles and shins were freezing. My legs were already half-buried. I stamped my feet and tried to get on top of the snow.

After what seemed like an eternity, the pounding changed back to pattering. I opened my eyes and peeked out from under the jacket. We lucked out. "I think it's over." Jake and Lars crouched next to me in only a meter of new snow.

They blinked and brushed snow off themselves.

"Cool." Lars stood up.

"We're okay! I can't believe it." Jake wiped snow off his clothes.

"Those rock formations above us must have diverted most of it away from us." I brushed snow off Jake's coat and handed it back to him. "Thanks a lot, Jake."

"So, where'd the snow go?" Jake glanced around.

Lars pointed back toward the physics building. "Look."

Our gaze followed his finger. Snow buried one side of the physics building up to the second-floor windows, and it looked like some of them were broken. That couldn't be good.

"Oh no!" The meeting was on the first floor there. I fumbled for my fon. "Ellen, call emergency services. There's been an accident, an avalanche, on campus at the physics building."

"Message acknowledged," Ellen said. "Calling emergency crews now."

"C'mon, you guys, we have to go help!" I said.

I tried to run to the physics building, but it seemed to take forever as my feet sunk in the snow. It was like some horrible dream where I could only move in slow motion.

After about a million years, Jake and I got to the front door and had to kick the snow away from it to get it to open. Lars was lagging far behind.

Jake and I ran towards the conference room past broken windows and through snowdrifts in the hall.

Inside the conference room, the snow had crashed through all the windows. People were already digging frantically.

Lily, the physics department's administrative assistant, saw us come into the room. She usually seemed like someone's granny with her quick smile, short gray hair, and conservative clothes, but today she barked orders like a drill sergeant. "You guys, come here, dig next to me. A bunch of people were sitting right here."

I went to where she indicated. I dogpaddled through the snow, shoving it behind me. My fingers felt so cold they burned, but soon they went numb.

Soon, some wiggling fingers appeared right in front of me.

I uncovered the rest of the hand and the arm, followed it to the torso, and exposed the face. I recognized Marcello, my old officemate. His thinning dark hair was plastered to his head, and his skin was red and blotchy. He gasped and opened his eyes. I unearthed more of him and found he still sat in a chair. "Hold on, Marcello! I'll get you out." I moved more snow, grabbed a chair arm, and rolled it out.

He gasped and brushed snow off himself. "*Grazie*, Kathy!"

"*Prego*, Marcello," I said.

I saw another chair arm sticking out of the snow. Quickly I turned my attention from Marcello and scooped snow away from where another head might be. Success. It was a woman, Gabrielle, one of the members of the fusion group. I finished exposing her face, but she didn't seem to be breathing.

I yanked the chair out of the drift.

Lily caught my eye. "Is she all right?"

"I'm not sure," I said. "I don't think so."

Lily moved towards us. "Here, let me check for a pulse. I know CPR; I'll take her. Keep digging."

I found another chair arm and tugged on it, but it wouldn't budge. I kept pulling on it. It had to move! I pulled some more. Did it move a little? I was starting to get frantic.

Jake reached over me and started brushing snow away from head level. "Uncover the face first." His voice was high-pitched with stress.

I started brushing snow away from the face area. "Right, I knew that." We uncovered a male head.

I felt his neck for a pulse. Nothing. "I can't find a pulse! He's not breathing!" I was barely breathing myself. I realized we had managed to clear all the way around the conference table. Most of the snow had been spread around the room. We had uncovered everyone. Several people were doing mouth-to-mouth resuscitation or CPR on fallen colleagues.

Gopal stood on the other side of the chair next to me. His neat beard had snow caked on it, and his brown eyes were solemn and unblinking as he examined the man next to me. "Kathy, get out of the way." He lowered the man onto the floor and started mouth-to-mouth resuscitation.

Lily came over. "I'll start CPR."

I scanned the room. "Is everyone accounted for?" There weren't any large piles of snow left. We must have uncovered everyone.

"Lars? Where's Lars?" Gopal asked.

"Still outside," I said. "Or maybe in the hall."

Now that the immediate danger was over, I was panicking. I leaned my head down, resting my numb hands on my knees. Between labored breaths, I said, "Lars is fine."

A piece of window glass fell, shattering on the floor. We all startled at the loud noise.

"Careful, everyone!" I yelled. "Move into the hall if you can."

I took the arm of a very pale Marcello and led him out of the room.

I felt exhausted and couldn't tell if I still had fingers, they were so numb. I put my hands under my armpits to try to thaw them. As I stood in the hall with my shaken colleagues, I heard ambulance sirens approaching.

We trudged down the hall, and someone pulled out a chair for me. "Kathy, sit."

How could I've been so idiotic with that last guy? I knew, I knew, I should have uncovered his face first. Did my mistake kill him? Gaia, I didn't even notice who it was. I leaned forward in the chair as my hands started to burn.

Off in the distance, far away, I heard talking. I rocked back and forth. Who did I kill?

"Miss!" Someone put his hand on my back. "Miss, are you all right? What's your name?"

I gazed at the medic leaning over me. His cheeks were flushed. "Do you know your name? Do you know where you are?"

I nodded. Kathy.

Jake came up. "That's Kathy. I think she called emergency services. She seemed all right a little while ago." He leaned down and peered into my face. "Kathy?"

"Jake. What? What do you want?" I focused on his face.

"Are you all right?" He gazed into my eyes, and his forehead was wrinkled in concern.

I nodded. "I think so. Who didn't I get to in time?"

"You did the best you could," Jake said.

"Who was it?" I asked.

"It was Professor Guy Cassou, one of the French guys in the fusion group. He didn't make it." Jake shook his head.

The medic straightened up. "I doubt you could have done anything more, but if you called emergency services, you saved lives. You're a hero."

"You hear that, Kathy? You're a hero." Jake rubbed my back.

I didn't feel like a hero.

"Anyway, Miss, if you're okay, please move into the other room. We're still assessing the situation." He pointed further down the hall, and we stumbled off in that direction.

Gopal stood in the hallway and checked us off on a list as we went into one of the classrooms. His clothes were soaked. "Thank Gaia, you are all right. Not everyone was so lucky."

I realized I was pretty wet myself. "Who?" My lips trembled so much that it was hard to talk. "Who didn't make it?"

Gopal consulted the list as if such horrible news couldn't be held in the brain. "Uh, let's see, we lost Professor Cassou and his student, Gabrielle." Gopal paused and sniffed, wiping his nose with his palm.

Gaia! That was awful. I nodded, not trusting myself to speak.

Gopal stared stony-eyed at his checklist for a few moments. "It's too horrible to believe …but we lost everyone in the fusion group. They're all gone."

Jake gasped.

"Jean-Phillipe? Everyone?" I asked. Jean-Phillipe was Gabrielle's significant other; they'd come here to Colorado together.

Gopal just nodded.

I collapsed against the doorjamb.

An EMT came up, and Gopal's face turned white as he conferred with him quietly.

Jake and I just looked at each other in disbelief.

I couldn't process this.

The emergency worker shook his head as he walked away.

Gopal's slack face seemed to grow more haggard, and his eyes more haunted as he looked at us. "That was, that was about the department chair, Joe Davidson. He didn't make it either. He had a heart attack."

"No." My eyes finally overflowed. This was just all too much and all wrong. I stumbled to the floor.

"Miss? Miss?" The EMT ran back to me. "Are you…"

Everything went black.